The Unex

The Unexpected Nanny

Published 2019

The Unexpected Nanny Copyright 2018
Cover design Copyright 2019 https://selfpubbookcovers.com/Frozenstar
Cancer Ribbon clipart by: Publicdomainvectors.org

All rights reserved. No part of this book may be used or reproduced in any manner whatsoever without written permission from the author.

This book is licensed for your own personal private use only. Any other use of the whole or part of this book (including, but not limited to, adaptation, translation, copying, issuing copies, unauthorized lending and rental, broadcasting or making available to internet, social media, wireless technology and application) is strictly prohibited. Thank you for respecting the hard work of the author.

This book is a work of fiction. Names, places, events, characters, situations and incidents mentioned in the book are products of the authors imagination and/ or used in a fictitious manner. Any resemblance to real or actual people, living or dead, places, brands, or events are purely coincidental and not intended by the author. Reference to public figures or brands are purely for the sake of fiction. The opinion of the characters does not reflect the opinion of the author.

Some events in the story may contain occurrences that happen in everyday life. This book is not intended as a substitute for the medical advice of physicians. The reader should regularly consult a physician in matters relating to his/her health and particularly with respect to any symptoms that may require diagnosis or medical attention.

ISBN: 9781097236121

Acknowledgements

I would like to dedicate this book to all who have, or who is going through breast cancer. As well as anyone who is dealing with or has dealt with a family member or friend with breast cancer.

I would also like to dedicate this book to Heather Teston, who helped me get to where I am today. She is not only a terrific person, but a great and wonderful friend. I'm glad to have met her through wattpad.

I would also like to thank one of my Wattpad readers who helped me with the first edit of this story; rudypooh37. Thank you so much, you were a big help!

To all my Wattpad readers and followers, you are also acknowledged by me. If it weren't for you, I wouldn't be putting this story out to be published! Thank you all so much!

I would also like to thank my husband Larry for encouraging me to finally publish this book!

I have also added just a little more to the story, while doing the second edit as well as while preparing to publish the story, hope you'll enjoy it.

Table of Contents:

Chapter 1: The news……………………………………………………….1
Chapter 2: The decision…………………………………………………..9
Chapter 3: Introducing Sadie…………………………………………..16
Chapter 4: The run in……………………………………………………..23
Chapter 5: Out of control………………………………………………..30
Chapter 6: Tension all around………………………………………….37
Chapter 7: Family time…………………………………………………..44
Chapter 8: Reality hits……………………………………………………51
Chapter 9: Her best interest ……………………………………………59
Chapter 10: Away from home………………………………………….66
Chapter 11: Time is near…………………………………………………74
Chapter 12: Birthday to remember……………………………………81
Chapter 13: Fly high………………………………………………………89
Chapter 14: Saying goodbye……………………………………………97
Chapter 15: Saving a life……………………………………………….105
Chapter 16: Heated passion……………………………………………113
Chapter 17: We need to talk……………………………………...…..122
Chapter 18: The talk…………………………………………………….130
Chapter 19: Uninvited guest…………………………………………..137
Chapter 20: Talking to Ethan………………………………………...145
Chapter 21: The date……………………………………………………153
Chapter 22: Confession…………………………………………...…..161
Chapter 23: Finding the journal……………………………….....…169
Chapter 24: Harlow's love……………………………………………..176
Chapter 25: Moving on…………………………………………………183
Chapter 26: Honoring Harlow…………………………………….….192
Chapter 27: A gift for Antonio……………………………………….200
Chapter 28: Antonio's love…………………………………………….209
Chapter 29: The guests…………………………………………………217
Chapter 30: The surprise……………………………………………….225
Chapter 31: Sadie vs. Giorgia…………………………………………234
Chapter 32: Visiting Harlow…………………………………………..242
Chapter 33: Birthday Surprise………………………………………..249

Table of Contents:

Chapter 34: Mystery woman……………………………………....…..258
Chapter 35: Explanation…....………………………………………..266
Chapter 36: Truth will set you free…....……………………………..274
Chapter 37: Feeling the love…………...…………………………….282
Chapter 38: Making decisions………………………………………..291
Chapter 39: Love of a lifetime……………….………………………..299
Chapter 40: Love all around…………………………………………..307
Epilogue: ………………………………………………………………314
Bonus chapter: ……………………………………………………….321

The Unexpected Nanny

Chapter 1- The news

The doctor walked into his office shaking Antonio and Harlow's hand, he then walked around his desk and sat down holding onto Harlow's mammogram, MRI and biopsy results. "Please, sit down." the doctor said, holding his hand out to the chairs across from him. Harlow sat down crossing her legs, nervous to hear what he has to say. Antonio sat down reaching for Harlow's hand, holding tightly onto her hand while waiting for the doctor to read them her results.

She heard the four words she never thought she would ever hear. "You have breast cancer." the doctor explained to her. She gasped when she heard the other words the doctor had to say. "You have metastatic cancer, which means you're at stage four." She put her head in her hands. "My girls." she cried out. Antonio lowered his head and started rubbing her back letting her know that he and their girls will be there for her.
Antonio then looked at the doctor. "What does all that mean, metastatic cancer?"

The doctor took in a deep breath while taking his glasses off and clasped his hands together. "What it means, and I'm sorry to say that the cancer is incurable, the cancer has spread to her lymph nodes, lungs, bones as well as her liver." he explained, handing Antonio the paperwork. Antonio took the papers, looking at them in shock. "I guess I don't understand how this happened? It doesn't run in her family, and she had no signs of lumps on her breasts until a couple weeks ago. She's only twenty-eight years old." Antonio says, choking up.

"Sometimes there are other signs if no lumps have formed, sometimes it could be discharge of the nipple, swelling of the breasts, breast or nipple pain-" the doctor began to say, being cut off by Harlow.

"I've noticed that I have been having shortness of breath, and some difficulty breathing, my breasts have also been feeling sore." she sighed "I've also been feeling extremely tired, and to the point where my body just hurts. I just thought I was coming down with the flu, or that I had something else going on. Breast cancer never even crossed my mind." Harlow said, cutting the doctor off.

"So now what? Antonio asked, feeling devastated.

"We can discuss options, we can't cure it at this point, but what we can do is treat it."

"Which is?" asked Antonio.

"We can start off with hormone therapy and see if her body responds to that, if it doesn't respond, that would mean we would have to start chemotherapy with the option of surgery. After surgery, then we would start radiation therapy. There are other options and treatments as well, some have even tried clinical trials." The doctor explained, giving them hope.

"Do we have to decide what we're going to do right now, or can we go home and talk about our options? I would like Harlow and I to discuss all of our options first, look at the pros and cons of everything, before we decide on what to do."

"By all means, think about it. Call me as soon as you decide on what you're going to do, we would need for her to start treatment right away, to try and prevent the cancer from spreading anywhere else."

Antonio helped Harlow stand up, then shook the doctor's hand.

"Thank you Dr. Walters, we'll be in touch."

Antonio looked at Harlow with sadness in his eyes, he placed his hand on the small of her back, and walked her back to their vehicle. The moment she sat inside, and placed her seatbelt on, she lowered her head in her hands and broke down.

He leaned over to her, and held her. "We will get through this together, you're not doing this alone." he tells her, squeezing her tight. He moved his head back a little and curled his finger under her chin, raising her head up, kissing her on the lips. "I know you; you can fight this."

"What am I going to tell the girls? They're only four years old, they won't understand any of this." she cried out.

His heart felt heavy while listening to her, seeing her with tears in her eyes, hurt him. After everything that she had been through the last few years, this was the last thing they needed to hear. He cupped the sides of her face, and looked her in the eyes with sincerity. Using his thumbs, he wiped away her tears. "We can wait to tell them, they don't need to know anything right now." he says, trying to stay strong for her. He sat up in his seat, and started the car.

On the way home, Antonio kept thinking about what he could do to help Harlow out and lighten up the load for her. With Harlow needing to start treatment right away, she will need all the help that she can get. "I can hire a live-in nanny to help us out, possibly finding one that can do more than just be a nanny for us. One who would be able to help with cooking, cleaning, or anything else you would need help with."

Harlow leaned her head against the window, stared up into the sky, not saying a word. She could hear Antonio speaking to her, but was too upset to speak.

"Hey." Antonio said softly. He turned his head to look at her, and reached his arm out, caressing her cheek.

The Unexpected Nanny

He lowered his hand to hers, placed his fingers inside hers and raised her hand to his lips, kissing the tips of her fingers, which only made her cry more. He breathed in a deep, and exhaled slowly as he was feeling sorry for her, hating that she must go through this. He didn't know what else to say to her to make her feel any better, and continued driving home.

When they got home, Harlow immediately ran up the stairs and into her bedroom, shutting the door hard. She stood against the door, taking in everything that the doctor just told them. She pushed herself away from the door and walked over to the bed to lie down, lying on her stomach, and pressing her face deeply into the pillow.

Antonio left to pick up the girls from pre-K school. He explained to them that mommy wasn't feeling well, asleep, and to not wake her up when they got home. "OK daddy." Gabriella says. "Mommy said she was going to play dolls with us when we got home." Isabella said sadly.

"Why don't I play with you girls when we get home, that way we can let mommy rest." he tells them with a smile, while looking at them in his rearview mirror.

After he got home, the girls grabbed onto his hands and pulled him to their playroom, to play with their dolls. While he was playing with them, Antonio didn't know it, but Harlow was leaning against the frame of the door watching them quietly, and smiling.

He looked over at her when he felt someone standing in the doorway watching them, and smiled at her. She walked over to them and sat down. Harlow picked up a doll and began playing with them until she needed to make dinner.

The girls continued playing, and Antonio followed Harlow out of the room and into the kitchen, so they could talk. While making dinner she discussed with him on what she wanted to do. "I've decided to try the hormonal therapy first, and see if that will work. From what I've heard and read, it's not as harsh as the chemotherapy."

"Whatever you decide to do, I'll back you one hundred percent." he says, wrapping his arms around her waist, looking at her concerned, and sighed "Did you hear me in the car earlier, when I brought up hiring a Nanny?"

"I did."

"What do you think about that?"

She shrugged her shoulders, still unsure of what to think about it, even though he had brought it up in the past. "I don't know, I guess it would help me out a bit, I'm sure I'll be at the doctors a lot, and more tired than I already am."

He smiled. "I'll go to an agency in the morning, and get all the paperwork filled out." he says, feeling relieved.

For the next couple months, Harlow tried hormone therapy, hoping that would work out for her. Antonio and Harlow also finally sat down with the girls, and explained what was going on with her. During those two months, they interviewed many caregiver's who had placed their applications for the job. Antonio started worrying about finding the right nanny, when not one of the interviewees were good enough for the job, and the girls were even turning their noses up to everyone who they interviewed.

Harlow had a doctor's appointment to see the results of how the hormone therapy was going for her. Harlow, Antonio and the girls sat in the room with the doctor, as he sadly explained to them that her body was rejecting the hormone therapy, that the cancer had spread to her brain and her spinal cord tissue, and that it was life threatening.

"We can prescribe medication to ease the pain, or we can admit her, and schedule for an emergency surgery procedure to remove as many tumors as we possibly can. Afterwards, she will have to do radiation treatment." The doctor explained, while scrolling his eyes back and forth to Harlow and Antonio.

Harlow cried as she held her hand with Antonio's, with Isabella sitting on her lap. Harlow looked over at Antonio, as she sniffled. "Let's just do the surgery and then we can go from there." she said heartbroken.

"I'll make a phone call to the hospital, and explain that you are on your way. You will be immediately admitted, and once you're into your room, you will meet with a team of doctors who will perform the surgery. I'll be honest, it might be a couple days until the actual surgery."

Antonio brought Harlow over to the hospital after leaving the doctor's office. Once she was admitted and into her room, Antonio and the girls sat in the room with her, reminiscing on the past; from when they first met, until they received the horrible news.

The girls were starting to get hungry, and when Harlow's nurse came in to examine her, Antonio figured it was the best time to take the girls to get a bite to eat, and to take them home. Antonio stood up and walked over to Harlow, kissing her on the lips. "We will be back tomorrow, get some good rest." he tells her. He lifted the girls onto the bed, so they could say their goodbyes.

While leaving the hospital, Antonio could feel his heart breaking for Harlow, feeling as if his heart was being torn to shreds. He could feel himself wanting to break down, but knew he had to be strong for their girls. He strapped the girls into their car seats, and drove over to a burger restaurant that recently opened in town. He heard good reviews about the food, their service, and that they were very kid friendly, and wanted to check it out.

The Unexpected Nanny

When they walked in, he was surprised to see how busy they were, and amazed at how many people were waiting to be seated. He put his name in with the hostess, and walked the girls over to where they had a variety of games for kids to play while they waited. "Daddy, can we have a balloon?" Gabriella excitedly asked, when she saw kids grabbing balloons as they were leaving.

"After we eat, then you girls can have a balloon."
After waiting a half hour, they finally were called to be seated.

"Kids eat free today." the hostess said to Antonio with a smile, as she sat them at a table, and handed out their menu's. "Wow, thank you." he said, while picking up the menu.

"Hi! My name is Sadie, and I'll be your server today." Antonio looked up from his menu, and noticed a very happy, smiley waitress.

"What can I get you all to drink?" she asked, sounding bubbly.

"I'll have a Pepsi, and two chocolate milks for the girls."

"Our mommy is in the hospital." Gabriella said to her.

"She is? I hope that she will be OK." she says to her. She kneeled while grabbing a crayon, and drew a heart on her paper.

"I want a heart too." Isabella says, handing her a crayon.
Sadie looked over at Antonio while drawing a heart on Isabella's paper, and could see that he was in a different world. "Are you ready to order, or do you need a few more minutes?" she asked, looking at him with concern.

"Sorry, I think we will need a few more minutes, my mind isn't all here right now. We just left the hospital, and found out earlier that my wife has terminal cancer." he said, placing his chin onto his hand as his elbow rested on the table, and stared down at the menu.

"Sure thing." she said, while looking at his twin girls with sadness in her eyes.

After they ordered their food and ate, Sadie walked over to Antonio's table and talked with them for a bit, wanting to see if she could try and cheer them up. Antonio sat there quietly, watching how the girls were interacting with Sadie, and liking how she was with his girls. He could see that his girls liked her as well, especially when they kept asking for her to come over to play with them. He decided to give her an offer that she couldn't refuse.

"I have a question for you…" he asked, while grabbing his wallet out of his back pocket.

"What question is that?" She asked curiously, nodding her head.

"How would you like to be my girls' live-in nanny, and someone who could possibly help us out with cooking, and cleaning?"

Sadie was surprised by his offer, and wasn't sure what to say. "Oh, I don't know?" she said, looking over at the girls.

"I'll pay you $20,000 a month, plus free room and board."

Chapter 2- The decision

"Twenty... thousand... dollars?" Sadie hesitantly said, slowly in shock. "Seriously?"

"Would you want more than that?" he asked, raising an eyebrow.

"Well no... $20,000 is already a lot. But the question is, why me?" she asked confused. She covered her mouth tightly, thinking about what he just asked her.

"I've been looking for a nanny for months, and the girls have not liked any of the women that we have interviewed. It looks like they have taking a liking to you in the short time that we've been here tonight, and after watching you with them, I can see why." he says, trying to smile.

She looked over at the girls, and smiled when they both looked at her with big smiles, she looked back at Antonio. "Hmmm..." she hummed, thinking.

"You're really pretty." Isabella said to Sadie, wiggling her body around in the booth.

"Awe, thank you so much. You know, both of you girls are really pretty yourselves." Sadie said, looking at both girls, and softly sliding her finger on Isabella's cheek.

Antonio pulled a business card out of his wallet, and handed it over to Sadie. She took the card and looked at it. "Think about it, my cell phone number is written on the back of the card as well." Antonio says to her, sounding desperate.

"OK, I'll think about it." She smiled while handing him the bill, and walked away.

The Unexpected Nanny

He opened his bill, and noticed that the bill was comped, owing nothing. He didn't feel right about that, leaving her a hundred-dollar bill, and writing a note on the ticket. *Thank you for the free meal, you didn't have to do that. It was very thoughtful of you, please think about my offer. ~Antonio~*

He closed the bill book, and held onto it. "Come on girls, let's go home." he says to them, while standing up. Sadie was walking by, and Antonio stopped her, handing her the bill book. "Thank you." he said, with a smile.

"You're welcome."

They began to leave and headed to the doors, stopping to grab a balloon for each of the girls, as he promised. He took the girls home, and played dolls with them for a while. The entire time he couldn't stop thinking about Harlow, and how scared she must be, alone in her room, and wishing he was there with her. He then realized that it was after eight at night, and way past the girls bedtime. He gathered the girls and quickly gave them their bath, read them a bedtime story, and put them to bed.

"Mommy will be home in a few days." he says, kissing both the girls on their foreheads. He walked to the door and turned to look at his girls, feeling bad for them. "Goodnight." he says, shutting the light off, and closing the door partially.

He went back downstairs, and decided to call Harlow to see how she was doing. When she didn't answer her cell phone, he called the hospital and spoke to her nurse. The nurse explained to him that she was in a lot of pain, and had given her medication, which helped put her to sleep. The nurse also informed him that she had been hiding all of her symptoms from him for months, how much pain she had been in, and also letting him know about Harlow mentioning that she didn't want him to worry about her, and that she didn't want her girls to see her in pain.

The Unexpected Nanny

Hearing what the nurse was telling him, and how he really wanted to be there for her, not being able to talk to her and to hear her voice before she fell asleep, he felt hurt. After hanging up with the nurse, he got on his laptop, and searched nationwide for the best doctors that specialized with her condition. At this point, he was willing to spend any amount of money on her, not caring what the cost would be.

He got out a notepad, and started writing down doctor's names, and their phone numbers. He figured he would start calling each one of them in the morning. He stayed up for hours searching the internet, that he ended up falling asleep on the couch, with his laptop still on his lap. The next morning, he awoke to Isabella shaking him "Daddy, wake up."

"I'm awake." he says yawning. He set the laptop on the couch and stood up. "I suppose you're both hungry?" he asked, while stretching.

"Yes." said Gabriella.

He walked into the kitchen looking in the cupboards, then inside the fridge wondering what to make them for breakfast. "I want scrambled eggs." says Gabriella.

He looked at them tiredly. "OK, that's what we're having then." he smiled, running his fingers through Gabriella's hair. The girls left the kitchen and grabbed their coloring books and crayons, and sat at the dining room table coloring while waiting for their food to be done.

While Antonio was cooking his phone rang, Isabella got up off the chair and ran to his phone, answering it. "Hello." she says happily in her little voice, while smiling. "OK, I'll get him… who is this?" she asked the person on the other end of the phone, she sat down at the table and began having a conversation with the person on the phone.

Antonio couldn't help but laugh while watching Isabella talk on the phone, acting like she was a grown up. "Who is it honey?" he asked her.

She looked over at Antonio grinning. "She says her name is Sadie."

Antonio walked over to her holding out his hand. "I'll take the phone, please."

"Bye." Isabella said to her, then handed him the phone.

"Hello, sorry about that." he laughed, as he walked back into the kitchen. "So… are you calling to tell me that you have made your decision?" he asked her, crossing his fingers. "Uh huh, that will be fine, I'll text you my address, it's pretty easy to find." he tells her.

An hour later the doorbell rang, as Antonio was opening the door, the girls ran over to him to see who was there at the door. There stood Sadie, he let out a slight gasp when he looked at her, she was dressed in blue skinny jeans, a white draped halter top with her long brown hair loosely hanging down with big bouncy curls. He thought she looked gorgeous, and had to shake what he was thinking out of his mind. He felt upset with himself for looking at her in a way, that he shouldn't have been.

"Come in." he says softly, opening the door wider for her to come inside. Isabella grabbed her hand, pulling her into the house. "Why don't you girls go play, that way I can talk with Sadie for a bit." Isabella ran off, but Gabriella stayed behind, keeping an eye on Sadie.

"Are you here to play with us too?" Gabriella asked her, spinning in a circle on her heels. Sadie leaned down to her level, smiling. "I can play with you later, I have to talk with your dad right now." she says to her, kissing her cheek. She stood back up and giggled, while looking at Gabriella.

"Go by your sister, so I can talk with Sadie please." Antonio says, lightly pushing her to leave. She ran off to go find Isabella. "Curious little girl." he laughed. "So, may I ask what your full name is?" he curiously asked.

"Sadie Marie Hart." she says, holding her hand out to shake his.

"Antonio Russo, nice to formally meet you." he says, shaking her hand.

"I wanted to fully go over all the details with you, before making my decision." she said, looking around, and thinking to herself that they have a very nice place.

"I can show you around, and I'll also show you where your room would be. Do you own, or rent right now?"

"I rent; I actually just signed a new lease a month ago."

"Well, if you decide to take this job, I'll pay your lease in full, and if you decide later that this isn't for you, you'll still have a place to go. Fully paid until your next lease is due."

"Wow, it's a nice gesture, but you don't have to do that." she said shocked.

"I don't mind, I know that this is last minute, and you weren't expecting this offer to become a nanny, but to be honest, I would rather pay your lease off, just to ease your mind in case it doesn't work out here for you. But my girls seem to like you so far, and I don't foresee any problems." he smiled. "I'm also pretty laid back, you'll still be able to do what you normally do, and go out whenever you like."

He began showing her the house starting with the first floor, showing the living room, kitchen, dining room and the patio door to go outside, accessing the pool and back yard. He then showed her the rest of the first floor, showing his den, the playroom, bathroom and music room. He brought her upstairs, showing her the master bedroom, the girls' bedroom, bathroom, as well as two more bedrooms.

"You must have wanted more children?" she asked curiously, after seeing the extra two bedrooms, already fully furnished.

"Yes, we had tried numerous times to have more children, but she kept miscarrying each time, and decided to quit trying. It took a huge toll on her, amongst other things that were going on. Then we got the devastating news about her having breast cancer, putting a damper on everything." he says hesitantly, after bringing up Harlow's breast cancer. She could tell that he was having a hard time speaking about it, as anyone would, and felt sorry for him. Right then and there is when she knew what her decision would be, and changed the subject, waiting to tell him that she would take the job. "How many more levels are there?" she asked.

"One more." He brought her downstairs, showing her the game room, wet bar, washroom, bathroom, and then opened another door showing her where her room would be, already fully furnished.

"If you don't like it, you're more than welcome to change it the way you would want it to be." he says to her, hoping she'll take the job.

"No, it's perfect just the way it is." she said in awe. She walked further into the room, looking around. She felt like she was in heaven after seeing that the room had a huge walk in closet, a full-size bathroom with a shower, a nice king-sized bed, along with a couple nice oak dressers.

"So, this is it, what do you think?" he asked, smiling.

"Your house is very beautiful, and bigger than I thought it would be." She giggled.

"It is big, Harlow hired people in the past to come over and clean the house whenever she got overwhelmed with work, the kids, and the miscarriages."

"Harlow?" she asked, with a curious look.

"I'm sorry, Harlow is my wife." he chuckled.

"Oh yes, sorry, I should have known." she said, covering her face in embarrassment.

"It's OK, I probably should have told you earlier that her name is Harlow." he says. They walked back upstairs and into the playroom where the girls were playing.

Sadie walked over, and sat with the girls. They were having a tea party with their dolls, she picked a doll up off the ground, and set it on a chair. "Can I play too?" she asked, with a smile.

Antonio stood inside the doorway watching Sadie with his girls, feeling confident that she will be the best one for them, not caring if she had experience or not. From what he could see already, she was a natural and began to relax. He felt relieved that he finally found someone his girls felt comfortable with, and adored. She seemed like she was good with kids, and acted as if she knew them since birth. He was feeling as if it was fate, that had him stopping at the restaurant the night before, and couldn't help but smile, thinking about it.

"So, does this mean you'll take the job?" he asked, finally being able to smile.

Chapter 3- Introducing Sadie

"I'm sorry, what was that?" she giggled, while playing with the girls.

"Oh, I asked if this meant that you'll take the job?" he asked, in hopes that her answer was yes. He looked at the girls, they're smiling, giggling and talking like they have known her for a long time. He knew then and there they liked her, and noticed they didn't act this way with any of the other caretakers he interviewed.

She turned around smiling. "Of course, I'll take the job, how can anyone not want to help care for these adorable little cuties."

He let out a sigh of relief. "Thank you, you have no idea how much this means to me. I can honestly say this is one huge relief off my shoulders." he sounded happy, relieved and desperate. "When do you think you could start?"

"I can start immediately if you would like me to." she says, while Gabriella sat down on her lap, handing her a doll.

"I would like that; will you be keeping your other job as well?" he asked curiously.

She smiled while looking at Gabriella. "I actually put in my two weeks notice last night." she said, turning back to look at Antonio and winked. She turned back to the girls and started playing with them again. He tilted his head to the side and looked at her with a questionable look, then realized she made her decision last night.

Being the girls had Sadie occupied now, he figured now would be a good time to call the doctors that he had found on the internet the night before. "Would you mind keeping an eye on them for a few minutes? I need to go make some important phone calls."

"I don't mind at all, do what you need to do, we'll be just fine." she said happily.

"Thanks." He walked away, leaving Sadie with the girls and went into his office, shutting the door, and praying that at least one of the doctors he found could help Harlow. After making several phone calls, one doctor was willing to fly out the very next day to visit her in the hospital, and look at her records. He was also willing to work with her current doctors, and see if they could come up with a new plan of attack.

Antonio walked back into the playroom, quietly standing in the doorway, and enjoying how the girls were interacting with Sadie. "We have to run to the hospital and visit Harlow for a bit, would you like to go with us and meet her?" he asked, thinking now would be a good time for the two to meet. He wanted to show Harlow who he found, and to let her know that the girls really liked her, hoping she will too.

She looked at him smiling, with Gabriella hanging from her hand wanting to play. "Sure, I'd love to meet her, I don't have anything else going on today."

"Great, I'm sure she would love to meet you as well."
"I can help get the girls ready, do their hair and find them something nice to wear."

"That would be wonderful, I'm going to make one more phone call while you're doing that... thank you." he smiled, loving the fact that he doesn't have to interview any another person.

Sadie helped get the girls ready, brushed their hair and pulling their hair back into French braids, she then had the girls pick out a dress to wear, wanting them to look pretty for their mother. After the girls were cleaned up and dressed, Sadie looked around and found some paper and crayons, asking if they would like to make something for their mom before they went to see her. "Yes." they both said in unison, they excitedly ran down the stairs and over to the dining room table, waiting for Sadie to bring the supplies down to them. She handed them the paper and crayons, and began drawing their mom pictures. "She's going to love these pictures we made her." Isabella said with excitement, while coloring.

After the girls were done drawing their pictures, Antonio drove them to the hospital. He couldn't wait to see Harlow, and was excited to let her know that he found a doctor that was willing to fly out the next day to meet her, and to discuss other options to help save her life.

When Antonio opened the door to Harlow's room, the girls went running to their mom, climbing up onto the bed and began handing her the pictures they drew for her. "Here mommy." Gabriella said smiling as she handed her, her picture. Isabella then handed her the picture that she drew, both still smiling when Harlow looked at the pictures.

The pictures gave her a smile "I love them, thank you!" she said kissing the girls on their foreheads, they were proud of their pictures and explained to her what they drew. "This is you mommy, I made you look like a princess." Gabriella pointed.

"I see that, I like it a lot, thank you so much!" she says, kissing her on the cheek.

"And this is you, with me handing you a flower. Do you like it?" Isabella asked.

"I do… thank you." she kissed her on the cheek, and held up both the pictures, smiling. "You both did wonderful jobs; you should be come artists someday."

Antonio walked up to her, handing her flowers that he had picked up in the gift shop on the way into the hospital, and leaned down placing a kiss on her lips. Sadie stood back, quietly watching them. She felt bad for all of them, being that Harlow was in the hospital and not home with her loved ones, she also was feeling a little nervous and out of place.

"How are you doing? he asked softly, after releasing his lips from hers. He missed not having her home, and hated that she had to be in the hospital alone.

She nodded her head, and sighed. "I could be better, and at home with all of you." she said quietly.

Antonio looked behind him, making sure Sadie was still in the room, then looked back at Harlow. "I have someone here for you to meet, we finally found a nanny, and she's here to meet you." he said quietly.

"Who is she?"

Antonio stood up straight and looked over at Sadie waving for her to come over to them. Sadie walked over to Harlow, reaching out her hand for her to shake.

"Hello Harlow, my name is Sadie, it's very nice to meet you." she said politely, with a genuine smile as she shook her hand.

Harlow nervously smiled back at her, she felt leery about her and thought she was too pretty to be their nanny, but she did like how polite she was. Sadie could tell the way she responded to her that Harlow felt nervous about her. Sadie then assured her that she was there to help them out in any way that she could, and to not worry.

Antonio could tell Harlow was unsure about her, he leaned down and whispered in her ear. "Don't worry, the kids absolutely love her." He stood up and looked at Sadie, then back over to Harlow. "Sadie has agreed to help with the kids, staying with us and help you out with cooking, cleaning, and also to help take you to your doctor's appointments if I couldn't take you." he says, trying to persuade her that everything will be OK.

"That would be nice." Harlow quietly said, feeling as if she was losing her family already.

"I also wanted to tell you that I found a top-notch doctor who specializes in your situation. He will be flying here tomorrow, and will be speaking with you and your doctors before your surgery." he says smiling, squeezing her hand, feeling hope. "He thinks there could be other options for you, and that you could possibly beat this."

Harlow leaned her head back into the pillow, staring at the ceiling while taking a deep breath. "I'm scared Antonio, I just want this over with, and I'm willing to do whatever I can to fight this."

"I know, and that's why I stayed up late searching for another doctor to help us out, I'm hoping he has more ideas to help you." he says in a soft tone, stroking his finger softly on her cheek.

Sadie sat down at the table, she brought extra paper and crayons for the girls to keep them occupied while they were in the hospital, when she pulled them out and set them on the table, the girls got excited, ran over to her, and began coloring some more pictures for their mom. Sadie also brought tape, for when the girls were finished with their drawings, and could tape them on the wall for Harlow to see. Hoping to give her smiles, knowing they would be much needed.

Harlow watched Sadie like a hawk, she wasn't sure what to think of her yet, and was beginning to wonder what her intentions were with Antonio and the girls. She watched how the girls interacted with her, and wasn't sure if she liked the idea that the girls liked her, she didn't want to lose them to another woman. She was hurting inside, knowing that she was their mother, and now must have someone else help her out with them.

Harlow did feel a little better, knowing that her girls felt comfortable with her, but at the same time she was feeling a little bit of jealousy. She wasn't liking the fact that Sadie was able to do things with them while she was stuck in a hospital bed, and wouldn't be able do anything with them that she normally does every day.

After being in the hospital for hours, the girls were getting bored and had wanted to go home. Antonio and Sadie were getting the kids ready to leave when there was a knock at the door, they all turned their heads towards the door while it opened slowly. A middle-aged gentleman walked in, and walked over to Harlow. "Hello, you must be Harlow Russo." he says, reaching for her hand.

"My name is Dr. Abraham Jacobson, your husband contacted me this morning, I was able to make arrangements, and fly out much sooner than what I originally told Antonio." he smiled, Antonio gasped in excitement that he was there. Antonio walked over to Dr. Jacobson, and introduced himself, shaking the doctor's hand with a big smile. "You have no idea how much this means to me, well to us actually." He was ecstatic that he came earlier than expected, relieved, and hoped that he would be able to pull off a miracle for the love of his life.

"I'm meeting with your doctor in about five minutes, I just wanted to come in, introduce myself, and say hi." he says sincerely.

The next day Sadie stayed home with the girls while Antonio went to the hospital to be with Harlow for her surgery. The surgery was long, and when the doctor finished with the surgery, he came out to the waiting room, explaining to Antonio that they did the best that they could, with removing as much of the cancer from her body that they were able to, he then explained that the next step is radiation.

A couple days later Harlow came home from the hospital. As much as she wanted to spend time with her girls, she was too tired and sore, and headed straight up the stairs, and into her bed to rest. Antonio received a phone call, with an issue at one of his properties, and had to leave to see what was going on. He went and checked on Harlow, wanting to let her know that he had to leave, but when he saw that she was still asleep he didn't want to wake her, and quietly shut the door, trying not to wake her.

The girls were also napping, so he went down to Sadie's room to let her know that he had to leave. When she answered the door, he was in shock at how she answered the door. He closed his eyes and looked down at the ground, feeling embarrassed.

Chapter 4 – The run in

"Oh!" Antonio says surprised. "I'm sorry, I didn't mean to bother you." He was trying not to look at her, after seeing her dressed in a black laced bra, black laced panties and a white button up shirt that wasn't buttoned. Looking like she just rolled out of bed.

"It's OK, I just figured to try and get a little nap in while the girls were sleeping." she said, sounding tired. She could sense that he was embarrassed, that she was only half dressed, and let out a little giggle. "I'm sorry, I should have thrown my robe on. Is there something you needed?" she asked, covering herself up.

"I just got a phone call that there's a problem at one of my properties, and I have to leave for a little bit. Harlow is still sleeping, so I was curious if you could keep an eye on the girls, which they're still sleeping as well."

"Properties? I thought you were an attorney?" she asked, sounding confused.

"I am, I also own various properties that I rent, and lease out."

"Oh." She said quietly, sounding amazed. "I do have to work tonight, is that going to be a problem?"

"No that should be fine, I will only be gone for about an hour, two hours at most." He assured her.

"OK, thanks." she smiled.

He turned and walked away scratching his head, she thought it was cute and funny that he stuttered a couple times while talking to her. She felt she shouldn't have answered the door like that, and could tell he was trying to keep his eyes focused only on her face, she shut the door and decided to shower, and change, before the girls woke up from their nap.

She quickly took a shower, put on her make-up, and pulled her hair up into a messy bun. She put on her work clothes, and headed upstairs to check on the girls. As she got to their bedroom door, she could hear the girls talking to each other, and slowly opened the door, walking in. "Did you have a nice nap?" she asked, walking over to them.

They both went running over to her, giving her a hug. "Is mommy awake now?" Isabella asked, with her arms up in the air, wanting Sadie to pick her up.

Sadie picked her up with a smile. "I'm not sure, I didn't see her, but if she's sleeping, we shouldn't wake her. She needs all the rest that she can get right now." she tells her, tapping her nose.

Gabriella walked out of the room while Sadie was talking to Isabella and peeked into her parent's room. She saw that Harlow's eyes were open, and ran over to her. "Hi mommy." she said, climbing up on the bed.

"Where's your daddy?" Harlow asked her.

"I don't know, but Sadie is here." she tells her, laying down next to her.

Sadie walked out of the girls bedroom with Isabella in her arms, looking for Gabriella, and noticed Harlow's door open. "She's in here." Sadie heard Harlow say, in a tired voice.

Sadie slowly walked in the room, setting Isabella down. "Sorry about that, I just told them not to wake you."

"Oh, it's fine I was awake. Is Antonio home by chance?" Harlow asked, squinting her eyes like she was in pain.

Sadie walked closer to Harlow, she could see that she was in pain and curious as to if she needed anything. "No, he left about an hour ago, he said there was an issue at one of his properties, and that they needed to be taken care of. He did say he would only be gone for about an hour, or two. Is there something you need that I can get for you?"

"I could really use a glass of water, and my medication." She said, trying to sit up. Sadie noticed her medication was on the nightstand next to her and pointed over to them. "Your medication is right there; I'll go grab you some water."

Sadie left the girls in the room with Harlow, grabbing her a glass of water. When she brought Harlow her water, her heart melted when she saw the girls snuggling up to their mother. She set the glass down on the nightstand next to Harlow. "I'll leave the girls in here with you if you would like, and I'll go start dinner." Sadie said, she figured that Harlow needed a moment with the girls and it would give her time to make dinner.

"Sure, I would really like some alone time with them." she says, as she hugged the girls, placing kisses on the top of their heads.

Sadie left the room, and headed back downstairs and into the kitchen. She began looking inside the kitchen pantry, and the fridge, trying to figure out what to make them for dinner. She found stuff to make lasagna and started to get everything ready, boiling the water, heating the sauce and browning the meat, she then grabbed the cheese out of the fridge and set it on the counter.

She was starting to get a little nervous that Antonio wasn't home yet, she looked up at the clock that was on the wall and saw that she had to work in an hour. She debated on calling him, but figured since Harlow was awake that it should be OK if she had to leave. Once everything was ready to prepare, she began layering the noodles, meat, sauce and the different cheeses, then placed it inside the oven.

She was busy getting dinner ready that she didn't hear Antonio come home, after she closed the oven and stood up, she turned around quickly and bumped right into him letting out a loud gasp as he held onto her arms when she was about to fall.

"You scared the crap out of me!" she said loudly, while looking into his eyes. She was mesmerized by how crystal blue his eyes were, just gazing into his eyes made her melt inside, and felt like her stomach were full of dancing butterflies.

"Sorry I didn't mean to scare you." he laughed, as he let go of her. "I was just coming in here to let you know that I was home. I'm sorry it took a little longer than expected."

"I was starting to get a little nervous that you weren't here yet. I made lasagna, and it should be done in about an hour." she says, as she walked over to the sink, and rinsed the dishes off that she left in the sink, trying to calm herself down. "I can set the timer for you, so you know when the food is done."

He leaned against the counter with a smile. "How did you know that was my favorite meal?"

"I didn't... I wasn't sure if I was supposed to make dinner tonight, it was getting close to dinner time so I looked to see what you had. I saw you had everything to make for lasagna, and made it. Hopefully it tastes OK." she smiled, and began loading the dishwasher.

"I'm sure it will taste just fine." he says, looking behind him. "Are the girls still napping?"

"No... they wanted to lay next to Harlow, so they are in the room with her. Harlow did wake up, asking for water and her medication. She sounded like she was in a lot of pain when I had talked to her."

"OK, thank you for your help."

"You're welcome, but I do have to get going." She set the timer, and walked to the entry way, putting her shoes on.

Sadie was just walking out the door when Antonio called for her, he walked quickly over to her, holding keys in his hand.

"I forgot to give you these.... they are the house and garage keys. I have each of them labeled for you, until you can figure them out."

"Thanks." she says, taking the keys from him. "I'm sure I'll be needing these tonight. I do have to close, but if you need anything, give me a call."

When Sadie left the house, she couldn't help but think about Antonio, wondering why she looked at him in the way that she did. She thought he was extremely sexy with those blue eyes, and dark hair of his, that it had her melting in ways, she knew that she shouldn't have been.

Antonio walked up the stairs and took a deep breath before walking in the bedroom, he couldn't help but think of what Harlow was going through, and felt bad that he couldn't do more for her. His heart broke when he saw the girls cuddling with their mother, and Harlow with tears rolling down her face.

"Are you OK?" he asked, as he walked towards her.

"I'm just scared, I'll never be able to watch them grow up, never be able to experience seeing them with their first boyfriend, comfort them from a heartache after a breakup, never see them get married, nothing." she cried, squeezing the girls tighter against her.

Antonio sat down on the bed next to her, curling his finger under her chin. He lifted her head up to look her in her eyes "Listen to me, you need to fight this, you can fight this, and you need to be strong for those two right there laying in your arms." he says to her, feeling frustrated. Frustrated that she was already giving up.

"Are you able to get up and get out of bed? Sadie made dinner for us, and it should be done soon."

The girls climbed out of bed, ran out of the room and down the stairs. "I think I could use some help getting up, I feel a little weak." Harlow says, trying to sit up.

He helped her out of bed and walked her down the stairs, sitting her at the table. "Smells good, what did she make?"

"Lasagna."

"You must have told her that was your favorite meal... where is she anyway?"

"She had to work, and no... I never told her that was my favorite meal." he says, wondering why she sounded jealous.

"Work?" she asked, giving Antonio a confusing look.

"Yes, she's still waitressing at that new burger joint in town, The Royal Burgers."

"You're telling me that you hired a waitress?" she said, sounding bitter. She rested her elbows on the table and placed her face in her hands, groaning at the thought of Sadie being a waitress, and not a caregiver.

Antonio could sense hostility in her, and let out a loud long sigh. "Harlow, the kids love her, and she's been really good with them so far. Who cares if she's not a licensed nanny, she's a natural."

"I suppose your right." she sighed. "I was no professional either when I became pregnant with twins. At the time I knew nothing about kids, and she seems to be good with them, from what I have noticed so far."

"Just give her a chance, she might surprise you... us that is."
The timer dinged, Antonio pulled the lasagna out and grabbed the garlic bread out of the freezer, putting it in the oven while the lasagna rested, so he could cut into it without it falling apart. The house was beginning to smell

like garlic once the garlic bread began to cook, making his stomach growl, making him hungrier than ever.

After the garlic bread was done cooking, Antonio got everyone's plates ready, set their plates in front of them, and ate. Harlow was amazed at how good it tasted, and enjoyed eating the home cooked meal rather than the hospital food that she had been eating.

"Well that's another bonus, she can cook too." he says.
Later that night after putting the girls to bed, Harlow was feeling sore and tired, and ready for bed herself. She went to bed, with Antonio following behind. He stripped down to his boxers, and climbed into bed, pulling her in his arms.

"When I die, promise me that if you find someone else to love, that they will love the girls just as much as I, and one who will take good care of them, just as I would have." she said sadly. He felt bad hearing her talk that way, and didn't know what to say to her. He just held her tighter and leaned over to her, kissing her lips.

"Just know that I love you, and that I don't want to think about that right now. You're all that I'm worried about, and all that I can think about. " he said softly.

Chapter 5 – Out of control

For the next few months Harlow had been receiving radiation treatments, and at her latest checkup they found out that the cancer had spread again, Dr. Walters explained to them that the radiation was not working, and that they also discovered that she had a rare form of aggressive breast cancer, still being at stage four. Antonio and Harlow were devastated to hear about the prognosis "So what now?" Antonio asked, choking up.

"Well... we never tried chemotherapy, we could try that, it would be our best option. Or she could even try some clinical trials that are out there. But I must warn you, the more we try different things on her, it could do more damage than good, if it comes down to it, we can order hospice care for her. They can make her feel more comfortable, and still be able to enjoy life. Whatever you decide to do, is totally up to you." Dr. Walters explained while taking his glasses off. He pinched the bridge of his nose, hating to tell her how things were looking for her.

"I need some time to decide what I would like to do." Harlow says sadly, she stood up and looked over at Antonio "I need some fresh air."

She left the room, leaving Antonio with Dr. Walters. Antonio looked over at the doctor after Harlow left the room, taking in a deep breath, trying to figure out the right words to the question he was about to ask him. "Can you be honest with me?"

"I can be, if I know the answer... which I have a feeling to what you're about to ask."

"How much time do we have left with her?" he asked, with hesitation.

"Honestly... about six months, the cancer is spreading fast... faster than I'd like to see it, I'm sorry."

"Don't be sorry, you've done what you could, as well as Dr. Jacobson." he says, running his fingers through his hair.

Hearing how much time he had left with her made his heart drop, he then stood up trying to hold back from breaking down, and shook the doctor's hand. "Thank you, we will be in touch."

Antonio left the room, inhaling deep through his nose, wiping away the tears that were starting to form. He walked outside looking for Harlow, and found her standing at the side of the building. "Ready to go home?" he asked her softly, he placed his hand on the small of her back and walked her to their car.

The ride home was quiet, when they got home, Harlow walked past Sadie and the girls without saying a word, and went straight to her room, slamming the door.

"What's wrong with mommy?" Gabriella asked, sounding scared. Antonio walked over to her, picking her up. "Mommy needs to rest, she wants to be alone for a little bit." he says, kissing her cheek.

Sadie was sitting down on the floor and stood up, and walked towards Antonio. "I take that it didn't go so well?" she asked quietly so the girls wouldn't hear.

Antonio put his hand on Sadie's shoulder guiding her over to the kitchen. "No, it didn't go well at all, the radiation isn't working and the cancer has spread." he says sitting down at the breakfast bar. He started to tear up, and rested his elbows on the counter leaning his head down, and rested his hands on the back of his head, while clasping his fingers together.

With his head down he mumbled. "There's more..." he says, pausing to breathe. Feeling as if he were about to hyperventilate. "Harlow doesn't know it yet, but the doctor didn't give her much time."

Sadie stood there listening to him, she didn't know what to say to him. Over the last couple months, she had developed some feelings for him, but hid it well. She felt sorry for him, and knew he was having a hard time dealing with Harlow's cancer. "Not much time?" she questioned.

"Six months…" he tells her, choking up. He stood up abruptly, scaring Sadie. "Excuse me, I need to go take a walk." Antonio walked past the girls in a hurry.

"Daddy where are you going?" Isabella asks, running up to him, and grabbing his hand.

"Daddy is going for a walk, you stay here with Sadie OK?"

"OK." she pouted.

Sadie looked over at the girls, and saw the sadness in their eyes. Harlow never said anything to them when she got home, immediately hiding in her room. Now Antonio left the house, not wanting to be around them. She figured she better step in and take the girls minds away from what was going on. She smiled at them, and tried to be cheerful. "Do you girls want to go swimming?" Sadie asked, knowing that would cheer them up.

"Yes." They screamed excitedly, and ran upstairs, to change into their swimsuits.

Sadie quickly went downstairs and to her room, changing quickly into her swimsuit, she then checked on the girls to maked sure they found their swimsuits. As she was walking up the stairs, the girls came running down the stairs with towels in their hand. Sadie had to giggle at them, at how excited they were to go swimming. Sadie saw their lifejackets hanging up as they walked outside and put them on. The girls excitedly walked over to the waterslide climbing up on the steps. "Sadie watch us!" Isabella screamed excitedly, before sliding down into the water.

"Sadie come in here with us." Isabella yelled, smiling while splashing water everywhere.

"OK, I'll be right in."

Sadie got into the pool, started playing, and laughing with them, getting splashed by the both of them as they tried to swim. The girls both then got out of the pool, and stood at the edge of the pool, wanting Sadie to catch them as they jumped in. "Catch us Sadie!" Gabriella yelled, as she jumped into the water.

Antonio finally came home from his walk, and had heard laughter coming from the pool. He walked over to the patio door, watching the girls smile and laugh. It made him smile, and then began to frown when he thought of Harlow. He decided to go check on her, and see how she was doing, he walked up the stairs and into the bedroom, he saw her sleeping and sat down on the bed next to her.

He tried to wake her, but she just rolled away from him. "Go away Antonio, I don't want to be around anyone right now." she demanded, with harshness in her tone.

"Harlow come on, don't do this."

"Antonio... I mean it, leave me alone. Please just go away." she snapped, grabbing a pillow and putting it on top of her head.

"Fine... is this how it's going to be?" He stood up, yelling back at her.

"Antonio, please…go!" she yelled. Her voice sounding muffled as her mouth was pressed down on the bed, with the pillow laying on top of her head.

He walked away slamming the door, feeling frustrated and hurt. He walked down to the bottom level of the house and over to the wet bar, looking to see what he had that he could drink. He grabbed a bottle of bourbon, and started to chug it. When he emptied what was left in that bottle, he looked around and found another one, chugging the entire bottle.

He then made himself a drink, and stumbled as he walked upstairs, he walked over to the patio door and stood there watching the girls play in the pool and talking with Sadie. *Damn* he muttered under his breath when he saw Sadie in her bikini, while she stood at the edge of the pool while talking to the girls. He slid the patio door open slowly and walked over to a patio chair and sat down.

"Daddy come in and play with us!" Gabriella yelled, smiling. Antonio took a sip of his drink, and threw his arm up into the air. "Not right now honey." he slurred.

Sadie gave him a funny look when she saw the drink in his hand, she could see that he was drunk, and could tell in his voice when he had spoken. The girls climbed out of the pool and walked over to Antonio, grabbing his hand, trying to pull him, wanting him to stand up.

"Daddy come on." Gabriella says, while pulling on his arm. "Not right now, I said." he snapped, with a slight slur to his words pulling his arm back.

Sadie got out of the pool and walked over to the girls, putting her hands on their shoulders. "Why don't you two go find some floaties or some more toys for the pool. I need to talk to your dad for a minute." The girls left Sadie with Antonio, and ran over to the storage bin to find more pool toys.

When Sadie saw that the girls were far enough away, she snapped at Antonio. "What do you think you're doing?" she whispered loudly, with anger in her tone.

"Having a drink, what does it look like I'm doing?" He asks, looking serious. Antonio went to take another drink, just as the glass hit his lips, Sadie grabbed the drink out of his hand, placing it behind her back.

"Hey, give that back!" he snapped, reaching around her trying to get his drink.

"NO, you don't need anymore." she says, putting the drink further away from his reach. He wrapped his arm around her waist, pulling her to him and stared into her eyes. "I'd like my drink back, please." he said slowly, and deep with sexiness in his voice. The way he spoke caused her breathing to become erratic. The way he looked at her, and the feeling of his arm around her, had her feeling weak in the knees. His hot breath that hit her skin while he spoke, and smelling like bourbon was giving her goosebumps.

"No." She snapped quietly, trying to look away from him, she then began to stutter a bit, as her heart felt like it was racing. She needed to get away from him, he was making her feel things that she knew was wrong. "You don't need it, those girls over there need you right now, you sound like you've had enough as it is."

With his one arm still around her waist, he took his other hand and began caressing the side of her face. "You know you're extremely beautiful when you're angry." he says quietly, making her feel as if she was about to drop to the ground.

He started to slowly lean closer towards her face, and her heart started beating faster. Thinking that he was about to kiss her, she turned her head away from him. He released his hand from her face, and reached around her, grabbing his drink back. He stepped away from her the moment he got his drink back.

She stood there not saying a word, she was at a loss for words as she thought about what it seemed like he was about to do, thinking that he was about to kiss her. She began to walk past Antonio to get over to the girls until he grabbed her hand, pulling her to him.

"Antonio stop... you're drunk, please leave me alone." she says, shaking her hand out of his, quickly walking over to the kids.

He finished his drink and went back inside to make himself another one. He sat at the bar downstairs, pouring himself another shot. As he was about to drink the shot, he could feel someone standing behind him, and turned around thinking it was Harlow. Instead, he saw that it was Sadie, standing with her arms crossed, giving him the evil eye. He stood up fast, nearly falling over.

He turned back around and slammed his shot putting the glass down on the bar. "Did you come down here to yell at me again?" he asked. "You might as well yell at me, today seems like the day to be yelled at by everyone." he says, with slurred speech, letting out a quiet chuckle as he leaned himself against the bar.

When she didn't answer him, he turned back around and walked towards her. "You need to sober up. I had planned on going out with some friends tonight." she said angrily. The closer he got to her, the more she backed away from him, and backed into the wall.

She started to get nervous the way he was walking towards her, with a strange look in his eyes, she pushed her hand against his chest as he got up to her, trying to stop him. He had her pinned against the wall and put his hands on each side of her, pressed hard against the wall trying to hold himself up, staring into her eyes, and not saying a word.

Chapter 6- Tension all around

As he stood there staring into her sparkling blue eyes, having her pinned up against the wall, his heart skipped a beat. He knew he had quite a bit to drink, and had a lot of emotions running throughout him, not even realizing what he was doing, and started leaning in to kiss her. Her heart began beating faster, and put her hand over his mouth. "Antonio, please..." she said quietly. Turning her head, and pushing him away.

When he finally realized what he was doing, he pulled his one hand away from the wall. "Sorry." he said quietly, looking down at the ground, feeling upset with himself. "I don't know what I was thinking." He felt embarrassed, and hoped that he didn't scare her off.

She hurriedly got away from him. "I'm going out, so you need to sober up… like right now." she growled. She went into her room and shut the door, then opened the door quickly, and peaked her head out, snarling at him. "I suggest you take a nap while the girls are napping, that will help you sober up." she said, shutting the door hard.

He looked up at the ceiling taking a deep breath *What the hell am I doing?* he mumbled. He shook his head, pushed himself away from the wall, and walked over to the stairs, stumbling while walking up the stairs. He walked into the living room, debating about going up the other flight of stairs to lay down with Harlow, he knew Sadie was right and that he needed to sleep it off.

He slowly went up the stairs barely making it up, wobbling on that last step, trying to hold on to the railing before he fell down the stairs. He caught his balance, and walked into the bedroom. He looked at Harlow and saw her back facing him, figuring she was sleeping, he tried walking quietly to the bed, but with all the alcohol he had drank he couldn't walk straight, and bumped into the corner of a dresser making a loud noise, causing some knickknacks to fall. The loud noise awakened Harlow, she rolled over and started barking at him when she saw him stumbling.

"Are you drunk?" she yelled, sounding upset.

"As a matter of fact, I am, do you have a problem with that?" he smiled, as he laid down on the bed, facing the ceiling and turning his head to look at her.

"Yes, I do have a problem with that, do you not realize what time it is right now? And where are the girls?" she snapped.

He couldn't believe what she just said to him, and felt angry. "Do I know what time it is..." he asks, pausing "The question is... do you know what time it is? You've been hiding in here ever since we got home, and now you're worried about them. If you want to know, then get your butt up out of bed and quit feeling sorry for yourself." he scoffed, while slurring his words. He looked back up at the ceiling, and took in a deep breath, groaning. He hated yelling at her, and knew it was the worst thing to do with what she was going through, but was frustrated, and hating the world right now.

"You're a jerk, how could even you say that to me?" she cried, crossing her arms.

"Instead of being in here hiding from everyone, you should be spending time with those girls of ours." he said quietly, closing his eyes.

She huffed, and shoved him hard, making him groan before she crawled out of bed. She walked out of the bedroom and headed over to the girls' room. She opened their door and saw they were sleeping together, she walked over to their bed and slid Gabriella over so that she could lay in between them. As she laid down next to them, she looked over at each of them, kissing their cheek. "I do love you two." she whispered to them.

The Unexpected Nanny

While Sadie was in the shower getting ready to go out, she kept thinking about how Antonio had come on to her, not once, but twice. She knew that he was drunk, and thought that it was uncalled for, all while his wife was upstairs, upset with the news that she just received. She didn't know what brought it on for him to drink like that, and was completely surprised by his actions.

She dressed in a short black low-cut dress that hugged all her curves, showing off her nice firm breasts. While she was putting on her makeup, Isabella came into the bathroom rubbing her eyes, watching her put on her makeup. Sadie noticed her watching her, and looked over at her with a smile.

"Would you like some makeup on too?" she asked, grabbing a tube of light pink lipstick, and walking over to her.

"Yes!" she said excitedly, jumping up and down. "I want to look pretty, just like you." she says, twirling around, and swaying side to side.

Sadie picked her up, and set her on the counter of the bathroom sink. She put the lipstick on, and told her to rub her lips together gently. "Now, close your eyes." Sadie tells her, and began putting a light shade of pink eyeshadow on her eyelids.

"Now, open your eyes and look up at the ceiling, I'll put some mascara on you." Sadie tells her. Isabella looked up at the ceiling, and she carefully put the mascara on her long eyelashes.

"There... how is that?" she asks, turning her around so that she could see herself in the mirror. She smiled big when she looked at herself in the mirror. "I look pretty, like you!" she says, in a high-pitched voice, and huge smile. They both could hear Gabriella calling for Isabella, Isabella turned around, yelling back at her. "I'm in here with Sadie!"

Gabriella ran into the bathroom looking at Isabella, and then looked up at Sadie. "Can you do that to me too?" Gabriella asked excited, jumping up and down.

"Sure, come here." Sadie says to her, picking her up and setting her down on the counter to do the same thing. When she was done, she showed her what she looked like, Gabriella smiled. "I look pretty, let's go show mommy!" Sadie lifted her off the counter and set her down, Gabriella started pulling on Isabella's arm wanting her to come with. "Come on Bella."

Sadie laughed as they ran out of the bathroom, and could hear them running up the stairs. She continued to get ready as the girls went to go show their mom that they had makeup on.

"MOM...MOM!" Gabriella yelled excitedly, running over to Harlow as she was grabbing a glass of water from the kitchen faucet.

"Look what Sadie did to our face, isn't it pretty?" Isabella asks, smiling.

"It is pretty, you both look much older than what you are now." she says, as she leaned down to their level running her fingers through their hair. "Don't you get used to it."

Antonio finally woke up, and slowly walked down the steps, trying to adjust his eyes. He could still feel some of the alcohol that was still in his system. He sat down on the couch, leaning his head back and rubbed his eyes.

"Have you sobered up yet?" Harlow asked harshly, walking towards him, with her hands on her hips.

"Not now Harlow." he snapped, looking over at her. "I really don't want to fight with you right now."

"Well..."

"Daddy look what Sadie did!" Gabriella said, cutting her mom off as the girls ran over to him smiling, pressing down on his legs and showing him their face, he sat up straighter to look at them and grinned.

"Very nice." He says, holding onto their chins as he looked at each of them, sliding his thumbs back and forth softly on their chin.

"Did Sadie leave yet?" he asked, sounding tired.

"Leaving?" Harlow asked, raising her eyebrows at Antonio.

"Sadie told me earlier that she's going out with her friends, so it'll be just us tonight."

Sadie walked up the stairs all dressed up, and ready to go out. Antonio couldn't help but stare at her, noticing how she was dressed. When he realized that he was staring, he quickly turned away so Harlow wouldn't see him gawking at her. Harlow took one look at her and glared at her with a disgusted look, she felt that she was revealing too much while being around Antonio and the girls.

"Wow, do you have a date?" Harlow asked, sounding annoyed, and with a hint of jealousy.

"Actually, I do." Sadie said cheerfully, looking over at Antonio with a smile. She could tell the annoyance in Harlow's voice, and looked back over at Harlow. "It is OK that I do go out, or am I not allowed to?" she asked curiously.

"You are getting paid to take care of the kids, are you not?" Harlow asks, giving her a dirty look.

Antonio looked over at Harlow shocked, and surprised at how Harlow was acting. "That's enough Harlow, she has done quite a bit for us since she has been here, she deserves to go out."

The Unexpected Nanny

Harlow didn't like the tone in Antonio's voice while he spoke to her, and stormed out of the room. "Come on girls, let's go play in the playroom." she said, as she walked away.

Antonio looked at Sadie, and sighed. "I'm sorry about that, she shouldn't have said that. I'm sure it doesn't help that she isn't too pleased with me right now."

"It's OK, she's going through a lot right now, it's pretty understandable." she said, walking over to the front window, looking out. "I see you have sobered up a little, so that's good." she says relieved. Watching out the window, to see if her ride was there.

Antonio looked over his shoulder and looked around, he stood up and walked over towards Sadie, stopping behind her and rested his hand on her shoulder, causing her to gasp and close her eyes. "I'm sorry about earlier, I shouldn't have done that, and I was completely out of line." she says, embarrassed.

She turned around slowly and looked at him with a serious look "You were way out of line, and Harlow has every reason to be upset with you." she said quietly, walking past him. "My ride is out there waiting for me, have a good night." she grabbed her purse, and headed out the door, not wanting to say another word to him.

Antonio stood at the window, looking out, watching Sadie get in her date's car. He rubbed his temples groaning, thinking about how rude Harlow was to Sadie, he then walked over to the girls playroom where Harlow was playing with the girls.

"What was that back there?" Antonio asked frustrated, trying not to raise his voice at Harlow again, especially since the girls were in the room. He didn't think it was right to fight, and argue with the kids being in the same room, but was also upset about how she was treating Sadie.

Harlow refused to look at Antonio, and continued to play with the girls. After a long silence, and knowing that Antonio was still standing there looking at her, she stopped what she was doing. "Does she really need to dress that way around us?" she said, sounding annoyed.

"What's the big deal, she was going out."
Harlow shrugged her shoulders. "I don't know." she snapped, wishing that she could wear something like that, wanting to turn Antonio on, instead of someone else turning him on. She knew Antonio was staring at her, and wished that it was her that he was looking at in that way.

Antonio upset, put his hands up in the air and walked away. He walked into his office slamming the door, and sat down at his desk. He had to do something to take his mind off what was going on and began looking over his client's file, getting things ready for his court case in the morning.

While Antonio was busy writing his notes down, he thought he heard the door opening and could tell that someone was standing there quietly watching him, he looked up and saw Harlow leaning against the frame of the doorway. "What are you going to yell at me now?" he asked, sighing while setting his pen down. He watched her walk up to the edge of his desk, waiting for her to start snapping at him.
He then gulped after hearing her speak.

"I think I made my decision on what I'm going to do next with the cancer."

Chapter 7- Family time

"I've made a decision and please don't get mad; I want you to hear me out." Harlow says to him as she stood across him, while leaning down on the desk. He leaned back in his chair, looking at her, not saying a word. His eyes stayed glued to her and watched her walk around the desk, standing between him and the desk, she leaned against the desk, and looked at him.

Antonio didn't like what he was about to hear, and leaned his head down in his hand, as his elbow rested on the arm of his chair. "What decision is that?" he asked quietly, and his heart beating faster, nervous to hear what she had to say.

"I'm not going to go through with anymore treatments, nothing is working anyway." she says, as tears rolled down her cheeks.

Antonio slid his chair closer to her, wrapping his arms around her, and resting his head against her stomach. She started running her fingers through his hair, trying not to cry harder. "I've been thinking hard about this, and I really do not want to go through chemotherapy, I have been reading all about it, and it doesn't sound like it will be easy to go through. As far as those clinical trials, I don't want to do that either, they are not proven to work, and I don't want to be a test to them either." sniffling as she spoke.

"Harlow, listen to what you're saying." he whispered, choking up. "You sound like you're wanting to give up, trying not to want to live." he says hardly getting his words out, wiping away the tears from his eyes. He couldn't believe what he was hearing, and wanted to try and change her mind.

She leaned down and cupped each side of his face, wanting him to look at her "I know what I am saying, what I am feeling, and I don't like it either... but this is reality. You do realize that if I were to start chemo, I would lose all my hair, I'll be more tired than I already am, I'll also be vomiting all the time, and lose my appetite, it's also a possibility for infections to start. I don't think I could handle all of that."

"You have to try it... for us." he whispered, pulling her tightly against him. "Those girls love you; they need their mother." he begged. Harlow cupped her hands on the sides of his head and leaned her head down onto his. "I just don't think I could handle it, and I don't want the girls to see me go through all of that either, it's a very harsh treatment." she whispered, kissing the top of his head.

If his heart wasn't broken enough as it was, it was more broken than ever. He wanted her to live, he wanted her to try and do whatever it took for her to live, to be with him and their girls. He imagined them growing old together, not this. He never imagined that this would stop all of that from ever happening, and it was killing him inside.

"I really don't want the girls to see me with no hair, I want to enjoy being with them, and not lay there watching them play without me, or playing with someone else either." she says, trying to take in a deep breath, to refrain from crying.

"We can get wigs, if that's what you're worried about." he says, holding her tighter than ever.

"It's not just that, I know I could do that too, but it's the other side effects I'm worried about."

He pulled back wrapping an arm around her waist and pulled her down, setting her down on his lap. She turned to face him, cupping his face and leaned in for a kiss. He pulled back to look at her, running his fingers through her hair, while looking at every part of her face, sliding some strands of her hair away from her face, and looked into her eyes. He saw sadness in those eyes of hers, and could feel that she didn't want to do what she decided.

All he could do at this point was respect her wishes, even if he didn't agree with them.

"I can't make you do anything, but I wish you would rethink this, you never know, it could save your life." he says, pressing his lips against hers, wanting to cry as he kissed her. They embraced in a passionate kiss before getting interrupted by the girls.

"Mommy, we're hungry." Isabella says, as she and Gabriella stood by the door looking at both of them.

Harlow pulled away from Antonio and turned around to face them "OK, I'll be right out, let me finish talking with daddy."

"OK." Isabella says, looking at them strange, trying to figure out what they were doing. The girls then turned around, and ran out of the office. Harlow turned to look at Antonio, smiling and giggled softly.

"We can talk about this later, I better find them something to eat." she says, touching the side of his face.

"Why don't we just order a pizza and watch a movie with the girls." he says "Let's just have a family night for once, and put everything behind us for now, it'll be like old times." he says, trying to smile.

"OK, I would really like that." she whispered, kissing his lips. Harlow left the room to order a pizza, while Antonio finished with his client's paperwork, getting it all ready for court, he had the next day. He sat at his desk thinking about what Harlow said to him, and finally broke down. He couldn't understand why Harlow wouldn't want to try something different to save her life. He remembered what the doctor told him, and wanted more than just six months with her.

He stood up and walked over to the door, shutting it. He went back over to his desk and turned on his laptop, searching chemotherapy side effects. He searched everything from reactions, side effects, to success stories and came across a story of a woman who had gone through the same as what Harlow was going through, and is a survivor. He read her story and started to have hope. He saw that she had left a number to call, that she was willing to talk about her success story. He grabbed his phone and was about to make a phone call when Harlow walked in, letting him know that the pizza had arrived.

"OK, I'll be right there." he says, starring at the screen of his laptop.

"What are you up to?" she asked, looking at him strangely.

He took a deep breath and smiled, waving for her to come over to him, wanting to show her what he had up on the screen of his laptop. She walked over and stood next to him, leaning down to look at what he was reading, when she saw what he had up she stood back up, crossing her arms.

"Antonio, I said I wasn't going to do it." she said, frustrated.
"Will you please just read this, then you can think about what you want to do after reading it." he says, standing up and having her sit in the chair. "Just read it... for me..."

Antonio left her in the office to read the story he found, and walked into the kitchen to grab a beer out of the fridge. He opened the bottle, and took a drink, then grabbed a slice of pizza and sat down at the table with the girls.

"Do you girls want to watch a movie tonight?" he asked.

"Can we watch Captain Underpants?" Gabriella asked.

He shook his head, not thinking that he heard her correctly. "Captain what?" he laughed. The girls started giggling as they took a bite of their pizza.

"Captain Underpants." Isabella said, with food in her mouth, giggling.

"Never heard of it." He says, taking another bite of his pizza. Harlow walked towards the table, curious as to what they were talking about. "Never heard of what?" she asked, sitting down.

"Captain Underpants? The kids said they wanted to watch that movie." he laughed, trying not to spit the food out of his mouth.

Harlow giggled. "It's an animated movie, they have been wanting to see it. I guess it's supposed to be funny."

Antonio looked back at the girls, leaning towards them. "I guess that's what we're watching then." he says laughing. The girls got excited, and hurried to finish eating.

The girls finally finished eating, and left to go wash up. Antonio looked at Harlow, asking if she read the story, wondering what she thought of it.

"I read it, and it may be a success story for her, but that doesn't mean it will happen to everyone, it's a miracle Antonio, and she was lucky... very lucky"

"It could be you too." he pleaded.

"I'm going to get the girls ready, I still need some time to think about what I will do, I was determined not to do anything." she says, as she stood up, pushing her chair in.

Harlow got the kids into their pajamas and went down to the kitchen to make them some popcorn to snack on. While she was doing that, the girls grabbed blankets, and pillows, and laid them on the floor in front of the TV. Antonio sat on the couch waiting for Harlow to finish getting the kids their popcorn, and couldn't stop thinking about the success story of that lady, hoping Harlow will at least give it a shot.

Harlow gave the kids their popcorn, and sat on the couch, cuddling up to Antonio. As they watched the movie, Antonio couldn't believe what he was watching, but got a kick out of the kids laughing, making him laugh, forgetting what was going on. Even if it was for a little while.

When the movie was done, they carried the girls up to their room and laid them into their beds. Harlow stood there watching the girls for a moment, thinking about what Antonio had her read earlier. She felt torn on what to do, she wanted to live for them, but didn't want the girls to see what chemo would do to her either. She gave them a kiss and left the room.

Harlow went in her bedroom, and found Antonio standing there looking like he was in a different world. She walked up from behind him, wrapping her arms around him, and resting her head on his back. He spun around, cupping her face, and kissed her hard. Their kiss was slow at first, then turned to a loving passionate, desperate kiss. He was enjoying the feeling of her lips against his, and felt tingly all over. She leaned her head back, giving him access to her neck. His lips moved down to her neck, and started kissing her all over, desperately wanting to make her feel good, and to forget everything that she was going through.

He lifted her up and carried her to the bed gently laying her down, lightly laying on top of her while kissing her lips hard and demandingly, her moans were muffled by his kiss, while his hands softly trailed all over her, feeling every inch of her body, that had her feeling warm inside. He helped take her clothes off, and quickly removed his, throwing each piece of clothing across the room as he undressed.

He thrusted in her slowly, trying not to hurt her and wanting to be as passionate as he could. Her moans were making him want her more, she wanted to be in control, and pushed him over to his back, straddling him. She placed him inside her, and began moving up and down on his hardened cock, until they both orgasmed, releasing at the same time.

She lowered herself down on top of him, she just wanted to lay there, and not move, while he held on to her tight. She raised her head up, and looked at him, wanting to remember every little detail of his face and placed a soft kiss on his lips before getting off him.

    She rolled off him and laid there quietly, content in his arms. He softly caressed her arm, sending goosebumps all over her body as she closed her eyes. He leaned over, kissing her lips. "I love you." he says quietly. She let out a sigh of happiness, and fell asleep in his arms.

Chapter 8- Reality hits

Sadie came home in the middle of the night, thinking that everyone would be sleeping at that time, she tried coming in the house as quietly as she could. She was taking her shoes off in the entry way, and jumped when she heard a noise from across the room, she didn't realize Antonio was in the kitchen drinking a glass of water.

"What is it with you scaring me all the time?" she whispered loudly, not pleased.

"Me? I was just drinking a glass of water, I assumed you were home already." he says quietly, as he walked towards her.

When he got closer to her, her heart started to beat faster when she realized he was only in boxers, and tried not looking at him.

"I should get to bed." she says quietly, wanting to avoid him. She started to walk past him so she could go to bed, he rested his hand on her shoulder as she walked by, making her stop.

His touch sent goosebumps throughout her body, when she stopped to look at him, the look in his eyes made her melt. "Antonio I'm tired." she whispered.

"I just wanted to ask you something about earlier, wondering if you could ever forgive me. It's been eating at me all night." he asked, looking at her desperately.

"I forgive you" she said quickly, wanting to get away from him.

"Can we talk about this another time, it's late." she asked, looking away from him.

"Thank you." he said quietly, taking a step back away from her.

He stood there watching her walk away, he felt like a heel when he realized he was starting to develop feelings for Sadie. He loved Harlow very much, and knew that he had to stop having these feelings for Sadie, every time he looked at her, or interacted with her, all he wanted to do was to hold her in his arms. He wasn't sure if they were exactly romantic feelings, or if they were just feelings of someone to help comfort him. He wasn't understanding where his mind was at, and it was killing him to be feeling the way he was.

The next day he left for work earlier than normal, wanting to avoid seeing Sadie. When he got to his office, he logged online quick to find the story he read the night before, and to get the phone number that he had seen at the bottom of her success story.

He called the number once he found it, and talked with the lady for about an hour explaining Harlow's situation. Although her situation was extremely similar to Harlow's, hers wasn't as aggressive, and rare as Harlow's was. She also was never told that she had so much time to live. The hope he had, suddenly turned to fear, and disappointment, thanking her for her time before he hung up.

He sat in his chair spinning it around slowly with his feet, and then stopped to face the window so he could look into the sky. He knew that he had to face reality, and to finally accept the fact that she will not be with them much longer. The more he thought about it, he broke down, and began praying for a miracle to happen.

His secretary knocked on the door, and walked into his office when he didn't respond to her. Knowing that he was in there, she figured that she better let him know that he was running late for court, and needed to hurry up.

"Thank you, I'll be leaving in a couple of minutes, please call and let them know I'm running behind." he tells her, with a crackle in his voice. After she left, he stood up and walked over to the small sink in his office, staring at himself in the mirror. He then splashed some water in his face, and cleaned up, getting himself presentable for court.

He walked over to the door, and stood there with his hand on the door knob. He couldn't get Harlow off his mind, and rested his forehead against the door, trying to get himself together, before walking out the door. He took in a few deep breaths to calm himself down, and cool off. He felt he was about to break down, and didn't want anyone in the office to see him that way.

He was finally able to calm himself down, telling himself to just get through the day, and all will be better once he was home, and opened the door.

******

While he was in court his mind was still elsewhere, and couldn't think about the case he was on. Every time it came for him to speak, he was staring off, and not acknowledging what was being said.

"Mr. Russo, will you please approach the bench?" the judge asked, in a serious tone.

Antonio slowly walked over to the judge, and stood before him, fighting back his tears.

"Is there something going on, that you are not focusing on your case?"

Antonio leaned over the bench and whispered to the judge. "May I please ask for a continuance?"

"May I ask why?" the judge asked, looking at him concerned.

"I'm sorry, my mind is elsewhere right now, and I do apologize." he says with a blank stare, he then covered his face and began sliding his hands down his face roughly. Taking some deep breaths in and out, trying not to lose it in the courtroom.

"And where is your mind at right now?" Judge Stevens asked, curiously.

Antonio leaned closer to the judge, talking quietly so others couldn't hear. "I just received news that my wife is dying, and she has been given only a few months to live, I'm sorry.... but I really need a continuance." he says hesitantly, looking away from the judge.

The judge looked at him in shock, he knew Harlow very well from previous functions they had attended together. He liked her a lot and had always thought of her as a daughter to him.

"I'm sorry to hear that." he sadly said, he took his glasses off and pinched the bridge of his nose, thinking about Harlow, everything she had gone through over the past few years, and how sorry he was to now hear about her health. "I'll grant the continuance, please let the court know when you will be able to set the next date for his court appearance."

"Thank you, sir."

Antonio sat down next to his client, and informed him what was going on, while the judge prepared for the next case.

After Antonio had left the courthouse, he took a long drive to think about everything that has happened, and what will be happening. He knew he needed to start preparing for the worse, and visited some funeral homes. He wanted nothing but the best of the best for Harlow, and looked for the best casket he could find, not caring what the cost would be.

The Unexpected Nanny

Antonio still never told Harlow that the doctor had only given her six months to live, he wanted her to fight, and to not give up. He knew that if he told her what the doctor said, she would refuse to do the chemo. She was already determined not to do anything, and he didn't want to say anything to her that would change her mind again. When he had got home, he was greeted by the kids running up to him "Daddy, Daddy." Gabriella said excitedly.

He picked her up giving her a hug, and kiss, and set her back down, he then gave Isabella a hug, and kiss when she reached up for him. Sadie was sitting at the dining room table, she was helping the girls make projects out of popsicle sticks, and they were excited to show him what they made. He looked at the boxes they made and smiled. "Very nice, girls."

He walked up to Sadie looking tired and wore out "Where is Harlow at?" he asked quietly.

"She's been sleeping for a while now, I wasn't sure if I should wake her up or not." she says, looking up at Antonio, she noticed that he had looked, and sounded depressed about something, and want to ask if everything was alright, but didn't want to intrude.

He walked over to fridge, and looked inside, debating on what to grab to drink, and reached for a beer. He opened the beer and sat down at the table, leaning back on the chair looking up and not saying anything.
"Bad day at work today?" Sadie asked, trying to figure him out.

"Bad day in general." he said sighing, rubbing his face. He leaned his head back down, to drink his beer. "I just need to face reality, but I can't.... I just wish there was more that I could do.... I could have all the money in the world, and it still won't change a damn thing." he says, frustrated.

While listening to Antonio speak, her heart was breaking for him. She was speechless, this was something she never had to deal with, at least nothing like this with anyone before. She knew what it was like losing someone that she loved dearly, but not this way. She didn't know how to react, or what to even say to him. She reached her hand across the table, and placed her hand on top of his.

"I wish that I could say everything will be alright, but I know that's not the case. Just remember you must stay strong for all of them. There are two beautiful girls over there, that need you." she says quietly, squeezing his hand.

He stood up holding his hand to his heart, breathing in deeply. "I better go check on Harlow." He took another drink of his beer, and set it on the table, before he headed up to see Harlow.

He headed upstairs and stood in the doorway, watching her sleep for a minute. He quietly walked in and sat on the edge of the bed next to her, running his fingers through her hair. He noticed she was turning pale, more and more each day, and it was breaking his heart. He leaned down kissing her forehead, which made her open her eyes.

"Antonio..." she whispered.

"Hi." he says softly, with a tight-lipped smile. He breathed out a heavy sigh, wanting to tell her about what he knew, but still not wanting to say anything to her, in hopes that she will fight this and to try living for them.

"I've had some time to think today." Harlow says sitting up, leaning against the pillows that were pressed against the headboard.

"What were you thinking about?" he asked inching closer to her, hoping that she was going to tell him that she will try the chemo.

"At first I thought about doing the chemo, but the more I thought about it, I changed my mind." she says quietly, resting her hand on his cheek.

"Why would you change your mind? You need to fight this Harlow, not just for you... but for all of us." He choked up, and had to look away.

She knew he was right, but it wasn't him that was going through this, he had no clue how she was feeling, he had no clue how much she was hurting, it was killing her to know that she wouldn't be around for them, and wanted to do everything that she could, to live. But where she was at with her stage of cancer, she knew the chance of living was slim to none. "I would have fought harder if there was hope, but there isn't any hope for me."

"Don't say that..." he pleaded, grabbing onto her hand, holding it tight.

"It's the truth Antonio, you need to realize that, and I know you know about how much time I have left." she says quietly, sounding hurt, she turned her head away from him, and looked out the window,

He shook his head, unsure of what she meant by that. "What are you talking about?"

"I called that one lady this morning, the one who's story you had me read. She said she talked to you already about everything, after I talked with her, I called the doctor to let him know that I decided to try the chemo. He was all for it, I was getting things all set up to start the chemo, until he told me that he had talked to you about how much time I had left. He proceeded to explain that the chemo might, or might not make me live any longer. That's when I changed my mind again, I'm just going to have to deal with it and try to live as long as I can."

Antonio closed his eyes after listening to what she said, he felt hurt that she was giving up so easy, and then began feeling angry with the doctor for telling her that she didn't have much time left on this earth. Harlow looked at Antonio and could tell that he was upset, after seeing how red he got in the face, she knew he was hiding it from her, and she also knew that he was keeping it from her for a reason.

"If you're angry with the doctor for telling me, please don't be... it's not his fault, I asked him to tell me, and I deserved to know."

Chapter 9- Her best interest

  A month had gone by, Harlow was getting weaker by the day and the pain that she has throughout her body had been getting worse. Sadie took Harlow to her doctor's appointment, since Antonio was to be due in court all morning.

  After Harlow's screening and her exams, the doctor prescribed her some more medication and a stronger medication for the pain. Dr. Walters explained to Harlow, as well as Sadie, that her bones were extremely frail right now, and to try avoid any activities that could fracture her bones. Sadie wrote everything down in a notebook, while the doctor was explaining where Harlow is at with her cancer, and what she should be doing at this point. She knew Antonio would be asking questions about it when he got home later, and figured this was the best way to let him know what the doctor said, so she wouldn't forget any of the information that was explained to them.

  The doctor also printed off paperwork with his findings, and instructions for what she is supposed to be doing at home. He also provided them with names and phone numbers for hospice care if they were to choose that route.

  "Harlow at the stage where you're at, it would be in your best interest to enter hospice. All they will do is help for you to stay comfortable, they will also help you with your medical care and with your pain management.... now, I'm not saying that you must do that, it's just something to think about." Dr. Walters explained to her.

  "Thank you, I'll have to talk about it with Antonio." she sighed, she didn't want to hear about entering hospice just yet, and it tore her up inside. She shook his hand, and looked over at her girls who were both sitting next to Sadie, and began to tear up. She sighed and looked at Sadie. "I'm ready to go home."

Once they got home, Harlow went straight upstairs and into her room slamming the door. She didn't want her girls to see her cry, she had been holding her tears back from the doctor's office all the way home, and couldn't hold back anymore. She dropped down on the bed, lying down on her stomach and let it all out, screaming into the bed. "Why me?" she kept asking over and over, while punching her fists down on the bed.

After she calmed herself down, she stood up and walked over to the bottom drawer of her dresser, and grabbed a journal that she had been hiding, she climbed into bed, covered herself with the blankets, and started writing in it.

Sadie had gone upstairs to check on Harlow, she knocked on the door and slightly opened the door, peeking her head in, Harlow grabbed a pillow, and put it over her journal, not wanting her to see it.

"I'm sorry to bother you, but I was wondering if there is anything that I can get for you?"

"No thanks, I'm OK for now."

"OK, let me know if you need anything." she says, before shutting the door, she then heard Harlow call out for her and re-opened the door.

"Did you need something?" Sadie asked, as she stood in the doorway, holding onto the door knob.

"I have a question to ask you." she says, patting the bed for her to sit down.

Sadie felt a little nervous, she wasn't sure what she was going to ask, she didn't think Harlow liked her that much, and was curious as to what she was going to ask her. She walked over to her, sat down on the bed next to her, looked at her, and could see that she had been crying. Harlow looked back at her nodding her head.

"What do you think of my girls?"

Sadie looked at her surprised, and confused by that question "What do I think of them?"

"Yes, I'm curious as to how you feel about them."

"Well... I think they are great kids, they are beautiful, very smart for their age, and I love them as if they were my own children. Why do you ask?"

"I was just curious.... they sure seem to like you. You're like a second mom to them, and I do appreciate everything you do for them. At first, I was nervous with you watching them, but they have clinged to you since the first time I saw them with you." Harlow says with a smile.

"I would never do anything to hurt them, I do hope you know that." Sadie says to her, assuring her. "And I'm glad I got to know them, they're very special... well actually, you all are special to me." Sadie says, smiling.

"Thank you, that's all I wanted to know, you can go now. I'm sure the girls are looking for you anyway." she says quietly.

Sadie left the room wondering what that was all about. She thought it was strange and unusual for her, since Harlow usually ignored her. She checked on the girls, and found them both asleep on the couch, she grabbed a blanket, and laid it over them. She knew they could use a nap and if she tried picking them up, they would wake up. Thinking she could use a nap as well, she sat down on the other couch, covered herself in a blanket, and quickly fell asleep.

Antonio came home from work, and walked into a quiet house, he thought it was odd since normally the kids are always running to greet him when he got home. He walked further into the house, and saw the kids sleeping and noticed Sadie sleeping also. He knew since Harlow wasn't downstairs, that she must have been sleeping as well.

He walked into the kitchen and noticed paperwork from the doctor, as well as Sadie's notes sitting on the breakfast bar. He picked them up, and sat down at the table, looking them over.

He started wiping his forehead as he read each page, his stomach dropped and let out a loud gasp when he got to the hospice paperwork. He stood up, and walked over to Sadie, wanting to wake her up to see what all the paperwork was about, he leaned over the couch, and got next to her ear. "Sadie!" he whispered loudly.

She could feel his hot breath on her, and opened her eyes. Her eyes widened when she saw him inches away from her face, with his eyes staring back at her.

"Can I talk to you for a minute?" he asks quietly, standing back up.

She slowly slid the blanket off her, stood up and followed him into his office. Once they were in his office, he stopped and turned around holding up the papers. She knew he was going to ask her about the papers, and what it all meant.

"What are these hospice papers about?" he asked, demanding that she tell him everything that was said by the doctor.

"Did you look at all the papers?" she questioned. She didn't feel like repeating anything, especially the way he was questioning her.

"I did, but what is this all about?" he asked, flashing the information about hospice care, and pushing the paperwork closer to her.

"Antonio, she's in a lot of pain, and she's very weak. The doctor thinks that it's in her best interest to hire a professional, to help care for her." she says pausing, she walked closer to him and grabbed the paperwork out of his hand. She felt a lump in her throat as she was about to tell him the next thing the doctor told them. "Her cancer is so aggressive, that it has spread everywhere, the way the doctor sounded, it's not good, not good at all." she said sadly.

Antonio stood there in shock, he looked at the papers in her hand, and looked back at Sadie, feeling broken. "You do know what hospice means, don't you?" he asked, feeling as if he was being stabbed in the heart.

Sadie nodded her head, quietly responding back to him "I do."

"This here means the end is near, and I'm not ready for that." he says, walking away from her.

"Harlow didn't take the news well either, she's been up in the bedroom since we got home."
Sadie thought about telling him what Harlow asked her earlier, but thought that it was best to not say anything, at least not right now.

"The doctor did say it was completely up to you and Harlow for the hospice care, but he did say that he highly suggests it, saying it would make life a lot easier for her." she said, as she walked up to him, giving him a hug.

He wrapped his arms around her, and held her tight while resting his chin on the top of her head. At first, she wasn't going to hug him because of the sparks she felt between them recently, but when saw how hurt and broken he was, she knew he could use a hug.

As they were holding each other, Isabella quietly walked into the room, tapping on Sadie's back. "I think mommy needs help; she was just yelling."

"Thank you honey, daddy will go check on her." he tells her. He released his arms rom Sadie and looked her in the eyes. "Thank you, I needed that."

She smiled at him, and nodded her head. "Go see what she wants." she says, pushing on his arm to leave.

Sadie leaned down, and picked Isabella up, hugging her. "Is mommy sick?" Isabella asked, as she rested her head on Sadie's shoulder.

Sadie's heart dropped when she asked her that, not knowing what to say to her. "Yes honey, she isn't feeling the greatest right now, how about I go play you a song on the piano?"

Isabella hopped down, and pulled on Sadie's hand, bringing her to the piano, excited to see and hear her play.

Sadie sat down at the piano, and started playing Ave Maria. Isabella sat next to her, watching her play with a smile. Gabriella came running in the room after she heard music playing and stood next to Sadie, watching her fingers as she played the song.

Antonio was upstairs helping Harlow out with her medication, his heart felt heavy seeing her in so much pain, and wished he could trade spots with her, so she wouldn't have to feel it anymore.

"Antonio..." she said softly. He looked at her and pulled her in his arms, holding her tight and running his fingers through her hair.

"Just keep resting you need it... I'm so sorry you're going through this and that I can't do anything more for you. I pray every day for a miracle, hoping that I could take it away from you." he tells her, pulling back and placing a kiss on her lips.

She pulled away from him, and laid her head back down on the pillow, taking in deep breaths.

"What would you say about all of us going on a family vacation? The girls birthday is next week, and I was thinking maybe we could take them to Walt Disney World, would you like to do that?"

She shrugged her shoulders "I don't know if I could?"

"Come on Harlow, we both know what is about to happen, wouldn't you like to take a family vacation, and see the girls happy? You have to be strong for them too, you're still here and you deserve time away from what's going on here as well."

"I guess you're right, I can try and be strong, and enjoy whatever time I have left, especially with you and our girls." she says quietly.

He leaned to her and kissed her lips "I'll go tell them." he happily says, grinning ear to ear,

As he walked back down the stairs, he heard the piano being played, and recognized the song. He thought that it was being played beautifully, and headed over to the music room to see what was going on. He stood in the doorway of the music room, he was in awe when he saw the girls sitting next to Sadie, while she played the piano.

He had no idea she knew how to play piano, and was flabbergasted. He started to walk in, and the girls turned around when they heard him behind them, clearing his throat. Sadie stopped playing, and turned around.

"Wow, I'm impressed... you never said that you could play the piano." Antonio said, surprised. "You were playing it so elegantly, it's also one of my favorite songs to play."

"Thank you, I've been playing piano since I was five years old. Hope you don't mind, I wanted to play them a song."

"No, I don't mind at all, you can play whenever you feel like it." he said thrilled, hoping to hear her play another song.

"I actually came down to let you all know, that I'm going to bring everyone on a vacation, the girls' birthday is next week, and Harlow could use a break away from everything, including me." He looked at the girls with a smile, and chuckled as they began jumping up and down. He looked back over at Sadie, and smiled. "Would you mind joining us? You also deserve a break from here."

Chapter 10- Away from home

Antonio waiting for Sadie's response, when she didn't respond, he tried again. "I'd really like it if you could join us, all expenses paid." he says, with a smile.

"Of course, I will, someone has to help watch the girls, and I wouldn't miss their birthday for anything." she happily accepted.

"Great, I'm just hoping that Harlow will be able to handle it, she's pretty weak right now." he sighed, trying to picture her having fun.

"Where do you plan on taking them?"

Antonio looked over at the girls, and smiled "Walt Disney World."

When the girls heard where he said he will be taking them, they got even more excited, and started jumping up and down.

"Oh, how fun!" Sadie said excitedly, while looking at the girls. She knew they would have a blast there, and couldn't wait to see their smiling faces when they get to meet their favorite characters.

"The girls have been wanting to go for a while now, and every time they see a commercial for it, they beg to go. I thought it would be nice for Harlow to see the girls enjoy it, and have their dreams come true before...." He realized what he was about to say, and didn't want to say it in front of his little girls "I just want Harlow to be a part of it, the girls experiencing Magic Kingdom, Hollywood Studios, etcetera."

"I'm sure she would like that, if anything I know they rent out wheelchairs, if she needed one.... it's just a thought."

"Yes, I'm sure she will probably want to use one while we're there, she may feel a little embarrassed by it, but who cares. It wouldn't be a bad idea, and easier for her to enjoy."

"Well, I'm going to go set everything up, and let Harlow know." he says sounding happy.

Sadie turned around and stared at the piano, she's always wanted a Grand piano, and here she was playing one. She started remembering when she first started playing, and was thinking that she could start teaching the girl how to play.

"Sadie, can you play us another song?" Gabriella asked politely.

"Sure." she smiled. Gabriella sat down next to her, and started playing her favorite song, one she always liked to play, Canon in D.

As she was playing the piano, Antonio stopped in the hallway, listening to her play. He thought she was playing the song perfectly, and was still surprised to see she knew how to play. He turned around to go back and watch her, and stood in the doorway, not wanting her to know he was there, watching and listening to her play. He leaned the back of his head against the wall and closed his eyes, while listening to the music, and couldn't help but smile.

He began to clap, when she finished, causing her to turn around quickly. "I thought you were getting things done?"

"I was, until I heard you play that song, and had to watch you play. You played it so beautifully, elegantly and perfect." he said in amazement. "I'm just so amazed that you can play, and play so well."

"Do you play?" Sadie asked.

"I do." he smiled. "I haven't played in a while with everything going on lately. Maybe I should start playing again, it might help take my mind off things, at least for a little bit."

She grinned. "You'll have to play for me sometime."
He nodded his head "I can do that." he says, giving her a wink. He turned around and walked away, and walked into his office to log into his laptop.

He booked the hotel, and called his pilot letting him know the details and to have the plane ready, then called his personal limo driver giving him the details.

******

A few days have gone by, it's now Sunday and the girls couldn't help but be excited to leave for Disney World, Sadie was getting the girls ready to leave, when she heard a loud bang. "I'll be right back." She tells the girls, as she stood up to walk out of the room. She walked around the upper level, checking the rooms out. When she got to Harlow and Antonio's room, she saw Harlow laying on the ground.

Sadie ran over to her "Oh my, are you OK?" she asked worried, trying to pick her up. She yelled for the girls, and Isabella came into the room. "Can you get your dad please?" Sadie asked her, she took off running and called out for her dad.

Isabella found Antonio in his office, and was busy talking on the phone. She walked over to him, saying his name over and over. "Daddy." she says again softly. Antonio held his hand up, wanting her to be quiet. Isabella looked at him with big eyes, and walked closer to him, tugging on his pants. "Daddy... mommy fell and Sadie needs you." she says, holding her finger in her mouth.

Antonio eyes widened and told the man on the other end of the phone that he had to go, and that he would call him back later.

"Where is she?" he asked, picking her up.

"Your room."

Antonio set Isabella down, and sprinted up the stairs to see what was going on, he walked into the room and saw Harlow laying on the ground, and ran over to Harlow, while Sadie was trying to help her up.

"What happened?" he asked worried, while lifting Harlow up off the ground, and laying her back on the bed.

"I heard a noise, and when I came in here, she was on the ground." Sadie says, trying to catch her breath, trying to calm her nerves.

Antonio looked at Harlow, sliding some of her hair out of her face "What happened?" he asked her.

"I was trying to get out of bed, and next thing I know I'm on the ground. I opened my eyes and saw Sadie, trying to help me up. I don't remember what happened."

"Should we not fly out today?" Antonio asked Harlow, looking at her worried.

"No, we have to go, those girls are too excited about going, and I don't want to be the one to take that away from them." Harlow says quietly. "I'll be fine."

Antonio sat down on the bed, and lifted her up to hold her in his arms. "You need to eat something, I noticed that you're not eating very much, and that could be why you feel so weak."

"I've been trying to, it's just that nothing tastes good, and I just don't feel hungry." Harlow says running her fingers along Antonio's cheek.

Sadie looked at Harlow and Antonio, feeling as if she shouldn't be in the room at the moment. "I'm going to go finish getting the girls ready, I'm glad you're OK." Sadie left the room, and gathered the kid's bags, bringing them down the stairs, and setting them by the door.

Antonio carried Harlow down the stairs and set her on the couch, while Sadie and Antonio started carrying the luggage out to the limo.

"Why would you hire a limo to take us to the airport?" Sadie asked.

He laughed "I own this, I just call him when we need a ride somewhere special."

"Oh." She was surprised, and began wondering how he got all his money. He was so young, and yet he had so much money.

Sadie grabbed the kids while Antonio helped Harlow to the car, placing her inside. On the way to the airport, the girls couldn't stop talking to Sadie about Disney World, and how they wanted to see Elsa and Anna from Frozen. Harlow sat and watched how Sadie was talking with the girls, and smiled while wiping a tear away that was strolling down her cheek. She hated the girls were close to Sadie, but knew she couldn't perform her duties as their mother at the time, and felt Sadie was like a mother to them. She also felt Sadie did it well, like any loving mother would. She looked away from them, and looked out the window, praying for a miracle that she knew was never going to happen.

When they got to the airport and pulled up next to an airplane, Sadie looked at Antonio. "Let me guess, you own this as well?"

"That would be correct." he smiled.

They all got inside the airplane and the girls began running around, they knew where everything was, grabbing their coloring books, and crayons out of the drawer, and sat down on a chair. Sadie buckled them in, and asked Antonio how long the flight was from Montana to Florida.

"It's about four and a half hours, give or take."

"OK, that's not so bad." she says looking over at Harlow, her stomach began feeling uneasy after noticing how pale and frail she was looking. "Will she be OK on the flight?" she asked, pointing over at Harlow.

"God, I hope so." he says, as he sat down next to Harlow, wrapping his arm around her. She leaned her head down on his shoulder and closed her eyes. He breathed in heavily, hoping he was doing the right thing and turned his head towards Harlow, caressing her cheek, and kissing the top of her head.

******

They finally landed in Orlando, and a private limo was there waiting for them. They then headed to the Ritz-Carlton hotel, and checked into their presidential suite. When they got into the room, Sadie was in shock at how beautiful the room was. She walked around and looked at the marble bathroom, living room, dining room, kitchen and was impressed with the five balconies, each displaying a different view. One showing a golf course, and the others with different views of the lakes, and one with a view of the pool.

"WOW." Sadie said amazed, as she stood on one of the balconies, overlooking a lake. While Sadie was admiring the view, Antonio walked up from behind, and rested his hands on her shoulders.

"Beautiful isn't it?" he asked softly, sending shivers up her spine.

"It is." she said quietly, taking in a breath of fresh air.

"Harlow is sleeping right now and the girls would like to do something, maybe we could take them to the pool for now until she wakes up?" He released his hands from her shoulders, and stepped away from her. She closed her eyes, feeling relieved that he backed off.

"We can do that." she says, turning around. She looked him in the eyes, and quickly turned away after seeing the look he was giving her. "I'll go get them ready."

Antonio walked over to the ledge of the balcony, staring off into the sky. His mind was going in all kinds of different directions, he's scared at where Harlow's life is at right now, afraid, and not wanting to lose her. He felt lost, and confused, angry, and depressed, all at the same time. He walked back into the room and over to Harlow, staring at her as she slept. He sat down next to her and whispered in her ear. "I'm so sorry my love." Placing a kiss on her lips.

"Daddy, daddy are you ready?" Gabriella yelled, as she ran into the room. He leaned back up and turned to her. "I'm ready honey, I'm just going to leave mommy a note, letting her know where we're at, in case she wakes up while we're at the pool."

He quickly wrote her a note, setting it on the nightstand next to her. He grabbed the girls, and headed down to the pool. They get down over to the pool, and the girls being as excited as they were, almost jumped into the pool, without their life jackets on.

"Hey you two!" Antonio yelled, stopping them from jumping. "Get over here and get your jackets on." He snapped, waving them over to him.

Sadie took her shorts and top off, and set her things down on a chair. Antonio couldn't help himself and looked over at Sadie while he was putting the jackets on the girls. Sadie saw the girls were getting their jackets on, and walked over to the pool, and got in, so the girls could jump in.

Antonio finished putting the jackets on them, and both hurried over to where Sadie was, wanting to jump in after Sadie. Antonio sat on the chair smiling, as he watched the girls laugh and splash water in Sadie's face.

Antonio decided to join them, and jumped into the pool, doing a cannon ball, splashing everyone.

"Was that really necessary?" Sadie asked, sounding bitter as Antonio came to the top of the water.

He laughed. "Of course it was, I wanted to get you wet." he smirked.

They continued playing with the girls in the pool, having a good time. The girls were screaming, and laughing, having a good time. Only thing that was bothering Antonio, was Harlow wasn't down there with them to enjoy playing with the girls in the water. He was beginning to feel a little guilty they were there having fun, while she was up in the room sleeping.

As they played with the girls in the pool, Antonio happened to turn around and looked up, he saw Harlow sitting on a chair watching them.

Chapter 11- Time is near

    Antonio was shocked, but happy to see Harlow made it down to the pool by herself. He got out of the pool, and grabbed a towel, drying himself off as he walked towards her. When he got to her, he leaned down pressing his lips to hers.

    "You made it down." he says happy, with a smile as he stood up.

    "I'm not dead yet." she snapped, as she looked up at him.

    He stepped back in shock, not expecting that kind of reaction out of her.

    "What's that supposed to mean?" he asked confused.

    "I'm just saying that I'm not dead yet, so don't treat me like I am." she says turning her head to look at the girls.

    "Would you like to go into the pool?" he asked, thinking that she might enjoy being in the water. It's been a while since she was in a pool and knew how much she enjoyed it. She hadn't even tried going in the pool at home, and figured he would try while they were at the hotel.

    "No, I'll just sit here and watch." she says, as she watched the girls splash Sadie.

    Antonio pulled up a chair, setting it next to Harlow, and sat down. He looked over at her, and reached for her hand. She looked down at his hand, debating on letting him hold her hand, she then placed her hand in his. He brought her hand up to his lips, softly kissing her fingers, and the top of her hand, trying to get a smile out of her.

    Harlow looked over at Antonio, she could feel in her heart that she would be gone soon, and it was breaking her heart. She hated feeling the way she did, and didn't want to fight with him. She stood up and walked over to Antonio, she sat on his lap and wrapped her arms around him, resting her head in the crook of his neck. "I'm sorry, it's just that I hate this, I hate feeling this way and I just hate knowing what I know."

He began rubbing her back, and leaned his head against hers. "I know Hun, I know... this hasn't been fun for me either."

Gabriella noticed her mom, and climbed out of the pool, with Isabella following behind, both walking over to their mom. Sadie figured she could have a little break after seeing Harlow was down by the pool. She got out of the pool, walked over to the bar, and ordered a beer.

Gabriella walked over and stood by her mom, tugging on her shirt. "Can we go see Elsa and Anna now?"

Antonio looked over Harlow's shoulder, to look at Gabriella. "We will go there tomorrow, it's getting late."

"OK." She pouted.

Sadie walked over to her chair and sat down, she set her beer down and grabbed her suntan lotion, and started rubbing it all over herself. A tall young man with blonde hair, built nicely with a six pack, walked by and whistled at Sadie, blowing air kisses towards her.

Antonio happened to see the whole thing and his blood started to boil, his face got red and was about to get up to say something to him, but then realized Harlow was on his lap and let it go. He watched the man and noticed how he kept staring at Sadie, smiling, and winking at her. He watched the man pucker his lips up to her, and got annoyed even more. He wasn't sure why, but he wasn't liking it one bit.

Antonio's eyes rolled back over to Sadie, she was lying in the chair with her eyes closed, tanning in the sun, and had no clue that the blonde guy was hitting on her. "What do you say we round up the kids and get some dinner?" he asked Harlow. He didn't get a response from her, and figured she might not have heard him.

Sadie sat up, drinking the rest of her beer. "Sounds good to me, I'm a little hungry myself."

Antonio felt Harlow becoming heavy while sitting on his lap, and could feel her breathing heavily on his neck, he pulled back enough to see her, and noticed that she fell asleep.

"I think we're going to just have to do room service, or have food delivered. Looks like someone fell asleep."

"That's fine." Sadie says smiling. "I'll grab the girls."

Antonio stood up and adjusted Harlow in his arms, making it easier for him to carry her. Sadie grabbed the girls, while she was walking, the young blonde man whistled at her as she walked past him, she stopped and looked at the man as he was asking for her to come over to him.

"What can I help you with?" she asked him.

"How about your phone number?" he asked with a grin, trying to give her a sexy smile. He handed over his cell phone, asking for her to enter her number into his phone.

"No thanks." she says, as she eyed Antonio. She noticed he was watching her and turned back to the man. "On second thought hand me your phone."

"Yes, I'll be glad to." He handed her his phone quickly, and looked over at his friend sitting next to him, he could hear his friend laughing at him. "I told you that I'd finally get her number." he says, shoving him.

She handed his phone back, and glanced at his phone. "Sadie... I like that name, sounds just like a temptress." he grinned, while he looked her up and down.

"You're saying my name sounds like a temptress?" she laughed. She turned to wave at the girls, waving for them to come to her. She could see Antonio was starting to get agitated, and figured that she better hurry.

"All I'm saying, is your name sounds tempting, and you're hot as fuck, you look like you would be wild in bed." he says. Sadie smiled at him thinking what an ass but didn't say anything, and let out a fake laugh. She saw Antonio walking over to them, and held onto the girls hands, as they walked over to her. "I have to go."

"Is there a problem over here?" Antonio snapped, looking at the man with an evil glare.

"No, we were just talking, chill man." The blonde man says to Antonio with widened eyes.

"Are you ready?" Antonio asks irritated, looking at Sadie with Harlow still in his arms.

Sadie held onto Gabriella and Isabella's hands and began walking back up to their suite. Antonio laid Harlow down on the bed, then called for food to be delivered.

When the food arrived, Antonio walked over to Harlow, trying to wake her up, and she wasn't having it. "I'm not hungry, please just let me sleep." Harlow said tiredly.

Antonio didn't like that she wouldn't eat, and got frustrated with her. "If you don't eat, I'm calling for someone to have tubes put in you, do you really want that?"

Sadie heard the way he was speaking to Harlow and didn't like the tone in his voice, she walked over to him, snapping at him. "Antonio! Was that really necessary?"

"She needs to eat; she hasn't eaten in days." he said worried. He ran his fingers through his hair, and pulled up on his hair out of frustration.

Antonio looked back at Harlow, pleading for her to eat. "Harlow the girls' birthday is tomorrow, and we have that party planned out for them, do you really want to miss that?"

"Of course not, I just have no appetite, and I can barely keep my eyes open." Harlow says exhausted.

Antonio threw his arms up in the air, and walked away. "I give up, I don't know what else to do." he snapped.

Sadie walked back over to the table and made the girls their plate.

"Antonio, come and eat, I'm sure she will eat if she becomes hungry." Sadie says to him encouragingly.

Antonio sat down at the table, he didn't have an appetite anymore, and tried forcing himself to eat. He kept looking over at Harlow, while he picked at his food, he could feel in his heart that his time with her was going to be shorter than what they were told.

Sadie watched Antonio play with his food like a little kid, and reached across the table stopping his hand while he held onto his fork. "Hey... maybe tomorrow she will feel better. She herself even said that she didn't want to miss the kid's birthday for nothing. Maybe she's trying to sleep this off, and have more energy for tomorrow."

Antonio stood up while picking up his plate, and set it in the fridge. "I'll be back, I need some time to myself."

Sadie kept quiet not wanting to upset him anymore than he already was, and watched him walk out the door. She hoped he wasn't going to the bar, but knew him to well and figured that was where he was heading. She figured if he wasn't back in a couple hours, she was going to go looking for him.

She pulled the couch, making herself a bed, and got the girls into their pajamas, and laid them down. Harlow had awakened, and pulled herself up slowly against the pillows, and began watching Sadie with the girls.

"Do we have to go to bed?" Isabella asked Sadie, while rubbing her eyes.

She touched her nose and smiled "Yes you do, you both have a big day tomorrow, and you need to sleep. You'll need all of your energy for tomorrow."

"OK..." she said slowly, sounding bummed that she had to go to sleep, she climbed into bed and got under the covers.

"Just think, you'll be able to see Elsa and Anna tomorrow, you do still want to go see them, don't you?" Sadie asked with a smile, knowing that would make her want to sleep.

"Yes, I do."

"Then close your eyes, and get as much rest as you can, you're really going to need it."

When Sadie was getting up off the bed after talking to Isabella, Harlow closed her eyes quick, not wanting her to know that she was awake, and she also didn't want her knowing that she had been watching her with them. Sadie tried calling Antonio, but his phone was turned off, and kept leaving him messages anyway.

"Where is Antonio?" Harlow asked, sounding like she was out of breath, shocking Sadie that she was awake and talking.

Sadie walked over to Harlow concerned. "Can I get you something?"

"Where's Antonio?"

"I'm not sure, he left saying that he needed to be by himself. He left pretty upset." she says, looking over towards the door.

Harlow sighed, holding her chest as she tried to breathe. "If you could get me some food, I'd like to try and eat something." Harlow says out of breath. "I could also use my medications; I'm having a bit of a hard time breathing."

"Oh sure, I'll be glad to do that." she says, with a smile, happy that she wants to try and eat, yet worried that she can't breathe.

She grabbed her food that Antonio put in the fridge, and heated it up for her. She grabbed her medication, and walked it over to her along with a glass of water.

While Harlow was trying to eat, Antonio walked in the door and was surprised to see Harlow with a plate of food. He looked drained, tired, and looked like he was hurting. He held his hand behind his back holding a bouquet of flowers as he walked over towards Harlow. He sat down on the bed next to her and smiled, while still holding the flowers behind him. "You're eating." he said softly with a half-smile, feeling relieved that she was trying to eat.

"I figured I would try and eat... just for you, it's not going so well, but I'm trying."

He sighed happily, and leaned over to kiss her. "I got something for you." He brought his arm around, handing over the flowers to her, with a smile.

"Pink flowers for you." He explained why he got the pink flowers, and showed her the pink vase to place the flowers in, then showed her the pink ribbon they put on the vase for her.

She pulled out a card that was inside the flowers, and began reading it out loud for him to hear:

My dearest Harlow, you have been the world to me since the first day I laid my eyes on you. When I said I do, I meant it. I will stick with you through sickness and health, for better, for worse, until death do us part. I never thought that would be so soon, and you will always be my wife no matter what happens. I love you with all my heart, and don't ever think differently.

I love you... Antonio

Chapter 12- Birthday to remember

Antonio sat on the bed next to Harlow, listening to her read the card he wrote for her. "I do love you." he whispered.

She closed her eyes while putting the card to her chest remembering her wedding day, and their vows they wrote for each other. "I'm sorry that you and the girls have to see me like this, this was definitely not my plan."

"Of course, it wasn't your plan, and you shouldn't be sorry, if anything, I should be the one who's sorry, I should have spent more money to help you..."

"It still wouldn't have mattered anyway, it is what it is... thank you for the flowers, I do like them a lot." Harlow set the card down next to her, and picked her plate up, trying to take another bite.

"You're welcome my love." he says with a grin. "So how does the food taste anyway?"

"I can't taste anything, but I'm sure it's OK." she says, shrugging her shoulders.

Antonio took her fork and tried a bite of her meatloaf. "Actually, it tastes pretty good, you should still try and eat it, to give you your strength."

Antonio stood up, grabbing the flowers and vase. He walked over to the kitchen, and set the flowers down to place water in the vase. He placed the flowers in the vase, and set the flowers down next to her. Harlow set the card up against the vase, and handed Antonio her plate. "I can't eat anymore."

Antonio grabbed her plate, and walked over to the table setting it down, he sat down and stared at her food. "She didn't eat much, but at least she ate something..."

Sadie sat down at the table, and looked at Harlow's plate. "The girls are pretty excited about tomorrow."

"I just hope Harlow will be able to handle it..." He took a couple bites of Harlow's meatloaf, then pushed the plate aside after he started thinking about her situation.

"I'm sure she will try her best to enjoy the day, it is her daughters birthday, and she was looking forward to it." Sadie says, as she stood up grabbing Harlow's plate. She put all the food away, and then got ready for bed. Leaving Antonio alone for the night, she figured that he needed to be alone and hoped that he would just go to bed.

******

"Sadie!" Gabriella said loudly while shaking her, to wake up. Sadie opened her eyes and smiled when she saw big hazel colored eyes staring back at her.

"It's our birthday today! Are we going to go see Elsa and Anna now?"

"Yes, you will get to see them soon, you just have to wait until your mommy and daddy wake up."

Gabriella and Isabella took off running, wanting to go wake up their parents, while Sadie got up and got herself ready. After the kids woke up their parents, they went back over to Sadie, asking to help them get dressed. Sadie got the girls dressed into fancy princess like dresses that she had bought for them, wanting them to feel like a princess for their birthday.

After they got their dresses on, they twirled around the hotel room like little ballerina's, making Harlow giggle when she saw them spinning around.

Harlow was able to get out of bed, and walked around on her own. She felt good today and felt like she had more energy. "See what a little food in you will do?" Antonio says to her, feeling relieved when he saw her walking around.

They headed over to Epcot Center, where Antonio had the birthday party set up. Elsa and Anna were to surprise Gabriella and Isabella for their party, the girls knew they would see them today, but didn't know they were going to be there for their party.

The girls got excited and started squealing when they got to the Frozen castle, they didn't realize that their birthday party was inside. When they walked inside the castle, the girls were greeted by Elsa and Anna, and both ran up to them squealing, and hugging them. Harlow had a huge smile on her face, that Antonio hadn't seen in months. He wrapped his arm around her, kissing her. "I'm happy to see you finally smile, it's been a long time."

"I'm just happy that I didn't miss this." Harlow says happily, looking at him, smiling again.

"Keep smiling, it's a good look on you." he says, giving her a wink.

The girls were in heaven as they partied, and played with their favorite characters for the day. By the end of the day, they were so tired they couldn't keep their eyes open. Antonio was amazed that Harlow was able to make it through the day, but by the time they got back to the hotel room, she was wiped out, and crawled into bed.

Antonio hired a photographer to take pictures for the girls' party, and to put all the pictures into an album, Antonio and Sadie sat at the table

looking through all the pictures, laughing at the girls expressions, they also talked about what they were going to do for the rest of the week.
By the end of the week, and after visiting all the attractions they had wanted to see, they were all beat, and couldn't wait to get back home, mostly Harlow.

******

Their flight home was a quiet one, most of them slept the entire flight, except Antonio. He couldn't sleep, and kept looking over at Harlow, he was happy she got to see the kids visit Magic kingdom, as well as make it through their fifth birthday. The more he looked at her, the frailer he noticed she had become. He wrapped an arm around her, and pulled her closer to him. He kissed her forehead, and began caressing her arm.

They finally arrived home, and the girls were still excited about their birthday, that they couldn't stop talking about how they got to have their birthday with all the Frozen characters. Harlow sat on the couch with the girls and looked through the photo album together.

"Look mom, that's when Elsa and Anna sang Happy Birthday to us!" Isabella said excitedly, pointing to a picture.

"That was pretty neat wasn't it." Harlow says, kissing the top of her head.

Harlow was starting to get tired, and had asked for some help getting her up the stairs. Sadie helped her up the stairs, while Antonio was on the phone in the other room talking business.

As Sadie was helping her lay down, Harlow stopped her, and gave her a hug. "I want to thank you for everything that you have done for all of us this past year, or however long it has been now. It means a lot to me. I may not have shown it at times, but you really are a great person, and I'm glad Antonio found you. I don't think my girls would have liked anyone else." Harlow tells her, hugging her tighter. Antonio started to walk through the door, but stopped when he saw the two together hugging, and stepped back out into the hallway listening to them.

Sadie pulled away from her and looked her in the eyes "Thank you Harlow, I'm sorry to see what you're going through, and I know all of this has to be hard on you. I may not be the one in your shoes, but if I was, I don't think I could be as strong as you have been."

"Just continue doing what you have been doing, you really are a great person, and I truly mean that from the bottom of my heart." Harlow says to her, as she pulled the covers up to her chin.

"I'll continue to do that, just promise me that you will continue to fight this, those girls really need you." Sadie says to her sincerely. "I'll go find Antonio, and send him over your way."

"No need to do that, I'm right here." Antonio spoke in a low voice. Sadie turned around when she heard Antonio speak, and saw him walking through the door. "What's going on in here?" Antonio asked Harlow, then looking at Sadie.

"I was just having a private conversation with Sadie." Harlow says tiredly.

"I'm going to check on the girls." Sadie says, leaving the two together so that they could talk.

Antonio sat on the bed next to her. "I have to go run and do some business deals, and I also have to stop at the office, will you be OK if I were to leave?" Antonio asked, while leaning down to kiss her on the lips. Harlow wrapped her arms around him, hugging him. "Yes, I'll be fine.... I just want you to know how much I love you, and thank you so much for the wonderful vacation, I truly needed that."

"I love you too, get some rest and I'll try not to take too long." "OK."

Sadie was downstairs playing hide and seek with the girls, Isabella was hiding behind a door, and thought Sadie had found her when the door moved. Isabella jumped out and screamed, making Antonio jump.

"What are you doing? he laughed.

"Playing hide and seek with Gabriella and Sadie. I thought you were Sadie, and I was trying to scare her." she says, smiling.

"I have to leave for a little bit, but I'll be back soon. I'm going to find Sadie and let her know too."

"OK, don't tell her where I'm at."

"I won't." he says, putting a couple fingers to his lips, pretending to be zipping up his lips.

Antonio walked away with a smile, and laughed. He found Sadie in the music room looking behind the curtains for the girls. He walked over to her, announcing that he was in the room, trying not to scare her.
"I'll be back in a little while, I have to take care of some things, can you keep an eye on Harlow please?"

"Yes, I can do that."

"What were you two talking about before I came walking in the room?"

"She was being very sincere, thanking me for everything that I have done for you guys, and how I have been with the girls."

"I too, thank you as well. You have been a lifesaver for all of us, and I want you to know that everything you have done, means a lot to us. But I should get going, so I can get back at a decent time, I told Harlow that I would try and not take too long."

"I better go find the girls anyway, before they get mad that I haven't found them yet." she giggled. She walked away from him, and looked around for the girls.

Sadie continued to look for the girls and found Isabella behind the door, and asked her to help find Gabriella. They both searched all around the house, and Sadie was beginning to worry, since they had looked everywhere and couldn't find Gabriella. She felt relieved when they found her laying in the bed with Harlow. "I want to lay with her too." Isabella said, looking at Sadie.

"OK, I'll start making dinner." Sadie says quietly, she looked at both the girls, and pointed her finger at them. "Just make sure that you let her rest OK?" she says, helping Isabella up on the bed.

Harlow smiled at Sadie "Thank you." she whispered.

"You're welcome, I'll come and get all of you when dinner is done."

Harlow laid there, looking back and forth at the girls, she talked with them for as long as she could, and then let them both know how much she loved them, kissing both of their cheeks, and giving them both hugs before falling asleep.

******

"It's been nice dealing with you, this will be a good investment." Mr. Olson says, as he shook Antonio's hand.

"Thank you, with the condition my wife Harlow is in, I just hope that I'm doing the right thing."

"By the way, how is she doing?"

"Not good." he sighed. "There's nothing more that they can do, and she refuses to do anything else. It's been extremely hard watching her wither away every day."

"Give her my best when you get home."

"I will..."

Antonio's phone rang while he was in the middle of talking to Mr. Olson, he looked at the caller I.D, and figured he better take the call "I'll be just a minute while I take this call."

Seeing who was calling, had him on edge, and afraid to answer his phone, he turned his body away from Mr. Olson and answered his phone quietly. "Hello?" Antonio asked, sounding nervous.

"I'll be right there...."

Chapter 13- Fly high

Antonio's heart dropped, his hands began to shake and dropped his phone. "I'm sorry… I have to go." he says, picking up his phone, and quickly leaving the office in a panic. He hurriedly ran to his car, and squealed his tires out of the parking lot. He ran every red light that got in his way, and hoped that no cop was around.

Antonio pulled into the driveway, leaving his car door open as he got out quickly and ran into the house, also leaving the front door wide open, while he ran up the stairs, skipping steps to get to the bedroom faster. He ran over to Harlow and lifted her up, and held her in his arms.

"Harlow! Wake up! Harlow!" he cried out, patting her face. He looked at Sadie in tears, and yelled frantically. "Call 911!"

"I already did, they should be here any second." she said in tears.

"Harlow, please wake up, please...." Antonio begged, with tears flooding his eyes.

The paramedics arrived, and Sadie directed them up over to the bedroom. They walked over to Antonio, and set their things down on the ground. "Sir, I need you to let go of her please."

As much as he didn't want to let her go, but knew he had to, he laid her on the ground, he stood up crossing his arms, and watched them work on her, then covered his mouth as he watched. The girls ran into the bedroom to see what was going on. "Daddy?" Isabella asked.

"Girls, you need to get out of here right now." Antonio said in a panic, pushing them out of the room, and calling for Sadie to grab them. He rushed back over to Harlow, not caring they were still working on her and kneeled on the ground next to her. He could see she was barely breathing. They asked him to step back while they placed her on a stretcher. They carried her down the stairs, and put her into the ambulance. "I'm coming with." Antonio said quietly, and shook up.

He had Sadie stay with the girls while he went to the hospital with Harlow. On the way to the hospital Antonio kept an eye on her vitals, panicking when he saw that her numbers weren't very good. Once they arrived at the hospital, they rushed her inside.

Antonio was then met with a team of doctors and nurses, asking what exactly happened. He insisted on going into the room with her after the doctors told him that he had to stay behind while they worked on her. At that moment there was no time to argue with him, and he got his way. He tried watching them as they worked on her, but had to look away, and looked down at the ground. He knew it was time, and placed his face in his hands, praying for God to help her.

They were tried their hardest with her, while Antonio prayed. He heard the noises of the machines, and just knew she was gone. He didn't even have to look up to know what the sounds were, and cried.

One of the doctors walked up to Antonio placing his hand on his back. "I'm sorry your-... "

"I know..." he blurted out, covering his head with his hands.

"I'm sorry." the doctor said sounding sincere.

The doctor pulled the sheet over her face, and Antonio quickly stood up. "Please, can you give me a few minutes with her before you take her away?"

"Certainly." One of the nurses said to him. "We'll give you a few minutes with her." she says, looking at him with sadness in her eyes. As the doctor's and nurses left the room, he walked up to Harlow and pulled the sheet down away from her face, and grabbed her hands, holding them tight. He leaned down and kissed her forehead, and moved down to her nose, then moved to her lips, giving her a long hard kiss, not wanting to release his lips from hers. When he finally released his lips from hers, he stood there staring at her, talked to her, and apologized to her, begging for her to come back.

"I'm so sorry Harlow... I cannot believe you're gone. You always were my angel, and now you literally are our angel now. Please watch over our girls, and keep them safe." he says, kissing the top of her hands, and placing her one hand on his cheek. "I'll always love you, my love for you will never go away..."

"Mr. Russo?" he heard from behind him.
Antonio turned his head, and looked at the nurse. "I'm sorry but we have to bring her out now." the nurse said sadly.

"OK." He looked back over at Harlow, and studied her face, giving her one last kiss before they took her from the room. "I love you, Harlow." he says to her, pulling away from her lips.

He stood there, watching them take her out of the room, and followed them out. He walked outside to get some fresh air, and looked up into the sky, hoping to see a sign from Harlow, but didn't see anything different. He pulled his phone out of his pocket, and called for his limo driver to come and pick him up.

When he got into the limo, he was asked where he was going. Antonio, still in shock didn't know what to say. He sat there quietly, ignoring the driver as he looked out the window, feeling lost and unsure what to tell the girls. "Mr. Russo?"

"Just drive for now, anywhere, I don't care where. Just please don't stop." Antonio said quietly, barley getting the words out of his mouth. He looked at his phone and sent Sadie a text *she's gone.*

"As you wish." the driver said, while looking in his rearview mirror at Antonio. He knew it was because of Harlow, and knew it wasn't good and was afraid to ask. He did what he was told and drove Antonio around for hours, until he finally spoke. Speaking quietly, and trying to clear his throat while he spoke. "Harlow passed away."

The driver felt goosebumps roam his body, and held the steering wheel tighter. "I'm sorry to hear that Mr. Russo, she will be greatly missed."

"I don't even know how I'm going to tell our kids, they're so young." Antonio felt a shiver go right through him, and believed that it was Harlow letting him know that she was there with him.

"You better bring me home, so I can start making the funeral arrangements." he sighed.

When he got home, he stood outside the door, hesitating to walk into the house. He stood, staring at the door for about ten minutes before he finally walked inside, and heard the girls playing, and laughing in the bathtub upstairs. Not wanting them to know he was home he went straight to his office, quietly shutting the door behind him.

He started making phone calls, letting his family know about Harlow, as well as her brother Ethan. He made another call to Judge Stevens, letting him know about Harlow, and that he will be taking some time off.

Antonio knew the time up with Harlow was coming, but didn't think it would be this soon. He stared across the room, and looked at a bottle of bourbon he had on the table, debating about having a drink or not.

Sadie got the girls dressed into their pajamas, she thought she heard the door earlier, and left the girls in the room to see if Antonio was home. She wanted the girls to say goodnight to him, thinking he could use a hug from them. She saw that his office door was closed and knocked before walking in.

She knocked and noticed the door was unlocked, and opened it peeking her head inside to see if he was in there, after he never responded to her knock.

"You are in here; would you like to say goodnight to the girls before I put them to bed?" Sadie asked quietly.

"Sure, send them in here please."

Sadie got the girls, and sent them to see Antonio. They both ran into his office jumping on his lap. He looked at them, holding them both tightly in his arms. As he held them, he felt hurt and lost, still unsure of how to tell them that their mother was gone, and not coming back.

"Daddy... why are you crying?" Gabriella asked, looking up at him, while she pulled away from his hug. He didn't answer her, and cupped the back of her head, pulling her back to his shoulder, and kissed top of their heads.

"I love you kiddos." he quietly said, choking up. "You should go get some sleep, and I'll talk to both of you in the morning." he says to them with a broken heart.

The girls ran out of the room, looking for Sadie. When they saw her sitting on the couch and walked over to her. She brought them up to their rooms and tucked them into bed. As she looked and talked to them, she could tell that Antonio didn't tell them about their mom, and her heart broke for them, wondering how they would take it, being as young as they were.

"Goodnight you two, we'll see you in the morning." Sadie tells them, as she shut the light off, and partially leaving the door open.

She went into Antonio's office to talk to him, and stood there looking at him, wondering what to say to him. He was covering his head, and sniffling.

"Antonio." she said softly, wanting to let him know that she was there. "I'm really sorry about Harlow."

He raised his head up and looked at her, pissed at himself. "I never should have left earlier."

She walked closer to him slowly. "Antonio... you didn't know, nothing would have changed."

"I still should have been here for her."

"It may not be the right time to say this, but I think she knew it was about to happen... she had been saying some strange things to me lately, and I could tell she was saying them with her heart. I wasn't understanding *why* at the time, but I'm understanding now why she was saying those things to me. Earlier tonight the girls went to lay down with her, when I let them lay with her, she looked at me and smiled, thanking me. She looked like she was at peace with them in her arms." Sadie said in tears. "Isabella was the one who came and got me, saying that her mom was making funny noises, and that she couldn't wake her up." she said hesitantly, choking up.

"Isabella? Oh god." Antonio said, leaning his head back. "I didn't have the heart to tell them that their mom was gone."

"I think they might know after the commotion earlier; I don't know for sure, but maybe they'll understand, maybe they won't. But you have to tell them." Sadie insisted.

"I do plan on telling them tomorrow, I just couldn't tell them tonight before they went to bed. Did they not ask about her?"

Sadie shook her head slowly. "No. They didn't ask about her at all."

Antonio sighed "I cannot believe she's gone, and this soon. It wasn't even the six months the doctor thought it would be.... but the more I think about it, he didn't sound so sure about that either."

"You'll have to come to understand that she isn't in any more pain. It may be hard to think that way, but towards the end there, she was in so much pain, and she could hardly breathe." Sadie says, inching closer to him.

She walked closer to him and leaned down to hug him. He sat there limp for a minute while her arms were around him thinking about Harlow, he finally reached his arms around her, and sobbed on her shoulder. "I'm here if you need to talk, just let me know and I'll be there for you." she says, as she stood back up. "I'll let you be..."

Sadie left the room to let him be alone, and Antonio started looking at what pictures he had on his laptop of Harlow, ordering for them to be printed off.

He opened the bottom drawer of his desk and pulled out a bottle of bourbon that he had hidden from Harlow, and started to chug on the bottle.

He guzzled, and guzzled on the bottle, wanting everything to go away for the night, even if it was only for the night. He continued drinking, thinking that all his problems would go away. Once the bottle was finished, he walked over to the bottle of bourbon on the table, and drank that until it was gone.

He sat back down at his desk, and grabbed their wedding picture he had sitting at the corner of his desk, and stared at the picture for a while, before holding it against his heart. He closed his eyes, remembering that very special day. It was the first best day of his life, before his girls were born, with that being his second-best day of his life.

"I'm so sorry Harlow, I'll always remember you, and this special day of ours." he muttered, sadly.

While holding the picture to his heart, he started remembering the day they first met, and how upset she was with him. He remembered their vacation in Cancun, and when he proposed to her there, worried her brother was going to ruin it. He set the picture back down, leaned back in his chair, closed his eyes and began begging for Harlow's forgiveness. Apologizing that he didn't do more for her, and wishing he was with her when everything first happened.

Chapter 14- Saying goodbye

For the next couple days Antonio had been busy with funeral arrangements, he took time off work, he let the courts know what was going on, and that he would be back when the time was right. He also called all his clients, letting them know that their court dates were going to be pushed back until further notice.

Antonio still hadn't told the girls where their mom was at, he had been trying to figure out how to tell them. They were all sitting at the dinner table eating lunch, Isabella stopped eating her sandwich and looked at Antonio. "When is mommy coming home?"

Sadie looked at Antonio, and gave him a funny look. She couldn't believe he still hadn't told them, "I'm going to leave." she says, standing up.

"No, stay here." he says quietly, resting his hand on top of hers. "Please." he says, looking at her in desperation.

Sadie sat back down, and leaned over to his ear, whispering to him. "You seriously need to tell them."

Antonio clasped his hands together, rested his elbows on the table, and leaned his forehead onto his clasped hands, trying to figure out how to say the right words to a couple of five-year old's. He took a deep breath and sighed while looking at them. "Oh God." he said and looked up at the ceiling.

"I really don't know how to tell the both of you this, but your mommy is up in heaven right now, she's our angel now." Antonio said, with tears filling his eyes as he spoke.

He choked up, got mad at himself for crying in front of them, and covered his face. "I'm sorry, I'm not being strong enough for you kids right now, but daddy is really hurting right now."

"Mommy isn't coming back?" Gabriella asked. She got off her chair, and walked over to Antonio. He wrapped his arm around her, with Isabella joining them.

"No kiddos, mommy isn't coming back, she's here with us right now in spirit, and as your guardian angel."

The girls cried wanting their mommy home, they didn't understand that she had passed away, and didn't understand that they would not see her anymore. Seeing them cry, hurt Antonio even more.

Sadie's heart broke seeing them all upset, and stood up sneaking out of the room to let them be alone. She figured that it was their alone time to grieve together.

Antonio released the girls from his hug, and looked at them.

"Tomorrow, we say our goodbyes to mommy."

"Can we make something for her?" Isabella asked.

"Of course you can, I'm sure Sadie will help you out with that." he says, looking over to where Sadie was sitting, and saw that she wasn't there anymore. He turned his head looking for her and stood up. "Finish eating your lunch, then go find Sadie, and have her help you. I have a couple more things that I need to take care of before tomorrow."

The girls finished their sandwich and ran around the house looking for Sadie. They found her downstairs doing laundry. "Sadie?" Isabella asked in a quiet voice.

"Yes Izzy?"

"Can you help us make something for mommy?"

"Sure, let me finish this quick, and then we can make something."

Antonio came down the stairs, looking for Sadie, finding her with the girls. "I have to go to the funeral home and finalize everything." he says, sounding tired, running his fingers though his hair.

"OK. I'll help the girls make gifts for their mom, while you're gone."

Once Antonio left, Sadie grabbed art supplies, and helped the girls make something for their mom. She used Antonio's printer, and printed off a couple pictures of Harlow with the girls, while the girls made frames out of popsicle sticks. She painted the frames, and grabbed some construction paper to cut some hearts. She placed a picture on each of the hearts, glued them, and placed them inside the frame. The girls also wrote their mom a letter, to place inside the casket.

Later that evening Sadie got the girls ready for bed, and talked to them about the funeral. Antonio finally came home, and was about to say goodnight to the girls, but heard Sadie talking to the them and stood outside the doorway way, listening to them talk.

"You're not going to leave us too, are you Sadie?" Isabella asked, as she sat up in the bed, while giving her sad eyes. She reached for Sadie, giving her a hug, scared she was going to leave too.

Sadie's heart dropped when Isabella asked her that, Gabriella sat up looking at Sadie, waiting to hear what she was going to say. "No. I'm not going to leave you; I'll always be here for you."

"Promise?" Gabriella asked.

Sadie held out her two pinky's and wrapped them around both of the girls pinky's. "I pinky promise." she smiled, assuring them.

Antonio walked into the room, looking at his girls. Sadie instantly got a whiff of booze, and turned around. She could tell he had been drinking, just by looking at him, and by the smell coming off him. She stood up, and walked past him giving him a dirty look. "I'm going to bed." she snapped quietly, as she walked past him. "Goodnight girls, I'll see you in the morning."

Sadie was upset he was out drinking, and didn't think he should have been drinking, when he has two little girls that need him the most right now. *He should have been home comforting them* she thought to herself. The more she thought about it, the madder she became. *He should know how they're feeling right now, especially missing their mom, knowing that she's gone and never coming back, and now they need their dad, now more than ever.* She mumbled, as she walked down the stairs.

After Antonio said goodnight to the girls, he went into his office, wanting to be alone. Sadie saw him walk in his office, and stormed in there after him, yelling at him. "Instead of going out and drinking, don't you think you should be home, and spending time with your daughters? They need you the most right now!"

Antonio sat in his chair, looking down and not wanting to look at her. "Sadie, I'm in no mood to fight, this is hard on me too, and I should have done everything that I could to save her."

She walked over to his desk, placed her hands on the edge of the desk and bent over. "You need to realize there was nothing anyone could have done, just know that she loved you, and those girls. There will always be memories, and you need to remember all the good times that you had with her. I know it'll be hard, but you need to be strong, if not for yourself, for Isabella and Gabriella. You need to move forward with your life, and make the best of it... especially for your kids."

Antonio sat in his chair listening to Sadie, not saying a word, and just listening. He knew she was right, but refused to acknowledge it, and spun his chair around, facing the back of his chair towards her.

Sadie threw her arms in the air, and left the room, frustrated. Somehow, she needed to figure out how to get through to him, hoping that he'll come around, so he could help care for his girls.

The Unexpected Nanny

The next morning Sadie made breakfast for everyone, as they sat at the table Antonio remained quiet, not looking at anyone. After everyone ate, she brought the girls upstairs and got them ready to leave. As they were leaving, the girls grabbed the things they made for their mom, as well as their letters for her, and headed outside to their limo waiting for them.

They arrived at the church, Antonio stepped out of the limo and stood outside the church staring up into the sky. He was having a hard time walking inside the church, not ready to say his goodbye to her yet. He took a deep breath, and grabbed a hold of his daughters' hands, and walked them inside to see their mother for one last time. After saying their goodbyes, the girls placed their pictures, and letters near their mom's heart and walked away.

Antonio walked outside with Harlow's brother after the service was finished, talking to him about Harlow's final days. Her brother Ethan, felt guilty for not visiting her. "Don't feel bad, not many people came to visit her. She didn't want anyone seeing her the way she was." Antonio assured him, trying to make him feel a little better.

"I know, but it still doesn't make it right." Ethan said sadly. "It makes me feel a little better that we talked on the phone, and that I talked to her before she passed away, but I still wish that I had made time to come see her." he says, lowering his head, feeling terrible.

Antonio gave him a hug. "Keep in touch." Antonio says to him, patting his back. "I do miss the days of us hanging out, and having fun. Remember how inseparable we were?"

Ethan smiled, and chuckled. "Yea I do, until Harlow put a stop to it."

"Oh, the good ole days..." Antonio says, finally smiling.

Sadie walked over to Antonio and Ethan with the girls, looking at Antonio, and sliding some of her hair away from her face, from the wind. "Gabriella wanted to be by you."

"Ethan... this is Sadie, Sadie... Ethan, Harlow's brother." Antonio says, introducing them. Ethan looked at her with a grin, and gave her a curious look.

"She has been our nanny since Harlow got sick, she's also been a huge part of our lives, and helped Harlow out quite a bit."

"Nice to meet you." Sadie said politely, shaking Ethan's hand. Ethan smiled, Harlow had talked to him about her, but had never got the chance to meet her. "Nice to finally meet you, thanks for helping Harlow out, I know she appreciated it."

"They became pretty close, especially towards the end." Antonio said, looking at Sadie.

The director came out, and had everyone follow him over to the gravesite. After the service was finished, Antonio sat on the chair staring at the coffin, holding hands with his girls, not wanting to leave.

Sadie looked around the crowd of people, looking for Antonio and saw him still sitting on the chair with the kids, and walked over to him.

"It's time to leave Antonio, everyone is heading over to the banquet hall." she said, reaching for Gabriella's hand. He slowly stood up, while keeping his eyes glued to Harlow's casket, not saying a word while holding onto Isabella's hand.

"Shall we?" Sadie asked quietly.

At the hall, Sadie noticed that Antonio was distancing himself from everyone, and walked over to him. "Need someone to talk to?" she asked, looking at him concerned.

"Sadie, I don't mean to be rude, but I need to be by myself right now, if you could get the girls home, I'd appreciate it."

She sat down next to him and glared at him "I understand you need time to yourself, just please don't ignore your kids."

"Please go."

Sadie gave him an evil look and sighed as she stood up, she didn't want to make a scene in front of everyone. Without saying anything, she walked away, and looked for the girls so they could leave. Antonio watched her leave, and felt bad for snapping at her. He knew she hadn't done anything wrong, and knew she was trying to help.

Antonio walked over to Ethan, and talked with him for a while, until Ethan suggested that they go to the bar for a bit, and talk there.

They left the banquet hall and headed for a bar they used to hang out at, sat down at the end of the bar, away from everyone, and had a few drinks while they talked. Ethan looked at Antonio, and leaned back in his chair. "That nanny of yours... Sadie is it?" Ethan asked with a grin.

"What about her?"

"Is she single?" Ethan asked, with a slight slur.

Ethan's question hit a nerve with Antonio, he looked at him wanting to tell him to stay away from her, but let it go, only shrugging his shoulders.

"So, she is single." Ethan asked again.

"No... no she isn't." Antonio said quietly, knowing that he was lying to him. He didn't know why he lied to him, it just came out quickly, without him thinking. He stared at his drink thinking to himself that he was an idiot for saying that to his brother in law.

"Well that's too bad, she's a hottie."

Antonio cringed again, and finished the rest of his drink. "I better go, those girls need me." He stood up, and placed cash under his glass.

"I'll be staying in touch." Ethan smiled, watching Antonio leave.

Ethan waved at the bartender. "One more please." he says, handing him his glass.

Antonio walked into the house and saw Sadie walking down the stairs, she wouldn't even look at him, still pissed at him about earlier. "If you even care, the girls are in bed, but they're still awake." she barked, while walking past him.

"Of course I care." he said loudly, clearly slurring, and trying to hide that he was drinking.

"You have a funny way of showing it." she yelled back.

Antonio groaned, and walked up the stairs. He walked into the girls bedroom and turned on the light.

"Daddy!" Gabriella yelled excited.

"Shhh, lay back down, I was just coming in to say goodnight."

"Daddy, is Sadie our new mommy now?" Gabriella asked, batting her eyes at him. She had a curious look on her face, and he didn't know what to say to her. He took a deep breath, and kissed her on the forehead.

"Go to sleep, it's late… you too Isabella." he says to her, and leaned down kissing Isabella on her forehead. "Goodnight you two."

Chapter 15- Saving a life

It's been a little over two months since Harlow passed away, and when Gabriella sked Antonio if Sadie was going to be her new mommy. He thought about her question often, and never responded to her about it, not know what to tell her, without hurting their feelings, or getting them excited for something that wasn't true. He already lied to Ethan, and felt guilty about that, but he couldn't lie to his little girls, especially something like that.

Each day without Harlow had been a challenge for him, he had been trying to go on with life without her, and couldn't stop thinking to himself about how to go on without her. Everything he did, reminded him of her, with her clothes still in the room smelling like her, when he laid in bed, he couldn't sleep from seeing the empty spot next to where he slept, it was becoming too much for him. After eight years of being together, and loving someone so much to where you thought you would be together forever, was killing him more and more each day without her.

Every time he looked at his daughters, all he could see was Harlow, and they were spitting images of her, hurting him even more. He began avoiding them, trying to stop the pain, he even avoided Sadie. Every day he would drive around for hours, go to parks and sit in his vehicle staring off into nowhere, and would even stay at work later just to avoid seeing everyone when he got home.

Antonio also visited her grave nearly every day, after his latest visit with her, he was at his wits end and not thinking clearly, he drove to a sporting goods store, and walked inside looking at various handguns. Seeing one he liked, he showed them his permit to purchase, and purchased the handgun. On his way home, he kept looking over at the gun he had sitting on his passenger seat, wondering when, and where he was going to do it. When he got home, he quickly went into his office avoiding Sadie and the girls.

He placed the handgun in the bottom drawer of his desk, and pulled out pictures of Harlow placing them on top of the desk for him to see. He pulled out a bottle of bourbon, and poured himself a drink. As he sat in his chair with the drink in his hand, he stared at her pictures for the longest time, then closed his eyes remembering when they met, where they met, and all the trips they took together. He began remembering some of their biggest fights, and her last days there on earth with him. He was still hating himself for not being there at the time, and trying to save her life.

Sadie was outside with the girls, and looked at the time, figuring it was time for their nap. She brought them inside and headed upstairs to lay them down.

She went back down the stairs, and was about to pick up their toys when she noticed Antonio's office door was closed. Seeing that it was closed, she knew he was home, and decided to go talk to him, wanting to give Antonio a piece of her mind.

She was fed up with him ignoring his kids, and doing everything possible to never be home. She was surprised he was home, and walked up to the door, taking a deep breath before barging in without knocking.

Her stomach dropped as she opened the door, taking one step in, shocked to see Antonio holding a gun to his head. "Antonio! Stop! What are you doing?" she screamed, running over to him, and trying to carefully pull the gun out of his hand.

Sadie finally got the gun out of his hand, and stepped back away from him, her heart was pounding hard, and her hand was shaking wildly, afraid to drop the gun, and have it go off. "I can't do this anymore." he sobbed, reaching for the gun she was able to get out of his hands.

"You can't do what? You do realize that you have two beautiful girls that lost their mother, and now you want them to lose their father too? What are you thinking?" she yelled. She looked over at Harlow's pictures that were placed in front of him, on his desk.

"Is this really the answer?" she asked loudly, and wide eyed. She grabbed one of Harlow's pictures, and held it in front of him. "Look at her! Is this what she would have wanted?" Sadie snapped. She turned half way and noticed a picture of his little girls on the corner of his desk, she reached over and grabbed the picture, placing it inches away from his face.

"Is this what Harlow wants, for you to give up on them?... Antonio! Think about what you are doing!" she yelled, shoving both pictures in his face. "LOOK AT THEM!" she demanded, when he wouldn't look.

He stood up taking the pictures away from Sadie, setting them down on the desk. His heart was pounding, and his fists pressed down on the desk, he lowered his head fighting back the tears. He felt relieved Sadie walked in when she did, and stopping him from doing something terrible. He thought, maybe it was a sign from Harlow, sending Sadie in his office when she did.

He really didn't want to end his life, but figured it would finally take the pain away for good. As he thought about it, and listening to Sadie yell at him, he knew he was in the wrong, and that he needed to snap out of the state of mind that he was in.

He turned to look at Sadie, and looked directly into her eyes. He saw terror and frustration in her eyes, and his heart started beating faster while looking at her. Without even thinking, he reached his arm round her waist and pulled her to him, using his other hand to cup the back of her head, he quickly pressed his lips against hers, kissing her hard. When she responded to his kiss, their kiss turned into a heated passionate kiss. He was out of breath and had to pull away. He leaned his head back to look at her, surprised she didn't resist him, and expected her to push him away, or slap him across the face.

She didn't say anything, and just looked at him. She was surprised, and shocked about him kissing her, and thought the kiss was nice. The way he kissed her, had her wanting more. He leaned in for another kiss, and while she kissed him back, it sent warm sensations throughout his body, as well as hers. His hands started roaming her back, pressing her tightly against him, exciting her more. The way he was kissing her, and how he was touching her, had her inner core throbbing with desire, and feeling wet below. She tightly wrapped her arms around him, kissing him with more urgency, and moaning as she felt the temperature rise inside her "Sadie." He moaned into her mouth.

He pulled away and cupped the sides of her face, and looked in her eyes. "WOW...." he said in amazement, and taking a deep breath. He felt like a whole different person after the kiss, and started thinking it was wrong of him to kiss her. "I'm so sorry, I probably shouldn't have kissed you like that... it just felt so right." he whispered, wiping her bottom lip softly with his thumb. He noticed her chest rising up and down fast, and looked back into her eyes. "To be honest, I expected a slap across the face."

She smiled at him, and wasn't sure what to say. She enjoyed the way his lips were pressed against hers, but she herself was unsure if it was right of them to kiss. "Promise me you'll get rid of that thing." she urged, pointing at the gun she set down on the desk. "And promise me, that you'll never think about doing anything like that ever again." she says, grabbing a fist full of his shirt, and pulling him to her while staring into his eyes.

"I'm sorry, I know that was stupid of me. It's just that every time I look at the girls, I see Harlow, and it kills me, it hurts. I've been feeling like I cannot go on without her." he said, sounding depressed.

"And that's a bad thing that they look like her? She gave you two precious gifts... don't ever take them for granted. They deserve you in their life, and I'm being serious when I say this, don't be doing anything stupid like that ever again, and I'll keep saying it over and over too, just to get it in your head." she says, picking up the gun, and emptying out all the ammo onto the desk. She made sure the gun was empty, and set it down on the desk, while grabbing all the ammo.

She looked back over to him, and pointed. "Don't ever say you can't live without Harlow, you can, and you will. Especially for Gabriella and Isabella, they can't lose both their parents, they're way too young." she snapped.

"Easier said than done." he spoke lowly, running his hands through his hair.

After sharing a kiss with him, she was nervous to tell him the other reason why she came into the room to see him. "I also came in here to let you know that I do have a date later today."

"A date?" he questioned surprised, looking as if he just lost his best friend.

"Yes I do, is that not OK? We're just going to a movie, and I told him it would have to be an early one so I could get back and put the girls to bed."

"What if I hadn't been around, what were you going to do with them?"

"I would have brought them with, or I would have kept calling you until you answered, insisting that you be here for your kids, and spend time with them. Something in which you've been neglecting, since she left."

"How did you even have time to find a date, when you haven't gone anywhere? What's his name?" he questioned, feeling like a heel. He walked over to the window and looked out, feeling like a dumbass for kissing her.

"His name is Ethan."

Antonio's heart dropped when he heard his name, and turned around quickly. "Ethan? As in my brother in law Ethan?" he asked surprised. He felt upset with himself when he remembered he told Ethan that she wasn't single.

"Yes, Harlow's brother... he has been coming here almost every day for almost two months to see and play with the kids."

"What? Why haven't you said anything?"

"Probably because you haven't been around, if you would have been here you would have known." she said, sounding bitter. She noticed how his demeanor changed when she mentioned she had a date, and more so after saying she had a date with Ethan. "Let me ask you this too... Why did you tell him that I wasn't single?" she asked, looking curious. Wondering what his answer would be to that, knowing damn well she was very single.

He placed his hands on his hips, and looked down at his feet. "I don't even know why, it just came out when he asked me." he said quietly, feeling embarrassed.

Seeing Antonio's reaction, she was second guessing going on the date with Ethan. "Do you not want me to go?" she asked, walking up to him. She curled her finger under his chin, and turned his head, making him look at her. She nodded her head when he didn't respond, trying to study his face "Is that a no?"

"I guess... I don't really want you to go, but you deserve to go out, so go." he says quietly, moving her hand away from his chin.

"If you don't want me to go, I won't go."

"Just go, go out and have some fun, you deserve it. Especially how I've been lately, you need a break too."

Sadie left his office quietly, hoping he would have told her no.

While walking away she thought about the kiss they shared, and started tracing her lips with a smile. She liked the way he kissed her, and liked the way his kiss made her feel inside. She hadn't felt feelings like that before, and loved it.

Sadie was down in her room getting ready to leave, when the doorbell rang. When nobody answered, it rang again. Antonio finally answered the door, giving Ethan a disappointed look. He was pissed at him for asking her out on a date.

"Well it's about time you're home." Ethan says, surprised to see him, and reached for his hand to shake. "Can we talk for a minute, while I wait for Sadie?"

Antonio didn't say anything, and turned his head, looking behind him to see if Sadie was coming. He walked outside when he didn't see her, shutting the door behind him. They walked and stood by Ethan's white SUV.

"Are you OK?"

"Yea... yea I'm fine." Antonio said disappointed, looking away from Ethan. He had a hard time looking at him, he felt Ethan was taking Sadie away from him. He knew she wasn't his, and knew he needed to stop acting like she was.

Ethan looked at him sincerely. "The reason I ask, is because Sadie says you haven't really been home since Harlow passed away, and you have been avoiding Gabriella and Isabella."

"Don't worry about it, I've got it under control." Antonio snapped.

"Well if you need anything, you know you can call me, just remember, I lost her too."

Antonio wanted to say something to him, but Sadie had come out and looked at the both of them. She gave a heartfelt look at Antonio, waiting for him to tell her not to go.

"Hello there, beautiful lady." Ethan says, pulling Sadie over to him, and placing a kiss on her lips. She wasn't sure if she liked his lips against hers, it didn't feel right, and she didn't feel any sparks like she did with Antonio. She placed her hands on each side of Ethan's neck, kissing him more, trying to see if she could get any sparks to fly.

When she didn't feel anything from the kiss, she pulled away from him. She felt nothing, feeling as if she were kissing her brother. She saw how Ethan was smiling at her, and gave him a smirk. She could see he enjoyed the kiss, and felt guilty for even trying to kiss him. She sighed and looked at Antonio.

"Antonio?" she asked, worried when she saw him staring off into the sky, not saying a word.

Chapter 16- Heated Passion

"Antonio?" Sadie said again, trying to get his attention.
Antonio was trying not to look at them, and looked the other way. He didn't know why, but it bothered him seeing Ethan kiss Sadie, and was holding back from saying anything to them, knowing that he had no say in what they do.

"Go have fun." Antonio said in a mocking tone, as he pushed himself away from Ethan's vehicle, and walked away. Sadie kept her eyes on Antonio, while he walked away from them. She could tell that he didn't want her to go, and wondered why he didn't try stopping her from going out with Ethan.

Ethan walked over to the passenger door, and opened it for her, closing the door after she was in. He walked around the car looking all around him, smiling ear to ear. He too, could tell Antonio was not liking him taking her out.

At the movies, Sadie was quiet, and couldn't get the kiss she shared with Antonio earlier out of her mind. Ethan noticed how quiet she had been, and wrapped his arm around her, hoping to get some sort of reaction out of her, and didn't.

After the movie was over, he took her out to eat, nothing fancy, but just to your typical burger joint, figuring that would be more appropriate, so that they could talk.

"So, you and Harlow got pretty close?" Ethan asked, while taking a bite of his burger.

"Yes, towards the end, she was pretty open with me. When I first started working for them, she was hard on me, and took a few months for her to finally accept me."

"At least, she's now back with my parents." He said quietly.

Sadie tilted her head to the side, giving him a questionable look. "I didn't know they were gone. When did they pass?"

"Two years ago, they were killed while riding their motorcycle." he says quietly, taking a deep breath. He sighed, and looked down at his plate, staring at his fries.

"Wow, what happened?"

"They went out riding after church, a young girl not paying attention and was on her phone, pulled out in front of them, killing them."

"That's so sad." She looked away, feeling bad for asking. She could see it still bothered him.

"Harlow took it pretty hard, she was really close to them, especially our mother."

"Sorry to hear that, I wondered why they weren't at the funeral, and never came around to visit with her while she was sick."

"I never did either, which I feel really guilty about. She did call me about a week before she died, and asked me to make sure the girls and Antonio remained happy."

"She wanted the best for everyone. I just hope that Antonio snaps out of the depression that he's in." Sadie quietly said, while staring at her food. Antonio then came to her mind, and started worrying about him, wondering what he was up to.

Sadie barley ate her meal, thinking about Antonio's gun he had earlier, pressed against the side of his head. Feeling a little relieved that she grabbed the ammo from him, hoping he didn't have any more hidden.

"I don't mean to cut this short, but I really should get home and check on the girls. Antonio was really out of it earlier." she said politely, not wanting Ethan to know what she walked in on earlier.

Ethan paid the bill, and brought her home. Once he pulled into the driveway, he put the car in park and leaned over to her, trying to kiss her. She ignored his advance, and turned her head quickly, grabbing a hold of the door handle to open the door.

"Whoa, hold on. I can get that for you." He opened his door, and hurried around the vehicle, opening the door for her.

"Thanks, it was nice." she says, smiling as she got out.

He smiled back at her and cupped the back of her head, pulling her in to kiss her. She didn't want him to kiss her, and only allowed him to peck her on the lips.

"Sorry, I need to brush my teeth. I've got a bad after taste in my mouth after dinner. Thanks again for dinner and taking me to a movie, I really appreciate it." she said politely, while looking at the front door.

"Hope to do this again soon." he smiled. She nodded her head and started walking to the front door, hoping he wasn't following her.

Antonio was standing behind the curtains, watching them after he heard Ethan pull up, as he watched out the window, his heart sank when he saw Ethan kiss her, and walked away from the window.

Sadie walked in the door and was immediately greeted by Isabella. "Sadie, you're home!" she screeched, running up to her and hugging her around her legs.

"How come you don't have your pajamas on?" Sadie asked, as she leaned down to her.

"Dad said we didn't have to put them on yet."

"Well it's late, we should get you two into your pajamas, where's your dad anyway?" she asked, as she stood up holding her hand and guiding her over to the stairs.

Isabella shrugged her shoulders and ran up the stairs. When Sadie got to their room, she saw Gabriella asleep on the floor. She lifted her up, carefully changed her clothes, and laid her in bed without trying to wake her. She then helped Isabella change, and into her bed.

"Did your dad even play with you today?" Sadie asked her quietly, running her fingers through Isabella's hair.

"Uh huh! We played hide and seek, then he got a phone call."

"Well that's good, I hope you all had fun." she smiled. "Go to sleep, and tomorrow if it's nice outside, I'll take you both to the carnival."

"OK!" She says, closing her eyes tight.

Sadie left the girls room, and looked for Antonio, she called out for him, but got no response. She started to worry, and looked around in his office making sure he got rid of the gun. She found it hidden in the bottom drawer of his desk, under a bunch of paperwork and grabbed it. Hiding it in a closet, on the top shelf in one of the spare bedrooms. She then headed downstairs to see if he was there, as she got to the bottom step, she saw Antonio shooting pool by himself.

He looked up at her when he felt her standing there. "Would you like to play?"

"Sure, I'm not very good at it though."

"I'll help you if you need some help, are the kids asleep?"

"Yes, and I can't believe you didn't get them ready for bed. Gabriella was sleeping on the floor, and Isabella was running around the house, where were you?"

"I received a phone call from my mom, my parents are still living in Paris and was checking to see how things were. I wasn't thinking, then I heard you come home. I've been so used to having someone help care for them." he says, shaking his head in disappointment. "They weren't by themselves long, maybe about fifteen minutes."

"Antonio, they're five years old, you need to watch them at all times, anything could have happened." she says standing with her hands on her hips, giving him a serious look, as he racked the pool balls together.

"I know." he sighed.

"Well, you're going to have to work on that." She watched him rack the pool balls, hoping he wasn't going to make her break. "I hope your breaking up the balls, I'm not very good at it."

"Come here, I'll help you." he says, waving her over.

After chalking up the pool stick, he placed the cue ball on the table and got behind her, placing her hand on the table, and resting the stick in between her middle finger and pointer finger, as he stood over her, speaking softly in her ear that sent goosebumps up her spine.

"Now concentrate on where you want to hit the ball, you want to hit the cue ball right there." he tells her, showing her the spot on the ball. With her other hand holding the stick he helped her pull it back and hit the ball scattering the balls all over the table.

"See that wasn't so hard." he smiled "You got two solid balls in, good job."

They finally got down to a couple balls left on the table, where her ball was located, and where the cue ball was at, Sadie had a difficult shot to make it into the pocket. He got behind her showing her where to aim at the diamonds on the pool table, and where she should hit the cue ball.

As he was bent over her, she could feel his warm breath against her skin, making her feel all warm inside. She pulled her arm back with the stick in hand, and felt him placing soft kisses along the side of her neck, she turned her head to the side, giving him access to her lips. His heart started beating faster, and went in for the kiss. She dropped her stick, turned around, and wrapped her arms around him, and kissing him passionately, while he had her pressed against the pool table.

His hands softly trailed down her body, and to her ass, gently squeezing them, while pulling her tightly against him. He lifted her up, and set her on top of the pool table, kissing her neck, and sending wonderful sensations throughout her body. She was enjoying how he was kissing her, and how he was making her feel inside. Her hands quickly moved up to his head, and tangled her fingers in his hair, tugging his hair, and letting out soft moans, as he hit the sensitive spot on her neck.

He slid his hand underneath her shirt, and started fondling her breasts. With her one breast filling his hand, he stopped and looked at her, nervous at what they were doing and what he was feeling.

"It's ok." she whispered, while pulling her shirt off. She grabbed the bottom hem of his shirt, and pulled it up over his head. She laid back on the pool table, and pulled him on top of her, kissing him.

Feeling uncomfortable on top of the table, he pulled her up, carried her into her bedroom, and laid her on the bed. She scooted herself back towards the pillows, and pulled him on top of her, kissing him hard and desperately.

Their lips moved in perfect rhythm, both getting hot and bothered, and she was starting to feel wet below. He pulled away from her lips and started trailing gentle kisses along down her body, and back up to her lips, kissing her passionately.

"I want you..." he groaned, in her mouth.

She moved her hand down to his hardness that she felt pressed against her, and began unzipping his pants. Her inner core was throbbing, and wanted nothing more than for him to be inside her. They wasted no time, and quickly took the rest of their clothes off.

He laid her back down, and stared at her while lying next to her with his head propped up by his one arm. He looked down at her lips, and caressed her bottom lip with his thumb. He was feeling confused, he felt like he was cheating on Harlow after having flashbacks of her, he knew she was gone, and not coming back and felt torn. The more he looked at Sadie, he wanted her. He slowly rolled on top of her, and pressed his lips against hers.

His cock was throbbing for her, and wanted her badly, his heart was pounding hard and felt extremely nervous about he was about to do. He spread her legs and placed his hand around his cock, and placed it at her opening, teasing her clit with the tip of his cock, that caused her to moan.

He closed his eyes, and thrusted in her slowly. "Oh God." he moaned, while opening his eyes to look at her. He liked that she was tight, and wet for him, that it sent shivers up his spine. She gasped as he slid into her, and dug her nails into his back as she felt him fill her insides, stretching to his size. Once she adjusted to his size, he started thrusting slowly, and lowered his lips to hers, kissing her hard.

"Antonio..." she whispered.

"Am I hurting you?" he asked, worried.

"No... it feels amazing." she quietly said, pulling his face back to hers, kissing him passionately.

His thrusts were becoming harder, deeper, and faster the longer they made love. Both were moaning, and groaning while pleasuring each other, and both were nearing their orgasms. She panted each time he hit her g-spot, that had her digging her nails further into his back, and started releasing all over his cock.

He thrusted deep and hard a couple more times, groaning and grunting while releasing himself inside her, he lowered his lips to hers and kissed her hungrily, while his cock pulsated inside her.

He pulled out of her, and rolled onto his back, he was out of breath and needed to catch his breath. He rolled his head to the side to look at her, and smiled. The back of his hand moved up to her face, and caressed the side of her face while looking at her. He felt himself getting hard again, and rolled back on top of her, kissing her slowly at first, then turned into a demanding, rough kiss.

"That was incredible, I could go for another round." he moaned, while kissing her wildly.

She pushed him over onto his back, and straddled him. She grabbed a hold of his cock, and placed him inside of her, taking full control. He squirmed and moaned loudly, when she took all of him in, and hit that wall of hers.

He liked how she took control, how she moved up and down, and how she used her hips to move around his cock. He still couldn't believe this was happening between them, but was enjoying every minute of it. Both started moaning out each other's names, while releasing together. Their bodies were full of sweat, he lifted her off the bed and carried her into the shower, showering together.

The way she was washing him, and how he was washing her, he couldn't stop himself from getting hard again. He wrapped his one arm around her waist, cupped the back of her head with his other hand, pulling her to him, and pressing his lips against hers, kissing her hard. His hands lowered to her ass, lifted her up while pinning her against the wall, and thrusted inside of her. He placed his one hand behind her head, to keep her from banging her head against the wall, and thrusted harder, taking her into another world with the way he was pounding into her, thrusting until they both released. He lowered her down after they released, and kissed her like a mad man.

Both were surprised at what they had been doing all night, they looked at each other, full of lust and smiled. Both trying to think about what to say to each other. He cupped the side of her face, and looked her in the eyes. "I never thought this day would ever happen, and I still can't believe it happened." he says, kissing her.

She smiled and pulled away from him, and looked in his pretty blue eyes, still feeling butterflies fluttering against her stomach walls, and pulled him in for another kiss, kissing him hungrily. "I never thought in a million years, this would ever happen between us." she said quietly, with a smirk. He picked her up, carried her out of the shower, and laid her on the bed, both soaking wet. As she laid in his arms, she closed her eyes with a big smile, humming with satisfaction and fell asleep.

While she laid in his arms, the thought of Ethan crossed his mind, hoping that he didn't have to worry about him seducing Sadie. He wasn't sure if this was a new beginning for him, and didn't want Ethan interfering. The more he thought about it, the more he couldn't sleep.

Chapter 17- We need to talk

Antonio woke up with Sadie still in his arms, he looked at the time and gently slid her off him, thinking it would be best to leave her room before the kids woke up. He quietly slid out of bed, and walked around Sadie's room looking for his clothes, finding his pants on the floor and remembered that his shirt was taken off by the pool table.

He walked upstairs, and over to the kitchen to make coffee. While waiting for the coffee to brew, he leaned against the counter thinking about what happened between him and Sadie, which made him smile.

The thought of Isabella's question popped through his head and it got him thinking, the more he thought about it, it was making his head hurt. He needed coffee to wake him up, thinking it would make him think more clearly. While the coffee was still brewing, he grabbed a mug and poured himself a cup anyway.

He walked into his office and stood at his desk, looking at all of Harlow's pictures that were still scattered on the desk, he picked one of her pictures up, and sat down looking at it. He felt he betrayed her by sleeping with Sadie, and began apologizing to her, asking her if it would be OK if he moved on, and letting her know that he still loved and missed her.

He also apologized to her about how he had been with their girls, not being there for them, and ignoring them. He sighed hard, apologizing again about how he was about to give up on everyone, and his life, just to be with her. He set the picture down, and gathered all the other pictures, putting them away in the bottom drawer.

Meanwhile Sadie was starting to wake up, and placed her arm across the bed thinking Antonio was still there. She opened her eyes, and looked over at where he was laying, and noticed he wasn't in the bed, she turned her head to the bathroom, and knew he left the room when she saw the door was open and the light off. She pulled the blankets off her, and smiled when she realized that she didn't have any clothes on. She laid there thinking about what happened between her and Antonio, humming at the thought of how the two made love all night, and the multiple orgasms that he had given her.

She got out of bed, put a robe on and threw her hair up into a loose messy bun. She walked up the stairs and into the kitchen to make coffee, seeing that coffee was already made, she poured herself a cup. Antonio walked up behind her and placed a kiss on her neck, making her jump. Spilling her coffee over herself, and all over the floor. She turned around about to yell for scaring her, and stopped when he cupped her face and placed a kiss on her lips.

"Morning." he said quietly with a smile, pulling only inches away from her face, staring down at her lips.

"Morning." she smiled "Thanks for scaring me again, you seem to have a knack for doing that."

He laughed as he walked over to grab some paper towels, and cleaned up the mess. "I'm sorry, I'll have to announce my presence from now on."

She started wiping coffee off her robe, when Antonio walked up behind her, wrapping his arms around her waist, and resting his chin on her shoulder. "We should talk about what happened last night." he said, quietly.

"I think so too, but the girls are going to be up soon, it would be best if we were to talk about it when the girls aren't around." She turned around and wrapped her arms up over his neck, and looked into his eyes. Just looking into his eyes, had her heart melting, and her inner core going haywire.

He kissed her lips softly. "That's fine, we can wait until later, I just need to make sure that we're on the same page."

"OK." she says turning around, and leaned against the sink. He placed his hands on her hips, and leaned towards her ear. "Just so you know, I don't regret anything that happened between us." he whispered.

She smiled. "I don't either, but we still should talk about what happened."

She turned around to look at him and smiled, feeling relieved that he didn't regret what happened between them. He wrapped his arms around her waist, and pulled her to him, studying every feature of her face. He kissed the tip of her nose, that sent electricity throughout her body. He lifted her onto the counter, positioned himself between her legs, and kissed her with passion. He pulled away when he heard the girls talking, while they were coming down the stairs. He helped Sadie off the counter, and gave her a warm hug.

Gabriella walked up to Antonio with a smile "Are we going to the carnival today?"

"Carnival?" he asked, confused. Not knowing what she was talking about.

"Yeah! Sadie said she was going to take us to the carnival today." Isabella said with excitement. She looked at Sadie and smiled.

Antonio turned his head towards Sadie with a questionable look, and scratched the back of his head. "What are they talking about?"

"I told Isabella last night, that if it was nice outside, I would take them to the carnival today."

"Is it nice outside?" Isabella asked, excited.

Antonio laughed. "Well this is the first I've heard of a carnival in town, but Sadie and I can take you girls later."

"It could be because you weren't around for a while." she winked.

"YAY!" they screamed excitedly, and started running around circles.

"The county fair started today." Sadie says. She looked at Antonio, hoping he would be free later. "Are you working today?"

"No, not today.... I took the rest of the week off."

"Good, then you can spend time with them." Sadie insisted, giving him a nudge.

Later in the day, it was getting close to dinner time, and the girls were getting hungry, and antsy, wanting to go to the fair. They ran around the house looking for Antonio, and found him in the bedroom changing.

"I'll be right down; I'm just changing my clothes." Antonio tells the girls.

Sadie called for the girls, wanting to see if they were ready to leave. They came running down the stairs, both nearly tumbling down the steps. "Slow down before someone gets hurt." Sadie says to the girls. "Are you ready to go to the carnival?"

"Yes, Daddy says he's changing his clothes." Gabriella says to her. Sadie happened to look up and saw Antonio walking down the stairs. Her heart fluttered, surprised to see what he was wearing. He had on blue jeans, and a black t-shirt, not a suit that she normally sees him in.

"Wow! I didn't think you even owned a pair of blue jeans." Sadie said amazed.

"I knew you would say something, I figured I wouldn't need to be dressed up for the fair." he winked and smiled. "What do you think?" he asked, trying to be funny, while posing for her.

Sadie giggled "You look nice, it's a nice change for once."

They all got into Antonio's SUV, and headed for the fair. As they approached the fair, and started looking for a parking spot, the girls eyes widened, and started jumping in their car seats when they saw all the rides.

"Look Sadie!" Gabriella screeched while pointing over at the merry go round.

"I see." Sadie giggled. She looked at Antonio and smiled. "Thanks for coming along, I think it's something that all of us needed to do, and to have a little fun, after all that has happened."

Gabriella and Isabella grabbed Sadie's hands as they walked closer to the fair, they stood and waited in line to get in, while Antonio paid for tickets.

"Time for some fattening foods." Antonio grinned, as he handed their tickets to a worker who was collecting the tickets.

"Can we go on the rides now daddy?" Isabella asked.

"Aren't you girls hungry?" he asked, as his stomach was growling.

"Yes, but I want to go on rides first." Isabella says, pouting. She pointed at the rides, and begged to go on them. Sadie gave him a look, and insisted that he let them go on some rides first. Letting him know, he will be just fine if he waited to eat.

Antonio walked up to the booth, and bought the girls unlimited ride bracelets, and placed them on their wrists. Antonio and Sadie stood behind and watched the girls smile and scream, as they were on their first ride, the kid's roller coaster. Antonio wrapped his arm around Sadie's shoulders, pulling her to him, and spoke into her ear. "I guess were going to have to have our talk later tonight."

"That's fine with me."

They let the kids go on the rides, until they finally got hungry. "What do you girls want to eat? he asked them.

"Cotton Candy." Gabriella giggled.

"You can't have that for dinner." he chuckled. "How about a corn dog?"

"OK." Isabella pouted.

"I'll get you girls cotton candy also, but you have to eat the corn dog first."

While Antonio went to get the food, Sadie and the girls found a table to sit at. She heard her name being called out, and looked around to see where it was coming from, and saw Ethan waving at her. He walked over to them and sat down next to her, and talked to the girls.

"Are you kids having fun?" Ethan asked the girls, pulling Isabella on his lap.

"Yes, we went on a lot of rides!" she said, excitedly.

Ethan turned his head towards Sadie, raising an eyebrow. "Is it just you here with the girls?"

Sadie started feeling uncomfortable, knowing Antonio would be back any minute with their food, she worried about him asking her out again, and wouldn't know what to say to him if he did.

"No, we're here with Antonio, he went to get us some food." Antonio started walking over to Sadie and the girls, holding a tray of food, drinks and the girls cotton candy, and stopped when he saw Ethan talking to them, he felt disappointed that he was here, but continued walking towards them.

"Ethan, what a surprise to see you here." Antonio said cocky.

"I figured that I would come check out the fair, just to see if it was worth bringing Sadie and the girls to, but I see you already brought them." Ethan says, hugging Isabella.

Antonio could feel his ears starting to burn, and his comment instantly hit him, he wanted to tell Ethan to stay away from Sadie, but didn't want to make a scene. The girls loved their uncle and Sadie wasn't his to fight for yet. As close as they were for years, he now felt threatened by him, and wasn't liking him being around them. *I should fire his ass that will make him stay away...* he thought to himself.

Antonio sat down and handed the food out, Sadie looked at Antonio, and could tell he had a little bit of an attitude, while talking to Ethan. She looked over at Ethan "Well, we should eat, and get the girls on more rides before we have to bring them home." Sadie says to Ethan, trying to get him to leave.

Ethan stood up, while looking at Sadie. "I'll give you a call tomorrow, I'm going to get some food, and head home." He hugged and kissed the girls, then shook Antonio's hand. "It was nice seeing you, and I hope that you're doing alright." Ethan says with a grin.

"I'm doing just fine, thank you." Antonio says, taking a bite of his food.

Ethan walked away, while blowing a kiss back at Sadie. Antonio wasn't too pleased with Ethan, and couldn't help but feel anger towards him. He finished eating, and remained quiet while they took the girls back to the carnival rides.

While the girls were on the rides, Sadie stepped in front of Antonio, poking him in the stomach. "Why are you so quiet?"

He looked over her shoulders, watching the girls as they rode by on a train. She cupped his face, turning him to look at her. "What's on your mind?"

"You."

"What about?" she asked, curiously. She noticed how he was acting different ever since Ethan stopped to talk to them. While looking at him she began to giggle.

"You have mustard on your face... come here I'll get it off."
She cupped the back of his head, and pulled him close to her. She licked, then sucked off the mustard that was at the corner of his mouth and upper lip. The way she licked the mustard off, made him feel warm inside, and had him melting. He thought it was hot the way she did it, and not caring who saw them, he began kissing her.

The girls were done with their ride, and ran up to Antonio and Sadie and stopped, the girls were excited to see them kissing, and just stood there watching them, and not saying anything until Sadie realized they were watching them.

Sadie giggled as she pulled away from him, and looked down at the girls. "What ride do you want to go on next?"

"We're tired now, can we go home and come back tomorrow?" Gabriella asked.

"We can go home, and will see about coming back." Antonio tells them.

The girls fell asleep in their car seats on the way home, both Antonio and Sadie carefully got them out of their seats, brought them up to their room, changed them into their pajamas, and placed them in bed.

They both made their way down to the living room and walked over to the couch, Antonio sat down and reached for Sadie's hand as she walked past him, pulling her down onto his lap.

"We finally have time to talk."

Chapter 18- The talk

Sadie looked at Antonio with lust in her eyes, wanting to badly kiss him. She liked how he makes her feel all warm inside. She also didn't want him thinking that she was easy, since she gave in too easy the night before. Normally it's against her rules, sleeping with someone when they aren't involved in a relationship.

"I wanted to talk to you about what happened the night before." he says, caressing her arm with his fingertips. "I know that I told you this morning that I don't regret anything, and I still don't."

"I don't regret it either, I'm just a little shocked that it happened." she says, resting her head on his.

"I know how you feel, I'm a little surprised myself that it happened. But I want you to know that it was wonderful, and have been thinking about it all day. Although I do have to admit, I felt a little guilty, like I somehow betrayed Harlow."

"You didn't betray her... now if she was still here, then yes you would have betrayed her. Besides I never would have allowed it to happen." She paused, looking away. She started thinking about Harlow, and some of the things Harlow had said to her. "You know, I have to tell you something... about a conversation that I had with Harlow. She asked me to make sure that you and the kids remained happy, and I never understood what she meant by that. She pulled me to the side a couple of times to talk to me, and each time I always thought that it was strange. Saying things that I didn't understand, almost like I was getting her permission."

"Permission?"

"I don't know how to explain it, it's how she said and asked me about things, about you, the girls.... and she always had a pen in her hand that she tried hiding whenever I would walk into the room, it just seemed strange to me."

"Hmm..... she never said anything to me that was out of the ordinary."

"I don't know, maybe it was nothing." Sadie says, shrugging her shoulders.

"I'm not going to lie to you, I do miss her." he says "But I want you to know that you gave me a wakeup call, and I thank you for that, had you not walked in...." he began shaking his head, and held onto her tight, thinking. He rested his forehead on her chest, and sighed. "I guess I don't even want to think about what would have happened."

She held his head up, and their eyes locked. "Just don't ever do that again, and I mean that."

"I will never do that again, I promise. I still feel like a coward about it, not only did I scare you, I scared myself, and I'm sure as hell that I let Harlow down for even thinking about doing that. She was probably looking down on me, cussing me out."

"I'm glad that you realize that.... now about last night-..."

"Yes, last night." he says, cutting her off. "I don't know if it should have happened, but to be honest with you, I'm glad that it did. Since we met and the more that I got to know you, I realized some things. I'm not sure what it is about you, but there's something special about you, those girls adore you, and they have since that first night at the restaurant... and I adore you."

"I love those girls; they make me laugh. You know, those girls made me promise them that I would never leave them." she giggled "They even had me pinky promise them."

He smiled, and caressed the side of her face. For a moment he didn't say a word, and just looked at her. He admired her beauty, and not only was she beautiful to him, she was beautiful on the inside as well. She had a huge heart and had a way with him, that always got him to listen. She was able to tell him off, and never had the nerve to yell back at her.

"I guess what I have been trying to say to you, or ask you..." he says, taking a deep breath. Thinking about how to ask the next question that he had for her, almost nervous to ask. "What or how do you feel about us?"

"Are you asking about us, as in a couple?" she asked, smiling from the inside.

"Yes... while you were on that date with Ethan, I started thinking, I really didn't like that he took you out, and had a hard time seeing him talking to you at the fair. I never said anything since I would have been in the wrong, it wouldn't have been fair to you, or him, being that we aren't a couple. Then I think about what happened between us last night, and feel like I'm alive again."

"Well..." she smiled. She looked down at his hands, and started playing with his fingers. "We can take it slow and see where things go, I just don't want to hurt or confuse those little girls if it doesn't work out between us."

Antonio smiled big, he felt relieved that Sadie accepted for them to try and be a couple, and was determined to not wreck anything between them.

"What about Ethan?" he asked.

She giggled. "You don't have to worry about him, I just went out with him to get out of the house. I also wanted you to spend time with your girls since you ignored them for a couple months."

"You kissed him." he sighed.

"I had my reasons why I did, and it wasn't because I had feelings for him."

Without wasting anymore time, he pulled her in for a kiss and laid her down on the couch, kissing until they were both out of breath. He pulled back, smiling. "I know you said that you want to take things slow, but right now, I'd like to carry you to your room, and make hot passionate love to you." he said, locking his lips to hers before she could say a word.

Feeling revved up, he carried her down the stairs, and laid her on the bed, both taking their clothes off in a hurry, and throwing them across the room.

As he got on the bed to get on top of her, she pulled him down on top of her, kissing him hard, and dominating her tongue in his mouth. A groan escaped his mouth, and moved his lips all over her neck, sucking the tender spot near her ear, and making her moan loudly.

He slowly kissed her all over, and moved down to her breasts. He still felt nervous to touch them, and loved the feeling of them, so soft but so firm. He began blowing air on her nipples, making them harder than what they were, and placed a breast in his mouth, licking and sucking on the nipple, and moved over to the other breast doing the same thing.

He licked his two fingers and moved his hand down to her pussy and slid his two fingers inside her. Feeling how wet she was, got him excited, that he started to slowly kiss down her body until he reached her clit, her breathing became erratic as he started spreading her legs, and her heart started pounding as his mouth covered her pussy, softly licking her clit up and down, then circling her swollen button with his tongue. Her back arched as he thrusted his tongue inside her, exploring her insides. She grabbed a pillow, and pressed it over her face to muffle the moaning sounds that she couldn't control.

She squirmed as he switched back and forth from teasing her clit to thrusting his tongue deeply inside her, tasting her sweet juices that began flowing. He continued pleasuring her below until she orgasmed, and grabbed a fist full of sheets as she released all her sweet juices onto his tongue, and loudly moaning out his name.

He wiped his face and slowly slid his tongue from her navel all the way up to her lips, hungrily kissing her, and groaning as she slid her fingers up his back, and up to the top of his head, grabbing a hold of his hair, as they kissed wildly.

"Sadie...." he groaned as he thrusted his cock inside of her. Her nails dug into his back as he continued thrusting deeply inside her, and hitting her g spot. "Antonio..." she screamed, as he slowly thrusted in and out of her, hitting all her magic spots. While they continued to be one, their kiss was also moving in perfect rhythm, and both moaning together.

She felt every inch of him inside her, her stomach full of butterflies. Every time he thrusted deep, she would arch her back and scream out his name. He was determined to satisfy her in every way until she came all over his cock. He couldn't hold out any longer, the thrill of making love to her again, had him aroused to the fullest. As he felt her orgasming, he felt warmness around his cock from her release and groaned loud. He pushed his body up with his fists, and thrusted a few harder deep thrusts, cumming inside her.

He dropped down on her, and rested his head in the crook of her neck, trying to regain his breath. As he got his breath back, he locked lips with her, kissing her passionately.

"You amaze me..." she moaned into his mouth, while they kissed.

He sucked on her bottom lip as he pulled away from their kiss, and looked at her. "Why is that?" he asked, whispering.

"You know all the right spots to hit while making love to me, my body goes numb." she says smiling, pressing his head back down to hers so she could kiss him, kissing until their lips were raw.

For a couple hours, Antonio laid on his back, wore out from making love to Sadie. He surprised himself to make it that long, and figured Sadie had to be feeling sore. Thinking she was, since he was told by Harlow, how sore he would make her feel.

She sat up looking at Antonio. "I'm going to go clean up." she says quietly, leaning down and pressing her lips against his. As she was getting up, he pulled her back down on top of him, making her giggle.

"Don't I get an invite?" he asked with a grin.

"You can come in, but I don't think I can survive another round." she giggled.

"Are you sure about that?" he asked, sliding her hair away from his face.

She took hold of his hand as she got up, pulling him "Come on, no monkeying around either, I can't do two late nights in a row."

They shared more tender kisses in the shower, as they were finished washing each other, Sadie decided to give him a surprise. She bent down, getting on her knees and kissed his cock, making it hard.

"Sadie what are you doing." he asked, in shock.

She placed his hardened cock inside her mouth, causing him to gasp as she slowly moved it in and out, and taking it in as far as it would go. He groaned loudly when he felt his cock hit the back of her throat. "OH MY...." It shocked him, to where his one hand pressed hard against the wall, and his other hand covered his mouth.

He never knew how good it would feel, feeling like he struck gold, or was in heaven. He kept looking down at her, and watching what she was doing to him. He couldn't believe she had him in her mouth, and leaned his head back, enjoying the wonderful feeling. He was about to cum, and leaned his head forward, pulling her up. "I can't let you do that." he said softly.

He picked her up, and pressed her against the wall, making her moan profusely as he thrusted in her. He held his hand behind her head, and thrusted harder into her. Not wanting her to hit her head as they were fucking like jackrabbits.

He set her down after they both released their juices together, and cleaned themselves off again. "Am I allowed to sleep in here again." he asked, cupping her face.

"As long as when I wake up, you're still lying next to me." she smiled.

She climbed in the bed after Antonio got in, and laid her head on his chest, smiling at the thought of how good she felt at the moment, and softly slid her fingertips along his chest. She was in a whole new world, and the feelings she felt for him, started to become even stronger. After over a year of getting to know him, they finally became one and a couple. Something she never thought could never possibly happen.

He kissed the top of her head, and wrapped his arms around her. She looked up and puckered her lips for him, wanting him to kiss her, which he didn't deny. "Goodnight." he whispered.

Chapter 19- Uninvited guest

The next morning Sadie opened her eyes, and saw a pair of big beautiful blue eyes staring back at her, and both smiled at each other. "I told you that I would still be here when you woke up." he says, sliding strands of her hair behind her ear.

She slid closer to him wrapping her arm around him, giving him a peck on the lips. He wanted more than just a peck, and rolled her from her side, onto her back, and laid on top of her, kissing her hard and demanding. His hand slide behind her head, gently tugging on her hair and creating moans between them, while they kissed.

His hand trailed down the side of her body, he got down to her thigh and moved his hand over to her pussy, teasing her by tickling her clit with his finger. He smiled in her mouth when she started squirming from side to side, up and down "The girls will be up soon, you know." she giggled.

"You're right." he groaned still kissing her, he wanted nothing more than to make love to her again. He moved his kisses away from her lips, and over to her cheek, along down her neck, and moving to her collarbone. Trying not to miss a spot.

He then rolled to his back, trying to calm down as he was getting hard "I'll just go take a cold shower then." he says to her, turning his head and watched her get out of bed.

"You'll be just fine, you've gotten plenty of sex the last couple nights." she said, giggling softly.

He kept a grin on his face while watching her get dressed. "You better get out of bed before the girls find you down here."

"What would be so bad about that?"

"I told you last night, I don't want to confuse them. If nothing works out between us, I'd feel bad that we let them down. They already had one heartbreak; they don't need another one."

"That's something that I don't plan on that at all." he says, being sure of himself. He slid out of bed and walked over to Sadie still naked, and wrapping his arms around her shoulders. She couldn't help but look down at the package he was packing, and grinned. He curled his finger under her chin, and lifted her head up.

"I don't plan on ever letting you go." he says, pressing his lips against hers.

"OK." She was happy to hear him say that, and smiled. She bent over, grabbed his clothes off the ground, and handed them to him. "Here... get dressed." she chuckled.

He dropped the clothes back on the ground, and reached out for her. Pulling her down with him as he dropped onto the bed. "Antonio..." she giggled.

"One more kiss?" he asked.

She smiled.

He cupped the back of her head, and pressed her down to him, giving her a long and very passionate kiss. Both were getting aroused, and Sadie abruptly pulled away. "The kids..."

Antonio groaned and pouted as she stood up, and left the room. She left to go make coffee, and to check on the girls. They were still sleeping, so she decided to start making breakfast, knowing that they would awake soon.

She started making sausage, and bacon, and got everything ready to make french toast. She poured two cups of coffee, handing one to Antonio when he walked into the kitchen.

"Thank you." he says, kissing her cheek. "Smells good in here."

"I know, I love the smell of bacon and sausage when it cooks, I hope you like French toast."

"I do, I haven't had that in a long time, I see you have the powdered sugar out, that's the best way to eat it with." he smiled, giving her a pat on the ass.

The girls could smell food cooking, and came down the stairs, sitting at the table while they waited for food. "I'm hungry." Gabriella said, bouncing on the chair.

Antonio looked over at her, grinning. "Calm down, it's coming... just sit there patiently and wait."

Sadie made the kids their plates, and handed them to them. "Do you want syrup on them, or powdered sugar?" They both told her syrup, which she figured they would. She then handed Antonio his plate. "Thank you." he says, taking the plate from her hand, and setting it down on the table. He then surprised her, as he pulled her down to his level and kissed her on the lips, in front of the kids.

Antonio released his lips from hers when he heard the kids giggling, and clapped his hands, rubbing them together. "What do you think kiddos? Should we dig in?" he looked back up to Sadie, smiling. "By the way the food looks and smells delicious."

"Thank you."

Antonio's phone rang while they were eating, he got up and grabbed his phone, answering it. His eyes widened while he was talking to the person on the other end, and hung up quickly. After hanging up, he hurried to finish his food. Taking a napkin, he wiped his mouth. "Thanks Hun, that was really good, but I have to leave and go take care of something. I'm not sure how long it will take." he says, standing up and walked to the sink with his empty plate.

Sadie looked at him confused. "I thought you took the whole week off?"

"I did, but one of my clients is in trouble, and got themselves put in jail."

"For what?"

"That's what I need to go there for, and to talk with him about. I have to see if I can get him out of there" he says, rinsing his plate off.

Sadie grabbed a washrag and clean the kids up, washing all the syrup off their hands and face, then cleaned up the kitchen while the girls looked for clothes that they wanted to wear.

Before leaving, Antonio walked in the kitchen. Wanting to be funny, he announced his presence. "I'm in here." he says, grinning.

"I heard you this time." she giggled "You're such a smart ass."

"I guess it's better to be a smart ass, than a dumb ass." he chuckled.

He walked behind her, and wrapped his arms around her, kissing the back of her neck, trying to give her goosebumps. "I have to go." he said quietly. He then placed his hands on her breasts, checking out her nipples. "I'm just seeing if the goosebumps worked." he smiled, as he lightly pinched her nipples. "Yep, I feel the antennas."

She giggled. "I'll see you later." she says, turning around and giving him a kiss.

"Thanks for breakfast." he says, feeling bad he has to leave.

Sadie checked on the girls after Antonio left, and walked into their room. "Your dad left for a bit, what would you like to do today?"

"Can you paint our fingernails, and toenails?" Isabella asked excited.

"Sure, I'll go grab my polish."

Sadie left the room and grabbed whatever colors she had, and brought them upstairs, calling for them to come to her.

The Unexpected Nanny

Isabella wanted to go first, and chose hot pink, Gabriella ended up choosing the same color after seeing Isabella's fingernails "Pink for mommy, right Sadie?" Gabriella asks, looking over at Sadie. Her heart dropped after hearing her say that, and smiled. "Yes, pink for your mommy." she says, touching her nose.

The girls sat nicely, while waiting for the nail polish to dry. Sadie ended up turning on cartoons, so the girls weren't bored while sitting there, waiting. "Remember no touching the nails, and let them dry."
After their nails dried, they wanted to draw pictures and make something for their mom. Sadie went and grabbed all their art supplies, and set them on the table for them.

Later, Sadie was putting the girls down for a nap, and heard the doorbell ring. "I'll be right back."

The doorbell rang again, and Sadie started running down the stairs. "I'll be right there!" she yelled. She quickly opened the door before they could ring the doorbell again, and her heart then sank when she saw who was at the door.

"Hello Sadie."

"What are you doing here?" Sadie asked, surprised.

"I know... I was going to call, but figured I would stop by instead, where are the girls at?"

"I was just laying them down for a nap when you started ringing the doorbell."

"I was going to see if they wanted to come with me, to go visit with Harlow."

"Oh... I think Antonio had planned on bringing them there today, he's usually there every day, for the most part anyway. Maybe when Antonio gets back, you can all go together." she suggested, figuring it would be good if they all went together.

"When will he be back?"

"I'm guessing maybe in a couple hours, I don't know, he didn't even know." she says to him, looking away.

"Well aren't you going to invite me in?" he asked, chuckling.

"Come in." she quietly said, opening the door further, and stepped to the side for him to walk in.

Meanwhile, Antonio was at the jail talking with his client, and looking over the police report. "I need more information out of you, what exactly happened?" he asked, getting his pad of paper out, and grabbed his pen out of his pocket to jot down notes.

After explaining his situation with Antonio, Antonio looked at him with a curious look. "Now you're sure this is everything? Because I must go to the judge and explain everything to him for you to get out. The judge will either lower your bail, let you out on a conditional release, or I can ask that they drop the bail amount, without conditions."

"Yes, that's everything." he insisted, sounding scared that he wasn't going to be let out.

"I'll see what I can do." Antonio says, shaking his hand. He stood up and left the room, then headed over to the courthouse to see the judge, explaining the situation.

"I'll drop the bail on a conditional release, he must remain law abiding, he's not allowed to leave the states, and he has to show up for his next court date, not a minute late. If he doesn't show, I'll issue a warrant out for his arrest." The judge said, signing the paperwork.

"Thank you, your honour."

Antonio went back to the jail, giving the officers the paperwork to release him. After a couple hours, he was finally released to Antonio, and brought him home. "Thank you for getting me out, I don't know what I would have done if I had to stay in there any longer." His client said, relieved.

"You're welcome, call me on Monday and we will figure all of this out."

Antonio stopped at the flower shop on his way home and bought Harlow flowers to put at her gravesite. He also bought Sadie a bouquet of flowers, hoping it would make her smile.

He pulled into the driveway, and was instantly upset when he saw Ethan's car parked in front of the garage. "I used to like the bastard, now I want him to just go away..." Antonio mumbled, putting his car into park. He grabbed both bouquets, and walked in the house. Sadie was in the kitchen and he walked towards her, laying the flowers down on the counter.

Sadie watched him walk towards her, and didn't like the look he had in his eyes. "Where is he?" he asked, with attitude.

"He's with the girls, up in their room."

"Why is he here?" he asked, sighing. "This was not something I wanted to come home to."

Sadie flung her hair behind her, and stood her back against the counter. "Just calm down, he came here to see if you and the girls wanted to go visit Harlow, he was on his way there and stopped by here first."

"I was already bringing the girls there."

"Well... maybe you can all go together?" Sadie said, hoping that he would relax. "He is your brother in law, your employee, and someone who you were once really close to."

"Yes, I know..."

Antonio picked up the bouquet of flowers, and handed them to her. "What are these for?" she asked with a grin. "They're beautiful, thank you."

"I just thought you deserved some flowers." he says, taking a step closer her. He stood in front of her, brushing her hair behind her back, and massaged the back of her head, smiling as he looked at her. He cupped her face, and planted a gentle kiss on her lips. Unable to control his feelings for her, he began kissing her more passionately. He pulled away to look at her, and kissed her again, nibbling and sucking on her bottom lip when he was done kissing her.

"Wow... that didn't take long." Ethan said, loudly for them to hear, as he stood there watching them kiss.

Chapter 20- Talking to Ethan

Ethan spoke sarcastically to Antonio, when he saw the two kissing, and noticed the flowers sitting on the counter. Sadie and Antonio turned to look at Ethan, both looking at him in shock, more so Sadie. She took a step away from Antonio, while wiping her lips with her thumb.

"What didn't take that long?" Antonio replied to his remark, smirking. He knew they were caught, and he didn't care.

"You getting Sadie flowers... which by the way are really nice. I also thought I just saw a heated kiss there, you two were on fire!" Ethan says, raising an eyebrow.

"Yes, you're right I did share a kiss with her, and enjoyed it, am I not allowed to?" Antonio questioned, sounding bitter.

"That's fine and all, but what about Harlow?"

"Harlow? Seriously Ethan?" Antonio angrily questioned, placing his hands on his hips.

Sadie began feeling uncomfortable and started to leave the kitchen, not wanting to witness a fight between them. She turned to look at the two. "I'm going to go check on the girls, please behave yourselves."
Antonio waited to speak to Ethan once Sadie was gone, and away from the kitchen. "Ethan, don't ever think I stopped loving your sister. I'm still *very much* in love with her, just as much as if she were still here. My love for her will never change.... you don't think that I miss her? You're very wrong if you're thinking that I don't love her, or have forgotten about her." Antonio says upset, while pointing his finger at him. He noticed Ethan had a smirk on his face, and it got him even more hot.

"What the hell is that smirk for?"

"Nothing, I was just seeing what you would say is all. Sadie said you were taking the girls to go see Harlow, I was on my way to visit her too, that's why I stopped here. What would you say if we all just went there together?"

As much as Antonio wanted to go alone with the girls, out of respect for Harlow he agreed. "We can do that, just don't ever question me about Harlow like that ever again."

Antonio walked out of the kitchen, still wanting to punch him in the face "I'll go get the girls and then we can leave." he says, leaving Ethan at the breakfast bar.

The girls were having a tea party in their room with Sadie, and Gabriella stopped playing, giving Sadie a serious look. "Sadie? Can we call you mom?"

Antonio was walking in the room when Gabriella asked Sadie the question, and stopped when he heard her question that again. Sadie didn't know what to say, she picked up Gabriella and set her on her lap, giving her a hug. "You can call me whatever you want." she smiled at her, she couldn't tell her no, but didn't want to say yes either, worried about what Antonio would say.

Gabriella smiled wide. "I'm going to call you mommy."

"Me too." Isabella says, sitting on Sadie's lap, next to Gabriella.

Sadie hugged the two of them tightly. "Just remember who your real mommy is, you don't want to ever forget her, she loved you two girls a lot, and I know she still does."

Antonio's heart dropped and felt his mind going all over the place, feeling all kinds of mixed emotions, he still never responded to that question when he was asked by Gabriella, and still didn't know what to tell them. "Hey girls, are you ready to go visit mom?"

They stood up from Sadie's lap, and ran over to Antonio. "Yes, can we go now?" Isabella asked. He looked over at Sadie and whispered thank you to her. "Go get your shoes on." he says to the girls.

"We need to grab our gifts that we made for her." Isabella says.

"I'll go grab them." Sadie tells the girls, following them out of the room. Antonio stopped her, turning her to face him.

"Thank you for being the way you are with those kids. Gabriella asked me that same question the night we buried Harlow."

"I hope you don't mind that I told her that she can call me whatever she would like."

"As long as you're comfortable with it, I'm fine with it." he smiled, resting his hands on her hips, pulling her to him, and giving her a quick kiss.

"I better go grab what they made for her."

Sadie stayed behind while they went to visit Harlow, figuring that this was their time together, and that she didn't need to be there. She cleaned the house for a while, and then decided to go play the piano to relax. She played for quite a while until the girls came running over to her, standing next to her and watching her play.

"Can you teach us to play sometime?" Isabella asked excited. Touching the white keys on the piano.

"Of course I can, not tonight though, it's late. Where's your dad?"

"He's downstairs with Ethan." said Isabella.

"Oh, great." Sadie said quietly. She figured that meant they probably made up, and were downstairs drinking. "Maybe this weekend I can teach you girls a song to play on the piano, looks like right now it's time for bed."

"Can't we stay up a little longer?" Gabriella asked. Being that Ethan was there, she thought that they would be able to stay up longer.

"Not tonight."

Sadie got the girls changed and into bed. "Good night girls." she says, shutting the light off.

"Good night mommy." Gabriella yelled out. Sadie giggled and shut the door.

She went down to where Ethan and Antonio were, and just as she thought, they were sitting at the bar talking and drinking. "Antonio, are you not going to say goodnight to your kids?"

"Oh, are they in bed now?" Antonio asked, turning his chair around to look at Sadie. He spread his lips back tightly when he saw her crossing her arms. "OK, OK, I know that look, I'll go say goodnight."

"I'll be right back." Antonio says to Ethan.

Sadie sat down on Antonio's chair, and picked up his glass, smelling it. "WOW, that's strong." she says, putting the drink back down on the bar.

"Would you like a drink? I'll make you one." Ethan says to her as he took a drink.

Sadie picked up Antonio's drink and took a swig, coughing as she was trying to finish swallowing the drink, it was burning her throat as it went down. "Whew, I'll have one drink, but not as strong as this one, I haven't drank in a very long time."

Ethan stood up quick, and walked over to the liquor cabinet, looking for something to make her, and something that she might like. He dug through the booze wondering what she would drink, he didn't know her very well, and wasn't sure what kind of taste buds she had. "What would you like, I don't even know what you like?"

"I don't care, surprise me."

"OK..." he says, grinning. He grabbed a bottle of Captain Morgan, and mixed her a drink. Pouring quite a bit of booze in the glass *oops* he mumbled under his breath, quietly chuckling. He then grabbed some soda, and poured it in the glass, stirring it up to try and mix up the alcohol. While Ethan was making her a drink, he kept looking over at her. "You know... Harlow talked very highly of you quite often."

"She did?" She looked at him surprised. "I would never think that she would do that, or think that. She hated me for the longest time..."

He slid her drink on the bar, over to her. "At first, she didn't like you at all, she didn't think you were here for the kids, she thought you were here for something else. But that all changed quickly as she watched you with her girls, and believe me... she watched *everything*, even when you didn't think she was, *she was*.... she actually liked you a lot."

"I liked her a lot myself, and I tried to do whatever I could to help her. I felt bad for her, and I couldn't even imagine going through what she went through. She went through something that I know, even I couldn't handle. She was a strong woman, much stronger than I ever would have been." She looked at her drink Ethan slid over to her and took a sip.

"Wow!" she said surprised.

"Too strong?" He laughed.

"Yes... very strong... but I'll drink it, it actually tastes pretty good."

Antonio came back down by Sadie and Ethan, he looked at Sadie and was shocked to see her with a drink. He picked her glass up and tasted it. "You're actually having a cocktail?"

"Is there something wrong with that?" she asked with a smile.

"No. In over a year, I have never seen you with a drink... well I saw you drinking a beer in Florida, but that was it." Antonio said surprised, he looked at Ethan, and squinted an eyebrow. "How did you manage that?"

"I just asked if she would like a drink." he says, putting his hands up in the air, grinning.

"I'm only having one, and then I'm going to bed, I don't know what you two are going to do. And since my room is right over there, I'm going to ask that you two keep it down."

Ethan saluted Sadie "Aye, aye, captain."

Antonio laughed, shaking his head. *Here we go, just like old times.* He thought to himself, thinking about how Harlow got with them when they drank.

The two continued talking, and talking about old times. Sadie finished her drink, and snuck away, going into her room. She shut the door quietly, and laid on the bed. The drink hit her pretty good, which made her dizzy. She stared at the ceiling for a while until she closed her eyes, trying to stop the spinning in her head, and fell asleep. Antonio and Ethan ended up staying up late, talking, drinking and doing shots.

"Harlow told me that she wanted the best for you, and wanted me to make sure that you and the girls remained happy, I also mentioned that to Sadie when I took her out."

"So... what are you saying?" Antonio slurred, taking another drink.

"Just curious, are you happy?" Ethan asked, finishing his drink.

"I guess, being the situation that I'm in. I'll admit, I'm much happier now than what I was about two months ago."

"Well that's good." Ethan says looking down at his glass, spinning it around in circles. Ethan's phone made a sound, and took his phone out of his pocket, looking at it. "I better get going, my ride is out there waiting for me... I'll get my car in the morning."

Antonio saw him out, after Ethan left, he stood in the doorway, wondering what Ethan was getting at, and shrugged it off. He walked up to his room and stared at the bed, the thought of Sadie came to his mind, wishing that she was in his bed. He turned around and went down to her room.

He quietly opened the door and saw that she was halfway on the bed and halfway on the floor, and laughed, laughing harder when it hit him that she only had the one drink. He took his clothes off, and climbed into bed, sliding her up to him and laying her in his arms.

He rested his head against hers, laying there thinking about everything that Ethan had brought up. His head began to hurt from thinking so much, and kissed Sadie's forehead. He closed his eyes and fell asleep.

Antonio woke up the next morning, and was liking that Sadie was still in his arms, he squeezed her tighter, wanting her as close to him as possible. She awoke, and looked at him confused, not remembering him coming to her bed, worried they had sex, and she didn't remember.

She lifted the sheets up, and looked under them, giggling. "I wasn't drunk last night, was I?" she asked quietly, when she saw Antonio was awake.

"Not that I know of, you only had the one drink, unless you had more when I was saying goodnight to the girls."

"No, I didn't, but how do you explain that I have clothes on, and you're naked?" she giggled. "I don't even remember going to bed."

"When I came in here, you were halfway on the bed and halfway on the floor. I just took my clothes off, and climbed into bed pulling you in my arms, I wasn't about to take your clothes off." he chuckled.

"Can I ask you something?" Sadie asked, while she yawned.

"Sure, I might have an answer for you."

"Was it just me, or was I imagining things about Ethan?" she asked. "He was acting weird, saying some things about Harlow, and was telling me things that she apparently told him."

"No, I noticed it myself. He was asking me things, and had talked to me about Harlow wanting me to be happy and wanting the same with the girls."

She rolled onto her side, propping her head up with her hand to look at him. "He told me that too, he's been really strange lately. At first, I thought it was because I wouldn't go out on another date with him, but now I feel that it's much more than that." Sadie says, scratching her head.

"I'll have to give him a call, or stop by the office, and find out what the hell he's up to."

Chapter 21- The date

It has been three weeks since Ethan was over, and witnessed the kiss shared between Antonio and Sadie. Antonio called Ethan trying to get information out of him, asking what has been on his mind and what he was up to with Sadie and himself, but Ethan wouldn't enlighten him on anything.

Sadie was teaching the girls how to play the piano when her phone rang. It was Ethan asking if he could take her out to lunch, and wanting to have a talk with her about some things. She was a little hesitant about going, knowing Antonio would probably get upset about it, but she was also curious about what he had to say, and agreed to meet with him.

Antonio was to be in court all day, and Sadie had no way of getting a hold of him to let him know that she was taking the girls out to lunch with Ethan. Since she had the girls, they decided to meet at Chuck E Cheese, that way the girls could run around, and play games while they were talking.

As Sadie and the girls walked into the pizza place, she saw Ethan waving for them, letting them know he was already there, and walked over to him.

"Thanks for meeting me." Ethan says, as he sat back down, he pulled out some money, handing it to Sadie. "Go get the girls tokens to play whatever they want, my treat."

"Wow, thank you." Sadie brought the girls over to the token machine, placing the twenty-dollar bill in the slot, and out came all their tokens. She picked them up and handed them some tokens. "Here, if you need more, I'll be over there, talking with Uncle Ethan." she says, pointing at Ethan.

"OK." the girls said happily. The girls excitedly ran away, going over to the play gym, while Sadie sat back down with Ethan.

"Has Antonio ever decided what he was going to do with Harlow's belongings?" Ethan asked curiously.

"I'm not sure...why?" she asked, while keeping her eyes on the girls.

"I'm just curious, she told me that she had some things hidden for the girls, and put aside something for Antonio. She never said what they were, or where she put them. Before he gets rid of any of her things, double check everything."

"OK, I will let him know... I do have to ask, why haven't you said anything to Antonio about it?" she asked, looking at him curiously.

"To be honest, I thought he would have gotten rid of all her things by now, and that he would have seen what Harlow left for him and the girls."

She tilted her head. "Why do you think that?"

Ethan grabbed her hand holding it tight, and looked into her in the eyes, like he had something important to say, her stomach dropped and she started getting nervous. She tried pulling her hand back, but he held on tighter. She turned her head to look for the girls, and didn't see them.

"Ethan let me go, I don't see the girls." she demanded, standing up. She frantically looked around for the girls, freaking out that she couldn't see them. Her heart was pounding, and ran over to Ethan, yelling. "I need help finding them!"

He stood up, and helped look for them. Sadie was standing near a jungle gym slide with tears in her eyes, and heard pounding noises above her, she looked up and saw the girls inside a clear tunnel with smiles, waving at her. She let out a sigh of relief, waving for them to come down.

The girls came down, and ran over to Sadie "You two scared me to death!" Sadie scolded.

"We have been up there." Isabella said, pointing up to the tunnel, that was also a maze.

"I'm sorry, I should have looked up there."

"Are you two ready to leave? I know I am…" Sadie wanted to leave, and to get away from Ethan, she didn't know what he was up to when he grabbed her hand, and wouldn't let go.

She walked over to Ethan with the girls. "I found them; I think we're going to head home."

"I haven't finished talking with you, I wanted to tell you about Harlow, and what she wanted you to know."

"Maybe another time, or maybe you can talk to Antonio about it, I really need to get them home." Sadie insisted, running her fingers through her hair.

He gave her a hug, and looked at her. "Harlow meant well, maybe you'll find what she wanted everyone to see."

"Thanks for lunch, and buying the girls their tokens to play games."

Sadie left Chuck E Cheese feeling uneasy, she thought about what Ethan had told her about Harlow, hiding things for the girls and for Antonio.

She pulled into the driveway and saw that Antonio was home, when they walked into the house, he had a big smile on his face.

"What's with the smile?" Sadie asked, looking at him strangely, since it was a different type of smile.

He walked towards her, wrapping his arms around her, picking her up and spinning her around. "I won a huge case this morning, so I would like for you to get dressed up tonight, to celebrate." he says, kissing her lips.

They both heard giggling, and Antonio slid her down to the ground, both looking at the girls, as they stood there watching them.

"Who's going to watch them?"

"I called Ethan earlier, he said that he would watch them." The girls heard Ethan's name and took off running towards their play room.

"Oh... I'd rather not have him over here." she says, watching where the girls went.

Antonio looked at her confused "Why not?"

Sadie walked away from him "We saw him today..."

"Where?"

"We met at Chuck E Cheese so the girls could play, and he had something that he wanted to talk to me about, but he got kind of weird on me, and made me feel uncomfortable."

Antonio looked at her not too pleased, placing his hands on his hips. "I would have called to let you know that we were meeting him, but you were in court. He called me saying that he had something to talk to me about-..." Sadie began to say

"Did he hit on you?" he asked, cutting her off.

"Not exactly, he grabbed my hand, and wouldn't let go when he was about to tell me something. I pulled away from him when I didn't see the girls, and after I found the girls, I told him that I had to leave."

"Maybe it was nothing, and you took it the wrong way." he says, hoping that he's right.

"Maybe I overreacted, I don't know." she sighed "I guess, at least you know that he can be trusted with them."

"Where are you taking me anyway?"

"A very nice restaurant." he says, smiling "Our ride will be here in about an hour."

"Ok, I'll hurry and get ready."

Sadie left feeling excited on the inside, this would be their first official date since they met. While she was getting ready, she began thinking of all the nice fancy restaurants in the area, and wondered which place he was taking her.

She dug through her closet, and put on a long sleek sexy red dress showing off part of her hip, with a long-slit opening showing off her one leg. She sleeked her hair back into a low ponytail, and finished her look off with red lipstick. She grabbed her stilettos and walked up the stairs.

Antonio was standing in the living room talking with Ethan when she walked up the stairs. Antonio immediately stopped talking the moment he saw her.

"Damn..." Ethan whispered.

Antonio walked over to her, and his heart fluttered the entire time while eyeing her. "Wow, you look amazingly stunning."

"Are you sure it's not my turn to take her out? You can stay with the girls and I'll take her out tonight." Ethan joked with Antonio, trying to rile him up.

Antonio turned around, and gave him an evil look. "Ethan, we talked about this earlier." he snapped, then turned around to look at Sadie again.

"Are you ready to go?"

Sadie nodded her head, and Antonio looked back at Ethan. "Don't keep the girls up too late."

Ethan saluted him "Have a fun time." he says smirking.

Antonio opened the back door of the limo, and helped Sadie inside. He had champagne on ice waiting for them, and instructed the driver to play some soft romantic music. Sadie felt like she just won the lottery, and was grinning ear to ear all the way to the restaurant.

He opened the champagne, and poured them each a glass. Before handing her, her glass, he curled his finger under her chin, and passionately kissed her. She felt her stomach drop, and could feel her inner core started to throb. He pulled away, and handed her the glass of champagne.

"This is really good." she said, as she tasted the champagne. He leaned over and kissed her again. "You're the one that tastes good." he says pulling away, while looking in her eyes with a smile.

She smiled back at him blushing, feeling that she was melting. When they pulled up to the restaurant, he opened the door, and grabbed her hand to help her out. He placed his hand on the small of her back, and walked her in.

The hostess smiled at Antonio. "Nice to see you again Mr. Russo, it's been a while." she says, looking over at Sadie. "Likewise." he responded back to the hostess.

Sadie looked around the building, and was loving the ambiance, it was dark, with candles lit up on the center of all the tables, and a beautiful softly lit chandelier in the center of the restaurant.

The hostess walked them over to their table, and handed them their menus. "Can we get two waters, and a bottle of my favorite red wine, please?" he asked.

"Wow, they know you here?"

"Yes, I used to come here quite often, one of my favorite places to eat at."

"No wonder she looked at me funny."

"Don't worry, they all know about Harlow." he says quietly, resting his hand on top of hers, and using his thumb to rub the top of her hand.

They ordered their food, talked about his win in court, and how he was up for the attorney of the year award.

They came with their food, and Sadie's mouth started watering when she smelled and looked at her plate. She ordered the roasted duck, and he ordered the escargot cooked in butter and garlic. He laughed when he saw her turning her nose up to his plate.

"So, I have to ask how you got Ethan to watch the girls so that you could bring me out?" she asked, wiping her mouth with the napkin.

"I told him that you deserved a special night out after everything that you have done for me, I also told him that if he didn't, I was going to beat his ass." he chuckled.

"I have to tell you something that he said to me, something that Harlow told him. Apparently, she has stuff hidden in the house for the girls, and that there is also something for you. He wants you to make sure you go through all of her things thoroughly, before getting rid of them if you were to."

"I wonder why he never said anything to me about it."

"I don't know, I asked him the same thing."

"He's been strange lately, he normally doesn't act the way he has been, and I can't figure out what it is, but he definitely has been a complete different person..." Antonio says, taking a bite of his food.

They finished their meal and Antonio grabbed her hand, kissing it "I want you to know that you have my heart right now, I feel lucky that you came into our lives, and I still believe that it was fate that brought me to you, do you believe in fate?"

"I do." she smiled. He leaned over the table placing a kiss on her lips. He sat back down, and Sadie looked around wondering if people were watching them.

"I'm ready to leave, how about you?" he asked, squeezing her hand.

"I'm ready, thank you very much for the dinner, it was nice and the food was good."

Antonio paid for the meal, and on their way out he pulled her to the dance floor, that was located at the corner of the building, he wrapped his arms around her waist and pulled her close against him. She felt the butterflies starting to flutter, and wrapped her arms around his neck, while rested her head on his chest, and shared a romantic dance.

When the song was done, they headed out to the limo, and the driver asked where he was to go to next. Antonio was willing to go wherever she wanted, and looked at Sadie, waiting for her answer. "Where would you like to go next?" She looked at the time, and shrugged her shoulders, she wanted to stay out a little longer with him, but he had her feeling excited below and wanted to go home and act on it. "Let's go home." she winked.

"Are you sure? It's my treat to take you anywhere that you would like."

"I just want to go home." she says, as she sat on his lap wrapping her arms around him. She began placing soft kisses along his neck, sucking on the soft spot behind his ear and started nibbling on his earlobe.
"You heard her Jake, bring us home." he blurted out quickly.

Chapter 22- Confession

On the way home Antonio couldn't keep his hands off Sadie, he laid her on the seat kissing her hard and very demanding. He slid his hand up under her dress, and suddenly stopped kissing her, and looked at her. Looking at her full of lust, and with a devilish grin when he realized that she wasn't wearing any panties.

An excited groan escaped his mouth, and crashed his lips back onto hers, while sliding two fingers between her essence, and thrusted inside her. She let out a thrilling moan, and arched her back while digging her nails into his back, loving the feeling that he was doing to her below. She was very wet and excited, and wanting him to place his cock inside her that very moment.

What he was doing to her, had her head spinning, almost as if she was about to pass out from the amazing orgasms, he was giving her. She covered her mouth and tried to muffle her moans, embarrassed that the driver would hear her.

She was just about to cum again, until they heard the driver announce that they were home. He pulled his fingers out of her, and tasted her sweetness. "Hope Ethan leaves right away, I want to finish this." he grinned, grabbing the extra bottle of champagne while they exited the limo.

They slowly walked towards the house, hand in hand. He wrapped an arm around her shoulder, and began kissing her neck while they walked, that sent goosebumps up her spine "God, you smell amazing." he groaned, quietly.

Ethan was sitting on the couch watching TV, when they walked in the door. "Wow, you two kids are home early, I wasn't expecting you both until later." he says surprised.

"We decided to make it an early night, I hope the kids were good for you." Antonio says, pacing back and forth, hoping for Ethan to get the hint and leave.

"They were good, no issues at all." He looked at Antonio, and could see that he had something on his mind, and wasn't sure if it was a good thing or a bad thing. He could tell something was up and thought about asking, but then had a feeling of what it was, and stood up stretching. "Well hopefully your dinner was good... I'm going to get going I do have to get up early."

Antonio smiled on the inside, happy that Ethan was leaving and hurriedly walked him to the door, shaking his hand and thanking him for watching the girls, practically pushing Ethan out the door as he took a step out.

Sadie stood at the counter drinking a glass of champagne, while he was with Ethan, she poured a glass for Antonio and set it on the counter. He was excited Ethan left, and walked over to Sadie, and nibbled on the back of her neck, making her giggle.

"I wasn't sure if he was going to leave, by the way he acted I think that he got the hint." he whispered in her ear, and kissing her cheek. She smiled as his warm breath tickled her ear, making her nipples hard. She turned around and stared into his eyes, the blueness of his eyes was causing her to melt and her heart began to race. "Kiss me." she demanded.

He cupped her face, and pressed his lips onto hers, with his tongue dominating hers in a heated kiss that had them both on fire.

"Wait." she says, pulling away from him. "Not here, in case the girls wake up."

She grabbed his hand taking him down the stairs. As they got to the bottom step, he pressed her up against the wall and devoured her mouth, while his hands uncontrollably felt her body.

He helped pull her dress up over body, and dropped it to the floor. He felt himself getting hot and revved up for her and began kissing her up and down her body, and as he reached her pussy, he gave it a couple licks before picking her up and carrying her to her room, laying her on the bed. She sat up, started pulling his belt off in a hurry, and pulled his pants down like a raging wild woman.

He quickly took his shirt off, and got a shock of his life when she grabbed his cock and placed it in her mouth. A loud gasp was heard coming out of his mouth, not expecting for her to do that, and surprised him.

He looked down at her while she was bobbing her head up and down, and taking him all the way in. His hands grabbed a hold of her hair as he felt her tongue circling the sensitive tip of his love machine, making him groan uncontrollably, while feeling all kinds of amazing sensations running through his body.

He was about to let release, and had her stop. She fell backwards onto the bed pulling him with her, crashing their lips together. He started trailing kisses down her body, and when he got down to her pussy, she stopped him by pulling him up to her, whispering. "Make love to me."

He looked at her with love in his eyes, and thrusted in her slowly as he spread open her legs, and raising her arms above her head while holding onto them, thrusting harder and deeper.

"Antonio!" she screamed out, as he kept hitting every possible spot, making her squirm, and wanting more. Her legs instantly wrapped around his waist, and wanted to feel every inch of him inside her. Her moans increased when she started feeling all warm inside, and began cumming all over his throbbing cock.

While thrusting deeply inside her he stopped, and leaned down to kiss her, kissing her passionately before pumping a couple more times, and releasing himself inside her. He fell on her, and rested his forehead against hers, pecking at her lips. "You're going to be the death of me."

"Why do you say that?" she asked whispering.

"Because... I just want to keep making love to you, and I don't want to stop. You just make me feel like a whole different person."

She cupped his face and kissing him hungrily, while rolling him over and laying on top of him. She lifted her head up to look at him, and her hair fell onto his face. Using his hands, he slid her hair behind her, and held onto it.

She leaned down, and started rubbing her nose against his, then sat up straddling him and pulled him up to her, having him sit face to face with her. "I want you to know that you have my heart as well." she says, smiling at him. "Ready for another round?" she giggled, as she leaned forward kissing him hard, muffling his response.

His cock instantly got hard for her, all it took was for her to kiss him, she placed him inside her and rode him like a wild animal. His hands roamed her body, while she was moving her hips around and started to bounce on him, he placed his hands on her waist, helping to guide her. Her movements kept changing from slowly moving up and down, to hard and fast. She stopped moving once she felt that he was all the way in her, and kissed him.

He wanted to take control again, and flipped her on her back, he lifted her legs onto his shoulders, and thrusted in her slow and hard, hitting her g spot and causing her to scream with excitement. With her legs resting on his shoulders, he was able to go in as deeply as he could, causing her to squirm.

"Fuck me." she moaned, shocking him. His thrusts became harder and faster, and she continued begging him to fuck her, and thrusted until they came together.

He was out of breath, and flopped down on his back, trying to breathe again. He laid there, not saying a word, he was thinking and debating with himself at the same time. Sadie felt like she did something wrong and rolled to her side to look at him, taking her finger, and lightly caressing his chest. "Is something wrong?" she asked, feeling hurt.

He looked at her, and pulled her on top of him, making her squeal and giggle. His arms tightly wrapped around her, held her tight and pressed his head harder against the pillow to look at her better. "I don't know if I should say this or not, or if it's even the right thing to say right now... but I think I have fallen hard for you... meaning that I think that I've fallen in love with you."

******

A couple weeks had gone by since Antonio took Sadie on their first date, and confessed his feelings for her. The girls were helping Sadie dig through Harlow's clothes, looking for what Ethan said Harlow left behind for them, while putting them into storage totes. Instead of getting rid of her belongings, Antonio just wanted to put them up in the attic, incase the girls wanted them later in life, for remembrance of her.

Sadie wasn't finding anything out of the ordinary, that had the girls or Antonio's name on anything. She hid nothing in the clothes and dug through all the drawers.

They started digging in the closet a little more, and Sadie noticed a box that was partially covered with a blanket, at the corner of her eye. She pulled it down, and opened it up. There were envelopes for each of the girls to open each year on their birthday, until they turned eighteen. There were also a couple more envelopes for each of the girls, for when they get married, as well as videos for the girls with instructions on when they could watch them.

Antonio came home from work, and saw Sadie sitting at the table with a box in front of her. He tilted his head and gave her a strange look when he saw the box, along with its contents sitting on the table.

"What is all that?" He asked curiously.

"I found some stuff that Harlow left behind. Ethan told me that she hid stuff for you and the girls, I found those. But I still haven't found what she left for you." she says, looking at everything in front of her.

He walked over to her, and looked at everything Sadie had spread out on the table, making his heart drop with seeing all the envelopes with the girls names on them.

"Wow, I had no clue she was doing this." he says quietly, and shocked.

"This is what she was doing when she was lying in bed, I knew I saw a pen in her hand."

Antonio picked up his phone and called Ethan, asking for him to come over.

"Ethan knows more than what he has told us, and this explains all the weird behavior with him." says Antonio.

"Maybe... but he did know about this, she must have confided to him about everything." Sadie says, standing up, and looking down at the envelopes, amazed. "What she did here... is beautiful, and smart. She made sure those girls will never forget her."

"I'm amazed at this." he says, shaking his head while taking a deep breath, and cupping the back of his head. "WOW, I'm going to have to put these in a safe, that way they don't get wrecked."

It didn't take long for Ethan to get there, and walked right into the house, like old times. He saw Antonio and Sadie at the table and walked over to them. He saw what was on the table, and smiled "Oh, you finally found what Harlow left."

"What all do you know?" Antonio asked, demanding he tell him everything he knows.

"Have you found everything?" Ethan asked, grinning while looking at Sadie.

"This is all I found, but you said she left something for Antonio, I haven't found that yet."

"Well, you have to find that, she explains a lot in that."

"In what?" Antonio asked, frustrated.

"I promised her that I wouldn't say anything until you found it all, but you're taking forever to find it, so I'll give you some clues... she left a daily journal, starting from the day she found out she had cancer, she also wrote a letter to both you and her."

"Ethan please, tell us what you know." Sadie begged.

Ethan groaned, not wanting to spill the beans. "Put it this way..." he started to say, and paused when he notices the two of them staring at him with big eyes. "Ah hell... Antonio, she wanted you to court Sadie. And Sadie, she wanted you to be the girls mom... there... I said it."

Antonio began rubbing his temples, not believing what he was hearing. Sadie's eyes filled up with tears, she didn't think that Harlow would have wanted them together.

"You need to find that journal, it explains it all in there... that's the best I can tell you." Ethan urged, pissed at himself for telling them more than what he was supposed to do.

"So, what was all this with Sadie? You taking her out, kissing her, all that bullshit?"

Ethan laughed "Don't you get it? Harlow asked me to take her out, wanting you to get jealous, and to make you realize that you have feelings for Sadie. She asked me to kiss Sadie, and to figure out a way to do it in front of you. I had strict instructions from her, how, what, and when to do it. Even if it meant getting my ass kicked by you."

"So, it was planned…" Antonio grinned, while still looking confused. "Just for that, I should still kick your ass."

"Why do you think when you finally went out on that first date, I was shocked that you came home so early, I thought it didn't go so well. I then started thinking of the next plan to get you two together."

"Well, I'm going to have to make a special visit to Harlow. I can't believe she did all of this. Was this her idea, or yours? Did you help her come up with this whole charade?" Antonio says with his hands on his hips.

"This was all her, I was shocked when she called and talked with me about it. She then sent me a letter with all of the instructions… if you aren't believing anything that I'm telling you, I can show you what she sent me if you'd like." Ethan said with his hands up in the air, trying to prove to them that this was all Harlow's idea.

"Here I thought you went off your rocker, and just turned plain weird on me." Antonio laughed. "I'm not used to this serious side of you, I need for the real Ethan to come back." he says, turning to look at Sadie. "I need Sadie to see who you really are."

Chapter 23- Finding the journal

"I'm sorry if you thought I was acting strange, I was only doing what I was asked to do, and then started to get frustrated that you two hadn't hooked up yet." Ethan says, resting his hand on the dining room chair.

Sadie began to giggle a little while looking at Antonio, she then looked over at Ethan, smiling at him nervously. "Well, we kind of have been together for a little while now, I told Antonio that I wanted to take things slow." Sadie spoke, scratching the back of her head.

Ethan's eyes got wide and grinned, waving his finger back and forth from Sadie to Antonio. "You two have? Since when?" He was surprised to hear that, and placed his hand on his heart, looking up at the ceiling. "What a relief."

Antonio and Sadie looked at each other amazed, both worried that he would have been upset about the two of them hooking up, Antonio smiled while looking over at Ethan "If you're that curious to know, we hooked up the night you brought Sadie out on a date. That night it sort of just happened, and I dipped the stinger into the honey hole."

Ethan chuckled "So the date with Sadie worked then..." he grinned, loving that they hooked up. "Harlow really was a smart woman, she saw things between you two, and when she realized that she was going to be leaving everyone, she watched everything, even when you didn't realize that she was. As much as she hated it, she came to terms with everything. She loved how Sadie was with the girls and how the girls loved Sadie, she didn't want someone else raising them, and had a lot of trust in Sadie." he looked over at Sadie, pinching his bottom lip as he thought for a minute "She also saw how Antonio would look at you, she felt that you would be the right choice for him once she was gone."

Sadie felt numb and sat back down, Antonio was in shock and couldn't say a word. He stood there covering his mouth thinking about what Ethan just told them, and then thought back to when Harlow was alive, wondering if she was giving him any clues that he never picked up on.

"My advice to you, is to find her journal. You'll get every answer that you want to know inside that. Everything that she wrote, she wrote from her heart. She also wrote it for you, Antonio. Just please don't feel guilty if you two are together, it's what she wanted."

"Is there anything else that we should know about?" Antonio asked, still in shock.

"I told you more than I already should have, I'm going to get going before I say anything more that I shouldn't be." he says walking to Antonio, placing his hand on Antonio's shoulder. "Call me if you need anything, or even if you just want to talk. I miss the old days."

He smiled at Sadie. "You're a good woman, keep doing what you're doing."

He turned back to Antonio, and smirked. "Antonio, your wife loved you very much, and this is what she wants. I give her a lot of credit for doing all of this for you, your kids and Sadie. Truly shows what kind of person she really was."

Ethan left feeling that he completed Harlow's wishes, hoping that the two of them will fulfill her wishes. Antonio and Sadie both sat down looking at each other, not knowing what to say to each other.

"I have to say, I feel a little better knowing that I have Harlow's approval to move on, I guess I do need to see it myself with my own eyes to feel even better." Antonio says quietly, tapping his fingers on the table.

Sadie stood up and walked over to Antonio, sitting on his lap and giving him a warm hug. She rested her head on his, whispering "I told you that she was up to something, I knew it. Now we know why, and what it was about."

She touched the side of his face, gently moving it to face hers and looked deeply into his eyes. "She seriously did a wonderful thing here for the girls, it was a very selfless act. I give her a lot of credit, with all the pain that she was in, and still did all of this." she says, kissing his lips softly "I'm going to go check on the girls."

Antonio sat at the table thinking while Sadie checked on the girls, she walked in their play room and the girls asked if they can play the piano.

"You girls should show your dad that you can play some songs." she said smiling.

Isabella ran out of the room and over to Antonio. "Daddy, come with me." she says pulling his hand. She brought him over to the piano and sat down.

"What are you up to?" he asked running his hand through her hair "Watch me." she grinned, excited to show him that she could play.

She started playing Amazing Grace, Gabriella ran into the room and stood next to Antonio, holding his hand. Antonio was shocked and looked over at Sadie. "Did you teach her how to play?"

"I did, I taught both of them."

He stood there watching as Gabriella anxiously waited to play. When Isabella was finished, Gabriella excitedly sat down "Now it's my turn."

She played You Are My Sunshine to him, Antonio wrapped his arm around Sadie kissing the top of her head "I've been working with them every day, they actually know quite a bit of songs."

"Can we play one more?" Gabriella asked her dad.

"Sure, one more then we will have to get some dinner."

The girls whispered to each other and decided to play a duet. They played Let It Be, Antonio was so amazed and had no idea that Sadie had been teaching them.

Sadie whispered in his ear "You still never showed me your skills on the piano."

"I will..." he whispered back.

The girls were done playing and turned around to look at Antonio.

"Did we do good?" Isabella asked happily.

"Of course you did." He leaned down, kissing their cheeks. "Keep up the good work." he smiled and gave them both hugs.

Later that night after the girls were in bed, Antonio and Sadie were searching his bedroom for Harlow's journal. "You would think it would be in here, she spent most of her time in here." Antonio says frustrated.

"It makes no sense, we checked everywhere in here earlier, I don't know where else to look, besides the rest of the house."

"I don't understand why she would make it so difficult to find, if she wanted us to read it?" Antonio says sighing, with a hint of disappointment.

"I'm sure we will find it eventually, it's obviously here."

Antonio sat down on the bed wondering where Harlow would have put the journal. Frustrated, he rested his head in his hands and groaned. Sadie sat down on the bed behind him, and started massaging his shoulders, trying to get him to relax.

"That feels good." He moaned.

He leaned his head back against her chest, she reached her arm around his face and softly traced his lips with her thumb. He quickly turned around and pinned her down on the bed, resting his forehead against hers "Think back to when you came in here, you said she was always trying to hide something, do you remember what it looked like?"

"There was one time, I thought I had seen a black book that I saw her shove under a pillow, but that was a book." she says, thinking back.

He kissed her lips hard and smiled. "What's that for?" she asked, as he sat up.

"I saw a black covered book earlier." He got off the bed and walked over to the dresser, opening her bottom drawer and pulled out a black covered book, opening it. "Bingo." he says, looking over at Sadie "It's been here the whole time. She hid it with another book cover." He says, setting the book on the bed, kneeling on the ground as he scanned through it. As he got towards the end of the book, two letters fell out.
He picked them up, and looked at them. One was addressed to Sadie, and the other to Antonio. "Should we read the journal first, or would you like to read the letters now?" he asked.

"Let's read the letters first, after talking with Ethan, I'm really curious as to what she had to say."

"Read yours first then." he says.

"Are you sure?" She figured he would have wanted to read his first, after all it was his wife who passed.

"I'm sure."

She started opening the letter while Antonio sat next to her, wrapping his arm around her as she read the letter out loud:

Dear Sadie,
I want to apologize to you, for me being a bitch to you from the beginning. I was afraid that you were there to steal my family away from me. I finally realized that was not the case. I watched you with the girls, and with Antonio. You're a strong, caring, loving woman and I liked that about you. I knew you had gotten on Antonio's case about his drinking and I admire you

for that. Thank you for that. Hopefully he's not drinking like that now, and I hope you have knocked some sense into that man. You have shown me how loving and caring you really are. I'm glad my girls fell in love with you, they talked to me every day about you, makes me feel good that they trust you. Those girls are special and they deserve someone special in their lives. To me that person is you, in my heart, I believe and I know that you will be a good mother to them, and I ask that you think about being their new mom. I really don't know who's reading their letter first, but I do ask that you give those girls a brother or a sister. I tried hard for years and couldn't, if you were to ask the girls what they wanted, they would say a brother. Haha... I just want you to know that I believe you and Antonio belong together. I saw how he looked at you at times, did it bother me? Of course it did, but I knew that I was going to be gone. I want him to be happy, he deserves to be happy and to not be alone, I honestly believe that you will be the right one for him and my girls. He's a good man, with a huge heart. What I'm asking is, will you please find it in your heart to be that girl for him? You definitely have my blessing.
Love, Harlow xoxoxo

Sadie finished reading the letter, holding back the tears in her eyes "Can you get me a tissue please?"

"Sure."

Antonio left the room and grabbed a tissue out of the bathroom. He walked back in with a tissue, Sadie was sitting on the bed, still staring at the letter. "Wow, I never expected this out of her. She really did mean well."

He took the letter and read it again, placing his hand on her thigh.

"Speaking of giving the girls a sibling, I guess I was used to not wearing a condom, and we have had sex *quite* a few times. I never really thought about using one, and it never even crossed my mind until now."

"Well...I have been on the pill." she said quietly.

He scratched his head, looking at her confused "You have?"

"I have been on them since I was a kid, to regulate my monthly cycle."

"Oh... I see." he says looking down, and away from her, thinking.

She noticed how his demeanor changed, and the look he gave her before turning away from her. "If you're thinking it's because I sleep around, you're wrong. I'm not like that at all, so get that out of your mind." she snapped a little when she saw his reaction.

His heart dropped when Sadie snapped at him, that was the last thing he wanted her to think, was that he thought that way about her. From the first day that she started working for him, she went out one time. He knew she wasn't like that all. He looked at her, and held onto her chin so she would look at him. "I wasn't thinking that at all, what I was thinking was, if you had become pregnant, I wouldn't have been upset about it, that's all." Leaning forward, he gave her a soft kiss "I also wouldn't be upset if you decided to go off the pill." he winked.

"Oh.... OK, well..." she said embarrassed "Maybe you should read your letter now." she says, handing him his letter.

He took the letter from Sadie, and his heart started beating faster as he held the letter in his hand, staring down at it.

"I don't know if I can read it." he says, wiping his forehead.

"I read mine, now it's your turn, you can do it."

Chapter 24- Harlow's love

"Antonio you can do it, you have to be strong for her, and just read what she had to say." Sadie says, caressing his back. She scooted closer to him and rested her head on his shoulder urging him to open the letter.

Taking a deep breath, he opened the letter, stuttering on the first few lines as he read it out loud:

Dear Antonio,
My dearest Antonio, how did we get here? This wasn't our plan, our plan was growing old together, watching the girls grow up to be beautiful women, watching them get married and to watch them have kids of their own. I hope that you're doing OK, and that you are taking good care of our girls. I may be gone, but that doesn't mean that I don't miss you, Gabriella and Isabella. I really do miss you and love you all still. God had a plan for me, it wasn't his plan for me to be on this earth, his plan was for me to watch over and to protect you and the girls. To be your angel, I may be gone physically but I'm still here in your hearts.
I want you to know that I don't blame you if you wanted to move on, I don't want you to be alone and I do not want you to be dwelling over the fact that I am no longer here, it isn't healthy. I really want you to be happy and I want the girls to be happy.
I have watched how Sadie is with the girls and she is perfect. She has helped raise them, just as I would have. I know I was hard on her in the beginning, but I had my reasons, and I fell in love with her (well not literally) but you know what I mean. She is a wonderful woman who I know will take good care of you and the girls, I have seen how you have looked at her and what man wouldn't? She's beautiful, young, and a lot like me really. I have seen

how big her heart is, she took on something many young women couldn't, or wouldn't have. Some would have only done it for the money. I saw that was not the case with her, she didn't care about the money and had shown how she cared about Izzy and Gabby. What I am getting at, is I really hope that you can fall in love again, and that doesn't mean that you forget about me either, but I really would like to see that you have a place in your heart for someone else to love, and that someone I am talking about is Sadie. I know in my heart that she would be the perfect mother and wife to my family. I would love it a lot.
I really don't want those girls raised by any other woman, other than her. I trust her with them and I trust her with you.
I ask that you give the girls what I couldn't, give them that brother they always wanted or another sister that they could fight with, haha. Like I said before, I know that Sadie is the one. Make her the mother of my children, please... You have my permission, and my blessings. I love you Antonio, don't ever forget me, I'll never forget you. You're free, free to love Sadie, love her as you have loved me.
I love you, make me proud.
Love, Harlow xoxoxo

Antonio folded the letter, and sat quietly for a moment. Surprised at what he just read, and for her to insist that he be with Sadie, to love her, to give her children, and to be their girls mom, had him amazed. He was flabbergasted, he really thought that she would be hurt if he moved on. She may be gone, but he knows that her spirit is around him always.

"It takes a strong woman to write something that beautiful. She had a really big heart, Antonio. Ethan was right... she meant well." she said quietly.

She looked at him and wiped away some tears that were strolling down his cheek.

"I do miss her a lot." he whispered "I'll have to read her journal another day, this was already too much."

"That's fine, it's not like she expected you to read everything all in one day, Ethan did say that she wrote in it every day, that's over a year's worth of what was on her mind. I'm sure she wrote it for you and the girls to read whenever you wanted to read something from her, what she was feeling or thinking. When you're thinking of her, just remember that it will always be here for you guys."

She continued holding her arm around him, her hand then began moving up and down his back in a loving way. She felt better after reading what Harlow had to say to them, and couldn't believe how she wanted her husband to move on, wondering what woman would ever say that to their husband. Her heart was bigger than she thought it was. Feeling free, she came up with an idea, for the two of them.

"Come on... follow me." she says, taking his hand while standing up. While they began walking out of the room, he set the letters on the dresser.

"Where are we going?"

"To relax, unwind, to take our minds off of things, and be free." She says, taking him outside and over to the pool.

"The pool?" he asked, looking up into the dark sky.

She started removing her clothes and placed them on the chair near the pool. "Yea... come on..." she said with excitement.

"You want to do this now?"

She giggled "Let's get our minds off of those letters... when was the last time you went skinny dipping?" she asked, jumping into the pool.

Antonio stood at the edge of the pool, watching Sadie swim laps around the pool, she swam up to him urging him to come in.

"Come on Antonio, it will take your mind off of everything." she says, then went under the water.

Antonio felt that Sadie was right, thinking about what Harlow wanted and asked him to do. He shook his head, smiling. He decided to take his clothes off and get in the pool. Sadie came up out of the water and her heart sank when she didn't see Antonio, thinking that he left her out there alone. She swam over to the edge of the pool, started climbing out, and was stopped by Antonio's strong arms as she felt them wrap around her waist.

She turned around cupping the back of his head, and kissed him hard on the lips. "I thought you left me out her alone." She says, pulling away from his lips and smiled.

"I wouldn't have done that to you. Besides, who wouldn't want to go skinny dipping with you?" he smiled, winking at her.

Her legs wrapped around him as he spun them around slowly in the water, kissing each other like it was their first kiss, full of emotions, full of love, hot and passionate.

She released her lips from his, and swam away from him, making him chase after her. He caught up to her grabbing her, and spinning her around in the water, water splashing into their eyes.

He took her to the wall of the pool, and started making love to her. The feeling of being free in the water sent incredible sensations throughout their bodies.

She leaned back into the water as he thrusted in her feeling every inch of him inside her, he held onto her waist and back, as her arms floated on top of the water, water splashing over her face each time he thrusted deeply inside her.

They both moaned and groaned while they came together, he pulled her up to kiss her, while he was releasing his warm juices inside her, hungrily and wildly kissing each other, as if it was their last day on earth.

They parted to catch their breaths and swam around for a while acting like two teenagers in love, while chasing each other and dunking each other under the water.

They were turning into prunes and figured that they were out there long enough and climbed out of the pool. Sadie walked over to the cabinet and grabbed a couple towels, handing one to Antonio before they walked into the house. Sadie started walking towards the stairs, to go down to her room to change, until Antonio stopped her.

"Why don't you come up to my room. Stay with me up there." he begged, pulling her to him, and kissing her forehead softly.

"I can't, it just doesn't feel right." she says quietly "At least not yet."

Antonio looked away, looking upstairs and feeling that he understood why. He didn't like sleeping in the room alone, and hated seeing the empty spot in the bed next to him. He looked back at her, picked her up and carrying her down to her room. "You're right, maybe another time, but that still doesn't stop me from sleeping down here with you." he smirked.

He laid her gently on the bed, and yanked his towel off him. He climbed over her and opened the towel that she had wrapped around herself. He moved his head down to her pussy and spread her legs, placing his face between them, and tickling her clit with his tongue that had her raising her hips up high. The moment his tongue hit her clit she grabbed a hold of his hair, pulling on it hard.

Licking her clit in circles, and softly up and down, then lightly sucking on her swollen button, had her squirming. The more he teased her clit with his tongue, her body shook rapidly, his tongue then thrusted inside her warm wetness, and tasted every inch of her insides that his tongue could reach, loving the taste of her warm apple pie.

She reached her arms behind her, and grabbed a hold of the pillows firmly, as her excitement grew, and electricity was running all throughout her body, sending jolts up her spine as she was reaching her peak. Her hips raised up, as she was about to cum. He placed his hands under her ass, and held her up to continue licking into her hole. He felt the warm juices sliding down his tongue and groaned, tasting her until she was finished releasing.

He lifted her one leg, and placed kisses along her inner thigh, and doing the same with the other leg before he moved up to her navel, slowly moving up and kissing every inch up her body, while gently massaging her breasts. As he moved his way up towards her breasts, he latched onto her nipple, licking and sucking on each one.

She lifted her head up to look at him, as he looked up at her, she ran her fingers through his hair gently pulling him up to her lips, and thrusted her tongue into his mouth, tasting herself.

Their kiss turned heated as he placed his cock at her opening and thrusted his cock deeply inside her, thrusting in and out slowly. She pulled away from his lips, and dropped her head back into the pillow, moaning. The deeper and harder he thrusted, sent strong tingles throughout her body.

He pushed her arms above her head, holding them with one hand as he thrusted harder and faster, her body squirmed and shook as she hit her arousal.

"Sadie..." he groaned, while she was moaning out his name.

They both continued moaning and groaning until they came together. He pumped his cock into her a few more times, while he released, making sure everything was out of his system. He laid on top of her for a while, just looking at her. He kissed her lips before sliding off her, and pulled her into his arms while he rolled to his back.

"Antonio?" she asked, as he caressed her arm, giving her goosebumps

"Yes?" he whispered.

"What if I were to tell you that I haven't taken my pills for a couple weeks?" she asked, whispering nervously "I've been out of them, and haven't been able to get to the pharmacy to pick them up."

He stopped caressing her arm and smiled, he rolled on top of her, and looked into her eyes, then lowered his lips to hers and kissing her with passion.

"I would say that is great news." he moaned into her mouth "I told you earlier that I wouldn't be upset if you stopped taking them."

She stopped kissing him, and looked at him with a serious look. "Well, I'm telling you that because it's true, and I didn't want to say it to you earlier, just to see what kind of reaction I would get out of you, I thought that you would have been upset."

"Upset? No... you just made my night even better." he grinned, rolling back onto his back, and rolling her on top of him. He held her hair behind her, wanting to see her face. "I'd be even happier if you would move into my room." he said, while smiling.

She laid her head into the crook of his neck, and laid there relaxing, and not saying a word.

"Please think about it, and reconsider it."

Chapter 25- Moving on

Antonio opened his eyes and looked over at Sadie, she was snuggled right up against him, and thought she looked extremely beautiful, and peaceful the way she was sleeping. While looking at her he thought of Harlow's letter, and what she expected out of him.

Resting his arm over her body, he leaned forward kissing her forehead. She smiled while her eyes were closed, and let out a happy moan. She puckered up her lips wanting him to kiss her, to which he wasn't going to deny and kissed them.

Upon opening her eyes, she saw Antonio's piercing blue eyes, sparkling back at her. "Morning." she says, with a morning crackle in her voice.

"Good morning." he says back, softly kissing her lips. She wrapped her arm around him and kissed him back, the kiss was so loving and passionate, that it got themselves revved up, and started rolling back and forth on the bed, kissing and moaning. Antonio stopped them from rolling around, and got on top of her, poking her with his erection. He thrusted his cock in her, and began making love to her. He quickly stopped when they heard Isabella outside the door.

"Momma!" Isabella yelled, knocking on the door, causing Antonio and Sadie to jump.

"Shit." Antonio groaned in disappointment, while moving off Sadie.

"What is it Hun?" she called out, as she sat up and covered herself up.

"Gabriella is in bed crying, and she won't stop."

"OK, I'll be right there, give me a minute."

Antonio looked over at Sadie, and sighed. "I can go check on her, you can just stay in bed." he slid out of bed, and realized that he had no clothes in the room while looking for them, and remembered they were outside. Sadie began to laugh when she watched him trying to figure out what to do.

"I have a couple robes hanging on the bathroom door." she giggled. "Put one of those on."

"You want me to put on one of your robes?" he asked. with widened eyes, and looking at her as if she were crazy.

"Well... what else are you going to do? Go upstairs naked? Or would you just like to wear that towel?" she asks, pointing over to the one laying on the ground.

Groaning, he walked over to the bathroom door and looked at his choices, a fluffy white robe or a silky hot pink robe. "You've got to be kidding me." he muttered under his breath, while he stood there staring at the robes.

He shook his head while grabbing the white one, putting that on. He walked out of the bathroom and Sadie busted out laughing "What's wrong with the pink one?" she asked while giggling.

"Very funny, at least I can hurry and make it up to my room, and throw some sweatpants on. This robe barely fits, and is just enough to cover my package if I held the robe together tightly." he says, trying to squeeze the bottom of the robe together, and peeking out the door, making sure Isabella wasn't still around.

He walked out, shutting the door while hearing Sadie laughing hysterically. She laid in bed thinking about her and Antonio, and what Harlow had written to them. As for Antonio asking for her to move into his room, she wouldn't mind it at all, but still felt weird about it. It was hard knowing that was the room he shared with Harlow. She would rather him move down in her room, or into another room. She knew she had to talk to him about it, and needed to let him know what her feelings were about the whole thing.

She put on her pink robe, threw her hair up into a bun, and walked upstairs. She got to the kitchen and could hear Gabriella still crying, wondering if she should go up there and help. She figured that she better wait and see if Antonio would ask for help.

Isabella walked over to Sadie, asking if she could have a bowl of cereal.

"Is Gabriella OK?" Sadie asked, feeling concerned.

"She misses mommy." she says, grabbing a step stool, and pushing it to the food pantry to look for cereal.

"Oh... I'm sure she does." Sadie grabbed a bowl and spoon, and placed it on the table, then grabbed the milk and set it on the table. Isabella found the cereal that she wanted and brought the box over to Sadie, wanting her to help pour it in her a bowl. Sadie spotted Antonio walking down the stairs with Gabriella in his arms, and her head resting on his shoulder. "Can you grab her a glass of water please?" Antonio asked Sadie.

"Is she OK?" Sadie whispered to him, handing him the glass of water.

He nodded his head and mouthed to her that she's fine. "I'll talk to you later about it; I have to get ready for work."

Sadie took Gabriella from Antonio, and sat with her on the couch.

"Would you like to do anything special today?"

Gabriella turned and faced her, wiping the tears away from her eyes. "Can we get a puppy?" she asked.

Sadie looked at her surprised "You're probably going to have to ask your dad that... that's up to him."

She jumped off her lap and Isabella shoved her bowl away from her. She hopped off her chair, and both ran up the stairs yelling.   "Daddy!"

He opened the door quickly thinking something was wrong, he was buttoning up his shirt when they ran up to him wrapping their arms around his legs.

"Can we get a puppy?" Gabriella asked.

"Oh... I don't know girls, that's a big responsibility."

"Please daddy!" Isabella begged.

Sadie walked up the stairs slowly, and over to the girls "Did you put them up to this?" Antonio questioned with a grin.

"No. Gabriella asked me if they could get a puppy, I told her that she had to ask you."

He looked down at the girls, unsure what to say. "I'm going to have to think about it, why don't you girls eat breakfast, and I'll talk with Sadie about it."

"OK." Gabriella sighed, sadly walking away from him.

Sadie followed the girls downstairs, and looked back at Antonio "I'll be right back."

Isabella grabbed her bowl, and started eating her cereal again while Sadie got Gabriella a bowl of cereal.

"Momma, you have to tell daddy that we can get a puppy." Gabriella says, as Sadie was walking up the stairs.

"Will see, I can't make any promises."

Sadie walked into the bathroom where Antonio was getting ready, trying to fix his tie. Sadie walked over to him, and helped him with his tie.

"What do you think about a puppy?" he asked her.

She shrugged her shoulders. "That's up to you, I don't think that they realize what kind of responsibility it is, but they are five years old and kids do like pets."

"Yeah... you're right, but you're the one that will have to deal with the puppy all day." he smirked.

She cupped his face and gave him a kiss. "If it makes the girls happy, it's fine with me, as long as you're OK with it."

"Good luck." he grinned and laughed. He pulled her to him, hugging and kissing her forehead. "Thank you."

"I better go check on them." she says, walking away.

"I'll be down in a minute."

Sadie walked up to the girls smiling, whispering to them. "You get to have a puppy." The girls got excited and screamed, and began running around the living room. They both ran over to Antonio hugging him when he came down the stairs.

******

While Antonio was at work, Sadie called numerous breeders that she had found online, as well as the humane society. She then took the girls out to see what was available. They first stopped at the store to get pet supplies, toys and food. On their last stop after looking at many puppies, the girls fell in love with a Maltipoo.

"Can we have two puppies?" Isabella asked as both girls were holding a puppy.

"No, you can have one, so you two pick together on which one you want." Sadie instructed.

They finally decided on a female puppy, and Gabriella wouldn't let her go. Sadie paid them the money, and was able to take the puppy home right away.

Once they got home, the girls immediately brought the puppy to their room and played with her, trying to figure out a name.

Sadie walked into the room with her phone and sat down next to them "Do you girls want to hold her and I'll take a picture to send to your daddy?"

"Yes!" They both said with excitement.

Sadie took a picture and sent it to Antonio's phone. At the time, Antonio was looking over his client's files when his phone made a noise. He picked his phone up from the desk and clicked on the message, smiling when he saw the picture.

Meet the newest family member, I (she) has no name yet. See you when you get home. -Sadie

******

The girls ran up to Antonio excitedly with the puppy, as he walked into the house. They were so proud and happy, that they wanted to show him right away.

"She doesn't have a name yet; can we name her after mommy?" Gabriella asked.

"Oh, I don't know about that, how about a different name?"

"Bella?" Gabriella asked.

"That sounds better." he tells her, taking the puppy from her to look at her. "How many did you go look at?" he asked Sadie, looking at the puppy.

"Eight of them, we drove all over the place, I was beginning to think that we weren't coming home with one. She was the last one that we looked at, from what I was told, they're supposed to be really good with kids, and are very loving."

"I'm sure she will be fine, but that dog is in trouble now with them girls." he laughed.

Later that night the girls had let the dog outside before they went to bed, while they were outside with the puppy, Antonio put the kennel in their room so the dog could sleep in their room, he then put the girls to bed, and the puppy into the kennel. "Now don't let her out, she's not potty trained yet, and we don't need any accidents in the house… OK?"

"OK." they said.

Antonio found Sadie cleaning up the dog toys that were spread all over the house. He walked behind her, and wrapped his arms around her tightly, while kissing the back of her neck, then whispered in her ear. "So, have you made your decision about moving in the room with me?"

"I thought about it, but I'm not sure if I feel comfortable with it."

"Why's that?" he asked, turning her around "I don't get it."

"Because, you shared that room with Harlow. It just seems weird and not right to me. I'd feel better if you would stay with me downstairs, I don't know."

"Well if you want to, and if it would make you feel any better, we can buy all new furniture and you could do the room differently, the way you would want it. I'd hate to switch rooms; the master bedroom has a fireplace, and a walkout to the deck."

She sighed, thinking. "I know, I guess we could always do that, and change it up a bit. Hopefully it would get a different feel. But as for tonight, I'm still sleeping downstairs."

"Sleep up there with me tonight... please? No sex... just cuddling, the girls have that puppy now, and I'm sure we're going to have to listen for it." he picked her up before she could even answer him, and carried her bridal style up the stairs.

"Just one night, give it a try... for me please." he says, setting her down on the bed.

"Since you said please and because of the dog, I will."

"I still have your robe in here." he says grinning, holding up her robe.

She laughed, grabbing it from him.

She stripped down to just her undergarments, and climbed into the bed, still feeling iffy about it. She was only doing it for him, wanting to make him happy. He climbed into the bed, pulling her on top of him.

"No sex I thought."

"Who said anything about sex? I wanted a kiss, that's all." He tucked her hair behind her ear for a kiss. Repeating what they were doing this morning, until they were interrupted.

Sadie snuggled up to him, and laid her head on his chest. "I've been thinking about this all day-..." he began saying.

"About me moving up here?" She interrupted.

"No… you didn't let me finish." he curled his finger under her chin, lifting her head, for her to look at him. "I was thinking about my feelings for you, and I don't think this... I know this..." He paused to kiss her, kissing her with love.

"I love you." he says kissing her again. Kissing her hard and demanding. "To be honest, I'm actually madly in love with you."

Chapter 26- Honoring Harlow

It's been a month since Antonio confessed his true feelings for Sadie, he also hired contractors to remodel his bedroom for her. That way Sadie would feel more comfortable staying in the room with him. They also went out, and bought all new bedroom furniture, letting her pick out everything that she wanted.

Sadie was in their newly remodeled room, getting ready for Antonio's big night. He snuck up behind her, as she was putting on a dress that she picked out of the closet, and held out in front of her, a beautiful red dress that he had bought for her, hoping she would wear it to the awards.

While showing her the dress, he kissed her cheek, and spoke into her ear "I bought you this dress this morning, I would love for you to wear it tonight, I think it would be the perfect dress. I also believe that you'll raise a ton of money wearing this." he grinned, as she took the dress from his hands and held it up for her to see it.

"I like it." She turned around, and gave him a kiss "Thank you."

"Personally, I think you look extremely sexy in red." he said, looking at her full of lust, and his eyes turning bluer.

"I think that it's great that they are going to help us raise money in Harlow's memory for breast cancer, and donating the money to the cause." she says, putting an arm around his neck, kissing him.

"Thank you again for the dress, I'll try it on right now." she said excitedly, and couldn't wait to see what it looked like on her.

"You're welcome."

The Unexpected Nanny

Antonio couldn't wait to see her in the dress, he watched her walk away. At first, he stood there waiting for her to come out, but changed his mind. "I'll just wait for you downstairs; Ethan is here anyway."

Sadie tried on the dress from Antonio, and stood there checking herself out in front of the mirror, loving the dress from him. She then finished her look off, by putting on her make up, and doing her hair. She thought her look was perfect and was excited to raise money in Harlow's memory, hoping that it all goes well.

Since Antonio was a well-respected attorney in the area, and with the other attorneys that will be there, and most of them knowing who Harlow was, she figured it should be a good turnout.

She grabbed her red stilettos, and carried them down with her. Her entrance into the living room turned the heads of Antonio and Ethan, with Antonio's mouth dropping, and Ethan couldn't stop looking at her.

"What do you think?" she asked Antonio, modeling the dress to him.

"Forget what he thinks, I think you look amazingly beautiful. You'll be making my sister proud, that's for sure." Ethan blurted out.

Antonio turned to Ethan, giving him a dirty look and not too thrilled about his comment. "First of all, your first remark was uncalled for, and yes she will be making Harlow proud."

"I was only trying to be funny, chill out man." Ethan grinned, he noticed that Antonio was still giving him the evil eye, and gave Antonio a shove from behind. "Relax... besides, I'd like to know, how were you so lucky to get two beautiful women, back to back like this?"

Antonio turned around and faced Ethan, wanting to smack him upside the head. Ethan's eyes got wide, and stuck his arm out. "Damn Antonio chill, all I'm saying is you're a damn lucky guy, that's all."

"That's right, I am a lucky guy, and don't forget that. You do realize that I still owe you a punch in the mouth." He says, grinning back at Ethan.

"You can do that another time, you two have somewhere to be." Ethan joked.

Antonio turned around and walked back over to Sadie. "You look wonderful, are you ready to do this?"

"I'm a little nervous, but I'm ready." Sadie put on her shoes and took Antonio's arm as he held it out for her, and walked her out to the limo.

Once they arrived at the banquet hall and began walking over to the doors, they walked past a group of attorneys that were outside talking amongst themselves, the attorneys stopped talking and were all turning their heads looking at Sadie, pointing and smiling at her, they then began talking quietly while still keeping their eyes on her. She reached up to Antonio's ear and whispered "I hope they aren't talking bad about me."

He placed his hand on the small of her back and leaned into her ear "They're most likely talking about how gorgeous you look tonight." he smiled "Shall we?" he asks, giving her a wink. He walked her to where she needed to be, so that she could get ready for the event.

He gave her a long passionate kiss before leaving, and headed to find their table. She stood in the rehearsal room memorizing her small speech that she had prepared, hoping to not screw it up.

The coordinator went into the dressing room to get the girls, letting them know that it was time. He walked them to the back of the stage, lining them up and instructing them on what to do as they walked down the stage.

Sadie was finally up next, she began inhaling and exhaling slowly, trying to calm her nerves down. Just as she was about to go on stage, the coordinator quickly walked up to her and began adjusting her hair and makeup.

"Have fun." he tells her, before she walked out there.

Sadie walked down the stage smiling, turning her head when she heard whistles from one end of the crowd, it was Antonio's group who were standing and whistling at her. She smiled and waved at them before heading back.

After all the girls walked on the stage, Sadie was called out by the speaker to come join him on the stage. He introduced her as she walked towards him, and mentioned to the crowd about the awareness that she was going to speak about. There was a white screen hanging behind her, that started flashing pictures of Harlow, as well as pictures of her with Antonio and the girls.

Antonio was shocked to see the pictures that were being shown, he had no idea that Sadie gave them pictures to display. His eyes were glued to the screen and had gotten teary eyed, each time it showed a picture of her. He was so touched by Sadie's heart, that it only made him love her even more.

"Good evening... before we get started with the awards this evening, we would like to take a moment of silence in honor of a very special woman who is no longer with us." Everyone got quiet and bowed their heads for a couple minutes, taking their moment of silence.

"Harlow Russo was a brave and courageous young woman, who was taken away from us way too soon at the young age of twenty-nine. In honor of Harlow's memory, we would like to raise awareness of breast cancer, and we would like to ask if you could donate what you can, in her honor. All proceeds raised tonight will go to the Breast Cancer Awareness Charity in her name, to help find a cure for this horrible disease. BCAC is a non-profit organization, that one hundred percent of its proceeds go to the cancer research. If you have any questions feel free to ask me, or Antonio who is sitting right over at that table." she says, pointing over at Antonio.

"I also would like to say; Antonio Russo will also be donating one million dollars." Antonio stood up waving, before sitting back down.

"Thank you so much." she said, smiling.

Sadie left the stage to have a seat next to Antonio. He stood up as she walked up to the table, giving her a hug, and kissing her on the lips.

"You did a wonderful job, you looked wonderful up there." he smiled, whispering in her ear.

Before they started handing out the awards, the waitresses walked the tables filling up everyone's glasses with champagne, and refilling their glasses of water, while servers were placing their meals in front of them.

Antonio leaned over to her asking if she would like anything else to drink while the waitress was there taking drink orders.

"No thanks, I'm good." she took a bite of her roasted chicken, and smiled.

"I'll have a double bourbon on the rocks, please." he tells the waitress.

During the meal, the presenter started to speak about the awards and the different categories, they started calling out the names for each of the awards, and having them grab their awards as their names were called. Antonio won three different awards, Attorney of the Year Award, Lifetime Achievement Award and Community Champion Award. His law firm also won an award for Best Law Firm of the Year.

After all the awards were given out, Sadie leaned over to Antonio giving him a kiss on the side of his lips "I'm so proud of you, congratulations."

Antonio was still amazed with Sadie for everything that she has done, he could see that her heart was full of gold, and had no idea that he could ever feel this way about anyone, other than Harlow. The more he looked at her, the bigger his smile was for her "I'm so proud of you for what you did for Harlow and I'm really amazed at what you put together in her honor."

"You're welcome." she smiled "Let's just hope that it was a good turn out tonight."

"I'm not worried."

The coordinator interrupted Sadie and Antonio, letting them know that they had received all the donations and were done being counted. "I'm excited to let you know that over three million dollars was raised tonight. I do have to tell you, there were also four very large donations."

"On top of the other amount?" Sadie questioned.

"Yes, all four totaling eight million dollars."

Both Sadie and Antonio gasped in shock, Antonio placed his hand on her thigh, while leaning back in his chair. He couldn't believe what he just heard, he looked around trying to figure out who would make such a large donation, four of them to be exact. He began rubbing around his mouth, thinking. "Are you going to make an announcement?" Antonio asked curiously.

"Yes, that is why I came over to let you know how much had been raised, I'll have you both come with me to make the announcement, which I will be doing right now."

Sadie and Antonio followed him to the podium, and got everyone's attention by tapping on the microphone. Once all eyes were on him, he began to speak.

"I would like to congratulate everyone on their awards tonight. I would like to also thank everyone for their generous donations to the BCAC in honor of Harlow Russo. Tonight, we raised over eleven million dollars, Antonio confirmed that he will also be donating a million dollars." Everyone began clapping, whistling and cheering. Antonio pulled out his checkbook and signed a check, signing the check for eleven million dollars, then handed him the check.

He looked at the check and coughed when he saw the amount that he wrote the check out for. "Everyone... he just wrote out the check for eleven million dollars, matching the amount raised." he announced, not taking his eyes off the check. He knew he was going to write one for a million, not eleven million.

Antonio and Sadie thanked everyone for their generous donations before exiting the stage. He grabbed his awards, and walked around shaking hands with everyone before going home.

When they got home, Ethan was asleep on the couch, instead of waking him up Sadie got him a blanket and laid it over him, while Antonio went into his office and set his awards on his desk. They both walked up the steps, trying not to wake up Ethan, the girls, and especially the puppy.

Sadie cleaned up and changed out of her dress, while Antonio got into bed, he was drained and ready to go to sleep.

She walked out of the bathroom smiling and climbed into bed.

"What are you smiling for?" he asked curiously.

She snuggled up to him, and laid in his arms. "I'm just happy that it turned out to be a good night, between the money raised, and the awards you got."

"There's something else about you, and for the life of me I cannot figure it out... but I like it." he said grinning, and kissing her before they fell asleep. "Good night."

"Goodnight." She said, inhaling deeply and opening her mouth, wanting to say something to him, then closed her mouth.

"Antonio..." she whispered.

"Hmmm" he moaned out quietly, nearly asleep.

"I love you."

He opened his eyes, and started caressing her lips while looking in her eyes. "I love you too Sadie."

The Unexpected Nanny

Chapter 27- A gift for Antonio

Gabriella woke up to Bella whimpering, and let her out of the kennel, carrying her to the bed with her.

"Gabby, daddy will be mad that you let her out." Isabella whispered.

"She was crying." Gabriella says, putting the puppy under the blankets, trying to get her to lay down with them.

Antonio woke up to hearing the girls giggling and talking, thinking that they are up earlier than normal. He put on his sweats, and headed over to the girls' room to see what they were doing.

"What are you girls up to?" Antonio asks, scaring the girls as he walked on the room. Both of their heads popped out from underneath the blankets, acting like they weren't doing anything, and trying to keep the puppy underneath the blankets.

"Nothing daddy." Isabella smiled, innocently. Antonio noticed the blanket moving, and looked over at the kennel.

He ran his fingers through his hair, trying not to get mad at them. "Why is Bella in the bed with you girls?"

"She was crying." Gabriella says, rubbing her eyes. Scared that they were in trouble.

"Come on, let's let her outside. I'm sure she has to go to the bathroom." he says, walking over to the bed and picking the puppy up, and carried her outside. The girls followed him outside and chased the puppy around until she did her duties.

"Come on girls, bring her back in, let's make some breakfast."

Ethan woke up to the girls running around the living room, playing with Bella. He lifted his head up, looking over the couch to Antonio "How did everything go last night?"

"Went really well, Sadie did a wonderful job raising money for the foundation, I also won three awards, as well as my firm. So, it was a good night."

"That's good, congratulations. Say... you wouldn't mind if I took the girls for the rest of the weekend, would you?" Ethan asked curiously.

"Why, what do you have going on?"

"I just figured that I would give you kids a break, so you could have some alone time for once. I was also thinking maybe taking the girls down to the creek and do a little fishing."

"I suppose, do you plan on taking their dog too?" Antonio laughed, as he flipped the pancakes.

"Yes, I can do that too. I can take them after they eat breakfast, and drop them back off tomorrow." Ethan removed the blanket from him, and folded it up. He then sat down at the table; his stomach started growling from smelling the food, and started to rub it. "Making enough for me to eat?"

"Yes, don't worry."

"Is breakfast done daddy, I'm hungry?" Isabella asked, as she stood next to him.

"Yes, why don't you girls go wash up, and then go sit at the table. Your food will be ready when you get back."

Antonio fed Ethan and the kids, then made a plate for Sadie and put it on a tray, bringing her breakfast in bed. He walked in the bedroom just as Sadie was waking up.

"Wake up sleepy head, you're sleeping in awfully late today." he grinned, handing her tray of food.

"Felt good to sleep in for once." she says, looking at the food he brought her.

Antonio sat down on the bed, picking a piece of bacon off her tray, having her take a bite. "Ethan is taking the girls until tomorrow, so it's just us." he says, still trying to get her to take a bite of the bacon. "He thinks we need some alone time."

"That's nice of him." she smiled, she looked at the food, turning her nose up. "I'm not sure that I'm hungry, but thank you anyway."

Antonio looked at her strangely "Are you sure?" he says, eating a piece of bacon.

"Maybe I'll eat it in a little bit, I'll go pack the girls some clothes."

Antonio brought the tray back down to the kitchen, and had the girls go by Sadie. She cleaned them up, and got them packed and ready to go. She then brought down the kennel and handed it over to Ethan.

"Have fun." she grinned, while handing him the kennel.

"You two have fun."

Antonio walked the girls out to Ethan's car and got them in their car seats. "You girls be good, and don't give Ethan any trouble." He looked at Ethan and then back to the girls. "On second thought, give him all the trouble you want." he chuckled.

Ethan laughed, shaking his head as he got inside his vehicle.

"We will be good." Isabella smiled, excited to hang out with Ethan.

Sadie got dressed and quickly wrapped a gift for Antonio, while he was outside with Ethan and placed it in her top dresser drawer.

Sadie figured since the girls were gone, she would finally be able to clean the house, and Antonio was also able to get his other work done with all his rental properties.

He hung up his awards, then went looking for Sadie, to show her and see what she thought. He found her asleep on the couch, and turned back around to let her sleep. He started heading back into his office, but stopped before walking in and looked over to the other room.

He walked over to the piano, and stood there debating on if he wanted to play. He hadn't played the piano in over a year, since before Harlow's diagnosis, and was worried about waking up Sadie. He sat down and hesitantly started playing. The more he played the more he had gotten back into the grove of things.

He started playing an Andrew Lloyd Webber piece. Sadie woke up to hearing Antonio playing the piano, and walked over to the room. She snuck up behind him, and leaned over, placing her hands on top of his, and playing the song with him, moving her fingers in rhythm with his.
He stopped playing and looked up at her. "You know this song?"

"Of course I do, its Cats." she smiled, impressing Antonio. "You can finish playing, I didn't mean to interrupt."

She stood back and watched, and listened to him play. He was finished with the song, and turned around in his seat. "I still got it." he says with a smile. She smiled back, handing him the gift she wrapped for him earlier.

"What's this?" he asked, taking it from her hand. He put it up to his ear, and began shaking it.

"A little something for you, from me." she says, as she sat on him, straddling him.

"I know, but you didn't need to get me anything, it's not my birthday or anything." he says, looking at her confused, and looked back at the long-wrapped box.

"Will you just open it!" she said happily, lightly shoving his shoulder.

"OK... OK, I'll open it."

He unwrapped the gift, and opened the box. His heart started to race in excitement, and looked up at Sadie, then back down to the box, pulling out a pregnancy test.

"You're pregnant?" he asked quietly, smiling.

"Uh huh, that's why I was only drinking water last night."

"How long have you known?"

"Almost a week, I've been trying to figure out ways to tell you, and wasn't sure when to tell you, I also have a doctor's appointment on Monday.

"Does Ethan know about this?"

"No." she giggled "Why?"

"I figured maybe that was why he offered to take the girls, and for us to have some alone time."

"No, you're the only one who knows."

Antonio hugged her tight, and started feeling all warm inside, feeling as if his heart just grew double in size. His excitement was well noticed by Sadie, he stood up with her in his arms, spinning her around.

He crashed his lips hard to hers, and kissing her hungrily while setting her down on the piano. Sadie pulled him closer between her legs and wrapped them around his waist. "So, I take it you're happy about it?" she asked, while grinning an evil grin. She already knew that he would be happy about it, and was thrilled to see his reaction.

He desperately kissed her lips, and moved to her neck and collarbone, kissing her all over while moving back up to her lips. "You just made me the happiest man on earth." he says, still kissing her.

She started tugging on his belt, wanting to get it off as fast as she could. "Right here?" he asked her, surprised.

"Why not? Nobody is here." She unbuttoned his pants, and pulled off his belt.

"You little temptress." he groaned.

He slid her shorts and panties down, dropping them on the ground. He leaned her back on the piano, placing his hands on her hips and pulled her closer to him.

He leaned down to kiss her navel, while thrusting his finger inside her. Groaning when he felt how warm and wet, she was. His mouth made its way down to her pussy, and slid his tongue softly between her sensitive folds, licking her until her back arched and began shaking, he continued slowly licking her nookie, not wanting to stop, and wanting to give her another orgasm.

He continued thrusting his finger slowly in and out of her, while his tongue circled around her clit, giving her another wild orgasm.

"Antonio." she moaned "I can't take it anymore... put it in me." she cried out.

He stood up and dropped his pants to the ground kicking them to the side, and pulled her to the edge of the piano, thrusting slowly in her. As his cock slid into her pool of wetness, his groans became louder.

"Antonio..." she moaned louder, begging for more.

She raised her head, looking at him while he was thrusting deeply inside her, she reached out for him to help her up, and pulled her to him. He picked her up and carried her over to the wall, pinning her against it while kissing her hard. Her legs wrapped tightly around him while he thrusted in her again.

Their kiss was passionate, the longer they kissed the harder and faster he thrusted, bouncing her back against the wall. They were both feeling tingles running through their bodies, and their kiss turned hotter and more intense. She pulled away from his lips and moaned into his ear while she was orgasming.

A groan loudly escaped his mouth, as he enjoyed the feeling of being inside her warm pussy, and feeling her warm release all over his throbbing cock.

He began grunting, and goosebumps formed all over him as he got excited, releasing his all into her, and having the most intense orgasm he's ever had. His lips crashed onto hers hard, and deeply thrusted his tongue in her mouth. He was all jacked up, excited, and couldn't help but wanting to kiss her until their lips turned raw. She was out of breath and had to pull away to take a deep breath.

He set her down and smiled "Whewwwww." he yelled out, in a high-pitched tone. His heart was still pounding hard, and held his hand to his chest. He could feel it beating hard and fast and placed Sadie's hand to his heart. "This is what you do to me." he whispered, giving her a kiss.

Sadie grabbed her clothes and walked back over to Antonio, grabbing his chin and giving him a kiss. "I love you so much." Her eyes sparkled when she told him that she loved him, causing Antonio's heart to skip a beat.

She went upstairs and ran water in the bathtub, getting it ready to relax and soak in the tub. Antonio walked in as she was getting in the tub, and looked at her surprised. "Am I not invited?"

"You can come in, I already figured that you were going to join me." she says, scooting forward so he could climb in behind her.

Antonio joined Sadie, climbing in behind her, placing his hands on her stomach and rubbing it softly. He kissed her cheek and whispered into her ear "I haven't been this happy in a long time."

She laid her head back against his chest, and held onto his hands that were resting on her stomach. "I knew there was something different about you, I said it last night. I should have known better... but then again, that was years ago." Taking a washcloth and a bar of soap, he started washing her body.

He couldn't stop smiling, knowing that he was going to be growing his family. "I'm finally going to be a dad again." he said, feeling like he was on cloud nine. "I haven't seen you getting sick, so I never suspected it."

"I've gotten sick a couple times; this morning was one of them. It was hard holding it back when you had that tray of food in here this morning, and when you tried getting me to eat that piece of bacon." she giggled "I immediately got up and let everything out, right after you left."

"Wait until the girls find out, they will be ecstatic."

"I want to wait to tell them, until I'm at least four months, or once we know everything is ok."

"Why? Why so late?"

"With everything that happened to Harlow, I don't want to see them get excited about it, and then for something go wrong. I know miscarriages can always happen in the first trimester."

"I understand, I was there many times with Harlow. She always miscarried within the first trimester. We had one that made it to a little over four months."

"You did? I didn't know that."

"Yes, we had a little boy, and named him Davide Amadeo."

Sadie looked at him with sad eyes, feeling bad for him. She could see that it still hurt him, and hated knowing that he lost so many loved ones the last few years. "I'm so sorry…"

"It's OK, now I know why she had been miscarrying all those years, it makes a lot of sense now. So, I understand why you want to wait."

"Now, keep your mouth shut." she insisted, wanting to change the subject. She reached her arm back behind her and cupped the back of his head, pulling him down to her lips to give him a kiss. "I have one more gift for you too."

"Another one?"

"Yep..." she says, wiggling her eyebrows up and down.

"Would you like a milkshake?" she asked, grinning. "Or a twinkie on a stick?" she paused, trying to hold back from laughing when she saw the confused look on his face. "What on earth are you talking about?" he asked, trying to figure it out.

"Oh Antonio... you're really in for a treat."

Chapter 28- Antonio's love

Antonio looked at Sadie confused, still unsure of what she was talking about. *Oh Antonio, you're in for a treat* ran through his mind, trying to figure it out.

She smiled, while slowly pushing him toward the bed, both still naked. She shoved him down onto the bed and climbed on top of him. Her mouth covering his, kissing him hungrily. She liked that the inside of his mouth was warm and wet as her tongue caressed his. His hands softly roaming her back while they kissed.

She slowly trailed her kisses along down his chest, and stopping when she got down to his hardened cock. He let out a low deep moan when he felt her warm mouth wrap around his cock, and began licking up and down, and circling her tongue around the tip of his shaft.

He let out a louder deeper moan, when she used her tongue to tease the soft spot on his cock, his body jerked and more groans escaped his mouth, when he felt her warm mouth covering his now even harder cock, slowly moving up and down, and lightly sucking when she moved her mouth up to the tip, grazing her teeth along the way.

So many emotions were going through his mind while he was enjoying the moment. Her warm wet mouth continued stimulating his cock, gasping as she went all the way down, feeling the back wall of her throat. She moved her mouth up and down him elegantly, causing his breathing to become erratic the way she moved her mouth and tongue along his cock, sending shockwaves throughout his body.

His orgasm was near and ready to release, she kept doing her magical touch on his wand, and tried stopping her before he released. She refused to stop, and her eyes rolled up to look at him when she felt his cock pulsating in her mouth, the intense sensations that she was giving him felt like he was floating on air, his body stiffened, and let out a loud groan while exploding his warm juices into her mouth.

He felt guilty, he never felt that wonderful feeling before, and it was the most intense orgasm he has ever had. He laid there for a moment, while his body was coming off the sexual high, feeling alive, and thinking about what Sadie said to him earlier. "So that is the meaning of a milkshake... now I understand" he said quietly, grinning while she moved up to him. "You really didn't have to do that... although I'm not complaining either."

"I wanted to do it, and I hope you liked it." she grinned, cleaning herself up. "You're always making me stop, and I wanted you to finally feel the full effect of it."

"That was actually the most incredible feeling that I've ever experienced." he groaned in awe. Still thinking about it, he pulled her in his arms, and kissed the top of her head.

He laid there feeling like a new man, thinking about what had just happened, and couldn't believe that he let her do that to him. He never thought the feeling could feel that amazing. He always heard guys always talking about it, but thought they were just fooling around, and talking typical guy shit.

******

A couple days later, the girls stayed with Ethan while Antonio went to Sadie's doctor's appointment. Sadie laid on the exam table while the doctor did an ultrasound. "Looks like you're about six weeks pregnant." Dr. Weston says, taking measurements of the baby.

Antonio stood there studying the screen, looking serious. "So, there is only one baby correct?" he questioned, while looking at the screen, all he saw was one little pebble.

"Yes, all I see is one, were you expecting more?" asked the doctor. "I can look again, and see if I can find more." he says, moving the wand over her stomach, looking at more views.

"No, no." Antonio laughed. "It's just that we have twins already, so I just wanted to make sure this wasn't another set of twins." he says, feeling relieved, even though his dreams were to always have a big family, and having lots of kids.

"If these were twins, it would have been just fine." Sadie says to Antonio. Playfully smacking his arm. "You're not the one who has to carry them." She looked back at the screen, and smiled.

The nurse came in the room giving Sadie a preparation packet before they left, explaining what to eat, and what not to eat, it also explained all the trimesters and what to expect each month, about labor, breastfeeding, etcetera. Basically, everything on what to expect during pregnancy, and after birth.

They arrived back home, and Antonio was full of excitement, it was killing him that Sadie wouldn't let him tell the girls. Ethan could see the excitement in Antonio's face, and wanted to know more. "How did it go?" he asked, looking at Sadie who was trying to hush him, by putting her finger to her mouth, and pointing over at the girls.

"Put it this way, everything is just wonderful." Antonio said happily. His phone rang, and left the room to answer it when he saw who was calling.

"The girls were just getting ready to put their swimsuits on and go swimming; I hope that's OK." Ethan asked Sadie.

"Yea, I'll go ahead and put on my swimsuit as well, I'll just go out there with them." Sadie says giving him a wink. "By the way, thanks for taking the girls the other night, I never got the chance to thank you, after you dropped them off yesterday."

"You're very welcome, I'll watch them anytime you guys need me to." he winked. "So how far along are you?" he asked whispering.

"Six weeks, more than what I thought I would be, I figured I was maybe four weeks."

"That's cool, I think you'll be a great mother, I know it." Ethan walked up to Sadie whispering in her ear "Do you not want the girls to know?"

"No, not until my first trimester is in the clear. I figured after everything is good, I'll let them know when I'm at least four months along, I would hate for them to go through another heartbreak."

"That's understandable, and that's also very thoughtful of you."

"It's going to be tough not saying anything, I just hope everything goes well." Sadie sighed.

"I'm sure everything will be just fine." he assured her.

Antonio walked out of the office looking frustrated. "Well, we will be having visitors for a while." Antonio says to Sadie, not sounding happy.

"Oh yea? Who's that?"

"My parents, they plan on flying here in about a month or so to visit, and they also plan on staying here, in the house."

"Here? Is that a bad thing?" Sadie asked, confused. "I'd actually love to finally meet them." she smiled.

Ethan laughed, while looking at Antonio. "All I can say is good luck to both of you, and have fun." Ethan looked at Sadie, and shook his head with a grin, remembering all the fun times he had with his mother.

"I'm glad that you think it's funny. Ethan, I swear your ass getting kicked by me, is getting this close." Antonio says, pinching his fingers closely together in his face.

"I'm so scared..." Ethan laughed, as he gave Antonio a shove.

"Just call me when they get here, I want to witness the show begin." he smiled wide, showing off his teeth.

"I guess I don't understand what the big deal is?" Sadie said confused, wondering what the two were talking about. "They're your parents."

Antonio rubbed the side of his nose, and laughed thinking about it. He wasn't too worried about his dad; it was more his mother that he was worried about. "They get on your nerves after a bit, nothing you ever do is right, they do mean well, but it's just that they like everything to be done perfect or has to be done a certain way." Antonio explained to Sadie. "It's not so much my father, it's my mother…"

"My sister told his mom off once, I thought it was going to be the end of her then." Ethan laughed. "His mom is way worse than his dad, his dad is actually sort of cool. I on the other hand, had some great moments with his mom, and if I have to, I'll have some fun with her again."

"Maybe I'll hire someone to build a guest house for them, then we wouldn't have to worry about so much." Antonio sighed, shaking his head.

"Ha! If you did that they would still want to stay in here." Ethan joked.

"I suppose that I could always stick them in our hotel here."

Ethan laughed "Yea right, look at the huge fit she threw the last time that you did that!"

"I suppose you're right…" Antonio sighed.

"I'm sure I'll be able to handle them." Sadie assured them. "I do have a way with people, and I'm sure that I'll be able to handle your mother, how bad could she actually be?"

Antonio shook his head with a smile, knowing that she was in for a surprise "If you say so." Antonio mocked, walking away.

Sadie saw the girls come down in their swimsuits, holding towels.

"I'll be right back, let me put on my swimsuit, and I'll go swimming with you two." she says, as she walked past them in a hurry.

"Daddy, can the dog come play in the pool with us?" Gabriella asked.

"No, she can go run outside, but not in the pool."

"Please daddy, please?" Isabella begged, pulling on his hand.

Antonio sighed as he looked at both girls, he felt bad and didn't want them to be upset with him. "Oh, I suppose. Just make sure she goes to the bathroom first."

The girls got excited and hugged him, he looked at Ethan who was shaking his head in disbelief "What? How can I say no to these girls, especially when they give me those puppy dog eyes."

"Sucker." Ethan grinned and laughed. "If they weren't kids, I'd say that you were pussy whipped." he says quietly, leaning to his ear so the girls didn't hear him.

Sadie walked with the girls outside, setting their towels on the chairs and put their life jackets on, before getting into the pool with them. Antonio and Ethan sat in the house talking about how life has been treating each other. "You know... Sadie just gave me a whole new life to live, she has been nothing but amazing. From the first day I met her, she has been nothing but a lifesaver. She has done nothing but think of others, before thinking of her own self. The way she took to those girls, and the way they took to her, it's like someone up above was looking out for all of us." Antonio says, opening up to Ethan.

"I'll admit, you're one lucky guy, and I know my sister, she would be so proud right now."

"Damn Ethan... I still miss her, more than anything. I still think about her daily, and what could have been. I can't change what happened, but I now know that I can move on, especially knowing that I have Harlow's permission."

"You've got a good woman right now, she obviously loves you and your kids, and she just gave you a new life to look forward to."

"That she did, and I couldn't be any happier."

Ethan gave him a little shove, and smiled. "I see love in those eyes of yours, brother."

"I do love her, and I love her even more today. Honestly I don't know what I would do without her." Antonio gleamed.

"So... do you think you'll marry her?"

"I haven't given it much thought really, Harlow hasn't been gone all that long, but to be honest with you it could be a possibility in the near future, especially with a child on the way." he looked away, taking a deep breath. "I actually could see myself with her, for life. I honestly believe that I could grow old with her."

"Just remember Harlow's letter, it's what she wanted." Ethan says, giving him a pat on the back. "If you don't want to... then hell... I will." he grinned, knowing that he was about to get popped in the face by Antonio's fist.

"Damnit Ethan, if you weren't Harlow's brother, and if I didn't like you, your ass would be on the ground so fast right now." he says, and started smirking when he saw Ethan grinning at him. He knew that Ethan was messing with him, and trying to get him worked up.

Ethan laughed, and gave him a brotherly hug. "You know I know how to get to you, and it works every time, just remember Harlow's wishes, you've got at least one of her wishes coming."

Antonio stood up, thinking of what Harlow wrote, and what some of her wishes were. "Yea, she did want me to give the kids more siblings, she knew that I wanted to have lots of children." he says, as he walked over to the patio door, watching Sadie and the girls play in the pool.

Ethan walked up to Antonio placing his hand on his shoulder.

"Think hard about everything, you know what you have to do. But I do have to get going, I've got a very hot date tonight."

"With Rosie and her sisters?" Antonio asks laughing.

"Ha ha very funny, actually her name is Krista, I've been chasing her for months, and she finally agreed to go out with me."

"She probably felt sorry for you." Antonio grinned a devilish grin.

Ethan shook his head at Antonio, he couldn't get mad at him, especially after all the stuff that he just pulled on Antonio, he knew he deserved what Antonio was saying to him, and laughed the more he thought about it.

As Ethan walked out the door, he yelled at Antonio. "Marry that girl will ya!"

Chapter 29- The guests

A couple months have gone by since Sadie was told that she would finally be meeting Antonio's parents. She was getting nervous after listening to Antonio and Ethan talk about them, and they were to arrive later in the evening. She ran around the house making sure the house was perfectly clean, and made sure there was no speck of dust to be found anywhere.

Antonio hired contractors to build a guest house towards the edge of his property. It recently had been finished, and fully furnished. The girls were with Antonio in the guest house making sure everything was cleaned up, looking perfect.

"Daddy can we go play now; this is boring." Isabella whined.

"Why don't you girls go play over on the play gym, Sadie's in the house making sure that it's all cleaned up inside."

"You mean, momma." Gabriella says, giving him a strange look.

"I'm sorry, yes momma." he smiled, patting the top of her head. "We are done in here anyway; you can go on and play."

Later in the evening Sadie was giving the girls a bath, when she heard the doorbell, and looked at the girls. "Your grandparents must be here." she says to the girls, sighing. Dreading about meeting them, hoping they weren't as bad as she was told, and worried about how they would act around her. Ethan pulled her to the side earlier, warning her about Antonio's mother, letting her know that she must show who was boss.

"Are we done taking a bath?" Isabella asked, standing up.

Sadie let the water out of the tub, and grabbed a couple towels for them. "Yes, first let's get you both dried off, and into your pajamas, then you can go visit with your grandparents."

Antonio let his parents inside, giving them both hugs. "Sorry about Harlow, wish we could have been here for you during that sorrow time..." Antonio's mom says, while giving him a hug.

"Thanks mom, please don't bring that up anymore." he sighed.

She looked at him disappointed. "Well OK, if you say so. I just feel bad that we weren't here for you."

"It is what it is, you can't change the past." he says, while looking at his dad. "How long do you plan on being in town for?" he asked, trying to change the subject.

"We haven't decided yet." his dad says. "Where shall we put our bags?"

"I will be putting you in the guest house, out back." he says, smiling from the inside.

"Guest house?" asked his mom, looking surprised.

"I recently had it built; you'll love it." he smirked after seeing the look on her face.

His mom curiously looked at him with an unsure look, her look immediately changed when she heard the girls running down the stairs, and quickly turned to them, reaching her arms out for them to come give her a hug. "Oh my, it's been a while since we last saw you girls, you're getting so big and tall."

"We're five now, grandma." Gabriella says with a big smile.

"I know." she says smiling, pinching their cheeks.

His mom stood back up, and looked around the home. "The house looks great, I see you have done some redecorating, you must have hired a better decorator around here."

"Actually no, this was all Sadie's doing." Antonio says, sounding frustrated with her.

"Sadie?" she questioned, looking confused.

Antonio looked at the girls, rubbing the back of his head. "Where is she anyway."

"She's cleaning up from our bath." Isabella says, holding her grandma's hand.

Antonio looked back at his mom. "I told you about her a while back, remember?"

Her eyebrows raised, wondering what he was up to now, hoping that it wasn't what she was thinking that it was. "Oh, the nanny? Why would she be decorating your home?"

"She's our new momma." Gabriella happily said. Antonio's eyes closed, knowing his mom was going to be asking many questions about why the girls were calling her momma.

His mom looked at Antonio confused. "Momma? Is there something going on here that I should know about?" sounding upset.

Antonio sighed and took deep breath, growing frustrated with her.

"The girls call her momma now, she's not only that, but my..."

Antonio stopped talking when he saw Sadie walking down the stairs, he could see that she was a little nervous, and met her at the end of the steps, he reached his arm out and placed his hand on the small of her back, walking her over to meet his parents.

"Sadie, this is my mother Giorgia, and my father Giovanni." he says introducing them. Sadie smiled while reaching out her hand, wanting to shake their hands. "Mom, Dad... this is Sadie... my girlfriend." he grinned.

"Nice to finally meet you." Sadie politely said, shaking their hands.

Giovanni smiled, happy to meet her. Giorgia on the other hand, was not so pleased, and gave her a sour look, causing Sadie's stomach to turn.

"So, is she the reason why we are staying in this guest house you just built?" Giorgia barked.

Antonio looked at Sadie, wanting to stick up for her, knowing that she had nothing to do with it "To be honest, this was all my idea. I figured that you would like it better, instead of staying downstairs, or in the hotel. You'll be by yourselves, and not have to worry about any kids running around, screaming. I'll take you out there right now, and show you around. I'll even help you with your bags." Antonio says, picking up their bags.

"Grandma you'll like it." Gabriella said, excited.

Sadie was feeling sick and stayed behind while Antonio and the kids brought his parents out to the guest home. Antonio set their bags down and turned the lights on, and began showing them around.

"Well this is nice and all, but we could have just stayed in your house." Giorgia scowled.

"At least being in here, you won't have to worry about getting awoken by the girls or their dog. You'll be able to cook whenever you like, and take your daily naps without getting bothered."

"This will be just fine." Giovanni says to Antonio, giving Giorgia a displeased look.

"Well let's go back in, I'd like to know more about who this Sadie person is." Giorgia says to Antonio.

Antonio pulled his mom to the side, not wanting his girls to hear. "Mother, she's a wonderful person, and there's no need for you to be rude with her. She has done a lot for the girls, and did a lot for Harlow before she passed away. I'd like to ask that you please respect her, those girls love her and she means the world to them."

"Don't you think it's a little too soon to be involved in a relationship, and with your nanny of all people?" she asked, snapping at him.

"First of all, that's my decision, not yours. Secondly, that's my business that you don't need to be sticking your nose in. You don't know her at all, and if you'll give her a chance, you'll see how wonderful she really is."

Giorgia didn't say another word to Antonio, and gave him an evil glare, she walked over to the girls, and kneeled to their level. "I brought you girls some gifts, would you like them now or would you like to wait until tomorrow?"

"I can wait until tomorrow, I'm tired." Gabriella says, rubbing her eyes.

"We can wait until tomorrow; I can help put you girls to bed if you'll like."

The girls happily accepted her offer on putting them to bed, and walked back into the house. Before the girls had gone to bed, they let the dog out. Sadie made sure to have Giorgia's favorite wine chilling and walked up to her "Would you like a glass of wine?"

"I'd love a glass, thank you." she said respectively. Antonio smiled when he saw that his mom being nice to her, and hoped she wouldn't be like she was with Harlow. Sadie poured Giorgia a glass of wine, while Antonio grabbed a couple beers out of the fridge, handing one to his dad.

Sadie handed Giorgia the glass of wine, smiling while handing it to her. She took a sip, and smiled. "Antonio must have told you that this was my favorite."

"He did."

The girls came in from outside with the dog, and walked up to their grandma, with the dog in Isabella's arms. "Grandma we're ready for bed now."

"OK, well let's go put you girls to bed." she smiled.

She brought them to bed and tucked them in, then read a bedtime story to them, helping them fall asleep. After the girls fell asleep, she left the room and headed back down the stairs. On her way down, she was wondering what Sadie's intentions were with her son, she didn't trust her and felt that she was using him for his money.

Antonio and Giovanni were deep into a conversation while the women sat quietly, listening to them. Giorgia sat there eyeing Sadie, and noticed that she was only drinking water. "Do you not like wine?"

"I do once in a while."

"Sadie hardly ever drinks, usually only on special occasions." Antonio blurted in.

"Well, what do you call this? I would say that this is a special occasion, isn't it?" she asked, eyeing Sadie while taking a drink of her wine.

"I'm good with only water right now, thanks." Sadie politely said.

Giorgia had a strange feeling while sitting there, studying Sadie. She then thought of what Antonio said to her, thinking that maybe he was right. She sighed, thinking she should give her a chance and get to know her. She was determined to end their relationship, if she ever found out that she was only after his money.

Sadie poured Giorgia another glass of wine, while she was being asked a million questions, and was getting quite annoyed with all the nonsense questions. "I'm pretty tired, I think I'm going to go to bed." she said, pretending to yawn, while looking over at Antonio...

"It was very nice to meet you." Giovanni said to Sadie with a genuine smile.

"Likewise." Sadie said, smiling.

"Goodnight." Sadie quietly said to all of them.

"I'll be up in a little bit." Antonio says to her.

Antonio stayed up late talking with his parents, and liked how his dad was pleasant with Sadie, and willing to get to know her. He was getting tired himself, and walked his parents out, handing his mom the bottle of wine. "Here finish this, otherwise it will just get tossed."

"Well we don't want to waste that, I'll take it." she grabbed the bottle from his hand and smiled. "See you tomorrow."

Antonio closed the door and rested the back of his head against it, feeling relieved that his mom was out of the house. He walked up the stairs and as he walked into the bedroom, he was relieved, and happy to see Sadie. He noticed that she looked drained while lying there watching a movie.

"Well that went somewhat well." Antonio says. She looked at him and shrugged her shoulders. "Your mother is ruthless. What was with all the stupid questions?"

Antonio took his clothes off and climbed into bed, pulling Sadie into his arms. "I warned you about her, she will eventually warm up to you. I think she's just trying to figure you out. I know her very well, and I'm pretty sure she's thinking that you're only with me for the money."

Sadie sat up, upset with what she just heard. "If she thinks that, she has another thing coming, I have never been about the money."

"Calm down, I know that. I'm just saying, I'm sure that's what is going on in her mind, she also thought that way with Harlow." he says, trying to calm her down.

"Well I hope she watches what she says to me, with these hormones that I have right now, I can't promise what I will do, or say." Sadie says, crossing her arms and sitting back against the headboard.

Antonio turned to her, curling his finger under her chin "Hey, everything will be just fine, just remember I'm here and I won't put up with her shit, I asked her to be nice and to try getting to know you. Let's just wait and see if she can be civil."

He kissed her lips and pulled back to look at her. "I love you." he smiled, kissing her again.

"I love you too." she smiled, pulling him back to her, kissing him passionately.

He laid her down, kissing her with passion as his hands caressed the sides of her body. "You're my world." he whispered to her, assuring his love for her.

"I don't feel like fooling around tonight." she says softly, caressing his cheek with her hand.

"I understand." he says, rolling on his back. She rolled to her side and laid her head on his chest, resting her arm around him, and holding onto him tight.

"Tomorrow is a new day, let's get some rest." he says to her.

Chapter 30- Surprise

Sadie was taking a shower when Antonio came in to join her, helping her wash up. He turned her around and wrapped his arms around her shoulders, looking down at her stomach with a smile. "You're really showing, and I'm loving this beautiful glow about you."

"I know, I can't hide it much longer."

"Have you thought about telling the girls yet? You're almost five months along now." he says, giving her a kiss. "My mom will figure it out you know."

"I'm sure she would, thanks for not telling her. I can honestly see her saying something about it, with the girls around."

"It's true, she doesn't know how to keep a secret very well." He placed his hand on her stomach, rubbing it. "We should tell them today."

He bent down, placing kisses on her stomach "I can't wait to meet you, little one." he grinned, standing back up "Don't you have a doctor's appointment today?"

"I do have one this afternoon, they were going to do an ultrasound and see if they could see what the sex was. We could always surprise them by having them there with us, they'll be able to know if they are possibly having a brother or sister." she smiled.

"If that is how you would like for them to find out, that's fine with me, they might even enjoy seeing it on the screen."

She bit down on her bottom lip thinking "How are we going to leave, and not tell your parents where we're going?"

"I'll just tell them that we have some running around to do." he says, kissing her before heading out of the shower.

Antonio took Bella outside for her to do her duties, his mom happened to be outside and walked over to him. "Nice morning isn't it." he says to her; he could tell that she had something on her mind after seeing the look on her face.

"It is nice out; I still don't see why you went through all the trouble by placing us out here." sounding snarky.

"Do you not like it? I really thought that you might enjoy it."

"It's nice, I'm just surprised about it since you never went through all this trouble before, we're here to visit, and right now I feel that we're not welcome." She looked at the guest house and back over to him, looking bothered. "It's like we're still so far away."

Antonio laughed "You're right outside my house, takes you about a minute to walk in."

"I still do not like it."

Antonio looked up in the air and sighed, then called for Bella. Giorgia stood there, still looking displeased with Antonio. "Sadie and I have some running around to do with the girls today, she planned on making dinner when we get back, you're welcome to the house while were gone."

"Where are you going?" she asked curiously.

Bella ran up to Antonio, jumping up for him to pick her up, he leaned down, and picked up and looked at Giorgia. "School is starting soon, and we have to get the kids signed up for kindergarten, we also have some other things we need to get done." he says, opening the door for her.

Sadie was in the kitchen making breakfast, and the girls were sitting at the table coloring. Giorgia sat down at the table, talking to the girls. She stopped talking when she saw Antonio walk up behind Sadie, and leaned over, kissing her cheek. She gave them a dirty look and turned back to the girls.

After breakfast, Antonio and Sadie left with the girls, getting them signed up for school, and then over to the doctors. Sadie was excited for the girls to finally find out that they were having another sibling soon.

They sat in the waiting room waiting to be called back, and Gabriella looked at Antonio with a strange look. "Why are we here daddy?" Gabriella asked, looking worried. He pulled her on his lap, and slid some hair away from her face "You'll see soon." he smiled.

She then looked over at Sadie with a scared look. "Oh honey, everything is fine, we have something to show you girls." Sadie says, not wanting her to think anything was wrong.

Sadie was called, and they followed the nurse back to the room. While Sadie sat on the table waiting for the doctor to come in, Isabella and Gabriella sat on the chair looking around the office, wondering why they were there.

The doctor came in smiling at the girls. "Well hello there, are you excited to see why you're here?" the doctor asked the girls. Antonio informed the nurse earlier, to let the doctor know that the girls didn't know anything yet, and that they were here to surprise them.

Sadie laid on the table while the girls stood next to her, watching what the doctor was doing. "Well here it is girls, you're both going to be a big sister." he smiled, pointing at the baby on the screen. The girls began jumping up and down, excited and full of smiles.

The doctor continued moving the wand around while looking at the screen taking measurements, making sure everything looked OK. A strange expression came across his face, one that Antonio noticed and wasn't sure if it was a good thing or bad thing.

"Is there something wrong?" he asked, feeling his heart become heavy. The look on the doctor's face, had him remembering the past with

Harlow, and thought it looked all to familiar to something being wrong with the baby.

The doctor smiled "No, no, no. Nothing is wrong, it's just that we have a little one here that likes to hide."

Antonio gave him a confused look "What do you mean by that?"

He pointed to the screen, and tapped on it. "Here is baby number one, and that right there, would be baby number two. I don't know how it was missed before, but it does happen. They both measure the same size and everything looks normal."

Antonio sat down, in shock "Wow, I'm just..."

Sadie laughed "Not only did the girls get a surprise, so did you."

"This is unbelievable." he says smiling, looking at the screen again.

"Would you still like to know the sex, or keep up with the surprises?" asked the doctor, chuckling.

"No more surprises." Antonio joked.

"Well then, baby number one is a boy, and your sneaky baby number two is a girl, congratulations."

"Awe." Sadie grinned while looking at Antonio. He was happy, surprised and had tears forming in his eyes, Sadie reached her hand up, and wiped the tears out of his eyes.

The doctor printed them some pictures, as well as another two sets, after Sadie asked for two more copies of each picture. On the way home Antonio was still in shock, and the girls couldn't stop talking about how they were having a new brother and another sister.

Sadie turned around to talk to the girls "Make sure you don't tell grandma and grandpa; we're going to surprise them." she instructed.

"OK momma." says Isabella.

"Promise?" Sadie questioned, lowering her one eyebrow.

"We promise." Gabriella said.

Sadie called Ethan, having him come over for dinner. Letting him know that they were going to be surprising him and Antonio's parents. Knowing Sadie was having a hard time with Giorgia, he couldn't wait to be there when they finally told her that Sadie is pregnant.

Sadie and the girls walked in the house, and her mouth dropped when she saw the living room. Sadie got upset, and went back outside to talk to Antonio.

He was grabbing the groceries out of the vehicle, and saw the expression on Sadie's face. *Oh Shit, if looks could kill I'm dead* he muttered under his breath. "What did she do or say now?" he asked, knowing that it was about his mother.

"I didn't want to go in any further after what I just saw, but she rearranged the damn living room." she snapped, crossing her arms.

Antonio took a deep breath, and sighed "I'll go talk to her, let me bring these in first."

Antonio brought in the groceries, and noticed the living room, shaking his head. He went to the guest house and saw her sitting at the table reading a book. "You're finally home." she smiled.

"What were you thinking?" Antonio snapped.

Giovanni walked into the kitchen after hearing Antonio snapping at Giorgia, and looked at Giorgia not too happy. "What's going on here?" he asked.

Antonio looked at him, upset "Ask her." He held his hand out to Giorgia "Ask her what she did."

"What on earth did you do now, Giorgia?"

She sat there smiling at the two, while sitting in the chair, and thinking that she did nothing wrong. "What? I just cleaned and made the house look more like it should. It makes more sense now." Giorgia says, looking down at her book.

Giovanni looked over at Antonio, shaking his head. "I'm sorry, she will go right back in there and fix it. I'll make damn sure of that."

Sadie was in the kitchen, making her famous lasagna that Antonio always craved for, and Ethan finally arrived while Giorgia was moving the furniture back to where it belonged. He gave Antonio and Giovanni a confused look while they stood there watching her.

He walked over to Sadie asking her what was going on.

"She rearranged the place while we were gone today, so they are making her put everything back to where it was." she whispered.

He leaned over to her and whispered with a big grin "She's over there sweating like a whore in church."

Sadie couldn't hold it, and busted out laughing. "Oh, my lord Ethan, where do you ever come up with those lines of yours?"

"What? Well she is." he laughed. "Look at her."

Sadie grabbed the lasagna out of the over and placed it on the table, letting everyone know that the food was ready.

During dinner, Antonio and Sadie couldn't help look at each other and smile. Antonio stood up and leaned towards Sadie, and whispered in her ear. He walked over to the counter and grabbed the two envelopes that Sadie put together, handing them to Ethan and his mother.

"What is this?" Giorgia asked, looking confused as she looked down at the envelope.

"We have a surprise for you, go ahead and open them." Antonio tells them.

Ethan had a feeling what it was and grinned when he saw that they were having twins. In his mind he thought Harlow had something to do with this, and couldn't be happier for them.

Giorgia opened the envelope as Giovanni sat next to her, curious as to what it was. She pulled the card out and opened it to find a picture of the twins.

"You're pregnant?" she asked Sadie, shocked.

"Yes we're 19 weeks." Sadie says, happily.

"Now she's got him really trapped." Giorgia says quietly to Giovanni as she covered her mouth. Sadie and Antonio didn't hear her, but it was loud enough for Ethan to hear.

"Congratulations." Ethan says "My sister is getting her wishes come true. She is probably up there jumping for joy." he says, trying to rub it in after hearing what Giorgia had said.

"What wish is that? She's gone." Giorgia asked confused.

"My sister's wishes before she passed, was for them to get together, for Sadie to be the mother to her girls, to give the girls more siblings and..."

Antonio cut Ethan off, as he looked over at his mom. "Harlow hid a journal, and a couple letters for Sadie and I, with her wishes. We found them after Ethan told us about them, and so far, some of her wishes have been coming true."

Giovanni smiled, and walked over to Sadie giving her a hug. "Don't mind my rude wife, I'll say it for her... congratulations."

"Thank you."

"And as for dinner tonight, thank you very much. It was excellent, I'm giving you two thumbs up, and you can make that for me anytime." Giovanni says, hugging her.

Later, Giorgia and Giovanni were getting ready for bed, and Giovanni was in the kitchen drinking some water, while Giorgia was in the bedroom. She walked over to the bedroom door making sure that he was nowhere near and grabbed the picture that Antonio gave her, while looking at it she smiled. She was happy to see that she was going to have a couple more grandchildren, her smile faded when he walked back into the room, and hid the picture not wanting him to know what she was doing.

Giovanni climbed into bed, and looked at Giorgia "You need to lighten up on Sadie, I think she is a terrific girl, Antonio seems happy and the girls are happy, why can't you just accept her? You never liked Harlow either, and you always gave her a hard time. I can see why Antonio had this guest house built, I'm sure it was because of you, to keep you from ruining things." He said, sounding stern with her.

"I just don't want him hurt, or anyone using him for his wealth."

"Giorgia, he's thirty years old, I think he can handle his own love life, he's done quite well for himself, and he did it all on his own. He doesn't need you harping on him, or you questioning who he falls in love with. His wife is no longer here, he's still very young and deserves to be happy. Don't you want that for him?"

"Well yes, yes I do."

"Then give it a rest and get to know her, let them be happy. From what he's told me, Sadie saved him from a lot of things."

Giovanni went to bed after lecturing Giorgia, and she sat in the chair thinking about how both Giovanni and Antonio asked for her to give Sadie a chance, she began to yawn and decided to go to bed.

"You're right, I need to get to know her." she says, letting out a deep breath. "I'll give her a chance, but if I find out differently of her, I will have her *ass*. After all she is pregnant with my grandkids." she says, pulling the blanket up over her.

Chapter 31- Sadie vs. Giorgia

Meanwhile, after Giorgia and Giovanni had left to go back to the guest house, Sadie felt that it went OK. Although she had hoped Giorgia would have been happier about the pregnancy, she felt hurt that she showed no emotions and had nothing to say about the news.

Antonio, Sadie and Ethan went downstairs to shoot some pool after the girls went to bed, so the guys could have a couple cocktails and to talk.

Antonio poured a couple shots, handing one to Ethan. "I'm glad that went well earlier." he says to Ethan, raising his shot glass to Ethan's for a toast.

"Yea it went OK, until I heard your mom smart off to your dad." Ethan says, touching his glass to Antonio's.

"Why? What did she say?" Sadie asked worried.

Ethan slammed his shot, wiping his mouth with the back of his hand and looked at her. "That you trapped Antonio really good now, for becoming pregnant."

"That Bitch!" Sadie yelled, she looked at Antonio after realizing what she said, furrowing her eyebrows. "Sorry, but she is, I swear if she doesn't knock it off, I'm going to say something that I won't regret."

Antonio sighed "She was like this with Harlow too. I just don't get it."

"Jealousy?" she questioned.

"I doubt it, she's always been over protective of me, ever since I was a little kid, but not like this. I guess I'm going to have to have another talk with her."

"No, let me talk to her. She owes me an explanation." Sadie says, walking over to Antonio giving him the look.

Antonio tilted his head back "Do you really think that's a good idea?"

"Yes, I want to know what her problem is with me."

Antonio's hands raised up, not thinking that it was a good idea. "Well that's completely up to you."

Sadie walked over to Ethan with a smirk. "By the way, I thought you were bringing your new girlfriend over for us to meet?" Sadie asked, playfully shoving his shoulder.

"Nah, she's pissed at me." Ethan says looking down at his drink.

"Why? How can she be mad at you already?" Sadie asked, furrowing her eyebrows.

He chuckled "I told her that I traded my bed in for a trampoline, she then came over to check it out and she hit the roof."

Antonio laughed "Really?"

Sadie looked at Ethan wide eyed "You aren't serious, are you?"

Ethan laughed "Hell no... I'm not serious, she's pissed at me because she wanted to move in with me, and I told her that I wasn't ready for that yet. Shit.... I just met the girl."

Ethan's phone rang, and looked at his phone to see who was calling. "Speak of the devil." he says grinning, getting ready to answer the phone. He placed the phone to his ear, and smiled, "What's up sweet cheeks?"

Antonio and Sadie decided to go to bed after Ethan's girlfriend picked him up. As they were walking up the stairs, Antonio kept thinking about how he was about to have two more kids, how his love for Sadie was growing even more each day, and stronger. He was so extremely in love with her, it was starting to scare him. He didn't think that he could ever love anyone as much as he loved Harlow.

When they started walking into the bedroom, he grabbed Sadie's hand and spun her around, pinning her against the wall. "You have no idea how much I love you." he says, crashing his lips hard against hers. "I am so much in love with you." he says, kissing her again.

The heat of the moment, they stripped each other's clothes off, he picked her up, and carried her over to their bed, and gently laid on top of her, not wanting to hurt the babies.

She rolled him over, wanting to take control. With how he had just told her twice about how much he loved her, and the way he was looking at her, had her throbbing at the core and wet as could be. Skipping the foreplay, she wrapped her hand around his hardened cock and placed it at her opening, and sliding it in her as she pressed her body down onto his.

He let out a loud groan, after feeling how warm and wet she was, and the way she was working his baby maker. His hands rested on her hips, while she moved up and down on his cock. She loudly moaned out his name each time she took him all in, and while swirling her hips around his cock. He closed his eyes, wanting to enjoy every moment of the way she was pleasuring him, as well as herself.

He was enjoying it way too much, and didn't want to release before her. He quickly sat up, pulled her to him and looked into her eyes with his sexy bedroom eyes, that had her melting, and her heart beating faster for him.

She pressed her lips to his and kissed him gently, while slowly moving her hips. The warmer her body was feeling on the inside, she kissed him with more urgency, and more demandingly. He laid her down and took control, thrusting in her slowly and pausing deeply inside her, to look at her. Wanting to look her deep in the eyes and to admire how beautiful she really is.

"Antonio, quit pausing and make love to me." she begged, wrapping her legs around him tighter. He smiled and started to thrust harder, and deeper causing her moans to become louder, and begging for more.

Her orgasm was intense, and her body shook wildly, causing him to release after feeling how tight her pussy tensed up around him, and the feeling of her warm juices flowing all over his cock. She then started screaming out his name while they released together.

He rolled onto his back, and placed his hand on his chest, trying to catch his breath. She snuggled up to him, and whispered in his ear. "I hope nobody heard us; I think we were pretty loud this time." she giggled.

He wrapped his arm around her, kissing her forehead. "If anyone heard us, I don't really care. Now if the girls heard us, then we're in trouble." he chuckled.

******

The next day while Antonio was at work, Giovanni took the girls out for ice cream and for a fun day over at the water park. Sadie figured this was the perfect time to have a heart to heart conversation with Giorgia. She grabbed a couple bottles of her favorite wine, and walked over to the guest house.

Giorgia opened the door, after Sadie knocked. Looking surprised to see Sadie at the door, and even more surprised that she knocked. "What brings you here on this fine afternoon?"

"We need to talk, I brought you some wine too." Sadie says smiling, flashing the wine at her. Giorgia opened the door wider for her to walk in.

Giorgia grabbed a glass, and sat down at the table. "I'd love to have some." Sadie opened the wine, and poured her a glass, setting it down on the table, and sliding it over to her.

Sadie could tell Giorgia was becoming nervous, as she kept slamming her glass of wine and pouring herself more. Sadie was sitting at the table, watching her guzzle the wine, waiting for her to say something.

"Are you ready to talk yet? Because I'm not leaving here until we do." Sadie says harshly.

Giorgia crossed her legs and crossed her arms, and leaned back in her chair.

"I want to know what your problem is with me?" Sadie questioned, giving her a serious look.

"My problem? I don't have a problem." she said, nonchalantly.

"Don't give me that, I'm not stupid. I can tell with your attitude towards me, the way you look at me, and the way you watch me, I could go on and on and on. I have not done anything wrong; I have gone above and beyond to make sure that you're happy."

Giorgia looked away from her not saying anything. Sadie out of frustration, slammed her hand down on the table. "Damn it Giorgia, this is not me. I do not like confrontations and I try to avoid them as much as possible, but I'm becoming really hurt and upset right now. One thing about me that you need to know and realize, is that I put everyone first before myself, and I think of everyone else, before I think about myself, unlike you...."

Sadie quickly leaned back in her chair, angrily crossing her arms while staring at Giorgia, waiting for her to say something and to cool off, before she says another thing to her, and one that may be something that she might later regret. "I'm waiting." Sadie snapped.

Giorgia looked back to her and spoke, questioning her. "What attracted you to my son? What made you want to be with him?"

Sadie smiled before speaking. "After Harlow passed away, it took a while for me to realize that I had feelings for Antonio. It even took going out on a date with Ethan, to finally figure it out. When I first met Antonio, I'll admit, I thought that he was an extremely sexy man, he was very handsome and very charming. His strikingly blue eyes and Italian accent drew me the most to him. But he was married, and hired me to help with his kids, as well as to help her out, when he couldn't. He may have been all those that I just mentioned, but I had a job to do, and I kept it at that. After she passed away, he asked me to stay on as his nanny to help him out. For about two months or so, the kids and I *never* saw him. He ignored them, and did everything possible to not come home, or come home so late after everyone was sleeping. The day he was finally home early and to where I could finally talk with him, I got on his case about ignoring his children, talked with him, and knocked some sense into him. The more time we spent together, with his charm, the way he talked to me, and the way he would look at me, is when everything just happened, and couldn't fight it any longer."

"Couldn't fight what?" she asked, pouring herself another glass of wine.

"My feelings for him."

"You knew that he had money, did that help persuade your decision on falling for my son?"

Sadie did not appreciate her asking that, and it instantly pissed her off. She stood up and grabbed the hard-covered book that was sitting on the table, and whacked her across the face with it, causing her to fall to the floor.

Giorgia slowly got up from the floor, holding her hand to her face and sat back on the chair. "OK, I guess I deserved that."

Sadie stood there wanting to cry, she didn't want to hit Antonio's mother, but she was so upset by her comment that the anger inside her, just came out. She sat back in the chair, and looked Giorgia in the eyes with hurt. "Did that answer your question? Because if you didn't understand that, then you're an idiot. And the answer to your question is No... I am not with your son for his money, I could care less about the money. I'm with him because I love him, I love those two girls of his, and I love the two the kids that we will be having together in about four to five months."

Sadie eyed Giorgia while she sat there holding the side of her face she hit, and began feeling guilty, when she saw that her cheek was getting red. "Do you want some ice for that?" she asked feeling bad.

"No, I'm fine." she said quietly.

"Are we clear now? Because I can keep on going. To be honest with you, you're lucky that's all I did, was smack you across the face. I was ready to do more. The last thing I wanted for you to think, was that I'm using Antonio, and for the record, that isn't true."

"I'll be honest with you also, I talked to Giovanni last night, I told him that I was willing to give you a chance, that I was willing to lay off and get to know you." Giorgia says with a half-smile "But, by you coming here gave me the chance to ask you, why you liked my son, and to ask something that I shouldn't have, so I deserved to be hit, and I do apologize for everything." She held her hand out for Sadie, wanting to shake. "Can I call a truce between us, and start over?" she asked, sounding sincere.

Sadie smiled "Are you being serious or is this another trick of yours?"

"I'm being serious, please accept my apology." Sadie looked at her hand that was still being held out, and shook it.

Giorgia stood up, holding her arms out for Sadie, she stood up and walked over to Giorgia, to which she gave Sadie a hug. "I'm glad we got this all straightened out."

"Me too." Sadie replied, sounding and feeling relieved.

Later that evening, Antonio never paid attention to how Sadie and Giorgia were getting along, and was busy talking with his father. Sadie had gone to bed early while Antonio sat in the living room, talking with his parents. He began begging his mom for her to lay off Sadie, wishing for her to give her a chance, and Giorgia started laughing.

"Antonio, did Sadie not tell you that we talked today?"

"No, she didn't." he said, looking surprised.

"We talked this afternoon; everything is straightened out between us. She even knocked some sense into me." she says, winking at him.

Antonio was shocked, and couldn't believe that Sadie was able to do it. He thought about Harlow, and how she tried hard with his mom for years, with nothing working. He looked over at his mom, wondering what she meant about Sadie knocking some sense into her, and noticed a bruise on her face. He smirked, and wondered if Sadie might have hit his mom.

"Quit sitting there looking shocked, just believe it. We made an agreement to start over." she says, standing up, and leaned over to him, giving him a hug, patting his back. "There's something about her that I like… I like her." she said with a smile. She kissed his cheek, and stood up. "I'm going to bed… goodnight."

Chapter 32- Visiting Harlow

Sadie laid in bed watching Antonio sleep, softly sliding her fingers through his hair. He opened his eyes and smiled when he saw Sadie looking at him. "Morning beautiful." he says, in a deep morning voice.

"Morning." she replied quietly, kissing him.

"I have to be in court today, are you going to be able to handle hanging out with my mother today?" he asked, grinning.

"We will be just fine, we had a very nice talk yesterday." she says, rolling on her back smiling, thinking about how she whacked her across the face.

"What are you smiling about?" he asked, propping his head up with his elbow, and chin in the palm of his hand. He looked down at her growing belly, and placed his hand on her stomach, waiting to feel movement.

"I was just thinking of the talk with your mom and how well it went."

"Yea, about that..." he sighed "I noticed that she had a nice welt on her face. What happened there?" he asked, curling his finger under her chin, and turning her to look at him.

"She pissed me off, asking me if I was only with you because of your money. I had enough and got upset... I am sorry about that, she just had me so angry. I also warned you that I wasn't going to take her crap, and with all these hormones that I have going on, I even warned you that I can't help what I would do or say if it had come to that point." she says, taking a deep breath.

"Well whatever you did or said to her, it worked. I talked to her last night and she said that you two had a nice talk, and that you were going to be starting out fresh. Believe it or not, she actually told me that she liked you." he says, sliding her in his arms.

"I stood my ground with her. I told her that I'm not this way, and that she brought me to that point. Must have woke her up when I knocked her to the ground." she giggled.

"I do give you credit, my mother is a very stubborn person... promise me, that you won't ever hit her again, even though I know she may have deserved it." he says, caressing her arm.

"You don't have to worry about that, I won't be doing that again, I got it all out of my system, and I think we're on the same page now."

She rolled over on top of him, giving him a kiss "As much as I want to continue on with this, I should get ready for work." he grinned, rolling her off him, and to her side. He smiled while caressing her cheek. "I'll see you later."

"Try and get home early or as soon as you can, I planned on making Chicken Marsala for dinner." she smiled.

"Excellent." he grinned, kissing her once more before getting out of bed. "I'll do what I can to come home as soon as I can, I can't pass that meal up."

******

Antonio was at the courthouse all morning, during recess he decided to go to lunch by himself, and to think about life, where he is at now, and to what his future holds. He could barely eat, as he was thinking about Harlow. He thought of her and what they would be doing right now, if she were still alive. The more he thought of her, the more Sadie came to his mind. He still believed in his heart, and mind that someone brought him to her. He wasn't sure if it was someone from up above, or if it was Harlow's spirit herself.

Whichever way it was, he was happy that they were united. If it weren't for Sadie, he wasn't sure where he would be today. He felt that he was just as in love now, as he was during the time he was married to Harlow.

After he was done with court, he took a long time driving home. He made a couple stops along the way, and on his last stop, it was a visit to Harlow. He cleaned the headstone off before placing flowers in the holder, and sat down staring at her headstone. Remembering the days and years they spent together.

"Oh Harlow.... There's not a day that goes by that I don't think of you, I thank you every day for what you had given me while you were here, and now I'm thanking you for everything that you have given me since you left. I miss you more than anything, and I know I haven't visited you lately, and I apologize for that, your favorite person is in town, and she has been a real treat, if you know what I mean." he says chuckling, stopping to think for a moment. He laughed again *"You would have loved it if you were here, Sadie left her with a nice welt on her face.... We have found all your letters, videos, and your journal. I want to let you know that I appreciate all of it. You have such a big heart, and what you did for our girls is amazing, it took love and courage for what you did. It was very special, and I can't wait to see what you did for them each year. I really want to thank you for what you wrote to both Sadie and I, it was such a selfless act. What you did there, I don't know of anyone who would have done what you did. For you to have Ethan try and set us up, your letters of your wishes of us to be together, it meant a lot knowing that it came from you, and in your own words. You wanting us to give our girls siblings and for me to marry Sadie. To this day, I just cannot believe that this is what you want. I thank you for everything.*

Sadie has been wonderful and yes, like you said she is a lot like you. I want to let you know that I have fallen very much in love with Sadie, I'm so very much in love with her, and I have you to thank for that. Your wishes have and will all be coming true. I love you Harlow, thank you again for everything."

    Antonio sat there for a moment, and talked some more to her. He then kissed her headstone before standing up and leaving, and walked back over to his car feeling free, while taking a deep breath of the fresh air before getting in the car.

******

    Isabella and Gabriella were in the music room playing songs on the piano that Sadie taught them. While Giorgia and Giovanni were in the room with them watching them play. They were in awe thinking that they played very well, for only being five years old.

    Sadie was in another room, worried about Antonio. He missed dinner that he was excited about having. She looked at the time, and saw that it was nine in the evening, she hadn't heard from him since before he left for work, and wasn't sure what she should do. She kept calling his phone, and it kept going straight to his voicemail.

    She then called Ethan thinking maybe they had gone out drinking, but he hadn't heard from him either. She hung up in a panic and decided to call the hospital thinking the worst. She was on the phone with the hospital when Antonio walked through the door, looking drained.

"Antonio!" Sadie loudly said, dropping her phone, and running over to him, and wrapping her arms around him. "I've been worried sick about you."

"I'm sorry." he whispered, running his fingers through her hair, and kissing the top of her head.

Her arms were still wrapped around him, and rested her head against his chest, happy he was home and that nothing bad happened to him. "I've been calling you for hours, and kept getting your voicemail. I even called Ethan looking for you. I was just on the phone with the hospital thinking something bad happened." she says, sounding upset.

"I must have forgotten to turn my phone back on, after court." He says, pulling his phone out of his pocket to look.

"Where have you been?" she asked, pulling back to look at him. Her heart was still pounding from being scared, and was still trying to calm herself down.

He gave her a tight squeeze, feeling bad that he worried her.

"After work, I did some running around, I stopped at a few places, then stopped to visit Harlow, and was there for a couple hours. I had to talk to her, and apologize that I hadn't been there for a while.... I also went there to thank her."

"Thank her?" Sadie questioned.

"Yes, to thank her about you." he says, kissing her lips "I had to thank her for everything. Everything she had done for the girls, for us, and all the trouble that she went through, trying to get Ethan to set us up."

"I'm just glad you're OK. I wish you would have called and warned me. I was really worried."

"I want you to know that I went there for a reason, and for a good reason." he says smiling.

"Please call me next time, before doing something like that again. Remember I'm pregnant, what if something was wrong with me, and I needed you." she asked, scolding him.

"I know... it'll never happen again." he whispered, assuring her.

She took his hand, and walked him to the kitchen "Well if you're hungry, I saved you some food, and the girls are in the other room playing the piano for your mom and dad."

"Actually, I'm not hungry, but I'll go and watch the girls play for a bit, and I'll put them to bed tonight. I have some things I'd like to talk to them about anyway." he says, kissing her cheek. He left Sadie standing there confused while he walked over to the music room, to watch the girls play.

He walked into the room, and stood in between his parents, watching the girls play the piano. "They play really good." Giovanni says to Antonio.

"Thank Sadie for that. She's the one who taught them to play." he smiled.

The girls finished playing their duet and turned around looking at their grandparents, proud of themselves.

"You can play one more song, then you have to go to bed." Antonio said to them. He looked at his mom and whispered in her ear. He then pulled her to the side, and talked to her for a bit. While listening to Antonio, she looked over at the girls and smiled when she heard them playing another song.

When the girls were done with their song, Antonio hugged his mom, kissing her cheek and waved for the girls to come with him so he could put them to bed. "Come on girls. It's my turn to put you to bed."

Antonio got them into bed, pulled the sheets over them, and smiled. "Can Bella sleep with us tonight?" Gabriella asked, batting her eyes, and holding her hands together, praying.

"Please daddy? She's potty trained now." Isabella says excited.

Antonio smiled, and couldn't help looking at the puppy eyes that they were always giving him, and gave in. They got excited and Isabella quickly got out of bed to let her out of the kennel, picking her up and brought her into the bed with them.

Antonio talked to them for a while, and asked them some questions before he read them a bedtime story. After they fell asleep, he kissed them on their foreheads, whispering good night.

Antonio looked around and found Sadie sleeping on the couch, he felt bad that he had her worried earlier, and picked her up, carrying her bridal style up the stairs. She awoke when he laid her on the bed. "What time is it?"

"It's after ten." he says quietly, while undressing. She took her clothes off, and climbed under the sheets.

"Did you want your night shirt to sleep in?" he asked, grabbing it off the bathroom hook.

"Nah, I feel like sleeping naked tonight." she says, pulling the covers over her.

Feeling excited, Antonio quickly got into bed. He leaned over and rubbed his nose against hers. "You're not still mad at me, are you?" he asked in soft tone, worried that she was still upset.

"No, I'm not mad." she says, cupping his face, and kissing him on the lips.

"Good, because I don't want you mad at me, I saw what you did to my mom, and I can only imagine what you would do to me." he chuckled.

Chapter 33- Birthday surprise

"Momma, there is someone on the phone for you." Isabella says handing her the phone.

"Who is it?" she asked, as she carried the laundry basket down the steps.

Isabella shrugged her shoulders "I don't know, some girl."

Sadie set the basket down, and took the phone from Isabella.

"Hello?" she asked. She then got quiet, her face turned pale and dropped the phone. She stood there stiff, after hearing who was on the other end of the phone.

She slowly sat down on the step, and picked up her phone, making sure the phone was hung up. She held her phone in her hand and leaned against the railing.

"Momma are you OK?"

"I'm fine, if you happen to answer the phone again, and you recognize the voice, just hang up OK?" she tells her in a shaky voice.

"OK." Isabella says, looking confused.

Sadie picked up the laundry basket and continued taking it downstairs. She stood in front of the washing machine still shaking and still upset about the person who just called her. She hadn't heard that voice in twelve years, and never thought that she would ever hear that voice again.

She walked back upstairs to make lunch for the girls, and Giorgia walked into the kitchen noticing that Sadie looked extremely pale.

"Sadie, why don't you go lay down, you look as white as a ghost, are you sure you're feeling alright?" Giorgia asked, looking concerned.

"I'm fine, thanks." she says quietly, grabbing a couple cans of ravioli out of the cupboard.

Giorgia walked up to her taking the cans of ravioli out her hands, and set them down on the counter. "Please... go lay down, I'll make the girls their lunch, you look like you're ready to faint."

"Thanks, you really don't have to do that, I'm fine... really." Sadie says, with a tired look.

"Well, you need all the rest that you can get, and don't forget that Antonio is taking you out for dinner tonight." she says, smiling "By the way, Happy Birthday."

"Thank you, you don't happen to know where he is taking me do you? With this big stomach of mine, I have no clue if I even have anything to wear."

"He never said, he just asked if we could watch the girls tonight, that way he could take you out for your birthday. So how old are you today? Nobody ever told us, how old you even were."

"Twenty-seven." she says, laying her head down on the arm of the couch, covering her eyes with her arm. "Knowing Antonio, I'm guessing that it'll be someplace fancy. You wouldn't mind watching the girls, so I can go shopping, would you?"

Giorgia walked into Antonio's office, and grabbed a package that Antonio had given to her, she wasn't sure when to give it to Sadie, but she figured that now would be a good time. She walked over to Sadie, handing her a box. "Here, Antonio asked me to give this to you." she smiled.

Sadie sat back up, taking the box from Giorgia. "What is this?"

"Just open it, you'll see." Giorgia grinned. She walked back into the kitchen to stir the ravioli, while keeping her eye on Sadie, and wanting to see her reaction after she opened the box.

Sadie opened the box, and pulled out a beautiful knee length mulberry colored laced dress, as well as diamond earrings, and a necklace.

She then noticed a card inside, and opened it. Antonio wrote her a little note inside, and smiled while reading it:

Happy Birthday Gorgeous, be ready by five o'clock. Love you! See you soon... Antonio.

Sadie smiled as she held out the dress, and couldn't wait to try it on. Giorgia set the girls food on the table, and called for the girls to come and eat. She walked over to Sadie, looking at the dress. "He does have good taste." she smiled "Go ahead dear, go take your time and get ready, this is your day."

"Maybe I might go soak in the tub, it might be what I need."

Sadie went upstairs and took bubble bath, she closed her eyes and relaxed, while lying in the tub for a while, the voice she heard earlier came back to her, thinking back to the day that she wanted to forget. She knew she wasn't supposed to get herself all stressed out, and talked herself into calming down.

The water finally got cold, and decided to exit the tub, she tried on the dress, and was thrilled that it fit perfectly. It also made her look and feel like a sexy pregnant woman.

She put on her makeup, giving herself the smoky eyed look, that brought out her blue colored eyes, added blush to the cheeks and put on a dark shade of lipstick. She finished her look, by adding some bouncy curls to the ends of her hair.

She walked downstairs to show off the dress he bought her, wondering what Giorgia thought of it. Her mouth dropped when Sadie walked up to her, posing. "How does it look?" Sadie nervously asked, unsure if she really wanted Giorgia's opinion.

"I love it, and I know Antonio will like it on you too." Giorgia says, placing her hand on her stomach. "It shows off your beautiful growing belly." she smiled. Her eyes then widened, and giggled. "Ooof! I felt them kick." Giorgia said excitedly.

Sadie laughed "They're so active, they kept me up all night last night."

"They will do that!"

Antonio walked in the door, excited about the night that he had planned. He noticed Sadie in the dress, and smiled as he walked up to her, giving her big passionate kiss. "Happy Birthday, my love." he mumbled into her mouth.

She pulled back and giggled when she saw lipstick left on Antonio's lips. "Thank you." she smiled, wiping the lipstick off his lips.

"For you." he says, handing her a big bouquet of flowers.

"Awe, thank you... they're beautiful." She felt like she was getting the royal treatment, and it was only her birthday. Something that she hadn't been big on in years.

"I'm going to clean up quick, our ride should be here shortly."

Sadie noticed that the girls were acting strange and goofy, and kept hanging on her, begging to come with. "Oh, I don't know. This is something that your dad planned, that would be up to him." she tells them.

"Not tonight girls." Antonio said to them, when he overheard them talking while he walked down the stairs.

"Ok." they both said bummed.

Antonio and Sadie left for their dinner date, on the way to their destination Antonio couldn't stop looking at Sadie, his smile was different, and it was making her heart melt. Her stomach felt like it was full of butterflies, and kept tickling her insides. "What's with your smile?" Sadie asked.

"Let's just say that I'm the happiest man on earth right now." he says in a deep low voice, as he curled his finger under her chin.

"Why is that?"

"Because I have a hot date tonight with the hottest woman alive, and she's pregnant with my children." he says, leaning forward to kiss her. "We have a lot of time before our reservation, what do you say I start off with the appetizer first?" he says, grinning.

"Appetizer?"

He groaned, and quickly laid her down, making her giggle. She looked over to see if the driver could see them and noticed that he was blocked by a wall, and couldn't see what they were up to. She turned back to Antonio, and pressed her lips to his.

Their lips were moving in perfect sync and with urgency. His hand slid up her dress, and let out an excited groan when he felt that she was wearing no panties. "I love when you do that." he groaned softly. He grabbed the remote and turned on music, wanting to muffle the sounds that were about to happen between the two of them.

He softly started kissing the side of her face, and slowly kissed down to her neck, sucking on the soft spot by her ear, and making her nipples hard as a rock. He felt her nipples harden against him, and unzipped the back of her dress, sliding the top down to suck and nibble on her nipples.

He moved down and slid up the bottom of her dress, placing his mouth over her pussy. Her back arched, and a moan escaped her mouth, when she felt him softly licking her clit. He began thrusting his tongue deeply inside her, causing her to arch her back again, and moaning even louder. Her moan was loud, and felt embarrassed that the driver could hear her, and tightly covered her mouth.

He licked two of his fingers, and thrusted them inside her as he circled her clit with his tongue. While reaching her peak, her body started to jerk and shake, and continued to pleasure her until her orgasm hit. Taking his fingers out, he thrusted his tongue back inside to taste the sweet juices, that she was releasing, her breathing hitched and began yelling out his name "Antonio!"

"Ti amo tanto." he said to her in a sexy voice.

Her head lifted, and looked at him confused "What did you even say?"

"I said, I love you so much." he smiled.

She giggled and smiled. "That was extremely sexy, and I love you too."

He pulled her dress down after satisfying her and sat back up, helping her up. "Now I need to clean up, I'm a little wet down there." she said softly.

He looked around the back of the limo and found a towel, he wiped his face and then handed it to her. "Our appetizer was served, how was it?" he happily asked.

"It was wonderful." she blushed. "Why are you blushing?" he laughed, caressing her cheek.

"I just hope he didn't hear me; I was pretty loud." she says, turning her head away from him.

"He can't hear us with the wall up, plus the music was on." They pulled up to the restaurant, and helped her out of the car. Before they walked into the restaurant, he pulled her in for a kiss.

"Hungry?" he asked her.

"Hungry for what?" she joked, with a smile.

"Wait for later, I've got a great night planned for you." he groaned. He placed his hand on the small of her back, and walked her inside.

Sadie's eyes got wide as she looked around when they walked inside. "WOW, this place is beautiful." she said, surprised.

She was admiring the chandelier in the center of the building, and loved how you could see the lights of the city from wherever you sat. The building had a very romantic ambiance, with candles on the center of the tables, along with music softly playing in the background.

The hostess walked them to their table, sitting them next to the window. "You didn't have to bring me somewhere this fancy." she whispered to him.

"Yes I did." he smiled, while looking at his menu.

She felt like a princess at the moment, she never had anyone take her out to anyplace that was so fancy, never had anyone treat her the way he does, and never felt the love from anyone that he has shown her. She looked over the menu, and couldn't decide on what she wanted.

"What are you having?" he asked.

"I don't know, I can't decide."

"Order whatever you want, it's your birthday, and I want this night to be a memorable one."

The waitress came back after a little bit to take their order, and looked at Sadie. "What can I get for you?"

"I'll have the filet mignon, medium rare with bearnaise sauce, and asparagus, no starch." she tells her.

"And I'll have the prime rib, rare with the roasted vegetables, and baked potato with sour cream." he says, handing her the menus.

When the waitress left, Antonio reached across the table grabbing a hold of her hands, and smiled. They talked while waiting for their food, and he couldn't help but stare at her. His heart kept fluttering, and the feelings that she made him on the inside, were strong. Had they been alone, he would've taken her right there on the table, and make her feel like she was in another world.

"You look absolutely gorgeous tonight, and I mean gorgeous."

"Thank you, you don't look so bad yourself." she said happily, with a grin. "And thank you for the dress, diamond earrings, and the necklace. That was too much just for my birthday, but I do appreciate it."

"Anytime, and I'll continue to buy you things, I like seeing you happy..."

"Please, you don't have to do that. I'm already happy, you make me happy, and just being with you makes me happy." she smiled.

He smiled. "I'm glad to hear that. You make me happy as well, and I love you so much, that at times it feels like my heart is going to burst from my chest, just from it growing so big... You know a week ago, when I went to visit Harlow?"

"Yes, what about that?" She nodded her head, curious as to what he had to say about that night. It still bothered her that he never called to let her know where he was, and had her worried for hours.

"I've been thinking about that night all week. It was wrong of me to not call you and let you know where I was, but I do want you to know that it was for a good reason, and I hope you'll forgive me for that. When I was talking to Harlow, I told her that I was very much in love with you, and I thanked her for her blessing to be with you. I pretty much poured my heart out to her, about you..."

The servers interrupted Antonio, wanting to place their plates on the table. He pulled his hands back allowing them to place their food in front of them. "Looks and smells great." Antonio said wide eyed, while looking at his plate.

Sadie kept looking at Antonio while they were eating, she felt that he was acting a little nervous, and could feel his hands trembling while he was holding her hands. She was trying to figure out what he was up to until he caught her looking at him. "How's your food?" he asked.

"It's really good, you got quiet there for a bit, and you seem a little nervous, what's on your mind?" she asked.

He looked around and wiped his mouth with the napkin. "Well... there is something on my mind, I was going to wait to talk about it, until after dinner but-..."

"Hello Sadie, it's been a very long time, hasn't it?" A woman standing next to Sadie says, interrupting Antonio.

"Dannazione, stavo per chiederti di sposarmi." Antonio blurted out frustrated.

Sadie's fork dropped out of her hand when she heard the voice next to her, she turned her head and looked, hoping that it wasn't who she thought it was.

As Sadie turned her head and looked at the woman standing next to her, her face turned pale and passed out, causing Antonio to rush to her side...

Worried about Sadie, Antonio yelled out for help and turned to look at the woman. "Who the hell are you?"

(Dannazione, stavo per chiederti di sposarmi= "Damn, I was going to ask you to marry me.")

Chapter 34- Mystery Woman

Antonio yelled for help, while he held Sadie in his arms. He looked at the lady who made her faint, thinking she looked a lot like an older Sadie. "Who the hell are you?" he asked frantically.

The woman bent down, feeling Sadie's forehead with the back of her hand, and kissed her cheek. "Oh God Sadie I have missed you, please wake up."

"I'm sorry who are you?" Antonio asked, giving her a strange look, wondering who the hell she was.

"My name is Grace, Sadie's mother." she says, while looking at Sadie, with a worried look on her face.

"Everyone please give her some space." Antonio hears a voice saying nearby, he looked up and saw a man walking towards them. "I'm a doctor, I can help her out." he says, as he laid her down on her back, checking her pulse and trying to wake her up. Sadie slowly opened her eyes, looking scared when she saw a guy kneeling over her.

"Will someone please get her some orange juice?" the doctor asked out loud. A waiter left to grab her juice, and came back handing the glass of juice to Antonio.

Sadie looked over at her mom, and then over to Antonio trying to sit up. "What happened?" she asked quietly, feeling embarrassed that a bunch of eyes were on her.

"You fainted, how are you feeling?" Antonio asked, looking worried as he handed her the glass of juice.

"I'm fine."

"You should really go in and get checked out, and to make sure that the babies are OK." the doctor said to Sadie.

"No really, I'm fine." Sadie insisted, looking at him strange, wondering how he knew she's carrying more than one baby.

Sadie looked back over at her mom staring at her, studying her, not saying a word. She felt like she was looking at a ghost.

"Do you know this woman?" Antonio asked her, raising an eyebrow while pointing at Grace.

"I thought I did." she says quietly, looking away from her mom.

Antonio helped her up, and helped set her back on the chair.

"So, you don't know her?"

"No... well actually yes, kind of... I used to know her. I used to call her mom, but I don't know her anymore." she stuttered, looking away and out the window.

Antonio looked over at Grace "I'm sorry, but you have upset Sadie, I would like for you to please leave her alone." he says to her, sounding upset.

"I really need to explain myself; I have been looking for her, for a long time now." she begged, looking desperately at Sadie.

"Look... mom, Grace, whoever you are, I was enjoying my night, and you just ruined it by showing up here."

Grace looked at her sadly "Please... I know it's your birthday, but I want you to please hear me out."

Antonio stood behind Sadie, resting his hands on her shoulders "I think that you should really leave, I don't like seeing her upset, and this wasn't the night to upset her."

Grace looked at Sadie sadly, she opened her mouth about to say something, but quickly shut her mouth and turned around leaving, without saying a word. She felt she was going to cry, and couldn't do it in front of everyone inside the restaurant.

Sadie sat quietly as Antonio went and sat back in his chair. "I can't believe she just showed up here.... how in the world did she even find me? I thought she's been dead this whole time." Sadie said quietly, still in shock.

Antonio listened to her talk, feeling bad for what just happened, and feeling bad that he didn't get to say what he had wanted to say to her, before they were interrupted.

"I suppose you're ready to leave?"

Sadie looked down at her plate and back up at Antonio "No, we can stay. I'm not ready to leave just yet, I still have asparagus to eat." she smiled, letting out a little giggle as she finished her last few bites.

"Maybe it's not the right time to talk about it, but that woman back there claiming to be your mom, do you want to tell me about it?"

Sadie nodded her head, taking a deep breath and exhaling slowly. "Well.... twelve years ago, on my birthday, which I turned fifteen, she had taken me on a trip to Las Vegas. One night, I woke up and didn't see her, I figured that she left to go gambling, so I went back to bed. The next morning when I woke up, she was still gone. I sat in the room for hours waiting for her to return, and she never did. I started wandering around the hotel, casinos, and the strip for a while, trying to find her. She left me with no note, no money, nothing. I didn't know what happened to her. At the time, we lived in Washington, and I ended up being stuck in Vegas for days. I was finally able to get a hold of my grandma, and she ended up flying to Vegas to come and get me. I never heard from her again until today."

"Where's your dad?"

She shrugged her shoulders "I have no clue; I've never met him in my life. She never talked about him, and he's not even on my birth certificate."

"Wouldn't you like to know what happened to her? She did have a worried look on her face when you fainted."

"No....not really." she said hesitantly "I thought she was dead, she's dead to me now."

Antonio looked around, waving for the waiter to come over "Can I get the bill please?"

Antonio paid the bill, he felt upset, wondering how Sadie's mom found her, and at the place they were at, out of all places. Antonio was quiet as they left the restaurant, when they walked out the door, Sadie's mom was standing outside leaning against the wall in tears.

"Please leave me alone." Sadie says, as they walked towards their limo.

"Sadie Marie Hart...please." Grace begged loudly. Sadie stopped walking, rolled her eyes and turned around to look at her.

"You have five minutes, we have plans, and we're late." Sadie barked.

"I didn't abandon you; I left that night to get you a birthday gift. I was then taken, drugged, abused and was forced to make money for them. I escaped about a year ago and have been looking for you ever since."

Antonio kept his arm around Sadie holding her tightly against him, listening to what Grace had to say.

"How did you even find me?"

"I posted a picture holding a sign with your name on it saying that I was looking for my long-lost daughter with your full name on the sign. Some friends of mine shared it online, and I was contacted saying that you were here in Montana, I was given your phone number and the address to where you live. I knew it was your birthday, and wanted to see you. Tonight, I went to your house and was told where I would be able to find you."

Sadie looked down at the ground, not sure if she wanted to believe what she was hearing. She had no clue if she was telling the truth or not, being that it had been years since she saw her last, she felt she didn't know her anymore.

"You may not believe me, but if you give me a chance, I can show you all my scars. I know you must get going, please, call me tomorrow I can tell you more. I want you to know that I've missed you so much, and I never stopped thinking of you." Grace tells her giving her a hug. She handed Sadie a piece of paper with her phone number "Happy Birthday, Sadie."

Sadie turned around and walked quietly to the limo, when they get in Sadie pulled Antonio in for a kiss, a desperate, hungry kiss "Thank you, I really needed that." she says, pulling her lips away from his.

"I don't know her... obviously... but I'm pretty sure that she was telling you the truth."

"Why do you say that?"

"It's my daily job remember?" he says, pushing her hair back behind her. She gave him a look that she didn't understand what he was trying to say "I'm an attorney remember? I have to be able to tell if they are telling the truth or not."

"I'll worry about that tomorrow, right now I want to enjoy the rest of the evening."

Antonio sat and looked at her, debating on what to do, he put his hand in his pocket and thought for a moment. He then pulled a box out, hiding it in his one hand and grabbed her other hand bringing her hand up to his mouth, kissing the top of her hand.

"Sadie, I know this isn't the most romantic place to say this to you and it wasn't my plan to say it in here, but I just can't wait any longer. Since you came into our lives, I knew that there was something about you, something very special. I have fallen deeply and madly in love with you, I think about you daily and nightly. You're just always on my mind, it drives me nuts sometimes because I can't get you out of my head. You're so beautiful, and you have such a beautiful heart, mind and soul, everything about you is just so wonderful, and I couldn't imagine my life without you. You took in my kids as if they were your own, and now together we have two more on the way. I want nothing more than for you to be my wife, and I want to spend the rest of my life with you. So, my question for you is..." he says taking the box out of his other hand and opened it for her "Will you marry me?" he asked.

He flashed her a beautiful big princess cut diamond, with numerous diamonds on each side of the platinum band. And he couldn't stop smiling as he held the box, showing her the ring.

Her heart was pounding hard while he talked to her, now she knew why he was acting so nervous. She had a feeling that he was getting ready to propose by the words he was speaking, and after he asked her to marry him, she pulled him in for a kiss, and wouldn't stop. She pulled away and smiled "Yes!" she excitedly said "Yes, I'll marry you!" He took the ring out of the box, and slid it on her finger, attacking her mouth with his.

They arrived home and walked in the door, they both were surprised when they saw a sign taped to the stairway: *House is empty, the girls wanted to stay with us in the guest house.*

Antonio grinned and picked her up, carrying her up the stairs. When they got in the bedroom Antonio set her down in the bed. She stood up and pushed him down on the bed, and climbed on top of him, straddling him.

"Oh no. This is your night; you're getting all the satisfaction tonight from me." he insisted in a low voice. He sat up and unzipped the back of her dress and took the sash off. He then rolled her to her back, and pulled the rest of her dress off.

He stood up and quickly took off his clothes, throwing them across the room "Now I'm ready for dessert." he grinned, while spreading her legs, and placing kisses along her inner thighs, working his way over to her clit. Flicking his tongue and circling the clit before thrusting his tongue inside her until he had her squirming and moaning.

The more wet she became, the more he groaned. She grabbed a pillow, and covered her face while screaming out his name, having a very intense orgasm.

He grabbed her legs and rested them over his shoulders, then thrusted his cock in her slow and deep. He let out a loud groan when he felt how tight, warm, and wet, she was. Her moans were still being muffled by the pillow, he thrusted harder, and deeper, and with his moaning getting louder. Loving the tightness that was wrapped around him. She threw the pillow and lowered her legs, pulling him down on her so she could kiss him. Their kiss was passionate at first, then turned into a demanding deep kiss, as their tongues both fought for dominance.

She pulled back to breathe, and took in some deep breaths when she felt that she had no air left in her lungs, he rested his head in the crook of her neck while thrusting a couple more times, both moaning out loudly while releasing together. He rolled off her and to the side of her, not wanting to lay over Sadie's growing stomach. He laid on his back with a smile, thinking about how he finally proposed to her. It wasn't the way he wanted to do it, but was still happy that he got to ask her, and that her answer was yes.

They both laid onto their sides facing each other, both full of smiles. He began caressing the side of her face, while he stared at her, and studied the beautiful woman lying in front of him. He slid some loose strands of her hair that was covering her face, behind her ear and leaned forward, giving her a nice loving kiss.

"I can't wait to make you my wife." he whispered.

Chapter 35- Explanation

Antonio got out of bed early, he couldn't stop thinking about Sadie's mother, and wondering if she had been telling the truth. He walked down into his office, shut the door and walked over to his desk turning his laptop on. He sat down and logged into his work site. Once logged in, he began doing a nationwide search on Grace. After searching for a while, he leaned back in his chair, staring at his laptop. He couldn't find anything on her, not even a traffic ticket.

He picked up his phone and called one of his investigators, asking to investigate Grace and to see where her whereabouts have been the last twelve years. He then began searching into Las Vegas police reports within the last couple of years, looking for any complaints on any hostage situations.

He came across a couple, there were reports filed a year ago, but the names didn't match. He leaned back in his chair again, and rested his hands behind his head thinking. He remembered hearing Grace mentioning to Sadie that she put out information about her, that she was looking for her and that a friend of hers posted it online.

He also remembered Grace telling Sadie that someone called her to let her know where she could find Sadie, and wondered who that would have been. The only one that came to mind, was his own mother.

Upon waking up, Sadie reached her arm out, and realized Antonio was not in bed. She got out of bed, put on her robe, and walked through the house looking for Antonio. She saw that his office door was closed and knocked. "Come in." Antonio called out.

Sadie walked in smiling "What are you doing up so early?" she asked, walking around the desk and sitting on his lap.

He wrapped his arm around her, and looked back towards his laptop "I'm working."

She rested her head on his shoulder, and began caressing his chest. "Working on what?"

He pointed over to the screen, showing her that he's been trying to find information on her mother. "Antonio, you don't have to do that. She abandoned me in a town, and in a state where we didn't even live." she said hurt.

"What if she was telling the truth?"

"Why would she have gone out so late to look for a birthday gift for me? She could have done that earlier in the day or the next day."

"True, but maybe she was trying to find something special."

"I doubt it. She never really bought me much growing up. All she did was provide a roof over my head. I was surprised that she even brought me to Vegas, I wasn't even of legal age to gamble."

"How long were you there before she disappeared?"

"We had just got there that day, we ate dinner at one of the hotels, I watched her play the slots for a bit, and then we went up to our room. Then she asked me what I would like to do for my birthday, asking if I would like to go see one of the shows, and telling me that I would enjoy seeing some of them."

"Hmm. Seems weird don't you think?" he asked, thinking there has to be more to her mom's story.

"I don't know." she sighed.

"I did call my investigator to have him look into her claims. Hopefully he finds something today, I asked him to get on it, and that I would pay him triple the amount if he got it to me around noon."

Antonio took her hand, and looked at the ring on her finger, sliding the ring back and forth. "On another note, that ring looks good on you." he smiled. Sadie extended her arm out, looking at the ring on her finger, smiling. She turned and faced Antonio, cupped his face and gave him a kiss. "I love it."

"If I were to call her, and ask for her to meet me somewhere, would you come with me?" she asked quietly. She couldn't believe she was willing to meet her, but was more than curious to see what she has to say.

"Of course I would go with you, I wouldn't let you do this alone. I do think you should hear her out, in case she is telling you the truth."

Sadie gave him a hug "Fine... I'll go call her." she said nervously, as she stood up.

Antonio heard the girls run into the house and his mother calling out for them to be quiet, thinking that he and Sadie were still in bed. He walked out of the office, and asked his mother if he could have a word with her.

She followed him into his office, and clapped her hands, excited to hear if Sadie said yes. "So how did it go?" she asked, grinning while sitting down in the chair. Antonio sat on his desk in front of her, and looked down at her with an unhappy look to his face. Her look went from a smile into a frown, when she saw his expression. "It didn't go the way you wanted it?" she asked worried.

"Put it this way, it could have been better."

"Oh Antonio, I'm sorry. I really thought that she would say yes." she said sadly.

"That's not what I'm getting at, everything was going great and to plan, until we had a *very* unexpected visitor, causing Sadie to get upset and to faint. "He says pinching the bridge of his nose "You wouldn't happen to know who that person was, do you?"

She lookup up at him and slowly shook her head no, she changed her expression when she saw the look on his face, and his one eyebrow raised. She knew he thought it was her, and figured she better fess up.

"OK, she stopped here looking for Sadie, wanting to wish her a Happy Birthday, I told her where she could find her. She seemed nice, and was desperate to see her." Giorgia says to him.

"Is that the only contact that you had with her?" Antonio questioned, having a feeling that it was her that let her know how to find Sadie in the first place.

Giorgia's head lowered, and sighed. "No."

"Explain." he demanded, not sounding happy.

"It started out when I was on one of the social media networks one day, and noticed some friends sharing a picture of a woman who was looking for her long-lost daughter. In the past, I had always shared those posts, and after I shared it, I noticed something familiar with the girl on the picture and stretched the picture out to look closer. The girl I saw in the picture was very young, with very long dark hair, blue eyes and resembled Sadie. When I looked at the sign the woman was holding, the name she was looking for said Sadie Marie Hart, and my heart instantly dropped. I called the number that was on the post and said that I think I may know the person who she was looking for. We talked a couple times on the phone, and then I gave her Sadie's phone number."

"You didn't stop to think that there maybe was a reason why Sadie never brought her mom's name up, *ever*?" Antonio asked quietly, and looked away from her, breathing in deep through his nose.

"No, I guess I never thought about it, I thought I was doing a good thing for her. I see those posts all the time, people looking for their birth mothers, fathers, siblings, etcetera, and thought that maybe she was a runaway, or that she had given her up for adaption."

Antonio looked back over at her, crossing his arms. "Sadie claims she thought that she was dead, that Grace abandoned her in Las Vegas when she was fifteen years old." Antonio sighed.

"Her story seemed so real. I'm sorry." Giorgia said, feeling bad.

"Well I hired my private investigator to investigate her claims as to why she disappeared out of Sadie's life. I don't need her prowling around here if there is something else going on, I have kids to look out for and I don't need Sadie upset and stressed out, hurting our unborn children."

Giorgia sat quietly listening to Antonio, feeling guilty. "I honestly thought that I was doing a good thing, especially after our other mishap." she said quietly.

"Sadie is pretty upset, however, she did decide to call her. If Grace agrees to it, our plan is to meet her somewhere. It would be nice if you could watch the girls for us again, and *please* do not do anything like this ever again, without consulting us first."

"That's no problem, we can watch them." she says standing up. She touched his hand, and gave him a sad look. "I want you to know, that I truly am sorry. I honestly thought that I was helping. Please forgive me."

"I forgive you, I'm not so sure about Sadie. That you'll have to talk to her about, with what you did. I just wish you would have told me, and talked with me about it, before getting a surprise like that myself."

It was noon, and Antonio still hadn't heard from his investigator. They were sitting at the restaurant where Sadie used to work, waiting for her mother to show up. They were about to order their food when Grace finally sat down. "Sorry I'm late, I had a little trouble finding the place." she said nervously, pulling her hair back into a ponytail.

She looked at Sadie, and nervously smiled at her. "Gosh, you haven't changed and still look so beautiful, you also look absolutely beautiful pregnant." she said in awe, while looking at Sadie's stomach.

After ordering their food, their table was suddenly quiet. Antonio sat there waiting for either Sadie or Grace to start a conversation, and looked back and forth from Grace then to Sadie. Sadie was watching a family where their kids were laughing, and smiling at their parents. He looked back over to Grace, and figured he better be the one to start talking.

"So, I guess you need to explain yourself to Sadie, she deserves to know the honest truth. All I ask, is that you do tell her the truth."

Grace sat up straight, and looked at Sadie. Hoping she will believe what she has to say to her. She closed her eyes, and breathed in deep, thinking back to that very night. "The night I disappeared, Sadie fell asleep, and figured since her birthday was the next day, I would go out and look for something nice for her. I wanted to surprise her with a nice gift, since I hadn't gotten anything for her yet. Earlier that day, I noticed a store nearby that was open twenty-four hours that sold gifts. Since Sadie was asleep, I went down to the casino and played some slots, trying to see if I could win some extra money to buy her something even more special. I won a thousand dollars, and was ecstatic about it knowing I could buy her something special with that money. I quickly left the casino and started walking over to the store. I had no idea that I was being followed, until I was grabbed from behind, and thrown into a van. I was then blindfolded, gagged and tied up.

We drove for what I felt was for hours, but was only driven to the edge of town. I was beaten, raped, and drugged by a bunch of men. They turned me into doing prostitution, and forced drugs on me. They also kept a close eye on me the entire time they had me making money for them. I was never out of their sight with them for all those years. They made a huge mistake the night I escaped, they had to leave after receiving a phone call about another one of their prostitutes taking off with the money, she had made for them that night. After they left, I jumped out of the window, and broke my leg and arm. A passerby saw me fall, and brought me over to the hospital. The staff at the hospital began asking me questions, and then called the police. I was then placed in a witness protection home, and that's where I had help trying to locate you. I tried calling my mother to see if she had known where your whereabouts would be, and found out that she had passed away. Everyone that we called, nobody had seen or heard from you in ages."

Antonio's phone rang and stood up when he saw that it was the investigator calling. "Excuse me for a second while I go take this." he says, leaning down to Sadie's ear.

Sadie sat still with tears in her eyes, staring at her cup of soup. She didn't know what to say, and was shocked to hear what happened to her. She took her spoon, and stirred the soup, thinking of what to say.

"Sorry about that." Antonio says, sitting back down.

"I'm telling you both the truth. I can show you all the scars on my back, my legs, and here… look at my arms." she says, sliding up her sleeves, showing the scars on her arms.

Sadie gasped loudly when she saw the scars, and tears started rolling down her cheeks. She grabbed a napkin to wipe the tears away, and pushed the soup away from her, unable to eat as she felt sick to her stomach after seeing the scars. Antonio started rubbing her back, letting her know that he was there for her, she lowered her head onto his shoulder, trying to hold back the tears, unsure if she wanted to hear anymore.

"I thought maybe your father found you, and took you in." she said quietly.

"I still have no idea who he is." Sadie whispered.

"The last time I saw, or heard from him was the day I told him that I was pregnant with you."

Antonio kissed the top of Sadie's head, and spoke quietly to her. "I know this is a lot to take in, but you should really try and eat something. Those babies need to eat too."

Sadie sat up and pulled her soup closer to her. "Grandma passed away three years ago." Sadie said quietly, taking a sip of her soup. "When she was sick, she kept saying that she hoped to see you again before she passed away."

Grace reached her hand across the table, and placed her hand on top of Sadie's "I never asked for this, please find it in your heart to forgive me. Every day I thought about you, and hoped that you were alright. I cried every night, begging for them to let me go so I could be with you."

A gentleman in a nice suit walked up to the table, and stood next to Antonio holding paperwork in his hand. Antonio looked up at him and grinned.

"Nadia Barker?" the man asked. Grace's eyes suddenly widened, and quickly looked over at the man standing next to Antonio.

Chapter 36- Truth will set you free

Grace looked up at the man, surprised that he just called her Nadia. "Excuse me?" she asked, scared.

The man took his eyes away from Grace, and looked at Antonio.

"Antonio, I have the paperwork you requested right here, may I sit down?"

Antonio stood up extending his arm out to the open seat next to Grace "Please sit down." Grace looked at the man worried as he sat down next to her, wondering who he was, why he was there, and how he knew to call her Nadia.

Sadie looked at Antonio with a confused look, and looked over at her mom studying her reaction, then looked at the man that sat down next to Grace "Who are you?" asked Sadie.

"My name is David, Antonio's investigator. He asked me to check into your mother's claims." He looked at Grace, giving her an apologetic look. "I'm very sorry, I didn't mean to scare you by calling you Nadia, I wanted to see if it was in fact you." He handed Antonio the paperwork he requested, and looked at Sadie.

"Your mother's claims check out, whatever she told you is the truth, Nadia is her hidden identity name that the witness protection program gave her."

Grace looked at Antonio in shock. "You had me investigated?"

"Yes... I wanted to make sure you were not here to cause any problems with Sadie, and I wanted to make sure that your claims were the truth. After all these years she didn't need someone coming into her life, causing any more pain." He looked at Sadie "When I found a couple reports that were filed a year ago, the names didn't match, Nadia Baker was listed as one of the names."

"The men who had kidnapped Grace, holding her for years have been arrested, they have been sitting in the Clark County Detention Center awaiting to be transported to prison."

Grace started feeling relieved, and looked at Sadie. "I wasn't lying, I'm really sorry that this happened, and for years I regretted my decision to leave the room that night."

"I'm sorry that I doubted you, but you have to understand my point of view." Sadie says, wiping away tears from her eyes.

"I understand."

Antonio looked at David, and smiled. "Thank you, you did good." He then looked at Sadie, and leaned into her ear, whispering. "Sure." she whispered back.

Antonio sat up straight, while tapping his fingers on the table, thinking. He was curious to know more about her, and felt that Sadie and Grace could use some alone time, and to sort things out between them.

"Well... you're welcome to come to our home, and talk more if you would like." Antonio says to Grace.

Grace smiled, she was happy to finally have found Sadie, and wanted nothing more than to catch up on what she missed. "I would love to. It would be nice to catch up on all the years that I have missed with her." She looked at Sadie smiling, with tears forming in her eyes. She couldn't believe this day finally came, and wanted nothing more than to hold her in her arms, and to never let go.

On the way home Sadie was quiet, and looked out the window the entire time. Antonio knew she was hurting, and rested his hand on her thigh "Are you OK?"

She turned her head towards him, partially smiling. "I'll be fine, I was just remembering that night, that's all. I was at that hotel for about a week until my grandma came and got me. The whole time I was there, I pretty much sat in that room waiting for my mom to return, and hoping that she would, it was the worst feeling in the world. All these years, I seriously thought that she was dead. When Isabella handed me the phone yesterday, and I heard her voice on the other end, I dropped the phone thinking that someone was playing a cruel trick on me."

"She called yesterday? You never said anything." he said surprised, whishing she would have mentioned to him that she called.

"She did, I thought it was a mean joke that someone was playing on me, and then to see her show up at the restaurant...."

Antonio rubbed her thigh, and gave her a genuine smile. "Well now you know the truth, and perfect timing at that. Just before you give birth to our children, and before we get married."

When they got home, Antonio took the girls out to the pool and left Sadie with her mother inside to talk. Grace showed Sadie all her scars, with her back being the worst, showing her the welts of where they whacked her with a rope and belt, and the cuts that never healed.

Sadie gasped again, as Grace showed her where she had surgery on her leg, to fix the broken bones that were damaged, and showing her the scars from the screws, pins, and plates they had to put in her leg.

"Wow mom, I'm so sorry this happened to you."

"Don't be sorry, if anything, I should be the one apologizing. I never should have left that night." she says as Sadie hugged her.

Giorgia sat down next to Antonio, and talked with him while the kids were in the pool. She was still feeling bad for what she done. Antonio kept his eyes on the kids while she was talking to him, and sighed. "Mom, don't worry about it anymore. Sadie is in the house working things out with her mother, her story came out to be the truth. So, all in all for what you did, was a good thing. I just wish that you would have at least said something to me."

"I know, and I'm sorry. I just really wanted it to be a surprise." Giorgia sighed.

"It was a surprise alright." Antonio grinned, while looking at her.

Later that night Grace was still at their home, catching up with Sadie, Antonio walked into the room and curiously looked at Grace. "So where are you staying?"

"I'm staying at the Cattle Inn, which actually isn't too far from here."

"I'm very familiar with that place. But I was thinking that we do have a room downstairs, and if you would like, you can stay here." Sadie looked at Antonio shocked, then looked at her mother, surprised Antonio offered for her to stay there.

Grace looked surprised herself, and was at a loss for words, unsure of what to do. She did like the fact that she would be here, and that she would be able to spend more time with Sadie. "Mom, it's quite alright if you would like to stay here. That was my room for well over a year, it's nice and you will have your own bathroom with a shower."

"If your absolutely sure that it's OK, then I would love to." she smiled. Antonio took Grace back to the hotel, and helped grab her belongings. While she was packing her bags, Antonio left the room to check out, and to pay for her bill.

"Thank you for paying my bill, you didn't have to do that." she said, while Antonio placed her bags in his vehicle.

"It's my pleasure. I'm just happy that Sadie has her mother back in her life. Sadie is a wonderful person; she has a big heart and holds a special place in mine. That woman deserves the best for all that she has gone through, and what she has done for me... she's very special."

Antonio began driving back home, and Grace got quiet for a bit, she was feeling overwhelmed with everything. She then looked over at Antonio, and smiled. "From what Sadie told me, and from what I've seen so far, you're a great person Antonio, thank you for finding her... I would also like to say, that I'm sorry to hear about what happened to your wife, I couldn't imagine the pain she went through, as well as your pain of seeing her go through what she had to deal with. I do however know what it feels like to never see someone you care so much for, ever again. I never thought I would ever see the day of being back into Sadie's life... Since she was a child, she always had a heart of gold, and she would always light up the room with her presence. I want you to know that your kids are in very good hands with her."

"Thank you, and I know what you mean about Sadie, she has shown me that life will go on no matter what happens, or what has happened." He looked over at her with a grin "I should be the one thanking you, for bringing her into this world..." he says looking back at the road.

Antonio paused for a moment, keeping his eyes on the road while he drove, thinking, and glanced back over at Grace. "Can I ask you something?"

"Sure, what is it?"

"Who is Sadie's father?"

Grace inhaled deeply through her nose, and closed her eyes, while leaning her head back against the seat. "He's a man that I met after graduating from high school. He was quite older than me, and someone who promised me the world, until I told him that I was pregnant. It was then that I found out he was married with kids, and that he wasn't planning on leaving his wife. He offered me money to have an abortion, and that was out of the question for me. Being that I'm against abortions, we got into a huge argument, and that was the last time I ever saw, or heard from him." she says, then sighed "His name was Scott Kline."

Antonio listened while Grace spoke, making sure to remember his name, and repeating his name over and over in his head, so he wouldn't forget. He wanted to know more about him, and wondered if Sadie might like to know who he is.

Sadie got her mom all situated in the room she once had, and talked some more with her. Now that Grace was back into her life, she didn't want to leave her alone, scared that she would leave again. They sat on the bed and Grace held onto her tight, apologizing to Sadie for what she went through all the years without her, and still apologized for leaving her that night.

"I'm glad that you found me, and now that the truth is out, I'm sorry for what happened to you. I still will never understand why you had to leave me alone that night, even if it was for a good reason. But I'm glad to know now, that my children will have their grandma in their lives."

Grace released her arms from Sadie, and looked at her with a smile. "You can thank Giorgia, for letting me know where to find you."

"Giorgia?" Sadie asked surprised. "Why her?

Grace explained to her how it all started, and what she did to look for her. "When I got the phone call that you were alive and well, I was ecstatic. She gave me your number, and when I came her looking for you last night, she told me where to find you." Sadie was surprised that Giorgia went out of her way, and contacted her. She never imagined for Giorgia to have a heart like that.

"Why don't you get some rest, I'm pretty tired myself. We can talk more tomorrow." Sadie says, giving her a hug.

Sadie walked into the bedroom, and saw Antonio lying in bed with his eyes closed. She quietly shut the bedroom door and took her clothes off. She was feeling over the moon, and happy for what Giorgia and Antonio had done for her. She was in a mood and felt like being frisky, wanting to show Antonio her appreciation.

She climbed into bed, and gently pulled the sheets off Antonio. She began working his cock until it became hard, and placed her mouth around it. He let out a shocked gasp, opened his eyes, and looked down at her, smirking "What are you doing?" he whispered in shock.

She looked up shushing him, and placed her mouth back around his cock. His head whipped back into the pillow, enjoying the moment. He groaned with excitement when she began fondling his balls, all while caressing his cock with her warm, wet mouth.

His back arched and moaned out loudly when his cock hit the back of her throat, causing his body to stiffen. His hands rested on her head, and began massaging her head, tangling his fingers in her hair. The warmness of Sadie's mouth, and the way she worked her tongue on his cock, had his orgasm going wild, and lasting longer than usual. "Sadie, oh Sadie." he moaned out, while his body moved around in excitement.

She slowly kissed up along his body, making her way up to his mouth, and demandingly thrust her tongue into his mouth, showing him that she was the one in control. Their kiss turned intense, hot and wild, both moaning loudly. He couldn't take her being in control anymore and flipped her onto her back, and began kissing and sucking along her neck. He moved down to her breasts and grazed his teeth along her hardened nipples, before flicking his tongue on each nipple, and wrapping his mouth around her breast, sucking hard as he released his mouth from her breast.

He fondled her breasts with his hands, while kissing her body along down to her navel, and spread her legs wanting to pleasure her below with his magical tongue. "Antonio." she moaned out, as her body became numb. She grabbed a fist full of the sheets, and screamed out his name over and over, when she began orgasming. He continued massaging her insides with his tongue, and couldn't stop smiling when her body jerk and shook uncontrollably.

"Antonio" she moaned out while he was giving her another orgasm, and forcefully pulled him up to her face. "Put your cock inside me." she demanded in his mouth, while he kissed her. He thrusted slowly and as deeply as he could, while passionately making love to her.

He continued making love to her until they both released, both sweaty and out of breath, he rolled onto his back "I'm telling you woman, you're going to be the death of me."

She giggled while rolling onto her side, and caressing his chest.

"You looked so sexy laying there while you were sleeping. I couldn't help it, and wanted to surprise you."

"You surprised me alright." he chuckled "I love you so much, and I cannot wait until you're my wife… I'm literally counting down the days." he says while smiling, and tracing her lips with his thumb.

She let out a happy moan when he said those words to her, and leaned forward to kiss him. "I can't wait until these children are born and to be your wife also. I love you so very much." she hummed.

"Dio ti amo così tanto, mi hai reso l'uomo più felice vivo." Antonio said in a low deep voice, grinning from ear to ear.

Chapter 37- Feeling the love

Sadie's stomach began to dance, while hearing him speak to her in Italian, she lifted her head up off his chest, and looked at him "OK, I understood the I love you so much part, but what was the rest of it?"

He chuckled "You've made me the happiest man alive." He says, squeezing her tighter, and kissing her forehead.

"I think I'm going to have to start taking Italian lessons, that way every time you speak the language to me, I'll actually be able to understand you."

"I don't speak it that much, only when you've got me revved up."

"All the more for me wanting to learn the language." she smiled, while laying her head back onto his chest.

The next morning Antonio walked in on Giorgia and Grace having a heart to heart talk, he stepped back and stood behind the wall after he overheard the two talking about Sadie. He heard his mother admit to Grace that when she first met Sadie, she liked her, but didn't want anyone to know that she had. She was putting up a front with everyone, because she never cared much for Harlow.

Hearing her say that to Grace, broke his heart, but had known all along that she never cared for Harlow from the start of their relationship.

Giorgia continued telling Grace that she once believed Harlow was just in it for Antonio's money, that she felt she didn't love him, and that her feelings towards Harlow changed after she passed away. She explained that she felt bad for not making it to her funeral, and for her not be there for Antonio. She then admitted to Grace that she was getting liposuction at the time, and didn't want anyone knowing. She confided to Grace, that after being here, and finding out what Harlow said and had done for Antonio, the girls and for Sadie, she felt even worse. She wished she had been nicer to Harlow, and wished that she had given her a chance. She then admitted, that she now knows that Harlow did in fact love Antonio, and wasn't there for his money.

"What made me wake up and stop with my nonsense, was having a talk with Giovanni, but then Sadie and I had a talk, and she stood her ground. I said something stupid to her just to see what kind of reaction I would get out of her, and she decked me across the face with a book." she says with a grin.

Antonio was still standing behind the wall, listening in on their conversation and covered his mouth, chuckling.

"It was then that I realized I needed to stop, and looked back at everything I had done, and said with Harlow, and wished that I was never that way with her." she says, as she drank a sip of her coffee.

Grace smiled; she was happy to hear that Sadie never changed her ways. "Sadie always had a knack of inspiration in her, she always brings out what others don't see. At least the first fifteen years of her life she was always like that. But I see in the twelve years that I have been gone, that has never changed with her."

Antonio decided that he heard enough, and walked into his office. At first, he was pissed and hurt about what his mother was saying, but after listening to her, he knew she had remorse for her actions.

While sitting at his desk, he started thinking about what Grace told him about Sadie's father, and started to do some digging. He searched online for him, and thought he possibly found the right one. He wasn't one hundred percent sure it was him, after seeing many names of a Scott Kline, but from Grace's description, his location and age, he was sure it was him.

Ethan stopped by to see how everything went the other night and to have a talk with Antonio, he walked into the living room and saw Giorgia and Grace sitting on the couch talking.

He did a double take when he noticed Grace, and his heart skipped a beat, he placed his hand over his heart and walked up to her smiling wide. "You don't mind if I sit down and talk with you, do you? My mother always told me to follow my dreams." Grace turned red in the face, and extended her hand out to his. "Hi, I'm Grace, Sadie's mother." she giggled.

"Even better." he said with a devilish grin "My name is Ethan, and very single." he says, shaking her hand. Sadie stood near the staircase watching Ethan with her mom, and shook her head "Ethan can you come help me with something?" Sadie asked him.

He turned his head and looked at Sadie, then turned back and looked at Grace. "I'll be back, I'd like to get to know you a little more, you're the type of girl that my mother always told me to bring home to her."

"Ethan!" Sadie called out, wanting him to get away from her mother.

"Excuse me for a moment." he says, kissing the top of her hand.

Ethan walked over to Sadie, and she smacked him in the back of the head. "That's my mom you're hitting on over there."

"I'm sorry, when I was talking to her, I dropped something, it ended up being my jaw." Sadie started giving him a dirty look, and placed her hands on her hips. "What? I can't help that she's a milf."

"Ethan, I haven't seen her in twelve years, the least you could do is be normal."

"I am being normal." he says, winking.

He put his hands on his hips, and took another look at Grace. He couldn't believe how beautiful she was, and how much she resembled Sadie. "How old is she anyway?"

The Unexpected Nanny

"Too old for you, but if you really want to know she's forty-six, now please be nice to her and quit hitting on her, besides... you have a girlfriend already."

Ethan sighed "Fine, you're no fun. I told her that I was single, so please don't tell her about me having a girlfriend." he says, praying to her.

"Where's Antonio anyway? He asked me to come by, he wanted to talk to me about some things."

"For one, you're not single. Two, it looks like he's in his office, just go right in. I'm sure he wouldn't mind."

Sadie walked over to Grace and Giorgia, and smiled "Sorry about Ethan, he has no manners." she says while looking at Ethan. Ethan overheard Sadie as he was going to see Antonio, and turned around blowing her a kiss, then laughed before entering the office.

"He's quite the character isn't he." Grace giggled.

"Yea, that he is, he has no filter."

"I know exactly how he's like, he was always trying to piss me off. We used to go round and round, he was always teasing me, and trying to get me worked up. He once told me that he slept naked, so it was easier for me to kiss his ass." Giorgia giggled. "I wanted to strangle him, but at least I can tolerate him now, I now see he was only doing that because of the way I treated his sister."

"Ethan is just being Ethan, but you gotta love him." Sadie smiled.

******

For the next couple months, Sadie bonded with her mother as well as Giorgia. Antonio allowed Grace to stay at his home until Sadie had the babies, and offered to help buy her a home nearby. He figured that it would be the best for Sadie and Grace if she was living closer to them, since Grace's home was in Washington.

Sadie was eight and a half months pregnant, and was home alone with the girls, teaching them songs on the piano, when she started to have some sharp pains. She continued teaching the girls until she no longer could stand the pain.

"Girls, I'm going to have to go lay down for a bit."

"What's wrong momma?" Isabella asked. touching her arm and looking worried.

"I just have some pain in my back and need to lay down, I'll lay on the couch if you girls just want to watch some TV for a little while, while I rest."

"Ok." says Gabriella.

The girls held onto Sadie's hands while they walked with her to the living room, Sadie grabbed the remote and turned cartoons on for the girls, then laid down on the couch.

"Where's daddy?" asked Gabriella.

"He's out with your grandparents doing something, not exactly sure what they are up to."

Sadie closed her eyes for a while, until the pain was so bad that she woke up telling the girls to call their dad. Isabella ran around looking for Sadie's phone, scared.

"I think it's by my bed." Sadie yelled out.

Isabella found her phone and called her dad.

Antonio was doing a walk through in a house that was a couple miles away, he was with Grace and his parents when his phone rang. He saw that it was Sadie and answered the phone. "Hello my love." He said smiling.

His smile faded when he heard Isabella's voice, telling him that something was wrong with Sadie. He quickly hung up the phone, and looked at his parents "That was Isabella on the phone, she sounded scared and said something's wrong with Sadie."

Antonio feared another repeat of what happened with Harlow, they quickly left the house, and rushed home. Antonio ran into the house and found Sadie laying on the couch, white as a ghost and full of sweat. He picked her up, and carried her out to their vehicle. "Please take the girls with you, I've got to get her to the hospital now." he said in a panic.

"What's wrong with momma?" Gabriella cried.

"Not sure honey, what happened?" Giorgia asked her.

"She kept saying she was in a lot of pain, she laid down and fell asleep. She then woke up asking for us to call daddy."

"Maybe she's in labor?" Grace asked, looking at Giorgia.

"She's not to full term yet." Giorgia says, as she was getting the girls ready to leave.

"She's having twins, usually they don't go full term." Grace explained.

"Let's hope your right." Giorgia sighed.

They gathered the girls, got them in their vehicle, and headed for the hospital. When they walked inside, they asked the nurse at the desk where they could find Sadie "She's on the fourth floor, when you get there, she will be in room 418." the nurse explained.

They walked into the room the nurse said she would be in, and saw nobody in the room. Grace walked back out, and found a nurse, asking where Sadie was. They walked over to the nurse's station and waited while the nurse looked her up. "Looks like they brought in, for an emergency cesarean section."

"Oh god." Grace cried out. "Is she OK?"

"I don't know what is going on, but you're welcome to wait in her room." said the nurse. "Once I find out more, I'll send a doctor in to talk with you."

They all sat in the room not knowing what to do, Antonio was nowhere to be found, and his phone was turned off. They decided to just wait it out, in hopes that someone would come in the room soon, explaining her situation.

"Where's mommy?" Isabella cried.

Giorgia wrapped her arm around her, she saw how scared she was, and it broke her heart. "She will be here soon, honey."

A couple hours later the girls were getting antsy and began crying, worried something bad happened to Sadie.

Giovanni stood up wanting to find a nurse, and to get the status on Sadie. When he opened the door, they were pushing Sadie in with Antonio following behind them.

The girls ran over to Antonio giving him a hug, begging to sit on the bed with Sadie. "Mom is sleeping right now, you can sit with her when she wakes up." Antonio says to them.

"What happened?" Grace asked worried.

"They had to do an emergency c-section, one of the cords was wrapped around the little girl's neck, thank God both kids are ok. They will be bringing the kids in soon after they examine them, and after they make sure nothing is wrong. On the way to the hospital, Sadie started bleeding. We weren't in the room very long before they decided to do the surgery."

There was a knock at the door, and in came the nurse with the babies. The girls were excited to see them, and ran to the crib, looking at them.

"I take it everything is OK with them, especially her?" Antonio asked, picking up his son, and holding him for the first time.

"They are fine, we will keep them in the nursery to keep a special eye on them later. We thought that you might want to hold them." says the nurse.

Sadie woke up feeling out of it, and once she realized where she was, she asked to see her babies.

Antonio handed her their son first, since that's who he was holding, and walked over to the crib and picked up his daughter, kissing her forehead. "I have a feeling you're going to be a little troublemaker." he laughed, while whispering. He then handed her over to Sadie.

The nurse walked over to the board on the wall, asking if they had picked out any names. Both Antonio and Sadie looked at each other, shrugging their shoulders "Well we have some names picked out, but haven't officially picked them out yet. We do have some time, right?" Sadie asked.

"That's fine. For now, we will call them Baby A, for the girl and Baby B for the boy." the nurse says, writing it on the board, as well as their weight. *Baby A: 5lbs 8 oz, and Baby B: 6lbs 4oz, both 20" long.*

Their parents and their daughters finally got to hold the babies, all while looking at them they tried to decide on names, wanting to help. Antonio and Sadie went down the list of names they already had picked out, and both not in agreeing on the names they chose.

Ethan came by to visit, and to hold the babies. He then gave his opinions on what they should name them.

"Will see, we still have time to decide. I just want to make sure we name them the right names. They will be stuck with these names for life, so I just want to be sure." Sadie says kissing their cheeks, as she held them both in her arms.

"I still think you should name her Harlow, or at least have it as her middle name." Ethan says, while looking at the little girl in Sadie's arms.

Chapter 38- Making decisions

It's been four days since Sadie had the babies. The doctors wanted to keep Sadie and the babies in the hospital a little longer to monitor them, and to make sure that everything was OK before they released them from the hospital.

Sadie and Antonio still hadn't come to an agreement on naming the babies, and continued going back and forth with the names, trying to come to an agreement.

"I like Harper a lot for a girl, and Luca for a boy." Sadie says to Antonio.

"I do like Luca, it's an Italian name." he smirked "But Harper is too close to Harlow." He looked down at his little girl and smiled at her.

"Well... how about Alessandra or Liliana? I believe those are Italian names, and they're a couple names that I had on my list." Sadie says.

"I like Liliana the best, is that what you would like to name her?"

"Hmm, I do like Adriana too." Sadie sighed, not wanting to make up her mind.

"We have to choose soon; they are expecting to release you and the kids today."

"Let's go with Liliana and Luca." Sadie says smiling, wanting to hurry before she changed her mind again.

"And the middle names?" he asked.

"I was thinking Hunter for Luca, and originally I had a middle name picked out for Liliana, but I don't think you'll like it... I thought of possibly Harlow, even Ethan brought it up the other day, but if not, we could go with maybe Harper? I just thought it would be a nice memorial for what she did for us."

Antonio sat there thinking for a bit "I don't know..." he sighed, still not caring to have her name involved with their children's names.

"Well... I guess that'll work, if that's what you really would like to do." He didn't want to argue about it anymore, and just wanted to get them all home.

"Are you sure?"

"If that's what you want, then it's fine with me, I'll go let them know that we decided on the names, and get us out of here."

Antonio handed her Liliana, and left the room to find the nurse, and to see about finally getting out of the hospital. Sadie sat in the bed holding Luca and Liliana and stared at them, she thought they were the most precious things she ever laid her eyes on. "I cannot believe your daddy and I made you two. I never thought that I could ever love anyone so much, as I do you two." She says quietly to them.

Antonio was able to get Sadie and the babies discharged, and brought them home. Once they walked in the door, the girls were ecstatic to see them and wanted to see the babies. Antonio carried them while in their car seats into the living room, and set them down for the girls to look. Everyone had to chuckle, watching the girls talk to them.

"What are their names?" Isabella asked.

"Luca Hunter, and Liliana Harlow." Sadie says with a smile.

"She has mommy's name!" Gabriella excitedly yelled "Can we hold them?"

Antonio and Sadie took the babies out of their car seats and had the girls sit on the couch. They sat down next to the girls and helped them hold their brother and sister.

Grace and Giorgia walked into the living room wanting to see the babies, Antonio and Sadie got up so they could sit next to the girls. Sadie figured it was perfect timing for her to go clean up and change. Antonio sat with Giovanni talking about his future, while keeping an eye on his little ones.

"Have you decided if you're moving here or going back home to Paris?" Antonio asked his dad.

"Well I think Giorgia wants to stay here, she says she's been away from you far too long, and that she wants to be able to see the grandkids more."

"I'm sure the kids would like that."

"We both would actually enjoy it." Giovanni says, thinking it would be nice to move away from the tourist attraction.

Ethan came over and brought his girlfriend along, wanting to see the babies and to finally introduce the girl that he has been seeing for about six months now.

Sadie was coming down the stairs as they were walking in. "Oh hi!" Sadie says, as she looked at Ethan and to the girl, standing next to him.

"Come in."

Antonio got up to shake Ethan's hand and then patted him on the back. Ethan stood behind the girl he brought holding onto her shoulders. "Antonio, Sadie I'd like for you to finally meet Melissa." He then started singing in her ear 🎶*Sweet Melissa*🎶 she turned around "Stop, you're embarrassing me." She said quietly, she turned around and her cheeks were beet red.

Sadie could tell that Ethan was embarrassing her and that she felt nervous being around them, she smiled at her and held out her hand "Nice to meet you, I'd have to say it's about time we met."

"Yes, it's about time." she said quietly, not sounding too thrilled.

Ethan looked over at Antonio smiling, mouthing *watch this* as he pointed to Melissa. "Melissa works at Little Caesars, cause she's hot and I'm ready." he says, while grinding on her.

"No, I don't!" she hissed, she turned around and gave him the stink eye. "Ethan, I swear, stop it... I don't even know these people." she whispered loudly.

"My bad. Simmer down there pretty lady, you should know me by now, I'm just having a little fun with you… I'm sorry...." he says caressing her arms "They already know I'm messing with you."

Melissa looked at him, not being impressed. She looked back at Sadie and changed the subject "I do love babies; I would love to see the little ones."

Sadie walked Melissa over to the babies while Ethan talked with Antonio, going into his office. "Have you had any luck finding Sadie's father?" Ethan asked, grabbing Antonio's hidden stash of bourbon from the drawer, then taking a swig off the bottle.

"Careful, don't be going out there smelling like booze, then Sadie will know I have a hidden bottle in here." Antonio says, grabbing the bottle away from Ethan "And no, I haven't found him. Well... he hasn't called back and I'm pretty sure he's the one."

"Where is he living? Maybe I can help and make a special visit?"

"He's living in Portland, Oregon. I'm not sure if it's worth going out there, talking to a man who abandoned his daughter, or should I say abandoned Grace while pregnant with Sadie?"

"It's worth a shot, he's older now, so you would think maybe he might want to know who she is? I don't mind going to talk with him."

"I guess it's completely up to you, I'll fly you there if you really want to do it. Otherwise we can forget it all. I'm sure Grace doesn't want to see him either."

The next day Ethan took a flight to Portland, looking to see if he could find Scott. Once he arrived, he checked into a hotel and ordered a cab ride, taking him to the address that Antonio wrote down for him. When he got there, he asked the driver if he could wait for a bit, letting him know that he would pay him extra, to which the driver agreed. Ethan walked up to the house, located at the corner of the street. It was an older home, and looked like a nice home, all it really needed was a paint job. He knocked on the door and stood there for about five minutes, then walked around the house making sure someone still lived there. As he looked around, there was a middle-aged man standing outside next door watering his plants, Ethan walked over to him, asking questions.

"Excuse me, you wouldn't happen to know if Scott Kline lives here, do you?"

"Ah, yea." he says, running a hand through his hair, looking at him cautiously. "He should be home in about an hour or so."

"OK, thank you. I'll just stop back later."

Ethan walked back to his ride, and had him take him back to the hotel. He walked into the bar of the hotel and ordered some food, and a beer, figuring that he should eat something before heading back over to Scott's home.

While eating his food, he checked the inside pocket of his jacket, making sure that he had the pictures that Antonio gave him. He looked at them for a minute, then put them back. A woman came over to him and sat down directly across from him at his table.

"Hello there." she says, batting her eyes at him.

He looked up while taking a bite of his burger "Hello." he says, mouth full of food.

"How come you're here all by yourself?"

"I'm here on business. Can I help you with something?"

"You could start with buying me a drink." she said smiling pretty, using her finger and sliding the diamond on her necklace side to side, trying to turn him on.

Ethan set his burger down and grinned. "You know, your eyes tell me a lot of things, but the only thing you haven't told me is your name."

"Kara."

"Look... Kara, I'm not here to meet anyone, I'm here on business, trying to eat my burger. I'm already involved with someone, and if she saw you here talking to me, I'd be putting my money on her that she would win the cat fight."

Kara stood up and huffed "Asshole." she barked.

"Yes, I have one, thanks for noticing." he laughed while she stormed away. He finished his burger and beer, after paying he went on his way.

He arrived back at Scott's house, and noticed a couple cars in the driveway. Figuring that he was home, he sent the driver away and headed back over to the door. As he knocked, he started feeling a little nervous, but calmed himself down when he thought of Sadie and her kids.

A beautiful woman with long dark hair possibly in her fifties answered the door, he figured that he better act professional since he wanted to say something else when she answered the door. "Can I help you?" she asked.

"Yes, I'm looking for Scott Kline, wondering if I can talk to him for a few minutes."

"What is this in regards to?" she asked, looking at him curiously.

"My name is Ethan, and its regarding a very good friend of mine and her mother."

She looked at him oddly, calling for Scott to come to the door. Ethan stood outside looking around until the door opened back up, and Scott walked outside.

"What can I help you with?"

Ethan extended his hand out, shaking his hand "My name is Ethan, I'm here for a woman named Sadie." Scott shook his head, confused "I don't know of any Sadie's."

"Of course, that's right... but you may know her mother Grace... Grace Hart?"

He stared at Ethan for a moment "I haven't heard that name in like thirty years."

"So, you do know her, at least her mother." Ethan says scratching his head.

"I do, what's this all about?"

"Her fiancé sent me to find you, Sadie just delivered twins a few days ago, and they're getting married in a couple months. He would have come, but with double duties of the twins, she needed all the help that she can get, plus helping with their older twins. Anyway, he would really like for you to come to their wedding, and for you to meet your daughter as well as your grandkids."

Ethan went on explaining about what happened to Grace and Sadie, and how Sadie was just reunited with her mother a few months ago. He then showed him a picture of Sadie. Scott sat in the swing that was on the front porch staring at the picture, Ethan then handed him a picture of the twins.

"Antonio said that you can keep the pictures."

"Antonio?"

"Sadie's fiancé." he says, handing him the wedding invitation. "Here take this, all the information is in this packet. I know that you don't know her, but I hope you find it in your heart to finally meet the daughter you never knew. You would be impressed with her."

Scott sat there looking like he was in shock, and wiped away sweat from his forehead. He opened the packet, looking at to what was all inside. "I'm not sure I can do this, I don't know her, and my wife has no clue I got another woman pregnant."

"Well then, that's too bad. You missed out on twenty-seven years of her life, it's not too late to get to know her now, but then again that's your choice." Ethan shook his hand "Thanks for your time anyway, think about it."

He left Scott's house and called Antonio, letting him know that he had found the right guy, he also filled him in that it didn't look good for him to be showing up there anytime soon.

"Sorry Antonio, I tried. I thought I had him convinced, he stared at those pictures for a while. Even forming a smile when he was looking at them. But he insists that it's a no go."

Chapter 39- Love of a lifetime

Ethan was in the hotel room getting ready to leave and head back home, when his phone rang. It was Sadie wondering if he could stop by the house, that she had something important that she wanted to ask him.

"I can stop by, but it won't be for another few hours. I'm out of town right now, and getting ready to head back home. I can stop by when I get back to town." he tells her.

During his flight he kept wondering what was so important that Sadie wanted to talk to him about, hoping that she didn't find out that he was out looking for her dad, and wanting to talk with him. Hours later Ethan made it back and headed over to visit Sadie, Antonio was out with Grace and his parents signing paperwork for Grace's new home.

He walked in the house and Sadie was in the living room, she was done feeding the babies and laying them in their bassinets.

"What's up sweet cheeks?" he asked, walking towards her.

She turned around, asking him to sit and that she had something important to ask him. She sat down next to him, tucking her hair behind her ears, acting nervous. "I wanted to ask you... since I have no father in my life, and nobody really that close to me anymore, I was wondering if you would like to walk me down the aisle?"

He smiled at her, it made him feel warm inside and special. He was loving that she asked him to do that for her "I would be honored, you're like a sister to me." Ethan says, giving her a hug.

Sadie perked up, she felt nervous asking him since she hadn't really known him that long "Thank you so much, you have no idea what this means to me. I didn't think that you would do it." she says, releasing from his embrace.

"Now why wouldn't I do that?"

"I don't know, maybe cause you're in no relation to me?" she says, shrugging her shoulders.

Ethan shook his head "Sadie... you're already family to me. Who cares if you're not blood? Look at Antonio, we're not blood and I still look at him as if he were my brother." Ethan paused for a moment "I do have a question for you."

"What's that?"

"What would you do if your father ever came around looking for you?"

Sadie shrugged her shoulders "I don't know, I never really thought about it, he left my mom when he found out that she was pregnant. I guess I would have a lot of questions for him. Why?"

"Just curious... you've got your mom back in your life, and I just wasn't sure what you thought about if your dad were to ever want to be in your life."

"Well... I've never considered him my dad. Just a sperm donor really, I probably would give him a chance to explain himself, I look at it that he was 10 years older than her, he should have been more of an adult. My mom was 18 when she got pregnant with me."

Ethan took it all in of what she was telling him, hoping that Antonio was doing the right thing. Sadie stood up and walked over to the babies when they started crying, checking on them.

Ethan looked at the time, getting antsy to be home "Well I should get going, I haven't been home for a couple days, and Melissa has been at my house waiting for me. I'm sure she's in a not so happy mood." he laughed.

"Is she ever?" Sadie asked, smirking.

The Unexpected Nanny

******

Two months had gone by and it's the day of their wedding. Antonio flew everyone to Hawaii to share their special day. Giorgia and Grace helped Isabella and Gabriella get ready, while Sadie was getting herself ready.

Sadie stood in front of the mirror with so many emotions running through her mind, when she put her veil on, she started tearing up. She couldn't believe that she was getting married, feeling sad that she didn't have a father to walk her down the aisle and hand her away. She then cheered up when she thought of Antonio, picturing his smile, and his beautiful blue eyes sparkling at her. She was in heaven, and feeling that she was marrying the man of her dreams, a man she never thought existed.

Grace walked in the room wanting to be the first person to see her daughter in her wedding dress. She looked at Sadie, and was in awe. She was dressed in a white silk chiffon dress featuring a sweetheart neckline and a long train, that she had specially made by Armani.

"Wow, you look really beautiful. I never thought I would ever see my baby get married." Grace says giving her a hug. "Antonio is a very lucky man."

"Thanks mom." She says, hugging her back tighter.

"Are you ready to do this? It's almost time to head to the beach." she says, grabbing Sadie's bouquet. Grace looked at the bouquet, and widened her eyes. "Wow, this is gorgeous." Her bouquet was all white, filled with gardenias and roses.

"I'm more than ready, where are the girls?"

"They're outside with Giorgia and the babies, they wanted to pick flowers." Grace says, helping her with her train.

When they walked outside, Sadie was in heaven when she saw the girls. She loved the flower headpieces that were made for them and couldn't wait for them to walk down the aisle before her.

"Look momma, we picked some flowers for you." Isabella said smiling, handing her the flowers.

"Thank you, but we have to get down over to the beach now. Remember what you're supposed to do with the petals, and make sure you don't lose our rings." Sadie instructed them.

"We know." Gabriella says grinning, grabbing Isabella's hand and walking down the hill to get to the beach.

The more Sadie walked down to the beach, the more nervous she was becoming, hoping that everything turned out as planned.

Ethan was talking with Antonio when he saw Sadie walking down to the beach, he saw her dress and veil blowing around in the wind, and looked at Antonio. "Don't look behind you, Sadie is coming and it's bad luck to see her beforehand." he says, pushing him to start walking.

"That's not fair, you get to see her before I do." Antonio pouted.

Ethan laughed, and patted his back "Tough cookies, you know the drill, you've been through it before." He continued to chuckle while grabbing Antonio's shoulders, pushing him to keep on walking. "Now go where you're supposed to be, and I'll go get Sadie. You'll see her soon enough, it's about to start any minute."

Antonio walked over to the arch, while Ethan walked over to Sadie, grabbing her to walk her down the sandy aisle.

Sadie and the girls got to the beach, and giggled when she saw the sign that they had out for the guests. It read: *Wedding this way, leave your shoes behind, and bury your toes in the sand, just like the bride to be.* She wanted a barefoot wedding, and didn't feel like wearing shoes on the sand.

She figured the guests would enjoy it, and would want to join in, if they wanted to.

Ethan walked up to the girls, giving them instructions "Are you girls ready? Now when the music starts, walk slowly up to your dad while dropping the flowers OK?" he says, smiling and touching their little button noses.

"We're ready." Gabriella says.

Ethan looked at Sadie, happy and with love. "Antonio is so lucky to have met you, and I'm glad that he did, if it weren't for you, I don't know where he would be right now. I hope that you realize that you're a special person, and I know that Harlow saw that in you as well."

"Thank you, Ethan, you're a true friend, a great brother and someone I can trust." Sadie smiled, kissing him on the cheek.

"By the way you look gorgeous, are you sure you're that committed to Antonio?"

She giggled "Of course I'm committed to Antonio." she says, playfully shoving him.

"Are you sure you don't want to kick him to the curb, and run away with me? There's still a little time to get out of here." he grinned a devilish grin, and laughed.

Sadie laughed "Nice try, what would Melissa say?"

"Damn you had to bring her name up, my chances with you are ruined again." he snickered, grabbing a hold of her arm "Let's do this." He got ready to walk her down to Antonio, and stood behind the girls.

He leaned forward "Start walking, you two." Ethan tells them, both watching them drop the flowers as they walked towards Antonio.

The girls smiled the entire time, and posed for the camera guy that was following them, and taking pictures as they walked.

Ethan was just getting ready to start walking her down the aisle, and looked at her quick "Just remember beauty fades and so will his eyesight." he says with a grin. Before she could say anything, he started walking her down the aisle.

Antonio stood there watching Ethan walk Sadie towards him, his heart started beating faster the closer they got to him, and getting more excited to say his *I do* to her.

Ethan and Sadie stopped when they got to the arch "Who gives this bride away?" the officiant asked.

"That would be me." Ethan says, kissing Sadie's cheek, and handed her off to Antonio.

Antonio and Sadie both looked at each other, not keeping their eyes off each other. They finally looked at the officiant when he started talking. They listened to what he had to say, he then looked at the two of them. "I understand you have your own vows for each other, if you could join hands we will start with Antonio's vows."

Antonio looked at Sadie smiling, melting as he looked at her "You are the culmination of a dream come true. I still can't believe that I'm standing here about to start a wonderful life together with you, you're my best friend, my greatest miracle, the mother of my children and the sexiest woman that I know, and love the most in this entire world."

Sadie couldn't help but chuckle when Antonio said sexiest woman, she was all smiles when he finished with his vows. The officiant then asked Sadie to say her written vows to Antonio.

Sadie looked at Antonio smiling, wanting to take him right there in front of everyone, she felt like she was drooling the more she looked at him

"You fill my life with meaning, thank you for welcoming me into your heart. I love that you're the father of my children and that I will be spending the rest of my life with you, I love the thought of growing old with you, and I'm looking forward to fighting through challenges and embracing joy from this moment until the end of time."

Gabriella and Isabella handed the rings to Antonio and Sadie.

They exchanged their I do's, and placed the rings on each other's fingers.

"I now pronounce you husband and wife." the officiant says to them "You may now kiss your bride."

Antonio cupped the back of Sadie's head, and placed a soft passionate kiss on her lips. He couldn't control himself, and started to kiss her hungrily and urgently. He stopped himself before laying her onto the sand and having his way with her, he pulled away from her, looking at her with a smile that was going from ear to ear.

"Non vedo l'ora di toglierti questo vestito e farti l'amore tutta la notte"

Sadie giggled, not knowing what he said, and turned around to face their guests. Antonio picked her up, and carried her bridal style down the sandy aisle, with the girls following behind.

Antonio set her down, kissing her again "What did you say to me back there?" Sadie asked, she thought whatever he said to her was extremely sexy by the way he said it, and was curious as to what it meant.

"I said, I cannot wait to get this dress off of you and make love to you all night long." he groaned, wrapping his arms around her waist, kissing her quick before the guests walked up to them.

While shaking guests' hands, Sadie noticed a couple in line, she didn't think she had ever seen before. She was curious to who they were, and looked at Antonio pulling down on his shoulder to get to his ear, and whispered to him.

"Who are those people back there?" she asked pointing to the older couple.

He stood back up and looked at the couple she was questioning, he recognized who they were and smiled once he saw them "When they get up to us, you'll get to meet them and find out who they are."

Ethan, Melissa and the girls stood nearby waiting for the Antonio and Sadie to finish greeting and thanking everyone for coming. Ethan grinned when he saw the familiar couple approaching the bride and groom, and started walking towards them.

Antonio placed his hand on the small of Sadie's back, when the older couple approached them, hoping that she wouldn't get upset. As they approached, Sadie studied the older couple, trying to figure out if she knew who they could be.

"Congratulations you two." the woman says to them.

"Thank you." Sadie smiled, shaking her hand.

The man looked at Sadie, and tears began forming in his eyes. He wiped away the tears, then wiped his hand on his pants "Congratulations, you are absolutely beautiful." he says, choking up.

Sadie looked up at Antonio and back over at the man, confused. "Do I know you?"

"No... but you should know who I am, and I'm so sorry."

Chapter 40- Love all around

"No... but you should know who I am, and I'm so sorry." She repeated in her mind, still trying to figure out who they were, until he spoke again.

"My name is Scott Kline." Sadie's heart dropped, her eyes got wide, and took a step back "Who?" she asked, shaking her head in denial, not believing what she just heard.

Antonio looked at Sadie worried she was upset, then looked back at the couple "The reception doesn't start for another couple hours, we were going to do pictures first. After we're done with those, do you think we can go somewhere and talk?" he asked Scott.

"We can do that." Scott says, looking at his wife.

Antonio looked at Ethan "Can you go get the kids so we can get our pictures taken?" He looked at Scott and smiled "Excuse us for a moment." Antonio took Sadie's hand and started walking over to the photographer.

"Antonio, seriously, who are those people? His name sounded familiar to me."

He stopped and walked in front of her, holding both her hands and looked her in the eyes "You're either going to be mad at me, hate me, or maybe you'll still love me, but ahh..." he started saying, running his fingers through his hair, as he eyed the couple behind them.

"Well... I found your father, and that man over there... is your dad." He looked back at Sadie and took a deep swallow when he saw the look on her face. She looked behind her and rested her hands on her hips while looking at who her dad was.

"Now remember our vows that we just said." Antonio said nervously, he curled his finger under her chin and turned her face to look at him "Please don't be upset, I found him a couple months ago. I had Ethan go see if it was in fact him, and he had a talk with him. I didn't know he was going to be here."

"How could you not know? I mean he had to know where we were getting married for him to be here."

"I gave Ethan a package to give him. I also placed tickets inside the package for him to fly here, if he wanted to be a part of your life. I offered it to him, and never got a response from him if he was going to accept it."

"Why didn't you tell me?"

"I wanted it to be a surprise, but honestly I hoped that he would have called me, and to warn me that he was going to be here."

"Well it is what it is now, does my mom know?"

"She knows Ethan went to see him, but didn't know that he was coming here. She may have noticed him sitting there."

"Well let's take these pictures, then we can talk to them and see what he has to say. I would like to go celebrate after that." Sadie says smiling.

Antonio and Sadie left to have their wedding pictures taken on the beach, while they were having their pictures taken, Sadie kept thinking about her dad, curious as to why he never wanted anything to do with her, and why suddenly now?

After they were done taking their wedding photos, Sadie walked over to Scott and his wife, with Antonio by her side.

Sadie talked with Scott for a while, and apologized to her for not being in her life. Telling her that on many occasions he thought about Grace, and the baby that they shared. He admitted that he often wondered if he had a son or daughter out there. He mentioned that there was a time where he once looked for Grace, and found out that she moved out of the state, and wasn't sure where they moved to, then decided to give up looking for them.

Sadie also found out that she has two older sisters and one older brother. He told her that they would like to meet her sometime, but only if she was willing to, and would understand if she didn't want to meet them.

"I would like that." Sadie says to him.

Scott nervously gave her a hug, then released himself to look at her "I'm glad that I finally got to meet you, you're a very beautiful woman, and I regret my childish decisions when I was younger. I had to answer to my wife about this, and let's just say that she won. She was pissed at me for a couple weeks, and was more upset with me that I walked away from you more than anything. I hope that you'll forgive me, and hopefully give me a chance."

She stepped back and looked away. Looking at the waves that were coming in while she thought about what he said "I'll forgive you; you'll have to give me some time to take this all in. But for now, I have a reception to join, maybe later I can steal a dance from you." Sadie says, wrapping her arm around Antonio's waist.

"I would like that." Scott tells her.

Antonio picked up Sadie bridal style, and carried her over to the reception area that had lights hanging from the palm trees, and candles on the tables lighting up the area. As he carried her into the crowd they were greeted with cheers, and the guests' wanting him to kiss her.

With love in his eyes, he looked at her raising his eyebrows up and down fast, kissing her passionately while still holding her in his arms, setting her down after the kiss. Sadie looked around and was in love with how they set up their reception. "They did this beautifully."

They started off by cutting the cake, so everyone could have a piece of cake after their meal. The cake had three different flavors, the top of the tiered cake was Chocolate Baileys Irish Cream, with the middle tier being Vanilla Mousse, and the bottom of the tier was Chocolate Mousse.

The Unexpected Nanny

After cutting the cake, Antonio lovingly wrapped his arm around her, both feeding his piece of cake to her, as she placed hers into his mouth. She took her thumb and began wiping off the leftover frosting off his bottom lip, before leaning forward, and licking the rest off while giving him a kiss.

After their meal, they danced their first dance as a married couple. Sadie chose the song When you Say Nothing at All, by Allison Krauss. While they were dancing, Antonio couldn't help where his hands kept moving to, causing Sadie to turn red in the face.

"You can wait until later." Sadie whispered in his ear.

He groaned "I just want to take your dress off right here right now, and take you right here on the dance floor." he says in her ear, then growled, giving her goosebumps all over her body.

"I'm going to check on the kids, then let's sneak out of here for a bit." she says with a grin, after their dance was over.

Sadie walked over to Giorgia to check on the kids, while Antonio met with Ethan over at the bar to do a couple round of shots.

Ethan raised his glass to Antonio, doing his typical toasts "Here's to you and here's to me, and here's to all the girls that lick us where we pee."

"You're something else you know it?" Antonio chuckled, nearly spitting out his shot.

"I was going to toast to something else, but figured I'd toast to that instead." Ethan grinned.

"Oh, now what was that one?" Antonio asked, unsure if he really wanted to know.

Ethan held up another shot, handing one to Antonio. He looked at Ethan with a curious look and a big smirk, wondering what was on his mind "Well... here's to the good ole nipples, without the nipples, titties wouldn't have a point." Ethan laughed, taking his shot.

The Unexpected Nanny

Ethan turned around and saw Melissa standing next to him listening, her hands were on her hips, and giving him a dirty look "Oh there you are! I was looking all over the place for you!" Ethan smirked.

Antonio knew Ethan was in trouble by the way she was looking at him, and decided to get away from them. "I'll catch you later, I'm going to go find my bride." he laughed, quickly walking away.

Antonio found Sadie and took her for a walk along the beach, enjoying the breeze while listening to the waves come in. They came across a very large rock, Antonio spun her around and pressed her up against the rock, crashing his lips hard against hers with urgency "I want to fuck you so bad right now, but we have guests to entertain." he moaned into her mouth.

A moan softly escaped her lips while he kissed her neck, and began rubbing his hand against her pussy "Fuck it, I'm going to satisfy you quick." he says. He kneeled onto the sand and raised her dress over his head, groaning when he felt her wearing no panties.

His mouth instantly went to her clit, and thrusted two fingers inside her, softly massaging her insides as he flicked his tongue on her clit. She grabbed a hold of his head while he was exciting her below, moaning. While she began to orgasm, he removed his fingers and thrusted his tongue inside her, tasting the sweetness she was releasing.

He removed the dress from over his head and wiped off his mouth, grinning as he stood up "That's just the appetizer, there's more to come."

"We should head back before people start wondering." she giggled.

"Can I steal a dance with the lovely bride." Scott asked Antonio, as they returned to their party.

"Sure, I don't mind." he says, handing her off to Scott.

Sadie felt a bit awkward while dancing with the man she never knew as her dad, but thought it was a nice gesture of him for trying.

"Again, I apologize, the more I see you, I feel like such a horse's ass for not being there for you while you were growing up. Had I been, it could have been me proudly walking you down the aisle." he says, pressing her closer to him.

She felt happy that she finally met who the sperm donor was, and thinking that he was nicer than what she thought he would be, he also showed her a caring side to him. He gave her a hug after their dance finished, and wished her the best, hoping to see more of her.

Later in the evening Antonio walked up to Sadie, while she was talking to her mom, and whispered in her ear "I'm ready to consummate our marriage."

Grace and Giorgia took the kids with them for the night, while Antonio and Sadie headed to their honeymoon suite. The moment they walked into the room, Antonio pinned Sadie against the wall, desperately crashing his lips against hers, and reached his hands around her, trying to unzip her dress.

She turned around and placed the palms of her hands against the wall allowing Antonio to unzip her dress. It dropped to the ground and he picked it up, and threw it on the chair. He quickly took his clothes off, not caring that they were on the ground, all he wanted was to make love to his wife.

With her facing the wall, he brushed her hair to the side and kissed the back of her neck, while reaching his hands around her and massaging her breasts, sending shockwaves throughout her body.

He kissed her down the backside of her body and to her ass, then spun her around and pleasured her below with his mouth, until she orgasmed. With his tongue he licked up her body and stopped at her breasts, licking and sucking on each of her nipples, before making it back up to her mouth.

He placed his hands on her ass, lifted her up, and carried her to the bed "You'll be sore in the morning, because I plan on making love to you all night long." he moaned into her mouth, as he laid her down.

"I'm alright with that." she smiled, pulling him tightly against her.

She pushed him over to his back while they kissed, then moved down to his throbbing hard cock, and wrapped her mouth around him. He moaned out loudly while watching her pleasure him, until he orgasmed. His head then flipped back onto his pillow, and enjoyed what she was doing to him, and enjoying the wonderful sensations she was giving him.

He pulled her up to him, and flipped her on her back, and climbed on top of her.

He stared into her eyes, looking at her full of lust, and still couldn't believe he was able to find love again. "Love you." he says, before kissing her, and making passionate love to her for as long as he could, while happily giving her many orgasms throughout the night.

They ended up making love until the sun came up, starting from the bed to the shower, and the last place they ended up was outside on the sandy beach, outside their patio door. They started falling asleep outside, until they heard people coming from not too far away. They quickly got up and ran back into their suite, laughing along the way back into the room.

He picked her up, and twirled her around, before they fell onto the bed. He climbed over her, and smiled. "With all that sex we had last night, I wouldn't be surprised if we made another little Russo."

Epilogue

Antonio laid on top of her still smiling "I'm literally the happiest man on earth right now, and I still can't believe you're now my wife." he says, lovingly rubbing his nose against hers.

"You better believe it, because I'm not going anywhere, and I'm here to stay." she says quietly, grinning.

"Good, because I'll be giving you the entire world."

His lips pressed hard against hers, kissing her with so much love and affection. Her heart melted by the way he kissed her, with his tender lips kissing her so passionately, made her wanting more, demanding a kiss that turned rough, kissing him harder. Her hands moved along down his body, and grabbed a hold of his ass "Fuck me." she moaned into his mouth.

He grabbed her legs and rested them on his shoulders, teasing her wet pussy with his cock, while rubbing the tip against it, and thrusting his cock barley inside her, just putting the tip of his cock inside her, slowly thrusting in and out.

"Antonio will you quit teasing me, and fuck me already?" she cried out, causing him to grin widely.

By her begging, only made him tease her even more, she got tired of him teasing her, and grabbed a hold of his cock shoving it inside her, while raising her hips up hard and making his cock go deeply inside her.

Loving how she took control, he leaned his head down and kissed her lips, a heated hungrily kiss, before he began thrusting and pleasuring her. He rocked her world, that had her screaming out his name with each thrust, hitting her g-spot each time.

"Oh Sadie." he moaned loudly, when he felt her insides tighten around him, and the warm fluids covering his pulsating cock, that was ready to explode inside her any minute.

After they released, he lowered her legs, and fell onto her and rested his head in the crook of her neck, trying to catch his breath. "I'm spent." he says, out of breath.

"I know... I'm really sore right now." she giggled. "I'm ready to close my eyes for a bit." She felt so alive, and so much in love, that she felt that she couldn't get enough of him.

Antonio and Sadie were able to get a few hours of sleep, until Antonio was awoken by the sounds of someone pounding on the door.

"Wake up you two lovebirds." Ethan called out, while knocking hard on the door.

"Hold on, hold on." Antonio yelled, trying to find his clothes.

Antonio looked around and couldn't find his clothes or his luggage, all he could find was Sadie's clothes. "Ah fuck not again." he mumbled out loud. Ethan kept pounding on the door yelling for them to open the door. He thought he remembered throwing his clothes across the room, but didn't see them and all that he saw was Sadie's wedding dress that he laid over the chair.

He sighed, shaking his head as he walked over to her dress, grabbing it and walked over to the door, partially opening it "Jesus Ethan, you couldn't wait?"

Ethan laughed and started pushing on the door to open it further.

"What are you hiding?" he asked, as Antonio let go of the door.

Ethan busted out laughing when he looked at Antonio standing butt naked, holding Sadie's wedding dress while covering his well-endowed love toy.

"You think that's funny? I can't find my damn clothes… and my luggage is missing."

Ethan couldn't stop laughing and turned his head, he bent over and picked up Antonio's luggage, that was sitting outside the door "Is this what you're looking for?" he asked, holding it up before handing it to him.

"You left it inside the limo, why do you think I'm here?"

"Oh, I don't know, so you could bother us?" he laughed.

"Well, I do enjoy doing that, but this time it was to bring you your luggage. Thought you might need some clothes to wear,"

Antonio grabbed his luggage shaking his head "Thanks, I owe you one." Antonio says, as he started shutting the door. Ethan peeked his head in through the crack of the door, and stopping Antonio from shutting the door. "Hurry up, the breakfast gathering is in a half hour. Go wake up your sleeping beauty over there."

Antonio shut the door, feeling relieved that Ethan found his luggage, and walked over to wake up Sadie. He stood there watching her sleep while she was laying on her side, he was so much in love that he couldn't believe it, he loved her so much that it hurt. He sat down on the bed next to her, causing the bed to dip, and leaned down to her ear, kissing it softly, causing her to get goosebumps on her arms. He grinned when he heard her moan. She slowly opened her eyes, and rolled onto her back, pulling him down on top of her.

He groaned while giving her a kiss "As much as I would like to make love to you again, we have a breakfast function to be at in about thirty minutes." he looked over at the time "Never mind I lied, we have twenty minutes to be there."

The Unexpected Nanny

Sadie pouted out her bottom lip, making Antonio wrap his lips around it, and sucked on her bottom lip, grinning as he pulled away. "We can always do this later."

"We don't even have time to shower, I'd say let's take a quick one but I don't think that will happen." she giggled, causing Antonio to chuckle as well.

They finally got up, and dressed quickly. They rushed out of their suite and hurried their way over to the restaurant. On the way, Sadie threw her hair up into a bun, trying to look somewhat decent. She couldn't wait to see her babies, and when they got inside, she rushed over to Grace and Giorgia, who were both holding them.

Ethan saw Antonio, and walked over to him, wrapping an arm around his shoulder "Man I have the worst hangover today." Ethan said chuckling while holding his head "When I was pounding on that door, man it was going right through my head."

Antonio laughed "Well that's what you get for pounding all them shots like that."

"It tasted good at the time."

"It always does." Antonio grinned "Where's Melissa? She wasn't too happy with you last night."

Ethan held up his hand, waving it in front of Antonio "Ah she's just fine, she gets what she wants from me after I've had a few, but now she's not too happy with me since we walked in here." Ethan grinned.

"Why now? She's mad at you an awful lot."

"That's all for show." he laughed "She's just embarrassed because when we were walking in, I held the door open for your mom and Melissa, I said ladies first, and when Melissa walked by, I said nice ass to her, she didn't think it was too funny."

Antonio shook his head "You're going to find yourself girlfriendless if you continue like that." he chuckled.

"She'll get over it." Ethan then stuck his nose up in the air, acting like he was sniffing hard.

"Issues?" Antonio asked "You look like a damn dog, doing that."

Ethan looked at him with a sly smile "I smell sex."

Antonio shook his head, grinning and walked away.

During breakfast Scott and Grace sat next to each other, Scott apologized to her for doing her wrong all these years. He told her that he was young and dumb, and that he wished that he never did what he had done, making amends.

For the rest of the week Antonio paid for everyone to visit wherever they wanted to go. Sadie and her dad bonded, which he also made her a promise to sell his home, and to move closer to her. He wanted to see her more often and to try and spend as much time that he could with her and his grandkids, and wanting to make up for lost time.

******

Nine months later Sadie gave birth to a baby boy, weighing 7lbs 8oz and 21" long. Sadie wanted to give him a traditional name, and named him Brandon Antonio Russo.

Antonio was holding and talking to his son, smiling as he talked to him, "Nine months ago I told your mother that I'm sure that we made another little Russo. I was right, and look who's here now." he grinned, kissing his forehead.

"I'm going back on the pill after this one." Sadie laughed.

"What? No more kids?" Antonio asked, looking at her questionably.

"You want more? I feel like I've been pregnant for two years now, I need a break already."

"Well I wouldn't say we need more right now, but I'd be open to it later on."

"We will talk about that later when the time comes. Right now, my body needs a break." she says, sounding tired.

Antonio looked at Sadie while she was closing her eyes, and laid Brandon down in his hospital crib, then sat down next to Sadie. Taking his finger, he caressed Sadie's cheek, still feeling like he was the luckiest guy alive. He was still in love, was happy, and was in awe that he had her, and five beautiful kids, what more could he ask for?

He lowered his head and began thinking of Harlow for a moment, thanking her in his mind for allowing him to move on, and prayed that he will never have to go through anything like that ever again.

He looked back over to Sadie, and stood up, kissing her forehead.

"I love you so much."

The nurse came in to take Brandon back to the nursery, and to finish with his tests. Antonio figured while Sadie was asleep, he would go run to a flower shop and pick Sadie up some flowers.

As he looked at all the flowers, he had a hard time deciding which ones to get, he liked them all and wanted to make sure the ones he picked out, were special. Once he decided on one, he saw another, and got frustrated, sighing. He finally decided on one that was mixed with Rose's, carnations and with beautiful stargazer lilies. He thought they were the perfect ones for Sadie, brought them up to the counter, and paid for them.

The Unexpected Nanny

When he got back to the hospital room, he walked in on Sadie nursing the baby "Am I next?" he asked, with a chuckle. She looked up and giggled at him, shaking her head. "You sound like Ethan." she says, giggling.

He held the flowers behind his back, grinning as he got closer to her. He pulled the flowers out from behind his back showing her the beautiful bouquet of flowers "They're beautiful, thank you." she said quietly with a smile, then looked back down at Brandon.

He leaned down kissing her lips then kissed his son's cheek, and set the flowers on the table.

"Thought I would put a smile on your face."

She looked back up at him, looking at the flowers "You always put a smile on my face. Besides, I already had a smile on my face after giving birth to him, and seeing him for the first time."

"To be honest, I think my life is complete. I'm married to the hottest, sexiest man ever, I have two beautiful twin girls that I think of as my own, and I have given birth to three of your children. I have my mom back in my life, and a father that I never knew, come into my life and has done everything that he can, to be a part of my life. I'd say my life is more than perfect, and I love you more than anything." Sadie said smiling wide, looking down at her baby.

"Ti amo di più" Antonio says with a grin, Sadie looked at him squinting her eyes "I know what you said, and we can argue later about who loves who more." she smiled.

(Ti amo di più== I love you more)

The End

Bonus Chapter

Three years later:

Isabella and Gabriella are now ten, Luca and Lilliana are four, and Brandon is three. The girls were running around the house with their Halloween costumes on, chanting as they were dressed up as cheerleaders.

Luca and Lilliana were dressed up as a cowboy and cowgirl, they were having fun with their hats and the sounds of their cowboy boots as they walked across the kitchen floor. Sadie was trying to get Brandon's outfit on, and was feeling sick, she then hightailed it to the bathroom.

She sat on the floor near the toilet feeling like she puked up her entire insides, and trying to think of what she ate that would have gotten her so sick. She had quit taking the pill about a year ago, because of developing some serious side effects from the pill, so Antonio had been using a condom the entire time.

She grabbed a glass of water and continued to put on Brandon's costume, dressing him up as a pirate. She had all the kids stand next to each other and took their pictures.

Sadie walked into Antonio's office and went over to sit on his lap. As she sat down, she wrapped her arm around him and sighed

"I don't know if I'll be able to take the kids out tonight." she says, caressing his cheek.

"Why, what's going on?"

"I have been feeling sick lately, and just got done puking my entire insides out."

"Pregnant?" Antonio asked, then chuckled.

"We've been using protection, so I don't think so."

Antonio curled his finger under her chin, and pressed his lips to hers, kissing her lips softly, he pulled back and looked in her eyes, giving her the look that made her melt every time he looked at her.

"Remember Ethan and Melissa's engagement party?" he asked with a grin

"Yes why?" she says, thinking back to it. She remembered that she drank a little too much champagne, and that they disappeared for a little while, having sex in the public bathroom and nearly getting caught by an employee of the banquet hall.

Sadie's eyes get wide "Oh no..."

Antonio was grinning from ear to ear, thinking that if she was pregnant, he wouldn't complain one bit. "I believe that night would have been your fault, you insisted on having sex that night, right then and there." he laughed "Go get yourself a pregnancy test."

Antonio looked at her, while rubbing her stomach "Ethan will be here shortly, you can stay here, and he can help with the kids if that's OK."

"I guess so. I'd hate to miss out on them going out in their costumes, they all look so damn cute."

"It's completely up to you, I'm not going to force you to go out if you're sick…"

Sadie got off Antonio's lap when she heard Ethan talking with the kids. She walked into the living and busted out laughing when she saw Ethan.

"What the hell are you wearing? You can't wear that out with the kids!" she said loudly, while covering her mouth to keep from laughing, then turned her head to look away from him. Antonio walked into the living room to see what the commotion was about, and couldn't stop laughing when he looked at Ethan. "Go figure…"

"What? I'm just a banana." he grinned an evil grin.

Sadie shook her head "If you get yelled at, that's your own damn fault."

"Wait until you see Melissa's, she's dressed up as a taco." he laughed.

Sadie looked at Antonio "You're right, I'll stay behind and you two can take them." she giggled.

"This is going to be fun and interesting." Antonio says gathering the kids, leaving to go out trick or treating.

Sadie grabbed her car keys, and headed to the store to buy a pregnancy test. Hoping that she wasn't pregnant, but then started thinking about when the kids were babies, and smiled.

At the store she grabbed two tests, one to see if she is or not, and the second one just to make sure the first one wasn't a defective one.

While Antonio and Ethan were out with the kids, she took the test, the first one instantly came up positive. Her heart dropped when she saw the positive and used the second one, a different brand. She sat there for a minute or so waiting to see what that would come back as, and picked it up. "Positive." she muttered and sighed.

When Antonio got back with the kids, they checked out all the candy they had gotten, and got the kids ready for bed.

Antonio was lying in bed when Sadie came out of the bathroom, holding her hands behind her back. She walked over to Antonio and climbed on top of him, straddling him.

"Oof." he groaned, as she sat on top of him, crushing his nuggets.

She set both tests down behind her and leaned forward kissing him "I have something for you." she grinned.

"Oh yea, what's that?"

She sat back up, and reached behind her, grabbing onto the two tests. "Hold out your hands, and close your eyes."

"You're not going to handcuff me, are you?"

"As much as I know you would probably like that, no, I'm not doing that." she laughed, placing the two tests in his hands. "Now, open your eyes."

Antonio opened his eyes and looked at the tests, grinning "I knew it." He set the tests down on his night stand, and pulled her down onto the bed, and laid on her, he happily smiled before giving her a passionate kiss.

"That's the best news I have gotten since we found out you were pregnant with Brandon." he says, moaning in her mouth.

The next day Sadie made an appointment with the doctor. After seeing the doctor, she found out that she was indeed pregnant. Three months to be exact, and it was from the night of Ethan's engagement party. The past few months she had been so busy, that she hadn't even realized that she was pregnant.

She was excited, and knew Antonio would be in heaven once she told him the confirmed news of the pregnancy. She decided not to complain about being pregnant, after he told her that his dream was to have as many kids the good lord would bless him with, and knowing Harlow wasn't able to do that for him, she knew that she couldn't take that away from him.

******

It's a week before Christmas, and Sadie was at her doctor's appointment finding out the sex of what they were having. After seeing the doctor, she was ecstatic with the news and couldn't wait to share the news with Antonio. This time around for the pregnancy he had been so busy with work, that he had missed every doctor's appointment so far.

When she got home, she wrapped the ultrasound picture up inside of a box and placed it near the tree. She couldn't wait to see the expression on his face when he opened his gift on Christmas, and that it was something that she had been quiet about the past couple months.

The kids were counting down the days until Christmas, and were getting more impatient as the days went by. They were excited to be opening all the gifts that they knew they will be receiving.

Antonio got home from work, curious as to what the doctor said he walked over to Sadie, and wrapped his arms around her.

"So, how did the doctor's appointment go?"

"It was good. Although, I still wish you had been coming to all my appointments with me, after all this is what you wanted."

"I know, and I feel bad that I haven't been able to make a single appointment... so what are we having this time?"

She shrugged her shoulders and giggled. "Well, since you have missed every appointment, that's for me to know, and for you to find out."

Antonio groaned, and pulled her in for a kiss, knowing that he can easily sucker her in, just by kissing her, only it didn't work. "Sorry, not working." she giggled, while pulling away.

"Can't you give me a clue?" he begged.

"Nope, sorry... you'll have to wait."

Sadie was laughing on the inside, she loved seeing him beg, and loved making him feel guilty for missing all the appointments, but even she herself couldn't hold it in any longer, and that was the reason why she wrapped it into a gift for him, and letting him find out on Christmas.

"Don't worry, I may give in and tell you." she says, giving him a wink.

******

It's now Christmas morning, Isabella and Gabriella ran into Antonio and Sadie's room waking them up, wanting to open their gifts.

"It's way too early girls." Antonio says in a morning voice, trying to open his eyes. He looked at the time, and saw that it was a little after six in the morning, and groaned.

Sadie sat up and looked over at Antonio, and smiled "They have the other kids standing in the hallway." she giggled "Might as well get up and start opening the presents."

Sadie was excited as well, she wanted Antonio to open her surprise that she had been keeping for him. She quickly got out of bed, put on her robe, and pulled her hair back into a ponytail.

She followed the kids down the stairs, and sat patiently with the kids, while they waited for Antonio to join them.

"Mom can we start opening the presents?" Gabriella asked.

"Hold on Hun, we have to wait for dad, he should be here any minute." she says, looking behind her.

"I'm coming, I'm coming." Antonio says, as he walked down the stairs, half asleep. He slowly made his way over to the couch, sitting down next to Sadie "You kids can start." he said, yawning.

Isabella and Gabriella excitedly started handing out the gifts, and once they were all handed out, they quickly tore into the presents.

Antonio stood up and walked over to the gift he had hidden for Sadie, and handed the gift to her, a big smile crept up his face as she saw what was inside "A Chanel handbag, I love it, thank you!" she says excitedly, hugging him.

"I'm glad you like it, it took me forever to find a gift for you." he says, kissing her cheek.

Sadie got excited and got up to grab his gift, pulling the box out of the tree, and sat back down next to him with a big smile on her face. "You should really open my gift to you." she says, placing the gift on his lap.

Antonio smiled while opening the present, his smile quickly faded into an expression to where he had a look like he was in shock while pulling the picture out of the box.

His eyes widened, and began choking while he spoke. "What's this?"

"What do you mean?" she asked with a grin.

"Why does it look like there are three heads in the picture?"

"Well.... Surprise! We're having triplets." She giggled hard.

Antonio's eyes got even wider and fell back against the couch "Is this a joke?" he asked, beginning to sweat.

She shook her head "Nope, no joke, you know how long I've kept this a secret? This is the newest picture, and the first one is hidden upstairs from when I first found out." she smiled "The sex of the babies are in the box as well." she then gave him a serious look "See, you should have came with to all of my appointments, then you would have known."

"Two girls and a boy." he says, picking up the paper "Holy cow... now I'm really going to be surrounded by girls." he says, taking a deep breath, feeling he was about to panic. "Now I'm going to have five girls that I have to protect from the boys." He says, sighing heavily.

"I was wondering why you looked a lot bigger in the stomach than usual."

Sadie laughed "Well now you know why."

Ethan stopped by with gifts for the kids, and for Antonio and Sadie. "Merry Christmas, Mommy Poppins." Ethan says to Sadie handing her a gift.

"Mommy Poppins is right." Antonio sighed.

"What's with the long face Antonio? You look like you've seen a ghost." Ethan laughed.

"Tell him Sadie." Antonio said, rubbing his face, still shocked about the news.

"I just showed Antonio that we are expecting two girls and a boy in April."

Ethan laughed "Woah! Your vagina is ruined now."

"Not funny Ethan." Sadie says, giving him a shove.

"I'm only playing, Antonio... Good luck is all I'm going to say..."

"I'll need it now." Antonio sighed.

******

It was the end of March, and Sadie was in the delivery room about to give birth. It was decided that she have a c-section to reduce any complications that could arise, had she were to give birth normally.

After a few hours, all three kids were born with no issues. They finally brought Sadie back into her room, along with the three babies. Antonio couldn't wait to introduce the family to their precious newborns, and was proud to show them off after they entered the room.

"So, what are their names?" Grace asked, as she looked at her newly born grandkids.

"We have decided to name them, Aria Mae, Carina Ava & Matteo Phillip Russo." Antonio says to the family, who had been anxiously and patiently waiting in the room.

"I think I'm done having kids. Eight is definitely enough." Sadie says, as she laid her head back onto the pillow.

Antonio laughed "You say that now, but there's always the what if." he chuckled.

"Yea right. This was enough for me. I don't think I could carry anymore." she sighed.

A week after Sadie had the babies, Antonio finally got the go ahead from the doctor, and was able to bring them home. After bringing them all home, and getting them all situated, Antonio decided to go make a special trip to go visit Harlow.

When he got there, he placed flowers next to her headstone, and sat down to talk to her.

I came by today to let you know that I still miss you, and to let you know that I still love you. I also want to thank you again for giving me the life that I have now. I do still miss having you in my life, and even though you're not physically in it, you're still in my heart. I have finally moved on, and I am extremely happy. I'm very much in love, and I owe it all to you, thanks to you and your big heart... Sadie and I now have a total of eight beautiful kids. Believe it or not we have five girls and three boys. Even though it was my dream to have a big family, I never in a million years thought I would see the day that I would have these many kids and I owe it all to you. I love you.

Antonio leaned down and kissed her gravestone, and attached a picture of all eight kids together on a stand, and placing the bouquet of flowers next to it. *Your daughters miss you so much, please keep doing what you're doing, and help keep them safe.* He says to her before leaving.

On the way home he couldn't stop thinking about all his kids, and it put a huge smile on his face. His life went from two kids, to trying to have more kids, to be told that he wasn't going to be able to have anymore, to now having a total of eight kids. He felt his life was now complete.

I will also be publishing the rest of the series; *The Unexpected Nanny 2,* **as well as;** *Antonio & Harlow; The beginning (Prequel to the Unexpected Nanny)*

About the Author

I was born in 1976 in Milwaukee WI, raised in Wisconsin and Minnesota. I have lived in Wisconsin, Alaska, and Minnesota, and currently living in the Twin Cities metro area. When I was growing up, my dream was to become an actress. When I was in school, I made sure to try out for every play, and was in all the plays at school. I loved learning foreign languages, and I also learned American Sign Language. I love music, and played different instruments. At home, I loved and enjoy playing the piano. It's relaxing and puts me in my own little world when I play, it has been something that I have been playing since I was a little girl.

When I was little, I used to write all the time, but quit writing, thinking that they were no good, and had gotten out of writing for a while... that was until I discovered Wattpad back in November 2017. I then started writing my stories on Wattpad in January 2018, just to give writing a shot again and to see where it would take me, I have written **many** stories since then.

I love to travel, and have been flying, and traveling since I was born. I'm an outdoors girl, and enjoy everything there is to do outdoors. In the spring and summer, you'll catch me on the waters fishing, as well as in the winter, I'll be out on the ice, ice fishing. I love camping with my family, and love camping alone with the hubby. Together we have 6 amazingly beautiful girls, and two little grandkids, a granddaughter and a grandson. How lucky are we to have two grandkids, exactly one year apart, two different mothers and born on the exact same day! Very easy birthday to remember! 😉

You can find me, and the rest of my stories on Wattpad under; JeniRaeD

The Unexpected Nanny

Made in the USA
Lexington, KY
01 September 2019